Voodoo

Alan M. Kent was born in St Austell, Cornwall and grew up listening to rock, punk and metal. He was educated at the Universities of Cardiff and Exeter. He now lectures in Literature for the Open University in South-West Britain and is a Visiting Lecturer in Celtic Studies at the University of La Coruña in Galicia. He is a prize-winning poet, novelist and dramatist. *Voodoo Pilchard* is the third novel in *The Trelawny Trilogy* – also comprised of *Proper Job, Charlie Curnow!* (2005) and *Electric Pastyland* (2007). Other recent titles include *Druid Offsetting* (2008), *The Tin Violin* (2008), *Surfing Tommies* (2009), *A Mere Interlude* (2010) and (with Nicholas Williams) an acclaimed bilingual novel, *The Cult of Relics / Devocyon dhe Greryow* (2010).

He has also written extensively on the literary and cultural history of Cornwall. Among his publications are *The Literature of Cornwall: Continuity, Identity, Difference 1000-2000* (2000) and *The Theatre of Cornwall: Space, Place, Performance* (2010). Further titles include a verse translation of the Cornish Mystery Play trilogy known as *Ordinalia* (2005) and he has recently co-edited *The Francis Boutle Book of Cornish Short Stories* (2010).

To R.J.D. (1942-2010)
– fur the voodoo, the maloik
and the music

Voodoo
Pilchard

Alan M. Kent

RYELANDS

First published in Great Britain in 2010
Copyright © 2010 Alan M. Kent

British Library Cataloguing-in-Publication Data.
A CIP record for this title is available from the British Library.

ISBN 978 1 906551 27 8

RYELANDS
Halsgrove House
Ryelands Industrial Estate
Bagley Road, Wellington
Somerset TA21 9PZ

Tel: 01823 653777
Fax: 01823 216796
email: sales@halsgrove.com
website: www.halsgrove.com

Printed and bound in Great Britain by Short Run Press, Exeter

"Ma canow vee wor Hern gen Cock ha Rooz
Kameres en zanz Garrack glaze en Kooz.
Poth'u an Coocoe devithes Treea
Durt Moar Tees Por Dega daga Creea."

[My song concerns pilchards with boat and net
Taken in the bay in the Grey Rock in the Wood.
When the boats came home
From the sea people cried, 'Tithe! Tithe!']

from John Boson
The Pilchard Curing Rhyme, 1710

"Alright, I've got something to say.
It's better to burn out than fade away!"

from Def Leppard,
'Rock of Ages' on *Pyromania*, 1983

Ten lessons learnt from being on a three-year long World Tour with Purple Haze:

1. Always fight yer Demons.
2. Be success savy.
3. Realise tha' the road takes its toll.
4. Develop a thick skin.
5. Beware of groupies.
6. Keep family ties goin'.
7. Don't be a tool.
8. Stay healthy.
9. Have some humility.
10. Know your enemy.

Whatever. Oh – an' one more:

No. 11: Keep yer roots.

Charlie Curnow – rock god – was back in Camborne.
Ut wuz good to be home.
Ee was tickled up ass.
The Press release went: 'After the madness of the past three years, we needed time to get back to our roots and recharge the batteries. We needed to be back in the Celtic West... to reflect... and write the new album...'
Like fuck.
That wudn' the real reason t'all.
The real reason wuz that after three years of tourin' the toilets and dives of Western Europe as Purple Haze, like boy Hendrix, they'd 'ad enough... enough ov 'Hey Joe', 'Crosstown Traffic' and 'Voodoo Child (Slight Return)', enough ov rock 'n' roll, and enough ov each other. The last straw was playin' the "prestigious" Hard Rock Hell festival at Prestatyn Pontin's

Holiday Camp in North Wales. That wuz if y'called "presti-gious" being bundled up in a freezin' cold chalet in the middle ov November, waitin' t'go on third on the second stage ov a Friday afternoon, or listenin' t' other shite rock bands on the way down the music industry's slippery ladder, with no-where else t'go. T'be honest, ut made a week in a tiny, mothball-smelling caravan down Gwithian Sands look like the penthouse suite on the top floor of the Khalifa Tower in Dubai. Yak wuz back t'being Yak, and Neil... well, Neil wuz somewhere else completely.

Trelawny Gardens wuz lookin' lovely. There 'twas – one ov the top 2% disadvantaged neightbourhoods in the whole of Britain – but lovely. Mind you, if you'd been on the road tha' long, anywhere wud look lovely. The reality ov ut was that the plaace still looked like a microcosm of Helmand Province, and tha' at any point an IED might go off in yer face. Trip wires everywhere you. *Hurt Locker* on speed. On Saturday nights you still needed t'suit up with body armour, and perhaps leave using a Jackal patrol vehicle. Taliban. ASBO-ite tackers. Naw dif-ference t'all.

NFC eh?

Normal fur Camborne.

That wuz wha' the triage nurses at Treliske hospital said, when anything came in from down there. The usual dangerous dog attacks, alcohol poisonings, overdoses, stabbings, gun-shot wounds, surface-to-air missiles, death by fuckin' frying pans...

Charlie wuz stroathin' 'long the end ov Centenary Street, just opposite the Vyvyan Arms, where moast ov the lunchtime regulars were already shit-faced. 'Twas a normal sort ov day in Camborne.

'Filthy fuckers..." came a low voice. "Dirty little bastards...'

Charlie recognised un right away. 'Twas the Methodist min-ister ov Camborne Centenary Wesleyan Church 'avin' a moan about some graffiti on the front of the building. This wuz the boy who'd 'ad one ov his eyes busted from a mine explosion a few years back. Ee was standin' there with a bucket ov soapy water, a hard bristle brush and a bit ov Wesleyan attitude, just behind one of the four columns that dominated the front of the building, all newly tarted up in terracotta an' cream, like ut 'ad just been on DIY SOS, or 'ad been flown in special from a

Mexican artists' colony. 'Twas all a long time ago now that Jimmy Pengelly 'ad tried t'shaw un the right path to enlightenment in this very institution. 'Es – the way of the Holman Climax Male Voice Choir. Jedi masters all ov um.

'Wozon?' went Charlie.

'This...' went the minister, pointun' down t' a bit ov the façade.

'Woz ut say?'

'Hard t'make out.'

Charlie entered through the open front gates and had a closer gake at ut.

'Voo... doo... Pil... chard.'

The minister looked at un.

'Make sense to you tha' do ut? Thaas' all the youngsters seem t'do now is this 'ere bleddy taggin' 'Tis all round the back too... I dunnaw wha' the world's comin' too. Ebm' um got nothun' better t'do?'

'That edn' taggin'' went Charlie, sizin' ov ut up.

'What ee mean?'

'Thaas' urban street art...'

'Street art?'

'Yeah. Like Banksy. See, there's a fish look... a pilchard... People pay fur tha' sort of thing nowadays y'knaw. In Bristol, they've got some ov Banksy's works, an' 'tis all preserved by the City Council...'

If there wuz one thing Charlie Curnow did knaw, and that was popular culture. Y'didn' spend the last three years ov yer life in a tribute band without knawin' tha'. Banksy was an anonymous street artist who'd won awards for his highly innovative and often political graffiti. It was street art with a social conscience, trying to make people think: rioters throwing flowers instead of Molotov cocktails, innocent children peering through concrete barriers between Palestine and Israeli settlements. Statements, see.

'It d'look a mess t'me...'

Charlie looked at ut again. It wudn' a mess. In fact, the graffiti was highly-skilled. There were some deft touches with stencilling an' black aerosol paint. In no way wuz this yer average piece ov Camborne street taggin'. Tha' wuz either just territorial pissing – marking their area - or about who'd shagged who

Alan M. Kent

recently, or who could be phoned up quicks'like fur covert homosexual activities.

'Clever really idn' ut?' went Charlie.

'Clever...?! What ee mean? '

'Well, the two elements are subtly juxtaposed' went Charlie, like ee wuz fuckin' Professor of English Literature at the Combined Universities of Cornwall.

'Well...' puffed the Minister, scrubbing like fury, 'I dun't care. It ov got t'be gone by this evening...'

'Why's tha'?'

'Concert here...'

'Here?'

''Es... a fundraiser fur Shelterbox.'

They wuz the cunts from down an industrial estate near Helston who boobed up everywhere in the world when there wuz some kind of disaster. Took on tsunamis, floods, earthquakes an' volcanos an' usually gived um bell tink back. They packed tents, an' tools and food in green plastic boxes and flew um out all around the world. Good crowd really. When no other bugger gived a damn, they wuz in there, quick as y'like.

'Jimmy Pengelly organised ut.'

Charlie smiled. This wuz the Cornwall ee liked. An' just like Jimmy tha'. Always thinkun' ov others. Charlie remembered his sessions with un, an' then smiled at the recollection ov lockin' Yak in 'is shed to do 'is rattle.

'Ee got they there Fisherman's Friends down... Knaw ov um do ee?'

Charlie knawed ov um. Not a bad crew either really. A bunch of boys from up Port Isaac who'd started singun' ov sea shanties and traditional Cornish songs. They was all filled with ballads like 'South Australia' ('bout the plaace buggers left Camborne an' Redruth fur because the mining went scat in the nineteenth century) 'Haul Away Joe', an 'No Hopers, Jokers and Rogues' (which sounded like ut ought t'be dedicated to anyone from Trelawny). You could see um standun' in front ov bits of fishun' gear an' lobster pots, in smocks and jerseys, lookin' all hunky, an' just like they'd stepped out of an Atlantic gale, with 'seben sorts ov' fish' ready t'feed 'ungry chieldurn. Mythic. Next thing they knawed, they'd cracked a million pound record deal. Their albums were sellin' like hotcakes over Tesco. They wuz livin' proof you could be Cornish an' still make ut.

'Suits ut really then dun't ut?' said Charlie.

'Wha'?'

'The pilchard an' tha...'

The Minister stepped back from the street art an' gived ut another geek with 'is one good eye. There wuz a moment where a flicker ov recognition went through the Minister – yeah, pilchards were about as Cornish as they comed, even though no bugger caught um any more.

'Cen't leave ut though,' ee went, an' went back t'scrubbin' ov ut off.

'See ee later...' went Charlie.

'You comin' tonight then?'

'Na,' said Charlie. 'Sorry. Got someun' else on...'

Charlie moved to click on his iPod again, and then the Minister spoke again. He pressed pause on the dial.

'Faather a'right is a? Ebm' seen un fur a bit.'

'A'right as ee'll ever be...' nodded Charlie.

'On as Shift Cap'n with Crofty again so I hear...'

'Well, price ov tin's up...'

'Good fur ee. We need some proper jobs back 'ere 'gain...'

Def Leppard's 'Photograph' full on blasted into Charlie's ear canal:

OH! LOOK WHAT YOU'VE DONE TO THIS ROCK 'N' ROLL CLOWN
OH OH! LOOK WHAT YOU'VE DONE

PHOTOGRAPH – I DON'T WANT YOUR
PHOTOGRAPH – I DON'T NEED YOUR
PHOTOGRAPH – ALL I'VE GOT IS A PHOTOGRAPH
BUT IT'S NOT ENOUGH

It was on 1983's million-selling album *Pyromania*. It was a suitable album t'play any time of the day. Joe Elliot, Rick Allen, Phil Collen, Steve Clark and Rick Savage kicking severe amounts of arse. Es – Rick Savage. That was a name. Real rock. None ov yer fuckin' guy-liner emo shit, all sleeve tattoos and 'Bring Me the Horizon' quirky throat roses. Produced by Robert John 'Mutt' Lange. Legend. A whole album devoted to creating the fire and

11

the energy of rock. From the Gods ut wuz: people like Moon, Bonham, Kossoff, Scott an' Dio. Even more so t'day considering some twat had set fire t'one of the empty shops in Trelowarran Street the night before, an' the fire brigade were still dampin' down. From 'ere, you could look back down the road an' see the blue an' twos still spinning. NFC pyromania.

His da had got un into ut. Ee'd been buyin' cheap CD versions ov all his 80s' classics off Amazon. Just recently, 'course, the twat had been in buoyant mood. Yeah – South Crofty 'ad properly re-opened. 'Twudn' just some Trevithick Society-style boys plaayin' at ut either – still pretendin' like 'twas 1850, an' the whole of the economy was merrily carryin' on vitty-like. Not all the levels had been re-opened though. Some of um remained flooded, but the new crowd who wuz runnin' ov ut – by the name ov Western United Mines - reckoned they could make ut pay, now tha' mineral prices 'ad gone up. Tin was a sought-after commodity again. Copper and tungsten too. Well, the scrapies over United Downs wuz offerin' good mony for old bits ov copper an' lead. Global recessions see – good fur Cornwall. So a few ov the old boys 'ad been takun' back on – an' were down there now with crowst an' tea on the 380 fathom level. Charlie cud see un' now – back on the SIG drilling machine, like ee'd dun fur half is fuckin' life. Natural see, fur men like ee. Anything else (wha', like a porn empire an' lapdancin' club?) just wudn' right. So yeah, 'Rock of Ages' was highly suitable fur boys who'd spent all their born days surrounded by ut, in ut and under ut. An anthem if y'like. Yes – Def Leppard, the John Harris ov the modern era. Pure rock poetry.

Headönizm Shampoo – the one that started it all.
Gentle Cleaning
• Mild formula, suitable for coloured hair – A mild combination of ingredients balanced to produce a rich lather and protect colour
• Enhances shine – Our activated shine blend of gorse, aloe, jojoba, henna and rosemary helps to add deep shine
• Improves manageability – Conditioners improve the surface and texture of hair

Voodoo Pilchard

Somethun' 'ad appened tha' changed things fur Charlie. Of all
the fuckin' twisted heap ov wreckage tha' wuz his first group
Balance, one good thing 'ad comed out ov ut. At the time,
'twudn' nothun'. But lookin' back, well, 'twas prob'bly the best
thing ee'd ever done. The financial guru and porn-star Kelvin
had suggested ut you. It wuz all t'do with their greatest hit
(not): 'What are you on?' This was their 'Smoke on the Water',
their 'Stairway to Heaven', their 'Enter Sandman', their 'All
Right Now'. The fuckin' thing had only been picked up by
some big-shot American producer, who gived ut to a new R&B
artist named Chakira, who'd only gone un funked ut up. Well,
the fuckin' thing went global didn' ut? No.1 in 20 countries.

What happened wuz this: Kelvin 'ad got Charlie to register
the song with a Publishing Company and what they asked fur
was the music and the lyrics, as well as a brief section of video
footage ov the song in performance. Kelvin had filmed Charlie
in his bedroom, singing ov ut with an acoustic guitar. It ud
spent about five years languishin' on their website 'til some
agent picked up on ut. Tha' wuz all ut needed apparently.
Chakira and her producer had a scan through that publishing
company an' found the song. Well, t'be honest, her version ov
ut felt very little like Charlie's original, time it had been souped
up with break-beats, dub bass, reverb and some other twat from
the Bronx rapping all over the top ov ut. It wouldn' helped by
the fact that the video on MTV wuz filled with about fifty vitty
maids all gettin' funky with ut in the middle of the Arizona
desert. You knaw the sort of thing: all tits an' ass, shakin' booty
an' wet t-shirts. When Charlie first knawed about ut, ee could
hardly believe ut. They were on tour in some hole somewhere,
an' an e-mail comed through. Ee gived permission an' signed
the contract. Didn't hear nothun' fur about six months. Then a
disc landed didn' ut? Radio One had ut on rotation. Then it
wuz top ov' the Dance charts. That wuz fuckin' embarrassing.
Charlie Curnow – rock god – with a dance hit.

This was often the way though. Charlie knawed ut. Some
cunt writes a song an' ut falls flat on its arse first time around.
Hardly makes the Top 40 perhaps, or in Charlie's case, not even
the top million. See what happened with the Northern Ireland
noiseneks Ash (the boys had played down Zennor a while back
on some back-to-roots tour), with their song 'Shining Light'.

First time around, ut didn't do much. Second time around with Annie Lennox, it becomes a huge hit. Thaas' the way 'tis sometimes. The songwriter makes a few quid but dun't get the glory. Now everyone d'think thaas' an Annie Lennox song – not one by Ash. Or check out Journey – fur fuckin' years an' years, Neil, Yak an' Charlie 'ad been extollin' the karaoke virtues of 'Dun't Stop Believin''. Now because of some American musical comedy series called Glee, the song wuz a hit, with everyone carryin' on like they've always knawed ut. Fuckin' thirteen year olds all singing along to ut like they'm Steve Perry and Neil Schon.

Still, Charlie wudn' complainun' – oh no. In fact, ee'd just been down the bank t'ave a geek at his royalties. Ut was funny really – ee was just a knobber from Troon, who'd 'appened to have written an international superhit. Charlie now knew wha' 'is knobber ov a da felt like when ee got his Crofty redundancy payout. Yeah – it felt like you'd won the National Lottery. Yak an' Neil had contributed to ut – s'far as he cud remember, so ee'd given they a tidy portion of ut too, but the words an' the melody, well tha' wuz his alone. They all knawed tha'.

Now Charlie wudn' about t'go out an blow ut though on some cruise around the Caribbean or brand new sports car. Maybe ee'd be in Trura an' buy some new gear – a new Marshall amp, and that Rickenbacker 4001 ee'd has his eye on. But na – ee wudn' be doin' any ov tha'. Instead, this was sensible Charlie Curnow – rock god, yeah – but Charlie Curnow in 'is mid-twenties, was a different beast. Ee 'ad ut in 'is mind tha' 'is dream of sex, drugs and rock 'n' roll wuz over. Y'ad to take stock at some points in yet life, an' this was one ov they kind ov moments. 'Twudn' na good goin' on forever thinkun' you wuz goin' t'be sellin' out the LA Forum, the Budokan or Hammersmith Odeon. Besides, Charlie had already sold his soul fur rock 'n' roll by traipsing around the world with Purple Haze.

This wuz Voodoo Pilchard see?

Fuckin' magic and stinkun' fish.

You cudn' have both. Sometimes however much y'wanted the magic, y'cudn' 'ave ut. Sometimes y'got t'settle fur the stinkun' fish.

Voodoo Pilchard.

Still, 'twudn' quite like tha' – not least, right now. Na, Charlie 'ad plans. Well, the cunt always 'ad plans – ever since ee could remember. Only this time, the plan wuz t'buy a house. Yeah – ee. Could ee have ever thought this way just a few years ago? Na – prob'ly not. But now. Well now, things were different. You live in a Mercedes Benz 311 Diesel Van fur three years with four other stinkun', burpin', gruntin', fartin' twats, and you'm just about ready to settle down. So this wuz Charlie's plan. He 'ad 'is eye on a new build up Troon – on School Lane – some bit ov' land tha' had been sold on. A company 'ad gone in an' put up three new houses there. Not bad: three up, two down, finished off vitty-like, with gravel drives an' slate porches. Well, road lesson No. 11 wudn' ut? - Ee wanted t'keep 'is roots didn' a? An' this money, this publishin' deal, that was goin' t'seal the deposit fur'n. That'd been the other reasons fur goin' bank – t'sort out the paperwork fur 'is mortgage. It hadn't been easy. Fur one thing, ee 'ad t'prove is income from music, but actually boy Spryer 'ad been on the ball there. Accounts were available – ee'd set um up all proper so there wudn' a problem. Fust off, the bloakey behind the counter (who wuz a bit like boy Yelland used t'be down the Dole Office) didn' like the look ov Charlie too much, but when Charlie shawed un the money in is account, ee started speakin' to un a bit better like. The cunts were always the same when ut comed t'the Cornish. Next thing y'knawed wuz they wuz offerin' un all sorts ov deals. 'Twudn' as if many people like Charlie walked in off the street on a daily basis in west Cornwall.

Hopefully this house was goin' t' give un enough space t'think 'bout wha' the hell ee wuz goin' t'do next as well. Fur certain, even though his da 'ad asked ov un, - an' there wuz a few jobs goin' if you wuz in the knaw - ee wudn' be goin' Crofty. Like always, Charlie 'ad ambitions. In 'is own house, Charlie could play 'is music as loud as ee wanted, convert one ov the bedrooms inta' a recordin' studio, 'ave as many people 'round as ee wanted, and first and foremoast, when ee wanted, get away from every other cunt who wanted a piece ob'm.

At the same time, ee might even be able to write a few more songs ov the quality of the one recorded by Chakira, an' collect the royalties. Maybe Charlie's kind of rock 'n' roll wudn' goin' t'be the Keef Richards, ju-ju beads, heroin, chicks and models kind of thing – it wuz goin' t'be a bit more real. An' havin' 'is own house, well, 'is mother ud be pleased. Everyone else prob'bly wudn' believe ut. Ownin' yer own house in Cornwall in the early twenty-first century wuz somethun' tha' just didn' 'appen. It awnly really appened t'twats from up the line, who 'ad money enough t'come down here. Years back, they wudn' touch plaaces like Troon – so you cud still pick up a bargain. Now though, the cunts wuz movin' in 'ere too – way from places like St Ives an' Carbis Bay. Leastways with the plaace ee 'ad in mind, 'twuz only a quick stagger down the road from Football Club, and 'twudn' that far either, from the Grenville Arms. 'Twas far enough away from Trelawny not t'be fuckin' attacked every night, but close enough fur Charlie t'keep 'is watchful eye on ut.

Troon – so this wuz where 'twuz goin' t'be then. Wha' wuz ut the old boys called ut? Obby Stanker County. Yeah – tha' wuz ut. Tha' wuz because years ago, all the boys up here wore hob-nailed boots an' when they comed inta' Camborne, you could hear ov um stankin' down past the station. Obby Stanker Country then. Not London, not LA, not New York - but Obby Stanker.

> Gwithian Shampoo – Go native with the goodness of Gwithian Sands.
> Super rich shampoo for hair and body
> • Leaves hair clean and fresh – A balanced blend of ocean ingredients provides rich lather and thorough cleansing
> • Helps prevent moisture loss – Our activated blend with Gwithian Sands helps balance moisture and prevent dryness
> • Provides body and fullness – Special conditioning agents help improve hair texture and provide added volume

'Is ma had progressed off ov the *Poldar*k an' her E.V. Thompsons.

Fuck me, she'd signed up fur some Open University course called *Voices an' Texts*, whatever the fuck tha' wuz about. This wuz goin' t'lead to er gettun' ov a degree.

''Twas time I used me brain a bit more...' she'd gone.

This wuz the Sally Curnow whose only other time she'd really used her brain wuz prob'ly outwitting her on-going twat ov a husband. In reality, tha' required a kind of Ph.D level of competence in coping with Charlie's da's twattishness. It was a twattishness that involved gettin' drunk, having affairs, wasting money, developin' a porn empire, goin' inta' business with Karen Mellow, and not actually realisin' that the twenty-first century – with all this inherent technology an' sophistication - wuz 'appenin' all around un.

She'd started with an Access course at Cornwall College – that 'ad got er back inta' studyin' again (She edn' dun nothun' since school really – well, er generation didn' did um?). This wuz initially good s'far as Tommy wuz concerned, because if she 'ad t'study, Tommy'd generally use ut as an excuse to get out of the house an' go get pissed somewhere: either one of Institute, Football Club, Grenville or of late, Trura City Football Club ('ome ov the White Tigers'). So, 'twas a convenient arrangement if y'like. But then, next thing she wuz on an Openings course with the Open University, an' then after that somethun' called *Approaching Humanities*. His ma wuz becomin' a proper student an' tha'. Tommy barely knawed wha' had hit un'. Now she wuz goin' on about the effects of the Enlightenment and Romanticism, an' applyin' ut on her daily work up Homebase. The crowd there thought she'd 'ad a brain transplant or somethun', she wuz that full ov ut. 'Twas hard you. She was findun' ov ut tricky applying the philosophy ov Jean-Jacques Rousseau an' Dorothy Wordsworth on decking sales and weedkiller, or the latest ergonomic kitchen and half-price bathroom designs.

'You want t'be readun' a bit ov John Harris maid... Ee's the boy...' went Charlie's da, and t'be 'onest, there wuz a flicker ov recognition there – that Harris might be worth 'avin' a read. Charlie's da knew some ov ut off by heart:

HAST EVER SEEN A MINE? HAST EVER BEEN
DOWN IN ITS FABLED GROTTOES, WALL'D WITH GEMS,
AND CANOPIED WITH TORRID MINERAL BELTS,
THAT BLAZE WITHIN THE FIERY ORIFICE?

But then, on the other 'and, the past few years ov marriage 'ad given Sally Curnow the view that moast things 'er husband ever suggested were best ignored. So right now, John Harris's romanticism went the same way: firmly stayin' in the realms of twatdom.

17

The day things really changed though wuz when Sally comed in with a new book for er *Voices an' Texts* course.

'Whaas' tha'? went Tommy inquisitively.

'Porn,' went Sally, t'get 'is interest.

'Really?' perked up Tommy. 'Now you'm talkin'…'

'No. You'd like that though, wouldn' ee? Actually, it's an essay by Virginia Woolf…'

Tommy went back t'watchin' the football, an' cracked open another can of Boddingtons. The Woolfster didn' sound like Tommy's kind of thing t'all. Sally Curnow carried on reading.

When the break came, an' the adverts kicked in – all DFS sofas and PC World computers an' iPads - Tommy went, 'Whaas ut say?'

'It's about women and writing.'

'Aw.'

Tommy scratched his ball-bag and went out fur a piss. Like usual, ee didn' close the door, so Sally could clearly hear the trickling waterfall.

'It's called *A Room of One's Own*.'

Ee shouted in, 'Whaa'?'

'*A Room of One's Own*.'

Tommy comed back in, and settled down again in front of the telly. Ee took some baccy an' started t'roll a fag.

'It says tha' a woman must have money and a room of her own if she is to write fiction… It's very interesting Tommy.'

'You got money.'

'Wha'?'

'You got money… from yer job.'

'I's not that though is ut? I's more about how women don't have their own space… I mean you have your own space dun't ee?'

Tommy knew 'zactly what she meant. She meant 'is mundic-block built shed out back – where if Charlie's da needed a cave to hide in, thaas' where ee went. 'Twas an essential component of 'is existence – tha' shed.

Tommy nodded, but was actually keen to continue watching the United v. Arsenal match.

'Wha' - you thinkin' ov writing a book or somethun'?' went Tommy.

'Maybe…'

'You?'

'Yeah – why not?'

Tommy didn' answer.

'I d'need a room ov me own though...'

'Whas' wrong with our bedroom?'

'Aw nothun' apart from all your crap in ut...'

Tommy knawed she was referring to 'is fine collection of dog-eared rock paraphernalia, old Crofty momentos and Cornish Pirates and Trura City football programmes (plus 'is hidden collection of 80s editions of *Razzle* and *Men Only* magazines). Ee lit is fag, and Sally gived un one er looks which meant tha' ee wudn' really s'posed t'be smoakin' indoors. Come t'think ov ut, actually, ee wudn' meant t'be smoakin' t'all. Thaas' wha' the doctor 'ad told un. She would soon be in one ov er flinks. Here it comed.

'If you adn' blawn all tha' redundancy money... perhaps we might 'ave been livin' over Lanner... in one ov they Wain homes. Then I might 'ave a room ov me 'awn...'

'Here we go...'

Time t'switch off Tommy went t'hisself. That wuz ut. She'd never let this go. What wuz the big fuckin' deal with Lanner anyway? 'Twas just as much ov a dump as 'twas 'ere. Only thing wuz, you cud go easy t'shop in Falmouth rather than Redruth. Tha' wuz top an' bottom ov ut. M&S, art galleries an' designer cafés there, rather than Charity Shops, Jimbo's Cash & Carry an' second-hand computer emporiums.

'Even Charlie'n afford somewhere new...' she went, 'with tha' song-writing money ee got.'

Tommy watched his wife carefully. She put down er Virginia Woolf an' went over to the window ov their house on Trelawny. Tommy knew what she would see. The same fuckin' thing as they'd seen fur near on twenty year. Only 'twudn' as good as ut used to be. There 'ad always been problems you, ever since they'd moved in – but t'be honest, Tommy knew as much as anybody else tha' the estate wuz goin' further downhill at an increasingly rapid rate. 'Twas like the luge at the Winter Olympics: slippery as fuck, an' just as dangerous. The latest 'ad been the rise ov mephedrone. Burglaries 'ad gone up ten-fold ov late with every little cunt under the age ov eighteen lookin' t'rob ee soon as look at ee, to pay fur their habit. Ee knew Sally deserved better. Thaas' wha' ee wanted with Club Rhino – only she wudn' 'ave ut.

Like we all do sometimes, the house over the road needed a bit ov love. It had had about twenty different occupants over the same number ov months an' ut wuz looking trashed. A good collection of seagull-ravaged bin bags littered the drive: Kentucky Fried Chicken bones an' Tesco Value baked bean cans. No-one 'ad touched the lawn in years. Ut didn't make fur much kind of social cohesion. That wuz from where a lot of the kids got their 'product' from. Some said the bloakey who wuz in there wuz manufacturin' ut fur the whole of West Cornwall. You didn't see un much. Then again, you didn't like t'ask too many questions. Ask the wrong thing, an' 'round 'ere, - well they'd take ee out. Give ee a good knee-cappin' over United Downs. Sometimes Tommy didn' get ut. His twat ov a son 'ad got out – toured the world – with that tribute band ov 'is, and now all the stupid cunt wanted t'do, seemed to be t'come back 'ere. Tommy told un: 'Buy somewhere down Treswithian' – where a posh new build wuz goin' on, but ee wudn' havin' none ov ut. The cunt wanted t'buy somewhere in Troon. They wuz wantin' t'get out, an' ee wuz wantin' t'get back in.

Tommy pondered all ov ut. Maybe Crofty wud be 'is solution. Just maybe, the boys might make a goodly bit, an' then, well, wages might be up – and then ee cud see if gettin' out might be possible. 'Til then though, Sally ud 'ave t'put up with ut. Tommy thought again – yeah – there wuz still brave few debts ee 'ad t'pay off with Club Rhino.

'They'm in there again Tommy,' went Sally.

'Who?'

'Youngsters…'

As one tacker comed out of the house opposite, ee noted Sally watchun' ov un from behind her nets, so ee flicked er the finger quicks'like. In his hand, was a little bag of 'fertiliser'. Nothun' new there then. As the tacker went past, Sally nawticed Jess an' Micky comin' down the path.

'Jess's 'ere,' noted Sally.

Over the years, Sally and Tommy Curnow 'ad warmed somewhat t'Micky an' Jess bein' together. All wuz goin' on well with their daughter an' the former DJ an' traveller. The fuckin' dreadlocked loser, whose 'angin' motor home'ad once stood on their drive 'adn' turned out t' be a bad ol' boy. Fur one thing, ee'd always looked after Jess, and fur another, the tool seemed t' 'ave a certain business sense. Australia 'ad kind ov sealed ut. Up t'then, well, they'd just seemed t'be hangin' out – but six months away in a camper van – running up from Sydney t'Cairns, then across t'Adelaide an' Perth seemed t'mature um boath. Micky though, wuz always a bit jealous of Charlie – like as if Charlie 'ad the lifestyle ee really wanted. Tha' wuz a joke really though, cuz if truth be towld, the Purple Haze thing, well, 'twudn' 'zactly the life of Bon Jovi or U2 now was ut? Separate tour buses an' dressin' rooms? No way.

As they comed in, Tommy grunted at um. Ee'd grown used t'um being back now – but sure 'nough, as soon as they wuz settled an' made a bit ov money, they wuz off somewhere on their travels again. Where wuz ut last year? South Africa. Time before Mexico. After Australia – it was California. Some ov ut wuz work; some ov ut wuz surfin', some of ut just seemed t'be sittin' on fuckin' beaches. Tommy reckoned there wudn' much point in tha' – not when you were only fifteen minutes from the ocean in Cornwall. Half the time ee 'ardly knew who Jess was anymore. She didn' even sound Cornish na more. Along the way she seemed t'pick up s'many different accents. Down mine, all the boys said the same thing 'bout their daughters. They didn' knaw who they were any more. Gone snobby 'alf ov um apparently.

'Well?' went Sally. 'What did she say?'

This was a crucial question. Micky an' Jess 'ad 'ad a plan.

They'd been down t'see Ursula – Sally's confidant and hairdresser.

The thing wuz that Ursula – who'd been fuckin' beyond ancient fur as long as anybody in Troon cud remember – 'ad finally decided t'shut up shop. She'd done er last blow-dry and perm a fortnight ago – an' tha' wuz it. She retired. Accordin' to Sally, she was lined up t'spend a few ov the winter months ov the year in Spain, an' then the summers back 'ere, toppin' up the tan on her flabby bingo wings. Well, Micky an' Jess went t'see if they could buy her old hairdressin' shop. They 'ad big plans see. Micky wudn' tradin' tapes an' CDs no more. Oh no – ee'd moved ut up a gear. Now, ee 'ad some fuckin' expansive website, dedicated t'sellin' DJ gear, vinyl and downloadin' music. Highly lucrative so ee reckoned. Iceland apparently, wuz where much of 'is business wuz comin' from. If 'twudn' releasun' ov a volcanic ash cloud to stop the entire world flyin' in or out ov Britain, or decidin' to cause financial meltdown to several million people who'd invested in Icelandic banks, they wuz obviously whacking down some ecstasy an' goin' out clubbing every night. Well, there wuz fuck all else t'do there, except stay in the dark reading the sagas ov the travels ov Lief Errikson.

So, that wuz one angle of Micky's enterprises. The other wuz his tattooing business. The tool 'ad always been messin' around with that particular art-form. Even back in the days of Balance, ee'd had one or two tribal designs on his upper arms. Now, well he'd gone Modern Primitive, reigniting the need for Celtic skin decoration. Woad an' knotwork wuz 'is mantra these days. There wudn' any on his face or neck, but his arms were covered, as was a good proportion of his torso. Charlie's ma 'ad got used t'ut. That wudn' t'say she liked ut much. In fact, prob'ly her studyin' ov voices an' texts wuz openin' up her mind somewhat.

Maybe she should've just dropped a tab ov acid, like the rest ov um on the estate, but then, there 'twas.

Jess meanwhile, wudn' doin' bad either. While her brother wuz away with the fairies, pixies and Jimi Hendrix, she'd done a'right fur herself. She used her jobs to finance her travel. Whenever she got back she always seemed t'land on er feet: gettin' jobs in salons over Trura, or down Penzance. Along the way, she'd won a few competitions too – you knaw the kind of thing. Stylist of the fuckin' year in Cornwall, or some other award fur Creativity from the Noble Society of Hairdressers. Charlie's ma had um all pinned up in the living room. There were *faux* bronze trophies in the cabinet too. Maybe it wuz a good thing Jess an' ee wuz out the country when it all kicked off a few years back. Jess knawed Clifford fairly well (she wuz always countering the dog-food eatin' an' goat-shaggin' stories), so 'twas well she didn't see an' hear all the drilgey 'bout ut. Jess's ma was of the hope that 'twudn' be long before they two would get married – and then well, scarily, some little Curnows might be on their way. Still fur now, there was good news.

'She's agreed,' went Jess. 'She's going' t'sell ut to us...'

Voodoo fuckin' Pilchard - right there an' then.

Voodoo Pilchard

Fate.
Destiny.
Hubris.
Ursula cud've stopped ut there an' then.

Thaas' what it felt like when news ov tha' came through. What wuz the plan? Well, 'twas simple enough really. Jess wuz goin' t'take ut over as a hair salon. 'Twud need a bit ov work mind you. Well, more than a bit ov work. In fact, the business on Fore Street wuz so old-fashioned 'twud need completely guttin' an' startin' over again. Expansion wuz on their minds. 'Twudn' just goin' t' be perms and blue rinses, for the pensioners over Boscean Close an' from down Treslothan. 'Twas goin' to be offerin' wider beauty services, like nails, waxin' bikini lines, facials an' tanning. The business. The full works.

Jess had a vision see. Fact was, she wuz just like Charlie an' Tommy underneath. Her idea wuz tha' she'd make a real go ov ut, an' tha' people would travel to there from all around Camborne, cuz ov the quality of service. Then, if tha' proved a success, she'd expand, go Cornwall-wide, then global. Be like Vidal Sassoon, that Nicky Clarke or Audrey Roberts off Coronation Street. Then, after tha', develop a Conrish beauty an' hair products range. Tha' wudn' half ov ut though. Micky wuz in too see. In their travels round the globe, they'd nawticed that lots ov hairdressers were offerin' piercin' an' tattooing services too. So, as well as cuttin', dyein', permin', an' straightenin' ov hair, Micky's studio wuz goin' to be in there too.

"Tidn' goin' to be naw rubbish', went Micky. 'Na. It'll be all designer stuff. Nothing off the shelf. All commissions. Bespoke tattooing and piercing...'

Bespoke? In Tommy's view what ee'd just said was laughable. The tool thought people would come up Troon – which spent half the year in mist an' the other half havin' Camborne's fly-tippin' dumped on ut – to have some designer tattoo.

The tool.

'Aw – thaas' wonderful love,' went Jess's ma. 'I knew Ursula wudn' let ee down...'

'We got the loan,' said Micky. 'No problem.'

'Thought banks wudn' givin' much out these days,' said Tommy, 'following the financial meltdown ov late...'

'Well, only if you've got a decent business plan,' said Micky.

23

'I think we have ebm' we Jess?'

He put his arm around Jess's shoulder an' kissed her.

'Well, I d'wish ee well with ut,' went Tommy. ''Tis hard though. I told ee 'bout Club Rhino didn't I? An' you heard the tale 'bout Clifford Mellow... See all the money ee 'ad to set up Pasty-Pronto. RDA money there. Went tits up too. 'Tis the economic climate see. Hard for any kind ov business t'make ut 'ere idn' ut? We'm too far away from the centre...'

Scarily, right at tha' moment. his da didn' even seem t're-member tha' Clifford's murder might jus' have prevented the further expansion of Pasty-Pronto.

'Crofty's doin' alright though edn' ut though da?' offered Jess in response.

'Es. Doin' a'right. But hard-rock minin's a bit different than hairdressin' or body piercin' bain't ut?

Ee 'ad a point, but nawbody cud be bothered t'argue widn'.

'Leave um be...' went Sally, protectively.

Except Jess.

'Da – I dunno... They're quite similar really...' she went.

'How d'ee mean?'

'Well, it's all about extraction idn' ut? You extract from the ground. We'll be extracting beauty'.

Tommy 'ad a think 'bout ut. Ee could see where she wuz comin' from. Considerin' some of the least attractive people on the planet were t'be found in the villages of Troon, Beacon an' on the estates ov Pengegon, Park an Tansys and Trelawny, 'twas goin' t'take some considerable industry t'extract some glamour. The hardest, strongest, diamond-tipped drill bits in the world cudn' make some local sow's ears inta silk purses – tan or naw tan. Tommy shuddered. Ee 'ad a sudden recollection of auditioning some of the dancers fur Club Rhino. It was the tattoos that 'ad dun ut. A bead of cold sweat formed on his forehead.

'Excitin' idn' ut?' went Sally. 'Both me son and daughter are buyin' somewhere...'

'I cudn' believe Charlie's buyin' somewhere over School Lane...' went Jess.

'Well, maybe ee's grown out of all that rock 'n' roll stuff,' said her ma, ever hopeful.

'Never,' went Micky. 'You're never too old to rock 'n' roll...'

'Thaas' right boy. You tell um,' said Tommy, momentarily thinkin' ee wuz Lemmy Kilminster of Motörhead, or Ian Anderson from Jethro Tull.

'An' Charlie – ee en't the type,' said Micky. 'Mark my words. Ee wun't be able to resist goin' back on the road again...'

'What about you?' went Sally.

'Me? Na... I've done my road stuff Mrs Curnow... Here's where I want to be now.'

Tommy cudn' resist askin'.

'What kind ov tattoos are ee goin' t'be doing?'

'Commissions. Arty ones like...'

'Just men's?'

'Na – men and women...'

Tommy thought fur a bit. He wuz thinkin' ov some of the sights ee'd seen at Club Rhino.

'Anywhere?'

'Yeah – anywhere...'

'Wha'?'

'Even there...'

'Need any apprentices do ee?'

Sally took the nearest available object and clobbered Tommy with ut. It happened t'be the Oxford University Press edition of *A Room of One's Own*.

'Ow,' went Tommy. 'Tha' Virginia Woolf d'hurt like fuck.'

Clotted Cream Special Shampoo – A vital experience.
Invigorating cleanser
• Cleanse impurities – A special combination of cleansers and Cornish clotted cream leaves hair feeling refreshingly clean, while enhancing vitality and adding lustre
• Stimulates – The combination of clotted cream moisturizer creates a cooling tinge
• Invigorates – The unique combination of clotted cream, lavender and peppermint creates a refreshing fragrant experience

Charlie's plan that evening wuz t'go up Troon Football Club an' sink a few. Ee needed ut. On the road, Charlie didn' touch much booze. No.8 ov road lessons tha' wuz: you 'ad t'stay healthy, or else you wuz shafted. Tonight wuz different.

Tonight wuz ritual. Alvin Sawdust wuz on. Alvin wuz a seven-foot tall, long-haired Primary School teacher from over Trura way, who dressed up in a pink glam rock outfit, and trawled through the best rock hits of the 1970s. It wuz the sort ov thing that went down well in Troon on a Saturday night. Alvin had stars painted around his eyes, an' wore a top hat, that had more than a passing resemblance to Noddy Holder in his heyday. The overall effect made un look like a camp Alice Cooper – fuckin' brilliant. He had a matching pink feather boa and Jesus creepers on. The fucker was full on. Throw a quite rummage through other rock hits (Focus's 'Hocus Pocus', Deep Purple's 'Black Night' and AC/DC's 'Whole Lotta Rosie') an' ut was the perfect night out.

There was karaoke on first though. The plaace wuz heavin' you. Every cunt around seem t'be there. Kelvin, Mel, Boy Bluett, that wanker Yelland too. Even Trescothick wuz in – sinkin' a few pints ov Skinners at the bar. Charlie nodded to un an' got a pint in fur'n. There'd always be a respect there. Despite his jihad on the Tamar Bridge, it wuz Trescothick who'd been there when the chips were down.

With this kind ov bash, moast people had been on the pop since mid-afternoon, and when the karaoke wuz fired up, it didn't take much for people to crack on an' give ut a go. 'Course, these days, every bugger seemed to be encouragin' un t'sing. Never mind the fact tha' ee'd been around Western Europe in a Hendrix tribute band, it wuz more the fact that he'd auditioned on *X-Factor* that moast ov um seemed t'knaw 'bout. That wuz the sad state ov' modern society in Charlie's view. More people seemed to know who Simon Cowell an' Cheryl Cole wuz than Noel Redding and Mitch Mitchell. Still, this is where ee wanted t'be. This wuz 'is people, 'is crowd. You hated um, but you loved um too.

The precise status of Charlie's relationship with anyone these days wudn' 'zactly clear. That ud never stopped maids before, an' it wudn' goin' to tonight either. One of Mel's mates wuz in. This wuz the crew ee'd once seen comin' home from Redruth on the Hoppa Bus years back. Christ, she'd grawed inta' some maid. 'Bout everywhere she stood at the bar, her massive tits kept hittin' people, so takin' her Pernod and blacks back to her table wuz quite a job. Moast of the bloaks didn' mind her being about. Eye candy wudn' ut? She wudn' 'zactly backwards at coming forwards, an' 'ad prob'ly got intimate with half ov Trelawny and the first team ov Troon AFC. Anyway she 'ad cornered Charlie fur a bit, halfway between the bandits and the gents' toilet, just as Neil, All an' Yak walked in. Ee saw the cunts laughin' at un. By now, this maid 'ad put her arms round Charlie's waist an' was gettin' a bit horny like.

'I always fancied you, Charlie...' she was goin'.

'Really!?'

Charlie wuz lookin' 'round fur help, to be removed from this hostile situation. Right out ov Sangin this wuz. No cunt looked interested t'all. Ee wuz on is own.

Next thing ee knawed wuz she was thrustin' her boobs inta' un an' tryin' t'lick 'is ear. Then it comed.

'Sowhenyougoin't'givemeonethen?'

Charlie 'ad forgotten how sex operated back in Troon. 'Twudn' the sophisticated dance tha' ee'd been witness to on the road. Oh no. Y'told ut like ut wuz 'ere. NFC. Voodoo Pilchard. The maid, whose name wuz either Sammy or Suzy (ee cudn' tell which – she wuz tha' pissed) wuz gazin' inta' 'is eyes, expectin' a quick grope, and maybe more. Charlie wuz flounderin'. It was Boy Bluett who comed in an' saved un.

'Come on Charlie – Summer Lovin's on...'

Bluett pushed un forwards out of the grasp ov the Pernod-wieldin' Medusa, an' 'eaved un on stage. Actually, the song wuz 'Summer Nights'. Bluett only knew the opening two words. Mel wuz already up there – ready t'do the Olivia Newton-John part. All ee 'ad t'be wuz John Trevolta's performance ov Danny. What the fuck? Ee wudn' normally touch this kind ov' thing with a barge-pole, let alone actually get up there an' sing. Still, ee 'ad t' weigh ut up: the prospect ov looking a tit in front ov everyone at Grouter Park or the prospect of further encounters with two ov them outside. On the face ov ut, ee wuz right t'choose the former. So off they went an' recreated the soundtrack to Grease is the Word:

WELL-A WELL-A WELL-A HUH
TELL ME MORE, TELL ME MORE
WAS IT LOVE AT FIRST SIGHT?
TELL ME MORE, TELL ME MORE
DID SHE PUT UP A FIGHT?

Charlie did 'is best. As they sung, ee looked around the plaace. It felt like ee wuz in slo-mo, that no time 'ad passed. 'Ere they were, all back together again, after all the shite they'd been through. But Charlie knew ee wudn' the same anymore. Neil, Yak, Ally – they wudn' either. 'Twas like the big bang – the universe pullin' apart. Tha' seemed t'be the way ov ut – gettun' older – you wudn' different t'all; it wuz just tha' the world got different. Road Lesson No.9 then – have some humility.

Charlie looked around the club as ee wuz on stage. The only one missun' wuz Clifford. Ee knew where ee used t'sit. Clifford wuz a fuckin' twat ov the first order, but you cudn' stop lovin' un. Charlie reckoned 'is spirit wuz ere at least, propping up the bar, an' getting' ready t'pass his belt under his kaks. Prob'ly there were little plastic Pasty-Pronto knockies still ferrying un across t'the Celtic afterlife right now.

For a moment, Charlie lost concentration on the lyrics passing across the television screen, and ee messed up the chorus. Nawbody much nawticed here. Ee gazed over the people. These were the buggers shafted by events elsewhere. All the money tha' ever seemed t'be put inta' Cornwall didn' come their way. Oh naw. They wuz still strugglin' – workin' the dark, scary an' black economy ov Cornwall – t'get by. Makin' a bit any which way they cud, up the scrapies, down lock-ups an' back in bedrooms.

Fur certain, this wudn' the Cornwall the government wanted y't'think 'bout. The latest wuz all eco-towns and fuckin' crap like tha' – an' more ways in which posh cunts from elsewhere could dump waste incinerators on people's doorsteps here rather than their own. There wuz hoardings all round Troon an' Beacon an' Camborne 'bout how everything wuz goin' t'have a bright future. Down Pool, they 'ad a big metal sign up where local school-children 'ad written their naïve vision ov the future. 'Twas full ov stuff like 'Pool is back with more beats so sound the trumpets', 'We are going to cast out nets all over the world and gather people together' and 'We will sail through the sea of knowledge'. Wha' wuz they fuckin' on? Must be drugs Charlie thought, coz no sane person would've thought anything like tha' 'bout the plaace. They knew what 'twas, an' what 'twas about. Some cunt must've bribed the kids with sweets, or Happy Meals, or mephedrone or somethun'.

Voodoo Pilchard

Mel gived un another nudge an' ee wuz back in the world ov karaoke – standin' on the seats of some American Football field, dueting with Sandy. When they finished, they got a bit ov a clap. More 'ad signed up fur the karaoke, but the committee wuz 'avin' t'call a halt t'ut – so the legendary Sawdust could get on. Ee wuz presently awaiting his stage time in the disabled cubicle in the gents' toilets. It wuz a moment, a time, a space Charlie knew all too well. By now, the usual head-bangers, druggies, football hooligans, old gits an' grannies were getting' trollied in the way tha' wuz traditional to do in Cornwall: the old Celtic folk custom of gettin' completely and utterly arse-holed t'escape where you lived.

Charlie grabbed a table an' Ally, Neil an' Yak moved some chairs so they cud sit together. A lot went unspoken. Tha' wuz the thing. They'd agreed on the old rock 'n' roll mantra – what went down on tour, stayed on tour. Tonight wuz important though. It was pre-arranged. They'd gather here like before, then do the deed. Ut had t'be done.

Charlie's phone rang. Ee looked at ut.

'Spryer..' he said softly.

The four ov um knew what ut meant.

'Dun't answer ut,' went Yak. 'Ee'll try an' stop us...'

All credit t'Boy Spryer – the boy had actually done a good job managing them. Ee'd done well out ov ut too – hence the reason fur phoning. But na, they cudn' respond to un. Ee'd break all the resolution they 'ad all garnered at this point.

'Leave the cunt,' added Yak, supping on a pint.

There were more serious things to talk 'bout. Charlie'd known the score for a while. It was one ov the reasons things started t'become fraught. When Purple Haze launched themselves across the Tamar, an' invaded England, the one person who didn' want them to go wuz Ally. Ally wanted Neil home, not fucking off on some European tour of Poland, Germany an' Belgium. Anytime, they 'ad a bit ov a break, Neil made 'is way back. Well, to an extent, Yak an' Charlie could understand ut. When y'had the body of a love goddess awaitun' ov ee back in Portreath, 'twas fairly temptin'. But tha' wudn' the issue. Na – the real issue wuz about Anthony.

Anthony wuz Neil's son. While Neil'd been on tour. Ally had grown increasingly worried 'bout Anthony's behaviour and how ee wuz getting' on. The last time Charlie 'ad really seen un, ee wuz still jumpin' around in a Spiderman outfit. Apparently, now, ee wuz inta' Iron Man and the Clone Wars; either pretend-in' ee wuz Tony Stark or Obi Wan Kenobi. Problem wuz ee'd kicked off at school several times (particularly with a length of 2x2 timber as a light sabre) so they'd taken un t'the education-al psychologist. The last few months, there'd been a series of tests, which had put the strain on Ally.

'So what'um say?' asked Yak.

'Ee've got a couple o'conditions...' said Neil. 'I's quite unusu-al...'

'Conditions?'

'Yeah – basically, one of um's ADHD....' went Ally.

Charlie'd heard ov ut. Ee knew wha' ut meant.

Yak looked sheepish. Ee didn' have a fuckin' clue.

'Attention Deficit Hyperactivity Disorder,' offered Neil.

'Wha' – ee goes fuckin' hyper do a?' said Yak sensitively.

'Well, we prefer not to see ut quite like tha',' said Ally. 'Moast people knaw i's the most commonly diagnosed psychiatric dis-order in children...'

It must be a disorder commonly found in Trelawny estate then, because half ov the little tackers there seem to be on one.

'So whas' a on?' questioned Yak – always thinkin' ov the 'medicinal' aspect, 'Ritolin kid is a?'

'They're not sure yet wha' to put un on,' said Neil.

'But wha's ut mean really?' asked Charlie. 'What are the symptoms?'

'Ee's easily distracted, misses details, forgets stuff, keeps swapping from one activity to another...'

Charlie could see Yak tryin' not to laugh. Ee wuz thinkin' 'twas soundin' 'zactly like Neil...

'He has difficulty focusing, daydreams a lot, has trouble doing homework an' tha'.'

It sounded grim. It sounded t'Charlie an' Yak a very good reason not t'become a parent. They both looked at each other. Yak thought ov all the little pieces ov Kernow ee'd... er... deposited over Western Europe, an' took a gulp ov air.

His eventual considered response was, 'Shit!' In the circum-stances 'twas about the best y'could 'ope fur.

'We'll try an' help like,' said Charlie.

'Yeah, well, the psychologist d'reckon it might be t'do with his da being away a lot...'

That was typical Ally tha'. Always throw ut back t'Charlie an' blame him fur takin' Neil on the road.

'Thaas' why I dun't want Neil goin' off again with you two...'

Charlie an' Yak ignored tha'. Old ground. Not worth goin' over again.

'You said two things though..,' noted Yak.

'Yeah – ee got Aspergers too,' said Neil off-handedly, as if 'twas nothun' tearin'. 'T'ave both ov they is really unusual like...'

'Asparagus?' deadpanned Yak, like a tool.

'Asperger Syndrome,' corrected Ally.

Yak 'ad 'eard ov ut. So 'ad Charlie.

'En't tha' someun t'do with autism?' asked Yak.

Fur once, Ally wuz surprised at Yak. Ee 'ad finally said somethun' remotely intelligent.

'Yes. Children with ut get focused, intense and show repetitive behaviours...'

'They have this narrow interest see.... With him, well, it's with Clone Wars idn' ut?'

Fuck. So this wuz what Ally an' Neil 'ad t'cope with. On the one level, the little fucker cudn' concentrate on anything, an' on the other level ee wuz concentratin' too much on the one thing. Ut sounded harsh – like you wudn' knaw wha' the fuck t'do widn'.

'They dunnaw what the fuck t'do widn' at school,' went Neil. 'Ee's basically in isolation all the time... Mrs Evans, the headteacher down Portreath reckon we should put'n t'a special school...'

To Charlie, ut sounded like Anthony wuz permanently in solitary confinement with a few bits ov' Lego by 'is side fur comfort. It didn' 'zactly sound like the perfect home life. Fur certain, Neil wudn' 'bout to go back on the road, an' neither wud ee be doin' much song-writin' or rehearsin' either. Y'cud tell the strain ov ut on Ally. Tonight, at least, her mother wuz lookin' after the kids. Megan, Anthony's sister was fine, so they thought. She didn' show any signs of either condition. Charlie went to the bar an' bought some more beers.

'Gorthewher vaze,' went Trescothick (the knobber always used a bit of Cornish when ee cud). 'I see the band's back then...'

Trescothick 'ad a black tam or beret on 'is head. The goon.

'Yeah – back fur now,' went Charlie, with a bit of hope in his voice tha' ut wudn' permanent, though judgin' by wha' Ally just said, it was lookin' more an' more like Neil wudn' be joinin' any enterprise in the future.

'How's the missile trade?' went Charlie.

Trescothick took a slow slurp ov his pint. A twinge ov old anger went slowly through un, then ut passed.

'Got bigger stakes now,' said Osama Bin Trescothick satisfyingly. He tapped his nose knowingly with his forefinger, an' readjusted 'is tam.

Charlie didn' answer un initially – but ut didn' sound good. When boys like Trescothick mentioned words like 'bigger' and 'stakes' you didn' want t'think 'bout ut too much. What was a on? 'Ad a gone nuclear now? - in cahoots with leaders in Iran.

'Catchee later,' went Charlie. 'Alvin's about to go on...'

'Proper,' went Trescothick, raisin' his glass.

Ut wuz as if Charlie cudn' escape un. That time down the Methodist temple tha' wuz Gwennap Pit 'ad sealed their fate together. The problem, the clear and present danger, wuz tha' Trescothick wuz a pilchard an' a half. Ee needed watchin'.

There wuz some voodoo there fur sure.

Never mind. Alvin wuz on. Ee 'ad style did Alvin. Ee comed on to the sounds of The Sweet's 'Block Buster':

AAH AAH
YOU BETTER BEWARE. YOU BETTER TAKE CARE
YOU BETTER WATCH OUT IF YOU'VE GOT LONG
  BLACK HAIR
HE'LL COME FROM BEHIND, YOU GO OUT OF YOUR
  MIND
YOU BETTER NOT GO, YOU'D NEVER KNOW WHAT
  YOU'LL FIND.

Fuckin' chuggin' base line an' police lights set up on top ov is speakers. It looked brilliant. Boy Bluett wuz down the front as usual, already with is legs apart an' is fingers in is pockets getting' down to some grebo, like 'twas still 1974. Charlie smiled t'hisself. Tha' wuz wha' wuz fuckin' great 'bout Cornwall. Up the line, no fucker wud have the sheer balls t'do tha' because they'd be too busy bein' fashion conscious an' up their own asses. Here, nawbody gived a shit. You just went fur ut. That wuz when the Cornish were at their best – when they just didn' care wha' people thought.

Thaas' wha' – more or less 'appened next. Whatever crap wuz goin' on in their own lives, the people ov Troon let go ov ut in the spirit of rock 'n' roll. Tha' meant goonin' round on the dance floor, startin' t'hit increasin' amount of the optics, an' joinin' Alvin on stage fur any possible sing-along. Ut wuz one ov they nights tha' guaranteed quiet on Trelawny all ov the next day – at least 'til six in the evening when they'd get ready fur the next session. The four ov them were more restrained these days – takin' ut easy an' knawin' their limits. Neil wudn' drinkin' t'all anyway – it 'ad been agreed tha' ee wud be drivin'.

'Ready now then?' went Yak.

'Yeah,' said Charlie. 'Time t'make 'iss, I d'reckon...'

What they were all about to do remained unspoken. You cudn' just talk about ut openly – not now, not now the decision 'ad been made.

They got inta' Neil's car – a Ford Focus estate, and made their way out ov the gates ov Grouter Park, then along Croft Common an' down t'Bolenowe. Ally didn' say much. Er mind wuz still on Anthony. The Purple Haze crew moved onta' the usual discussion of guitars. With 'is money Neil had just invested in a new Gibson Explorer (ee kept ut a bit secret from Ally).

'I's the business,' ee wuz goin'. 'Good enough fur The Edge an' James Hetfield – an' good enough fur me...'

'I's gotta' a good sound,' went Charlie. 'Powerful like... Matthias Jabs ov the Scorps uses ut an' all...'

Y'cud hear Ally thinkin' 'twas a waste ov money. Tools. All three ov' um.

'Y'getting' anything new Charlie?' asked Yak.

Charlie'd stuck with a Fender Precision bass fur the past two years – as used by Steve Harris, Glenn Hughes, John Paul Jones an' Phil Lynott. Legends all.

'Mine's pretty cashed,' Charlie said. 'Could get ut re-built I s'pause...'

'Na. Y'wanna' get someun' new,' said Neil. 'The Fender Jazz is s'paused t'be very good…'

'Well, said Charlie, 'if I do, it'll prob'ly be the Rickenbacker 4001.'

'4001?' went Yak. 'Tidy bit o'kit tha'… Me an' you with tha' Charlie… fuckin' kickin'.'

Yak wuz right. The 4001 wuz some kickin' gear. The likes ov Geddy Lee, Lemmy an' Chris Squire thought so too. But Charlie 'ad 'is doubts. Even though, ee'd been the Noel Reading ov Purple Haze, the bass really wudn' where ee wanted t'take things. In 'is mind, ee'd never wanted to lob an instrument around on stage. Ee'd always wanted t'be spinnin' the microphone stand – in the style ov the greats: Paul Rodgers, Robert Plant, Ian Gillan, Ronnie James Dio, David Coverdale and Bruce Dickinson - an' standin' on the stage monitors tryin' t'get the crowd clappin' along. 'Twudn' the sort ov thing y'cud do with a Precision bass around your body. In Charlie's view, tha' role 'ad always been fur Bev – but there 'twas – water under the bridge: polluted water under a bridge, an' a very long way away.

Neil drove up through Carn Moor's tight hedgerows and then turned right to Polgear. Carnmenellis mast was flashing away in the distance. Just over the way there, past Lancarrow, wuz Stithians Reservoir where they'd found Mrs Williams' wasted body. Thaas' how y'saw the world when y'got older: y'viewed ut in terms not of the names of places but ov where stuff 'ad 'appened. Everything wuz familiar now – the desolate-lookin' Four Lanes, and then the turn down to Higher Carnkie. Just across the way, stood the remains of mining activity at Treskillard, and then Carnkie itself: a fuckin' dump ov the first order, full ov Cornish twats who reckoned they somehow lived down Mylor or Feock rather than here – all trendy designer stuff boobed up in their gardens.

'You got ut all ebm' ee?' asked Yak, as they made the turn by Bowling Green, up the track to Carn Brea, a dark, malevolent form in the distance.

''Course,' went Neil. 'The whole fuckin' lot…'

''As a phoned again Charlie?'

They all knew who Yak wuz talkin' 'bout: Spryer.

'Couple times,' said Charlie.

No-one responded. They were resolute. It took guts this,

wha' they were about t'do.

Neil's exhaust clanked a couple ov times against the dirt track. Lord de Dunstanville's Monument peered down on um, watchin' their every move. Compared to Alvin's session back at Troon, all was still now. Charlie broke the silence.

'Hey – I read ut on the internet a couple ov days ago – the first ever guitar burned onstage by Jimi Hendrix has just been sold at an auction fur £680,000...'

Considerin' wha' wuz about t' 'appen, it seemed apt.

'No way,' went Neil.

'Fuckin' way,' went Charlie. 'Apparently, 'twas a '65 Fender Strat tha' ee set fire to at a gig in London in March 1967...'

This wuz Charlie Curnow all over, Neil an' Yak reckoned. Just the kind ov' fuckin' nerdy information tha' they'd 'ad to put up all the way from the fuckin' mud-filled Wacken Festival in Germany t'the shitehole named Guilfest in Surrey.

'Yeah – well, we'll soon imitate tha' a bit,' said Neil ominously.

'That idn' all,' went Charlie.

Fuck, wha' wuz the loser goin' t'say next?

'They're goin' t'release some new material: Jimi Hendrix an' the Ghetto Fighters...'

'The Foo Fighters?' asked Yak, thinkin' ov Dave Grohl's post-Nirvana noise-sters. .

'Na, y'cunt. The Ghetto Fighters...'

It sounded the kind of cats in Be-Bop hats Hendrix ought t'have been leading. Revolution from Harlem. Black Panthers an' that.

'Yeah – there's goin' t'be a DVD with recordings. a film script an' drawings and stuff by Hendrix an' the Aleem Brothers...'

No-one gived a shit.

No-one had even 'eard ov the Aleem Brothers. Besides, their own fuckin' dabble with Hendrix wuz 'bout t'come t'a glorious an' spectacular end.

Neil parked the car an' they got out.

Suddenly ut seemed sacrilegious t'do wha' they were doin'. Charlie felt around his neck, fur the piece of Hendrix's guitar string tha' 'ad guided un fur the past few years. All courtesy ov Druid Dave the roadie. Obviously, the others didn' feel the same way.

Alan M. Kent

'Where d'ee want ut Charlie?' shouted Yak.

'Anywhere y'like. Ut dun't matter…'

Yak was haulin' out a brazier from the back of the Focus, an' fillin' ov ut with newspaper and wood. Ee 'ad 'is ciggie lighter ready t'go.

'You sure 'bout this?' asked Charlie fur a final time. Charlie wudn' sure. Not really. Ee looked out over electric pastyland. There below, wuz Clifford's factory – now taken over by Ginsters, an' in the distance, the boarded-up skanky remains ov Club Rhino. There too, South Crofty's head-frame. To the west, Obby Stanker land. To the east, cunting Trura – all middle-England twattishness, coffee bars an' designer shops. Out there, all the fuckin' dumps and drongos they'd played to. Beyond tha', t' the north, the Atlantic. America. Purple Haze hadn' got there. Unlikely to – considerin' wha' wuz 'bout t' 'appen next.

From the back ov the Focus, Neil wuz gatherin' up a set ov bundled clothing, all wrapped in bin liners, ably helped by Ally – who arguably hated the fuckin' stuff anyway. Y'knaw wha' 'twas by now. 'Twas all their Purple Haze stage clothes – the bleddy lot. Yeah – they wuz goin' t'ritually burn them. Put an end to ut. Despite wha' Spryer 'ad wanted – fur them t' 'ave a break from ut fur a bit – an' then return in the future – 'twas time fur ut t' all go. You cudn' justify carryin' on forever pretendin' t'be somethun' you wudn'. 'Twudn' right anymore. Other people cud do ut – just not them. Charlie, sentimental twat tha' ee wuz, ee knew 'twas the right line t'take. On some level, ee didn' want ut t' 'appen. On the other hand though, ut 'ad to, fur all ov um t'move on.

'Burn, you crazy motherfucker, burn!' went Yak in the Trelawny-style - givin' a bit ov a fist pump - who wuz by now, takin' each costume, piece by piece, an' squirting lighter fluid on them, an' placin' them in the lit brazier. The 'House', so to speak, was 'burning down.' There wuz still a bit ov Hendrix left in un – even now.

It felt like they were ancient West Britons makin' some sacrifice t'the Gods. The flames lit up the druid temple ov Carn Brea. 'Twas the final, final, final part of '…And the Gods Made Love.' In a way, ut 'ad t' be.

None ov um said much. At that exact moment, Charlie wuz thinkin' ov one ov their biggest gigs at the Pop-party in

Voodoo Pilchard

Amsterdam. That 'ad been a blast. Some adulation there – the kind Charlie 'ad always wanted. Neil was recollecting them playin' a big Hendrix convention in Rome. Great audiences. Massive crowds. Italian rock fans – mental as y'like. Yak wudn' thinkin' ov much tell the truth – perhaps all the new kinds of drugs ee'd managed t'collect when they'd done Rhodes Rocks – like Club Ibiza but with metal instead ov rave. Still, 'twas over now. Their dabble with boy Hendrix wuz dun. Dun an' dusted. Road lesson No. 3 tha' wuz: realise tha' the road takes its toll.

The smoke rose up high in the night, an' drifted westwards down towards Tregajorran. Little known to them, this wuz the exact spot where Clifford 'ad met one ov Markie's boys – and well, that 'ad eventually led t'his tragic downfall. 'Twas the same plaace too – where boy Trescothick went on 'is Kernewek Jihad training missions. But then, all ov tha' wuz a long time an' space away wudn' ut?

Right now. Purple Haze, wuz seeming like somethun' ov a dream. Like the past three years 'ad been spent on quaaludes or LSD.

Yak an' Neil prob'ly viewed ut less ov a dream an' more ov a nightmare… but still.

Yak fished in the last ov their gear – Charlie's military jacket: the ultimate late '60s' garment. Fur a moment, Charlie wanted t'stop ut – t'put that on his bedroom wall, and remember… but na, fuck ut, sometimes y'just gotta' move on. Neil wuz oldin' tight onta' Ally. Charlie cudn' read Ally's face. It wuz as expressionless as the g'eat weathered an' indented rocks that they stood around. Maybe she wudn' even thinkun' ov Hendrix. More likely she wuz wonderin' how the hell they wuz goin' t'cope with Anthony fur the rest ov 'is life. Yak didn' seem t'show any feelings too. Then, tha' wuz always Yak. Ee took each day as ut comed. Never looked ahead. Never looked back. Lived fur the right here, right now. Very metal tha'.

So that left Charlie. All ee could do wuz watch the flames an' the embers. Wuz tha' ut then?

Everything wuz burnin' – like napalm dropped on 'Nam.

Out there in the distance, Charlie caught the white beam ov Godrevy Lighthouse spin over the Stones reef of St Ives Bay. Ut jerked un out of the trance ee wuz in. Es - to quote Boy Jimi, 'the moon was turning the tides…gently, gently.'

'Wha' now then?' went Yak, in hope of knowing their next musical direction.

The brazier burned bright.

Nawbody seemed t'answer ov un. Nawbody cud.

'Voodoo pilchard,' mouthed Charlie under 'is breath.

Seaweed Conditioner – Get hair into shape with the original leave-in conditioner.

Leave in moisturizer and conditioner

• Balances moisture – Moisturizing conditioners and our Activated Cornish Moisture Blend with seaweed helps balance moisture and prevent dryness.

• Improves texture – Conditioners smooth the surface and reduce static

• Excellent for hair and skin – This unique water-based formula is excellent for both skin and hair

Momentous changes were occurring. Not just small shit, but big changes; the kind of changes that are life-shifting. They were the kind of changes that you could never come back from. They were changes that you never thought would actually come. The next fortnight would see Charlie start to move into his new house on School Lane. There was a lot of stuff to sort out. His ma an' da were chipping in a bit, an' ee found hisself beggin', stealin' an' borrowin' bits of furniture. 'Course, 'is ma was doin' her level best t'find un all sorts of bargains from Homebase, so every day she wuz comin' home with a new kitchen implement, or something fur the bathroom. All this wuz between her literary studies. She'd finished *A Room of One's Own*, an' had now progressed onto to *To the Lighthouse*. This wuz Woolf's modernist classic from 1927 – the story of the Ramsay family and their visits to the Isle of Skye between 1910 and 1920.

'I's a complex psychological exploration that skilfully manipulates temporality an' the impermanence of adult relationships,' she wuz goin', whilst tryin' t'sort out the colour of Charlie's curtains with un. Multi-tasking see.

Y'cud tell tha' sometimes, when she wuz off on one like this, she wuz imaginin' wha' life might have been like if she had managed to go off with her old boyfriend, and t'be perfectly honest, loser and complete tool - Ronnie Phillips. This wuz, of course, when Charlie's da wuz shacked up with his ma's nemesis, Karen. 'Course all this had actually given his ma a complete an' utter understandin' ov the novel's themes.

Charlie wuz proud of his ma fur doin' this though. 'Mean, 'twudn' the kind ov discussion you heard very much in the kitchens round Trelawny. More often than not, 'twas how they wuz goin' to score their next batch of weed, or in the posher plaaces, who they'd reckoned wuz goin' t'win *Britain's Got Talent*, an' what bargains there wuz t'be 'ad over Tescos this week. Fuck, Charlie's mum wuz doin' somethun' amazin', incredible, superheroine-like. It wuz like her fuckin' avatar had stepped inta' their house, an' she wudn' there no more.

'I's all based on Godrevy lighthouse y'knaw,' said his ma, 'when Virginia (she said this like she knawed ov her personally, an' saw her over the Co-op every Friday) lived at Talland House in St Ives... She used to gaze out onta' it, and the whole thing inspired her... only she set ut on Skye rather than in Cornwall...'

'Great ma,' said Charlie. He gave 'is ma a hug. She wuz some proud ov un – t'knaw that ee wuz movin' in t'his own plaace an' that. Bugger the fact that ee'd managed t'tour half ov Western Europe. Apparently, fur his ma, this wuz wha' counted.

'I still be worried how you'm goin' to find money each month fur ut...'

It wuz a genuine concern. But Charlie reckoned somethun' would come 'is way soon enough. There was no oracle or anything, but ee'd be alright. Anyway, ee'd have a year's grace sure enough, with the money ee had in the bank – enough t'keep un goin' fur a while.

'Thought of takin' a lodger in 'ave ee? Might help...'

Ee knawed 'zactly where this wuz goin'. This was really code. What it actually meant wuz that Charlie's ma had spoken t'Yak's ma about the possibility of Yak movin' in with un. She wuz keen as mustard fur the cunt to get out of her plaace (messun' ov ut up with all 'is drums an' tha'), and the natural place fur un to go wuz with Charlie. Charlie wudn' s'keen though. Though Yak was a mate, y'wudn' 'zactly want un as a member ov yer household. Besides tha', the whole point ov movin' out wuz t'gain 'is own space, not t'share ut with another cunt. Virginia Woolf wudn' be havin' any ov tha'. Charlie wanted a room ov his own too. an' jus' like always, there were other plans too.

If this wudn' keepin' her busy enough, then there wuz Jess and Micky t'think about. Fur his ma, the fact that Jess wuz takin' over Ursula's wuz just about the ultimate thing y'cud possibly do in Troon. To slightly mis-quote Metallica, in one ov their more sensitive moments, nothing else mattered. See, the very fact tha' her maid was about to engage in this enterprise shawed all the disbelievers out there that the Curnow family could actually do something worthwhile. T'be fair to her, there'd been quite a lot ov ground in the respectability department to make up, after Tommy's recent endeavours, so this wuz her chance to pose. She knew she'd be talkin' 'bout all the latest styles an' cuts tha' Jess would be offerin', over bus stop and down Homebase.

Charlie cudn' help but think 'bout Micky though. Wuz a really ready t'settle down with er? Well, maybe. Ee wuz 'bout the same age as Charlie. Perhaps 'twas time. Perhaps ee wudn' s'much of the cunt he used t'be. Maybe neither ov um were.

The bottom line ov ut wuz that no sooner had they signed the deal on the salon, then the builders an' shopfitters had moved in. Well, in these days ov economic uncertainty, you took on jobs where you cud. It needed gutting. Some of the gear in there – the sinks and the dryers an' tha' – were from the 1970s an' had seen better days. All ov ut got 'eaved in a skip outside. Someone had already nicked the old copper water tank fur cash over the scrapie's. Sixty quid they wuz makin' at the moment – enough t'keep ee in mephedrone fur a week.

The tackers on the estate were finding fun things to do with bits ov ut – like playin' Doctor Who monsters with the perm dryers, and then smashing up all the old mirrors one by one. Yeah – all the Formica needed strippin' out too – an' upstairs, well, tha' wuz where Ursula used to store all the old perming lotions an' boxes ov unused curlers an' tha' – so all ov that needed t'go too.

When Charlie went over t'have a geek at wha' wuz on, the plaace looked like a bombsite. There wudn' nothun' left really – but Micky wuz there pretendin' t'co-ordinate stuff, while Jess

wuz out visiting manufacturers, an' sourcin' all the products
she wanted t'sell. Y'knaw the kind of crap they have in the windows – like as if some anti-frizz is goin' t'help out in the middle of wintry, mizzly day in the middle of Bolenowe Moor.
Apparently she had several options: Tigi, Bedhead or
Rockaholic.

'Comin' on then,' went Charlie, soundin' like an old fucker.
It wuz one ov they things you have t'say when y'dun't knaw
how the fuck it is actually comin' on.

'Gettin' there mate,' went Micky. That wuz one of they sort
ov things y'd'say when you'm clueless as to how it wuz actually progressing. There ee wuz, the cunt Micky. Called ee mate
like ee didn' mean ut.

Builders were goin' in an' out of the shell of the old shop
that used to be Ursula's, bringing out wheelbarrows full ov crap,
an' loadin' in new kit to do the conversion. Suddenly, Micky
wuz looking like the kind of enterprising business man, the
Tory MP for the area wanted, to help develop the economy of
Camborne and Redruth.

What the fuck had happened?

Change is what had happened.

Pilchards.

An' voodoo, see.

In a way, they both knawed ut. They both knawed that their
lives were altering big time. Charlie cudn' just up sticks an'
leave to go on some tour now, an' neither could Micky. Stuff
was becoming permanent. Charlie reckoned thaas' what happens when you become older. Nothing's temporary any more.
It all becomes fixed – unmovable, motionless. Tha' wuz positive
in a way though. It wuz all the homeless cunts down Camborne
who still had that temporary sense of life, an' thaas' why they
ended up pissing their pants every night an' kung-fu-ing the
cars by Aldi. Yak, Yak, yeah, ee wuz still in tha' temporary
unfixed world of non-progression. Neil, na. Ee wudn' anywhere
close t'Yak. Neil been like ut since he'd left school. If Charlie
'adn't dragged un out on tour with Purple Haze, ee'd have been
settlin' down t'retirement as Manager of Camborne Tescos.
Havin' said tha', 'is world had been somewhat unfixed by the
news about Anthony. Tha' had wrong-footed both Ally and ee.
Charlie understood tha'.

Charlie an' Micky were cut from the same cloth really. Tha' 'ad always been the cause of the tension between um. Now though, they didn' need t'say very much. There wuz shared understanding see. Charlie still thought Micky wudn' rock enough – all tha' fuckin' dabblin' about with keyboards, DJ-ing and samples an' tha' – all very Linkin Park nu-metal; and well, Micky thought Charlie wuz still too old school fur 'is liking. Matter now did ut? Prob'ly not, now both ov um wuz mort-gaged t'the hilt. 'Least, Micky an' Jess 'ad the keys to their plaace. Charlie wuz still waitin' fur 'is.

'What ee goin' t'call ut?' asked Charlie.

'Dunnaw... nothun' tacky though...'

Fuck, thought Charlie. This wuz Troon. Tackiness wuz ut's middle name. Thaas' wha' ut lived by.

'Jess an' I've got a few ideas...'

Ah shit, thought Charlie. Knawin' her it'ud be somethun' pretentious. Ee hoped t'fuck his dad wudn' have anything t'do with ut either, fur Club Rhino had forever sealed his fate as a knobber when ut comed to the name of new enterprises.

Charlie's da had changed too. When ee looked back on the last few years, ee cud see now how being made redundant 'ad fucked un up. 'Mean, there ee wuz in the early noughties doin' a'right, still listenin' t'his 80s' glam metal albums by bands like Dokken, Ratt and Keel, enjoyin' life, drilling the fuck out of the ground beneath them, and carryin' on like that wuz all 'twas ever goin' t'be. 'Twas like evolution had made un that way: gen-erations of his family working the mines locally. Aw yes, ee'd been an' researched ut all over the Cornwall Records Office. Like ee could tell ee how 'is great, great uncle wuz the shift cap'n over Tolcarne – that sort ov nerdy shit tha' people ov a certain age in Cornwall seemed t'love. Then there'd be so-an'-so Curnow who'd made an' lost a fortune over in some gold mine in Colorado (like tha' wuz ever goin' t'appen again!). Tha' wuz ut, see. His da liked the romance ov ut all, liked the idea ee wuz doin' somethun' age old. So now, Charlie could under-stand all the fuck ups, all the mistakes, the affairs, the strippers, the pole-dancers, the porn empire, an' 'is general lack ov under-standing of just about everything. When Crofty 'ad closed ut wuz like some ancient Celtic god had pulled the carpet from under his feet. Ut scat un flyin' you. But now, the da ov his childhood seemed to be there a little more. Obviously things 'ad changed but the cunt wudn' getting nearly half s'wrecked each week, nor wuz a being a total tool. Ee had purpose see – back underground. A proper job. That way ee wuz doing what ee wuz meant t'be doin'.

In his youth, Charlie'd been down Crofty with un a few times. 'Twudn' 'zactly wha' Health and Safety wanted, but all the boys did ut at some point. If y'dun't knaw ut, then you'll never realise how vast the operation is underground. It's like a small fuckin' invisible city under yer feet. You wudn' believe the gear down there – nor how the fuckin' ground above dun't collapse around ee, pullin' half ov Camborne's housin' in weth ut. Charlie cud remember the moment, when they locked the cage an' down you went. Cold first ov all, but then the heat buildin', like you was entering the layers ov Hell itself. Down there, the boys had their own rules – same as those you learned on the road. Do's and don'ts. When t'do stuff and when not to. Who t'respect and who t'slag off. Getting' all tha' back again wuz hard first of all when the mine re-opened. 'Mean, that's what y'd'lose first of all, that lore, that legend, that shared understanding that d'make a plaace tick. You'n soon buy new gear an' that, but the expertise down there is what you wanted. Fuck, tha' was the whole reason half the fuckin' world got dug out, 'cause of boys like tha' crowd. Six months on, and 'twas slowly comin' back. Some days, Tommy felt like ee'd never been gone. One of the stopes ee'd started work on, wuz the last one tha' they were on when the mine shut down the first time. Apparently, the tools wuz still there, still ready fur work the next day. Charlie's ma didn't really like his da goin' back down. Aw 'es, 'twas safer now than ut ever wuz, but still, there wuz tha' thought lurkin' in the back ov er mind that anything could happen underground. The names and the accidents in Troon cemetery told her tha'.

So after the collapse of Club Rhino, how wuz his da occupying hisself? Well, backalong, when ee wuz a tacker you, ee'd been a supporter ov Trura City Football Club. These days, ee wuz devoting a bit more time to ut.

'Only bleddy way we'm goin' t'put Cornwall on the map is t'have a proper team in the football league...' ee'd argue.

In a way, ee wuz right. Channel the energy of football inta' supportin' a real Cornish club, an' you might just take the rest of Cornwall – and its political aspirations ov devolution - with ee. Tommy's dream might well match the kind of future Cornwall someone like Trescothick wanted. Right now, you had yer Cornish Pirates, Redruth an' the Cornwall rugby team, but this wuz somethun' different. Football. Tommy didn't really get people in Cornwall who supported Plymouth Argyle. Yeah, a local team like, but they wuz over the border. They might have St Piran's flags (courtesy of Ginsters Pasties) on their shirts, but they wudn' Cornish. They wuz an English team no matter how you shook ut up. Tommy had dreams see. Ee wanted a Cornish team in there.

'Imagine,' ee wud go, 'just imagine if we wuz in the FA Cup... or Football League Two... We might have Man U or the Arsenal come down t'play at Treyew Road...'

Thaas' wha' ee wanted see. Enough clout t'take on the big boys. What a day tha' might be.

Sadly, Charlie knawed all about the cunts. Ee'd had their hist'ry drilled inta' un one day while his da wuz turning out all his old Uriah Heep an' Yes albums a few years back. See, right now they wuz in the Conference National Division following four successful promotions. This wuz the point, you. They wuz in striking distance of Football League Two (the old fourth division). The club had been there a good while – they were the founding members of the South Western League in 1951, an' 'ad had quite an illustrious history, culminating a few years back with them winning the FA Vase trophy. Half ov Cornwall went up t'Wembley Stadium t'see um win ut. His da wuz doin' the best ee cud t'make ut happen.

'This is why Cornwall idn' on the map...' ee said, obviously frustrated. 'We ebm' got naw foothall club... Getting' a football in the league'll be the best thing tha' could happen... You'n have yer bleddy Mebyon Kernow an' tha' fightin' for we, but 'tidn' naw good. Get Cornish flags in a football stadium an' we'm on...'

So fur his da, football seemed t'mean revolution. Ut meant devolution. Ut meant St Piran's flags in Europe. Ut might even lead t'a national team like Wales or Scotland. Yeah – St Piran's flags at the World Cip then, next t' the fuckin' row ov the vuvuzela horns.

Voodoo Pilchard

Ee'd heard Trescothick an' his da debate ut a few times up Institute. 'Course, Trescothick knew the value ov supportin' the 'White Tigers' or 'The Tinmen' as they wuz knawn, but then again, ee wuz prob'ly still thinkun' of setting off a million ton of explosive t'separate Cornwall off from England, so the place'd float a few more miles west inta' the Atlantic. Tha' wud then hopefully stop all the second-home cunts and other twats who reckoned Cornwall wuz some part ov South-West England from takin' over.

'Bleddy interlopers,' his da called um.

'White settlers,' went   Trescothick. ''Tis time the worm turned...'

Kernewek Jihad – yeah, yeah – only with the footy. KLF = Kernow Liberation Footy.

Charlie's ma hadn' got a lot ov time fur his footballing ambitions, but even so, him fartin' around with ut wuz at least better than un developing websites an' DVDs ov 50-year old cougars from over Rosewarne dressed up in Cornish tartan basques. The point wuz that ultimately Trura City just needed a bit ov investment. With the right financial backin', the Football League wuz in striking distance. Then, they could give Plymouth Argyle bell tink – an' any other football club in the south-west Britain a run fur their money.

So this wuz Tommy – back on the core, an' backin' Trura City.

This wuz the way things were changin'.

Charlie knew ut. He whacked Black Sabbath on his iPod; always comforting to know that Ozzy. Geezer, Tony an' Bill had been through the same feelings:

I FEEL UNHAPPY
I FEEL SAD
I'VE LOST THE BEST FRIEND
THAT I EVER HAD
SHE WAS MY WOMAN
I LOVED HER SO
BUT IT'S TOO LATE NOW
I'VE LET HER GO

I'M GOING THROUGH CHANGES.

When ee heard the song, ee cudn' help but think about Clifford an' then Bev as well. Too late now, Charlie told hisself. Ee mouthed ut as Ozzy's plaintive voice sang: 'I'm going through changes'. This wuz the kind exquisite love song that Sabbath cud turn their hand to, even those moast cunts just though they turned out doom and gloom old school riffage. Ah no, there wuz much more to ut than tha'. But still, the song reflected Charlie's mood. Ee cudn' help ut. Tha' wuz road lesson No.4 – develop a thick skin.

Elsewhere though, the same old shit was goin' down. Well, actually, 'twas the same old shit, just done a different way. Here's wha' happened: jus' as Charlie and Jess were getting their future lives sorted, it all kicked off on the estate. In the house next door t'Charlie's ma an' da (No.40 t'be exact), lived an old bugger by the name ov Arnold Crago. Everyone called un Arnie. Ee wudn' a bad ol' boy like. Mrs Williams used t'be good friends with un – makun' un yeast buns ('Without the orange peel mind…') every Thursday. Used to moan a few years back when they had the big all-nighter house parties. But other than tha' ee kept hisself t'hisself. Didn't harm nawbody or nothun' like. Only thing wuz, ee wuz very fucking proud ov the fuckin' prize-winning roses he wuz grawin' in his back garden. Ee'd spent a bit of money on um mind, got them from some posh nurseries down Tehidy way. Well, the flowers wuz lookin' grand, until one night, some fuckin' little gang of tackers went past an' – fur a laugh – cut all the heads off ov um.

Ol' boy Crago wuz indoors tuckin' inta' a plate ov fresh mackerel an' seen what happened through the patio doors. T'be honest, ee didn't give a fuck naw more. Well, the cunt wuz eighty somethun' – what could they do to un? Very calmly, ee went t'his shed, and brought out a Stihl MS 200 high-performance chainsaw, an' started ut up. Normally 'twudn' the sort of thing ee wud do. In fact, ee took special care ov ut, always greasin' ut up and oilin' ut down after dealin' with next door's Leylandii trees. Now though, ee wuz goin' t'use ut as a close-quarter weapon an' sort they little fuckers out fur good. Yeah – ee'd slice their fuckin' arms an' legs off – an' see how they liked tha'. So, the come uppance ov ut wuz tha' the tackers went screaming up the street, with Arnie Crago followin' on, buzzing like fuck, an' goin', 'Come here y'buggers! I'm goin' t'lop your heads off now...'

Apparently, Tommy Curnow seen ov ut tha' night after comin' 'ome from afternoon core.

'A'right Tommy?' ee'd gone, nice an' polite like.

'Jus' goin' t'sort these kids out...'

''Twas like the bleddy Texas Chain Saw Massacre... Boy Crago wuz full on with ut...'

The police wuz called by a neighbour, who heard the screamin', an' in the end they had t'take un out with a taser. So ee's standin' there buzzing away like some sort of crazy arborist, being fried by two electrodes. Some cunt managed to take a picture of ut on their mobile so 'twas all over the telly an' internet. In the meantime, ee'd managed t'run amock in some of the tackers' gardens, while they'd runned indoors, takin' out some trampolines, Wendy houses and a couple of bicycles. Apparently, some garden gnomes an' a clothes line got damaged too in the attack.

The BB-gun kid - now a bit taller - who'd helped Charlie t'take out Trescothick down at the Tamar Bridge, comed down the road, going, 'Arnie's flipped. Ee's like a Terminator...'

What did the coppers do? Well, tha' wuz ut wudn' ut? You wudn' believe ut. The Chief Constable ov Devon an' Cornwall wuz on the radio an' telly immediately, workin' in conjunction with Cornwall council. Apparently, Trelawny wuz goin' t'ave a fuckin' huge CCTV system set up, linked t'their control centre in Exeter. No cunt would be able to move, fart or do anything. Honest, 'twas shaping up t'be like George Orwall's *1984*. Big Brother wuz goin' t'be watching y'scratch yer ass, pick yer nawse an' whether you'd come home tanked up from a night up the Grenville Arms. Not only tha' though. Old boy from the coppers wuz talkin' 'bout a pilot scheme called Operation Goodnight. A strict curfew wuz goin' t'be introduced. Anyone under the age of sixteen wudn' going to be allowed out after 9pm unless they were accompanied by a responsible adult. This wuz the necessary crackdown on anti-social behaviour tha' wuz needed apparently – especially in the light of the chainsaw incident. The scheme wuz t'be extended down Park an Tansys and Pengegon, just in case any other tiny tools wanted t'kick off.

When ut comed on the telly, Charlie just laughed t'hisself. If they thought tha' would sort out the estate, then they had t'be fuckin' joking. The real issue wuz 'bout 'responsible adults'. The problem wuz, there wudn' that many ov um about. Charlie reckoned ut might work fur about a week, but after tha' the local coppers ud get pissed off, an' rather not be monitoring little knobbers up Trelawny. Meanwhile, they prob'ly best put a lot more energy inta' monitoring chainsaw sales down B&Q at Pool.

But then, y'had t'laugh. About a week after Operation Goodnight wuz introduced, the police got caught off guard didn' um? They wuz monitoring so closely wha' wuz goin' on in Trelawny, Park an Tansys an' Pengegon, the cunts failed to stop a serious robbery. It wuz the kind of serious robbery tha' just about near demolished the Co-Op in the middle ov Troon. See, of late, the powers tha' be, running the Co-Op had installed a cash machine in the wall of the shop, so they could charge fuckers in Troon a few quid extra to take out money, instead ov goin' down Camborne. Well, Charlie an' Yak heard the yarn. A few drunk buggers on their way home from football club nawticed what happened. Some party had driven down through Troon with a six-tonne JCB, bouncing along like – along New Road. This was all 'bout one in the morning. The cunt comed to a standstill opposite the fish an' chip house, an' then swung his rear bucket into the wall of the Co-Op where the cash machine was. After a few strikes at the concrete, they used the front loader to dig at the entire cash machine box, and lifted the bugger right out. Tens of thousand went apparently, fur ut had been newly stocked tha' week.

So, with the front bucket filled with the cash machine, they pissed way off down Treslothan. The busted cash machine wuz found in some fields down there, just beyond the church, near t' Carwynnen Quoit. They used the same pneumatic drill used t'smash up concrete to break ut open an' take the money. Fuckin' hell, y'had t'hand ut to um. 'Twas far easier than goin' inta' a bank or a Post Office with some shooters, an' askin' fur cash. This way, y'took the whole kit an' caboodle. No messun' see. Clean. Easy. Fuck. The usual local plod wuz first on the scene: Constable Combellack. Well, Combellack 'adn't seen the like ov ut. Apparently, ee looked proper adle-headed as he stepped out of his Focus to have a gake at the g'eat hole in the wall.

Voodoo Pilchard

'Course, the story attracted a lot of media. Troon wuz used t'ut by now. Satellite trucks an' BBC Spotlight an' Westcountry News down there. Ol' boy, the Chief Constable, wudn' too happy mind. It distracted the Devon & Cornwall Constabulary's work fur community safety under the auspices of Operation Goodnight, so just about every media cunt goin' wuz askin' ov un whether police resources were goin' in the right direction. The nice take on ut wuz an interview with another ol' boy who'd support Arnie's chainsaw attack. Georgie Angov 'twas.

'I'm ready fur um...' ee wuz goin', revving up some huge sized beast of a chainsaw. 'The police dun't protect me see. Thaas' why I got this... You gotta' take the law inta' yer own hands... I tell ee straight: 'tis the Wild West down here...'

Sales ov chainsaws was prob'ly hittin' double figures down B&Q inspired by Arnie Crago an' Georgie Angov. No doubt the Chief Constable would be hauled in t'see the Minister for the South West 'bout ut all, an' whether the right strategy was being developed in Cornwall. It made Charlie laugh. The story in *The West Briton* explained how the 'normally quite village of Troon, was subject to a JCB raid'.

Normally quiet? When?

NFC this wuz.

'Who do ee think dun ut?' asked Charlie's ma.

Nawbody answered. But everybody 'ad their suspicions.

Instead, they were meant t'be talking about what the new salon wuz goin' t'be called.

'Curl up and dye,' said their da. 'Or maybe Ali Barber...'

Jess groaned.

'What about Soul Scissors or Talking Heads?' chipped in their ma thinkin' she wuz being trendy.

'Hair & Now,' went Charlie.

'Fuck off,' went Micky. 'Thaas' pants...'

It wuz really, but y'had t'take the piss.

'Streaks Ahead then,' went their ma.

'Na.'

'Hair Kutz,' said their da in a German accent.

'No da. That's been over-used...'

'An it's shite,' went Charlie.

'See, we want somethun' that combines the hairdressing with the piercing and tattoos an' tha'...'

'You'll be lucky then,' went their da.

The gags went on all night. Y'had Close-Shave, Hair Force, Shear Luck, Mane Man, Locks Smith, Choice Cuts. Fuckin' hell, they were gettin' really terrible.

'Well, you dun't have t'name ut right away do ee?' offered their ma.

'No, but we want to start advertising soon ma,' went Jess.

'My last attempt,' went their da, 'Crowning Glory... How 'bout tha.?'

No-one even bothered t'respond to un. It wuz so shite. 'Twudn' worth ut. His da went back t'watchin' the telly.

'My idea,' went Micky, 'is tha' it should be called Headonizm.'

'Headonizm... Wha'... like someone who believes in pleasure?' asked Jess.

'Yeah – only spelt h.e.a.d. instead of h.e.d., an' with a z instead ov a s.'

The cunt Micky might have nailed ut.

'I like ut,' went Charlie. 'Y'can't go wrong with z... very metal. Put an umlaut in there an' thaas' ut...'

'H.E.A.D.O (with an umlaut) N.I.Z.M. then,' said Micky, spelling un out.

'Well I think ut sounds stupid,' said their ma, who was prob'-ly favouring somethun' like Making Waves.

'I agree,' grunted their da. But then wha' did ee knaw?

'It's good, I d'reckon,' said Jess. She wuz lookin' some tickled with ut.

'I's got the right attitude, I think,' said Charlie, 'not that I knaw much about marketing a hairdressers...'

'Your choice I s'pause,' said their ma, an' went upstairs t'carry on reading her Virginia Woolf.

'I'm on the bit where Charles Tansley claims tha' women can't paint or write...' she announced, as if everyone wuz as familiar with the narrative as she wuz.

The problem wuz, everyone ignored her. 'Twas lookin' there fur a moment, like the fucker Tansley wuz right.

So that wuz ut. The salon wuz goin' t'be called Headönizm. Charlie 'ad t'hand ut to um. 'Twudn' a bad start really. Jess an' Micky stayed downstairs playin' around with designs fur ut, while Charlie went upstairs to his room.

It felt weird being back in there after all the time away. Some of his stuff had been there since ee wuz a fuckin' kid. 'Twas time to get rid ov a lot ov ut – take ut t' a car boot up Pool Market or dump ut over United Downs. When ee moved, thaas' when he'd sort ut. Then again, what usually happened is that you just take this sort of crap with you. There was song-writing t'be done. Ee had a mind t'pick up his guitars, an' try an' write how he wuz feeling. If not with chords, then perhaps try an' assemble some lyrics. But na, fuck ut – not now. Ee wudn' really in the mood t'write.

Charlie checked his e-mails. There wuz one in from Kelvin an' Mel. Apparently, they had moved inta' the world of film extras since ee'd been away. Some Rosamunde Pilcher drama wuz being filmed over St Agnes way, an' they'd got part in ut. Then they wuz hopeful of a part in a new film being shot down Mowshol 'bout the Spanish Raid there back in 1595. Some step up you, from filming gonzo porn down an industrial unit in Pool. Still, Charlie congratulated them on ut. Boy Kelvin had been quite helpful in advisin' Charlie which mortgage deal to go fur. Somethun' else in from Spryer too – callin' them a bunch ov cunts fur not being in touch widn'. Charlie pinged un an e-mail back sayin' how they wudn' be doing naw more Hendrix stuff. Ee'd already told un they'd all ritually burnt all their stage clothes. Charlie cud imagine un somewhere cussin' an' swearin' an talkin' about all the lost opportunities to make a bit ov money.

In another e-mail there was a link t'a You Tube video from Piotr Zbarashchenko. It was a Celtic Frost reformation gig shot somewhere in Poland ee'd been too. Good ol' Piotr Charlie reckoned. Even though ee an' Yeugen wuz now ancient history, er da 'ad kept in touch. Didn't say much 'bout her though, whenever Charlie asked. Best t'let sleepin' dogs lie maybe. Was this road lesson No.5 maybe? Beware ov groupies. Not groupies perhaps, but previous girl-friends maybe.

Ee closed down Outlook Express, and logged in t'his Facebook page. Fuckin' Facebook. In reality, ee hated the crap. You could spend hours in there, sharing shit nawbody else needed to knaw about, but 'twas necessary. How cud y'be a twenty-first century rock musician without ut? The answer was, y'cudn'. Ee'd been thinkin' 'bout Yeugen a fair bit ov late. Deep down, ee felt sad 'bout what had happened, before Purple Haze went away on endless European tours. Charlie'd 'oped they cud've got over whatever glitch had happened: principally tha' last return t'Bev ee'd had. Fuckin' twat, ee mouthed at hisself. Charlie'd have moments where ee really worried 'bout the Curnow gene inside ov un. An' Bev – well, ee'd reckoned ee'd lost that one a long, long time ago, back when Balance split.

'Mean, Bev wuz too intelligent fur him wudn' she? Tha' wuz the reality ov ut. She wuz headin' fur a glitterin' academic career in somethun or other, an' ee, well, now ee wuz back in Troon – home of the chainsaw massacres and drive-by cash-machine wrecking. The last ee'd heard wuz tha' Bev wuz back down in Cornwall again. She'd got a flat down Falmouth, an' wuz studying fur an MA down the University of Exeter in Cornwall. What wuz ut she wuz lookin' at? Somethun' t'do with witchcraft in Early Modern Britain. She had plans t'do a Ph.D as well. Given time, Bev would be fuckin' running the plaace down there. An' tha' wuz ut wudn' ut? When ee'd met her accidentally shoppin' in the middle ov Trura, round Christmas time, she told un she wuz thinkin' ov sellin' all her gear an' that. Wha' a fuckin' waste.

Charlie thought back t'his own efforts in education. How the fuck did a end up with a 2.2 in Media Production? Ee didn' rightly knaw. Moast of his assignments an' work ee'd just about managed t'cobble together before headin' off to some toilet t'play. An' then well, when Purple Haze kicked off, ee'd just about managed t'keep ut all goin'. Lectures though, wuz something ee'd have to write off as a non-event. Basically, at tha' stage, ut 'ad become a correspondence course. So now, there ee wuz with a fuckin' degree in a subject no-one wanted. Given the decline of the local pornography industry, there wudn' much call for media production duties in Obby Stanker. On one level, ee'd considered journalism. Ee 'ad the musical knowledge fur sure. Yak an' Neil kept remindin' un ov how much ov a musical nerd ee was. But then ee reckoned ee'd have to spend a while workin' for a local paper, and be someone like local music journo Sam Polglaze, and that, ee didn' go much on at all. Na, 'is song-writing wuz the way forward. Ut 'ad t'be.

Then came the surprise ov the day. Ee clicked around his Facebook page some more, an' found a couple ov new messages. One wuz the same stupid message from Kelvin as on his e-mail, and another wuz from somebody asking when the next Purple Haze tour was. But another message had come in from Bev Bennetts an' she wuz asking un t'be her friend.

'Meet up for drink sometime?' the message said. 'Heard you were back.'

In a single instance, like you do, Charlie felt all the kisses and cuddles ee'd ever had with Bev, and they went through his body like a Pete Townsend power-chord. Ut gived un a deceptive boner just thinkin' about her. Then reality bit back. Na – she wuz just being pleasant thaas' all. Bev wuz like tha'... even when she'd been goin' out with tha' tool Mike in Bristol. And up there, tha' wuz a real fuckin' mistake. Best leave ut, ee reckoned and so ee switched off 'is laptop. Ee pushed 'is iPod inta' the docking speakers he'd installed an' twirled the dial. At moments like this y'needed Deep Purple's 'Child in Time'. Gillan, Glover, Blackmore, Lord and Paice. Ten minutes and eighteen second of existentialist angst. A bit ov seriously mad screamin' too. Jus' the right thing.

Below un, Jess an' Micky were conceiving of Headönizm (with a z), while in her bedroom is ma wuz devoting her time t'various studies of Virginia Woolf's literary genius.

Hi da wuz just downstairs, getting' pissed on cheap lager from the Co-Op, oh, an' plottin' ov how the White Tigers could eventually be in the Premiership.

Outside the coppers were monitoring everything from the safety ov Exeter, and tackers were driving their parents mental coz they cudn' go outside an' tempt chainsaw murderers. Usually, this meant turnin' up the blood splatter factor on their Zombie-themed computer games: from green t'red.

Down Godrevy, the lighthouse beam lit the known world, not knowin' ov uts fame or reputation.

The Saffron Detangler – Triumph over tangles with this super rich conditioner.
Instant detangler
• Instant detangling and conditioning – Strands of saffron provide instant conditioning, detangling and shine
• Smoothes and softens – Special conditioning agents and our activated moisture blend with saffron help smooth,

soften and prevent moisture loss
• Helps protect against sun damage – Saffron is a natural
UV absorber

Ut wuz the morning an' Charlie wuz in that beautiful world
between being asleep and awake. Ee wuz dreaming about being
interviewed for some magazine. The questions were coming
thick an' fast:

Is it important to stay in touch with life at street level and
for success not to take you away from that?

What is your worst character trait?

What's you best character trait?

What's your biggest vice?

Have you already written your best song?

Have you ever been in therapy?

Is there anyone special in your life right now?

Are you now the finished article?

Charlie woke up. The last two questions put un in a sweat.
When ee woke up, ee realised they 'adn't woken un up. In fact,
Micky wuz standin' at the end ov 'is bed, with a cup of coffee,
rifling through his CD collection.

'Coffee fur you,' ee went. 'From yer ma…'

'Do you ever sleep Micky?' went Charlie.

''Course…'

'Then…?'

'Been down t'Headönizm. Builders start at seven, see…'

'So? What you tellin' me fur?'

'Come down there with me Charlie… Somethun' I want you
t'see…'

'Fuck off,' went Charlie. 'I's too early…'

'Not this,' said Micky, 'eavin' off Charlie's duvet. 'You'll like
ut…'

A fuckin' ex-traveller orderin' un about. Thaas' all ee fuckin'
needed wudn't ut?

About ten minutes later, Charlie'd finished 'is coffee an'
struggled inta' Micky's van, and they'd wound their way up
Polgine Lane an' inta' Fore Street, where Headönizm wuz goin'
to be located. Jess, apparently, had gone inta' town t'visit the
Tigi styling products plaace on one ov the industrial estates
over Pool.

Micky pulled the van outside ov the salon. There wuz already a lot of building activity taking place.

'Look,' went Micky.

'Wha'? Wha' am I meant t'be looking at?' said Charlie still in a bit ov a daze.

'The fuckin' hoarding outside the salon.'

Charlie turned his head and squinted.

'See ut do you?'

'What? What am I lookin at?'

'Tha' there…'

Micky took his arm and pointed across Charlie's chest.

Charlie turned his head. Ee cud see shopfitters goin' in an out with various bits of suspended ceiling and fluorescent lights.

Then he saw ut. Right in the middle of the hoarding was a piece of street art. Charlie looked at ut. He read ut aloud: 'Voodoo Pilchard'.

'Yeah,.., thaas' a blessin' that is,' said Micky.

'A blessing…?'

'Well, yeah, I mean this Voodoo Pilchard artist – the "Pilchard" I call un. Well, ee's the main man idn' a? You got tha' on your buildin' an' well, you'm 'in' ent ee? See what I mean…'

Fuck. Micky wuz near shakin' with excitement.

'I's just a piece of street art Micky…' went Charlie nonchalantly. 'You'm goin' on like 'tis the Second Coming or somethun'…'

'It's a sign…' said Micky.

'Here we fuckin' go,' Charlie thought. 'I thought ee'd left all this New Age crap behind when he stopped selling wooden toadstools t'grannies on the A30…'

'The Pilchard… here in Troon… Charlie…'

Charlie looked over at the graffiti again. None ov the builders seemed t'be takin' much nawtice ov ut.

'Proper mystical is ut?' asked Charlie.

'Yeah – as good as,' went Micky, the tool. 'See the fish shape look?'

'I'n see ut,' went Charlie. 'Same as on Centenary Chapel…'

'Just like you told me Charlie… Just like you said.'

Ah fuck. Who needed knobbers down Penwith dancing

round standing stones, lookin' fur ley lines an' reverse polarities, when you had first-class fuckwits like Micky.

'So, The Pilchard's been here.... So what?'

'Well, I'm goin' t'keep ut. When the hoardings come down, I'll keep ut – mount ut on the wall above me tattooing machine... fur good luck an' that...'

'Beauty,' went Charlie. 'Make sure you have trip wires an' a alarm on ut, or some art thief may come along an' nick ut...'

He wuz reminded ov another time.

'Yak'll...'

But then ee stopped. Ee realised what ee wuz about t'say. Na. That wuz all a long time ago now.

There wuz a pause.

'You en't takin' me seriously are ee Curnow?'

'When 'ave I ever?' asked Charlie, smiling.

'Cunt,' went Micky. 'I thought you'd be impressed...'

The reality wuz tha' Charlie wuz impressed. Ee'd even seen ut comin' all over Obby Stanker Country, all over electric pastyland. Ee wudn' about t'admit that t'Micky though, not yet, at least.

Charlie looked down the road. There wuz the old chapel they'd first rehearsed in – bashing out the old Free and Led Zeppelin numbers. The plaace wuz closed now. No-one t'keep ut going see. Even worse now that old boy Crago was locked away. 'Least ee used to weed the gravel outside. 'Twould soon be converted inta' flats and the last of John Wesley's presence in Troon would be swept away. Trundling up past ut comed Jess. She pulled up behind Micky's van and got out ov her Ford Ka.

'Got me products,' she said excitedly. 'What you two doing?'

'Nothun',' went Charlie. 'Just checkin' out the conversion...'

'Well, give me a hand then... Can you help load in this lot?'

Fuck. It looked like Jess had just bought out Vidal Sassoon. Fur the next fifteen minutes they were loadin' in Brunette Goddess shampoo, Foxy Curls, Control Freak anti-frizz, Moisture Maniac conditioner, Dumb Blond straightening stuff, Superstar volumizing spray, Small Talk Soothing lotion an' Spoil Me heat resistant serum. Then there wuz the Ego Boost hydration spray an' the Self-Absorbed Mega-nutritional conditioner, an' the Power Trip Hair Gel and Mastermind texturizing spray (whatever the fuck tha' wuz). Finally, the tins of Maxxed Out o-zone-friendly hairspray and the Hard Head Hard Hold hairspray.

Fuck me. It wuz like another language - Klingon or somethun'.

'D' y' really need all ov this lot?' went Charlie. 'I mean, I thought y'was jus' cuttin' hair an' tha'... not makin' everyone south of Camborne inta' models an' film stars...'

'It's how you make them feel Charlie...' went Jess. 'You should know tha' by now...'

'Jess wants to give them the 'Headönizm' experience...' went Micky, like ee wuz her fuckin' manager or somethun'.

'Okay, okay, I get ut,' said Charlie. 'Now, I'm off...'

'Where ee goin'?'

'Home.'

'Wha' for?'

'I need a room ov me awn...'

Charlie went past Grenville and Troon Motors. He still wanted solace from the hectic Hendrix schedule. So far, ee wudn' really findin' ov ut.

Those questions came back to un, as ee walked along. Ee tried to give some answers:

Is there anyone special in your life right now?

'No, no-one special right now.'

Are you now the finished article?

'No, I'm not the finished article. I might be settled, but I'm a long way from achieving all I want to...'

Yeah, tha' sounded right.

Back at Headönizm, Micky admired once again the street art and began unpacking the Power Trip Hair Gel.

Power trip – yeah – tha' wuz fuckin' Curnow all over wudn' ut?

Dozmary Hair Repair Treatment – Get together with this power-packed weekly treatment.
Strengthens and rebuilds.
• Replenishes strength, elasticity and shine – A special combination of heather conditioners helps build inner strength
• Helps prevent breakage – Essential Dozmary Pool

heathers, vitamins and wheal proteins help repair and
prevent further damage
• Hydrates – A powerful combination of ingredients helps
to bind moisture to the hair

Tommy Curnow understood 'the temporality an' the impermanence of adult relationships' better than 'is wife thought.

Now, ut wudn' like there wuz anything goin' on – or anything like tha'. Na. This wuz the new, improved, biological
Tommy Curnow. After core, sometimes Tommy'd nip in an' see
Karen. Now, everyone knew wha' went on between um years
ago like, but well, now, things wuz different. 'Mean, when
Clifford 'ad 'is head staved in, that made Tommy re-think
things completely. Even though ee'd denied ut, there wuz
always that bit ov jealousy there, that the cunt Clifford wuz
shaggin' 'is ex, an givin' her one right before 'is eyes. Ee cudn't
help ut. Well, 'twas human nature see. But since ut 'ad all happened, Tommy kept a watchful eye on Karen. Not that she
cudn' do whatever the hell she wanted, or even see who see
wanted, it wuz jus' Tommy wantin' ov the best fur her and the
kids. For one thing, despite everything, ee'd been more like a
father to um than anyone else, and fur another, ee didn't like
to think ov her rattling round Clifford Towers on her own.
She'd just about managed t'keep the house after Clifford's passing. The sale t'Ginsters helped, but course, there were a lot ov
debts, half ov which Karen didn't knaw about. Clifford cud be
a tool, but she still loved un. She cudn' help ut.

Mainly Tommy went round there, so they cud talk about the
murder case, and the on-going investigation inta' ut. Problem
wuz, the case had gone fairly cold, and the coppers didn't seem
too bothered on pickun' ut all up again. 'Course, Tommy 'ad
helped Karen makes presentations t'solicitors and so on, but
'twudn' goin' very far t'all. Both of them knew there wuz people out there who knew stuff, but naw-one was goin' t'say anything fur fear of them being found dead in a World Heritage
Site as well. 'Twas true too, tha' Tommy had t'be careful. Sally
knew a little bit ov ut, but perhaps not the full tale. She'd have
gone spare if she knew Tommy was slipping her a few quid, to
help her get by, fur the kiddies an' tha'. But strikin' up any sort
of relationship with her wudn' Tommy's idea t'all.

Voodoo Pilchard

Karen, on the other hand, always 'ad the idea tha' ee might come back to her – 'specially now tha' Sally wuz readin' all that there feminist literature. Maybe deep down, somewhere below the surface, she wuz hoping Sally might go back t'Ronnie Phillips an' then Tommy might seek solace with her. But fur now, she accepted ut as 'twas. They wuz just friends. Christ, Tommy even took her up cemetery last few months so she cud put flowers on Clifford's grave.

This wuz it on Obby Stanker see. Amongst the voodoo and the pilchards, morality – as the Jehovis Witnesses knew all too well - took new turns every day.

Godrevy Seal and Shine – Shiny, hydrated hair, is gorgeous head-turning hair.
Heat Protection and Shine
• Thermal protection – Helps protect against damage caused by blow dryers, smoothing irons and other thermal appliances
• Prevents moisture loss – Thermal protection and our Activated Moisture Blend help balance moisture and prevent dryness
• Adds shine – Essential fatty acids and conditioners help provide added shine

When Yak lacked direction, thaas' usually when serious shit happened. Like a few years ago when ee fucked up the gig in Newquay, an' then when ee decided t' assist Markie Phillips in his raid on St Day Post Office. See, everybody else seemed t'be sorted. 'Mean, Charlie sorted hisself out a house an' that, an Micky an' Jess wuz doin' up Ursula's, an Neil, well, Neil wuz settled down good an' proper, despite all the current problems with Anthony's Asparagus syndrome.

There'd been lots ov temptations on the road the last few years. Ee wuz proud ov hisself: ee had managed t'resist a few ov um, if not all of um. When some time came up fur a bit of kickback an' relaxation, well, 'twas only natural tha' ee'd indulge in a few substances. The way ee saw ut these days, s'long as ut didn't affect is playin' then naw-one could say anythun'. Still movin' back inta' 'is mother's wudn' quite t'his likin'. Fur a start, she wuz crampin' 'is style in all kind ov ways. Yak always did quite well fur maids, an' well, now, bringin' some BBW boiler 'ome t'his ma's plaace didn' quite have the attraction – with her in the next bedroom listenin' t'his gruntin' and groanin'. Then she wuz always moanin' on at un fur not doin' this or that. Ee felt like ee wuz fuckin' back at school again. Then there wuz the fact tha' ee cudn' really rehearse any more. Purple Haze wuz naw more. No cunt seemed t'have a new idea. Ee usually relied upon Charlie's guidance an' direction, but now, Charlie'd seemed distracted; not up fur ut anymore. Perhaps 'twas just him maturin' a bit – thinkin' through 'is options. Fuck, 'twas borin' though. Yak liked t'live on the edge – always 'ad done, always would. Better t'burn out than fade away. That's wha' the rock-'n'- roll-poet Joe Elliot said, wudn' ut? Wha' wuz road lesson No.7? Dun't be a tool. Well, ee wuz tryin' not t'be.

So, a combination ov factors wuz impacting on Yak when ee made a new business decision. Ov late, ee'd invested in a new i-Phone an' wuz transferring numbers onta' ut from 'is old phone. There were a lot of good new apps on ut, an' ee reckoned tha' this wuz the kind of new technology ee needed. See Charlie Curnow, wudn' the only man on a mission in Troon. Yak's plan wuz simple. Ee wuz fuckin' sick t'death of there bein' naw plaaces fur new bands or tourin' bands t'play in Cornwall. Ee 'ad a model in mind. Ee wuz goin' t'open a new venue – a rock club, jus' fur this kind ov thing. If ee plaayed 'is cards right, ut might even become his own pad – then ee cud shift all 'is gear from 'is ma's, an' be sorted.

The model fur ut wud be the legendary rock venue in Manhattan, New York City: CBGBs. That stood fur Country, Blue Grass and Blues, an' although the venue wuz originally goin' t'feature tha' kind ov music, during the new wave era in the late 1970s, it featured up an' comin' cunts like the Ramones, the Misfits and the Patti Smith Group, but latterly, wuz more famous for its hardcore punk bands like Agnostic Front, Bad Brains an' Sick of It All. Yak 'ad done 'is research. Ee knew ut started in 1973, 315 Bowery on Bleecker Street, but wuz closed down in October 2006. Years ov rock history wuz in there. Thaas' wha' ee wanted for Cornwall – the kind of plaace they'd needed when Balance had first started out. That way 'twould be there forever. 'Twould be Yak's legacy, his gift t'Kernow. There'd be a picture of un on the wall, and drum skins mounted on picture frames.

Ee'd have a bit ov a battle on though – fur the plaace ee had in mind wuz Tommy Curnow's old Club Rhino site. Problem wuz the whole area wuz up fur re-development wudn' ut? The government wanted t'put a whole new eco-town in there, and make Pool all fuckin' designer – eco-homes and zero mile work units. Moast people didn't have much faith in ut you, but tha' didn' stop the RDA marchin' round putting compulsory purchase orders on plaaces. Yak had t'ope 'twudn' go through – that in the wave ov the new Government spending cuts, the planned reconstruction wudn' happen. Yak wuz 'opin' the economy would stay shafted fur a bit, then ee might just make ut. Perhaps the government might even scrap the RDA altogether, but then 'twud only be replaced with somethun' equally as shite, like some new Local Economic Forum. They wuz talkin' all 'bout ut on the radio.

Yeah, Yak wud have every type ov alternative music goin' on there: anything s'long as ut wudn' manufactured fuckin' non-threatening pop fur twelve year olds. No non-threatening teenage boys an' na' booty-shakin' girl bands. Ee reckoned ut wuz just the sort ov half-way house venue between the pubs an' clubs, an' the bigger plaaces like the Pavilions in Falmouth. Marketed the right way, ee cud make a killun'. You never knaw, the whole plaace might take off. Ee wanted ut t'be like some of the better venues they'd plaayed up in England – and on the continent – with Purple Haze. Inside ut would be painted black, some kind of skull and crossbones logo on the doors, an' after a gig, the ceiling drippin' with condensation and the carpets all sticky. Since ee'd been back, ee'd had a geek in the old building ov Club Rhino. Not much ov ut 'ad changed. Still some ov ut hadn't been done up since the big fight took place between the Polish, the Lithuanians an' the Cormac boys tha' night. Boy Bluett wud give un a hand surely, an' once Charlie knawed 'bout ut, ee reckoned ee'd be up fur helpin' out as well.

Ee cudn't tell un yet though. See part ov the problem wuz financin' ov ut. Well, banks didn' give fuckers like ee any kind ov loan. Ee wuz typical Cornish in tha' way - they didn' want t'knaw:

'Speak dialect do ee?'

''Es...'

'Well, cunts like you we just dun't lend to... Fuck off home t'yer clotted cream, saffron cake an' pasties...'

Thing wuz, 'twas goin' t'take a bit ov money t'set ut up. Well, Yak 'ad weighed up his options. There wuz always Markie wudn' there? Despite everything tha' had happened, Markie knew Yak's weakness, knawed tha' with the right job, the right deal, Yak wud always go fur ut. But not this time, na. See, even Yak reckoned that – despite all the bullshit – all his so-called 'community work', the police's interests in Markie's activities wuz gettin' hotter an' hotter. 'Twudn' goin' t'be long 'til they brought un down. Na. Not Markie. Not this time. Yak had thought about the music. Wuz there any possibilities there? Na. not really. Like Neil, Charlie'd given um both a good wedge off tha' song-writing deal – but ee knawed the truth, 'twas Charlie who'd made the songs. Ee wuz grateful fur ut, make naw mistake, but a wedge like tha' wudn' goin' t'come 'is way again soon. What ee decided wuz t'use that wedge to invest. With the right deal, ee cud come out of this very sweet, very sweet indeed.

Ov all the plaaces on the earth, Newlyn wuz where Yak 'eaded. 'Twas the only plaace t'go really fur what ee wuz after. Newlyn wuz the largest fishing port in the whole of Britain. It had an annual turnover ov over twenty million quid. Newlyn wuz world famous fur fish, yeah, stinkun' bleddy fish. Well, maybe. But the problem wuz, moast ov the edible species 'ad either been fished out or 'ad fucked off, knowing that their chances of living a bit longer might be better out in the middle ov the Atlantic where the boats cudn' go. See, years ago, the plaace wuz fuckin' heavin' with fishermen and jowsters, plaaces barrelling up pilchards all over the shop. G'eat schools of um used t'come in – an' with they sorta' quantities, 'twas easy 'nough t'make a bit, an' pay tithes t'the church. Thaas' when all the artists wuz about painting pictures ov long-bearded old sea dogs repairing their nets: Thomas Cooper Gotch, Henry Scott Tuke an' cunts like tha'. Well, all tha' stopped in the 1960s, when the pilchards got over-fished and decided not t'come back anymore. Perhaps the fuckers woke up t'the fact that every season they'd get netted in their millions. Tha' wuz ut. The whole market collapsed, an' Cornwall cudn' provide tins any more fur demand in Catholic countries round the

Voodoo Pilchard

Mediterranean. Tha' really fucked the economy up good an' proper, conveniently jus' as the las' tin mines were closin' too.

Since the 1960s, well, things've been goin' along but moast ov the boys down there ent tha' keen on any sort ov European Union policy on fishin'. You'n just about guarantee tha' whatever quotas gone in, they ent goin' t'be happy with ut. So what with all the environmental restrictions, the health an' safety, an' the dear price of diesel, 'tis a wonder any cunt down there can even be bothered t'take a boat out over Gwavas Lake an' inta' the Channel. Worse than tha', now all the houses down there've been bought by artists an' potters an' so on, so when, years ago, the fishermen cud come in an' stroll up the hill t'the cottage, now they 'ad t'drive in from plaaces like Camborne just t'live.

But some fishin' wuz still goin' on. Well, 'twas like mining wudn' ut? It defined ee, didn' ut? Stop ut, an' you'm lost. So some buggers wuz still on ut down there - beam trawling, gill netting, potting or fishing inshore. Then every few years, there wuz a scrappage scheme – basically, y'got paid money t'have yer boat scat t'bits, an' say you wudn' be fishun' any more. Despite the buildin' ov a new fish market (2.3 million quid courtesy of the EU), the whole system wuz fucked. Y'had fish packed in ice being transported up the M5 t'plaaces outside Bristol, t'have ut sorted out by some supermarket, and then transported back down the M5 t'be sold in shops in Cornwall. Ask any fisherman and they'd tell ee 'twas all fucked up.

So wha' do ee do? Well, you find alternatives, dun't ee?

Well, perhaps not alternatives, just an update of old practice – more or less. Yeah, if 'tidn' pilchard an' pasties Cornwall wuz famous fur, then 'twas smugglin' an' free-tradin' – so, yeah, talk t'anyone in Newlyn these days an' they'll get ee what you need: yer own peculiar so t'speak. Yeah – 'twas like fuckin' e-Bay or Amazon on the Atlantic. What ee want? Bit of immigrant labour. No problem. Prostitutes. Take a bit longer – but they'n get um. Extra strength Viagra. Here, in twenty-four hours. Cheap tobacco? Easy as fuck. Cannabis? Too easy, these days. Alcohol fur sellin' cheap back St Just or over St Ives. Naw problem. You name ut, you'n 'ave ut.

Yak named ut. What ee wanted wuz simple. Ee wanted a couple ov crates ov cocaine. Yeah – these were the pallet loads –

63

stacked up with about fifty bags of ut on each, wrapped around with industrial cellophane. A little bit ov ut – perhaps a bag or two – would be fur 'personal use', an' then the rest ee'd sell on. Quite good sales apparently these days, down Penryn an' Falmouth – s'many students see. Easy pickings. Tha' way ee'd make enough money t'invest in the venue. Livin' the dream ee told hisself, thaas' what 'twas about, sure 'nough.

How did ut work? Well, the boys would link up with some of the big vessels in the Western Approaches. Easy see, t'just load a couple ov crates overboard onta' one of the trawler decks. Then crane ut down below in the hold. Nice little haul like – well, ut beat bein' out there in a Force 10 gale after a few cod t'sell back at market. Ideally, 'course, you'd do the two – bit ov fishing by night, and then when dawn comed, meet up with the regular suppliers. These were the South America ones – comin' over from Bolivia an' Brazil an' headin' up t'Milford Haven an' Liverpool. Twenty years ov managin' ut 'ad made fur a slick operation. 'Twas the perfect distribution method really – just like years ago – comin' in off the big clippers an' puttin' in t'some isolated cove. Get a van down there with a crew ov boys an' bob's yer uncle. All sorted. Then off down Hayle McDonalds fur a breakfast (the usual sausage an' egg McMuffin, hash brown an' coffee), and a quick line of coke in the toilet.

So thaas' why Yak found hisself wanderin' round down Newlyn harbour. Out in the distance ee cud see St Michael's Mount, an on Gwavas Lake, a few trawlers comin' in from the Western Approaches. Ut stunk t'fuck down there (worse than Trelawny after a curry night) – wha' with bits ov old fish guts kickin' round everywhere – that the seagulls wudn' even have a go at. The fucker looked – well, like a fish out ov water (moast of the boys down there wuz hard cunts you) – but ee soon found the bloakey ee'd needed t'have a yap with.

'Whaas' up me andsome?' ee went. 'Believe you'm after a bit ov gear are ee like?'

'Yeah. Work someun' out cen't us?' went Yak, like ee wuz fuckin' Long John Silver.

'Proper job! Come'st you in, an' le's 'ave a yap...'

Fuckin' hell, thought Yak fur a moment. With this knobber, 'twas like ee'd stepped back in time t'*Poldark*. But then, with their satellite tracking, mobile phones and high-speed delivery system, it very much looked like a special kind ov FedEx fur the coke users an' head-bangers ov Cornwall. Bewdie. 'Twas free-tradin' on a whole new global scale. Back Prussia Cove, Harry and John Carter ud be turnin' in their graves – happy as Larry.

> Holy Well Special Conditioner – Promotes healthy look-ing hair.
> Energizing Body Builder
> • Thickens – A unique blend of well waters of Penwith both volume and thicken limp locks
> • Strengthens – Traditional, magical waters strengthen damaged hair and reduce the formation of split ends
> • Energizes – Natural extracts of fern and bramble help stimulate the senses and provide an energizing experience

Ally an' Neil wuz at an 'Individual care plan' meetun' about Anthony. 'Twas meant t'be one of those cosy get togethers where all interested parties discuss the best way forward fur Anthony. Apparently, so Charlie heard ut from Neil, there wuz a lot ov cunts there: Anthony's head teacher, 'is doctor, social workers and the Asperger's Syndrome and ADHD support group: basically half ov' Cornwall, tryin' t'work out how t'deal widn'. Everything 'ad quickly become very formal like. There wuz reports on his behaviour, on his cognitive ability, on his literacy and numeracy, on his brain pattern, on how ee operat-ed with other kids, on what his dislikes and likes where, and all the recent violent shit ee'd been up to, since the last meetun'. Things wuz gettin' a bit serious. His headteacher, Mrs Evans, wuz kickin' ut all off. She'd 'ad enough.

'It's clear that we, as a school, are unable to continue to man-age Anthony's behaviour... We neither have the time nor the resources to cope with the high level of disruption he is caus-ing. My staff also feel that his levels of violent response are increasing...'

'Can you give us an example?' one of the social workers asked.

'Well, of late, when asked to complete a task that he didn't want to do, he went through the infants' classroom, turning over all the tables, and punching anyone who got in his way... About a third of the class had to be hospitalised over Treliske.

The governors had to have a special meeting about the incident. The Chief Education Officer's involved now...'

NFC see.

Ally held Neil's hand even tighter. It wuz all goin' out ov control – like all these people there, didn't really knaw un t'all. 'Twas like whatever they said now, didn't seem t'matter. Everyone seemed t'have made their own mind up 'bout un.

'Is there anything more we can do medically?' asked Neil.

'Ee's on the highest dose of Ritolin I can give him safely... Any more and I'd be worried about the long-term side effects...' their doctor said.

All this discussion got side-lined by some bloakey called Geoff Hawkins, who wuz one of the senior social workers on Anthony's case.

'We need to establish a comprehensive care plan for Anthony...'

'We already tried that,' went Mrs Evans.

'Is there anyway of altering these behaviours ee has?' asked Ally. 'I mean, Neil an' I we've been lookin' ut up on the internet... Some people have had success...'

'The material I've read so far points to music as being good therapy for ADHD...' said their doctor.

'Often these kind of conditions are best solved with soothing music... It can make a difference,' said a seemingly encouraged Geoff Hawkins.

There wuz a pause while everyone thought about it.

'What kind of music do you play at home Mr Davey?' asked their doctor.

'Well...' said Neil, clearin' his throat.

Ally looked at un. She didn' want un t'say anything. Ah naw – here it was.

'Metallica at the moment... moastly... an' a bit ov Black Sabbath...'

Everyone's eyebrows were raised.

'Do you think that kind of music's good fur him?'

''Ee likes ut,' went Neil. 'We bought un tha' Guitar Hero game – the Metallica one – an' tha' seems to focus un... I's the only thing at the moment... well. apart from the Star Wars Lego obviously...'

'I see...'

Voodoo Pilchard

'You do know they use heavy-metal music like that to torture prisoners in Guantananmo Bay Mr Davey?' noted Mrs Evans.

She spat out the term heavy metal like it wuz poison.

'Yeah – I knaw – but it seems t'calm un down…'

'Have you ever thought that it might be causing him further anxiety?'

'Not really,' said Neil. 'I don't feel it does. Calms me down, so why not him?'

There wuz a pause. People sipped on their cups ov coffee, an' reached fur more custard creams.

'Behavioural therapy seems the best way forward,' went one of the social workers. 'We need to address Anthony's poor communication skills, and try and circumvent his repetitive routines.'

Neil sort ov understood wha' she meant.

'The intervention must be based on multi-disciplinary assessments…'

'Yes, I agree,' went their doctor, 'but I am more concerned about the ADHD. The clinical trials of Dexedrine have proved successful… beyond what Ritolin can do. Maybe we should try that…'

It seemed a good idea, though t'be honest, nawbody didn't much knaw about the effects ov either. The fundamental problem wuz tha' when one drug fixed one set ov behaviours, ut only seem to exacerbate somethun' else.

'We need t'find out more about the way Anthony sees the world…' offered Geoff Hawkins. Ee wuz a fuckin' old hippy really, wuz Hawkins, even though ee wuz boobed up in a three-piece suit these days. Ee tried t'pretend ee wuz the voice ov reason, when in reality, ee prob'ly wanted t'just lock Anthony up an' thraw away the key.

Fuck, sometimes Neil reckoned all ee needed wuz a couple ov weeks out on the Trelawny estate. Maybe they wuz wrappin' un in too much cotton wool. Maybe the only solution wuz t'drop in the deep end an' see if ee cud swim. A dose ov skateboards, chainsaws, mephedrone, zombie-killun' an' BB guns might sort un out. Perhaps a week up trainin' with Tommy Curnow might do ut. Neil'd survived ut. Why cudn' 'is son?

'Perhaps some more tests at this stage,' offered one of the concerned social workers.

Neil wuz holding tight onta' Ally's hand. How the fuck did ut come t'this? 'Twas like they wuz all blamin' them. Right there and then, she wanted t'blame Neil, but she knawed she cudn'. Since ee'd been back off the road, Neil'd been brilliant with un really. 'Twas all getting' to her though.

She caught the doctor there gazin' at her tits as they were talkin'. She still had ut then. But why the hell wuz this happenin' to they? Wuz it the time she'd spent away from Anthony when ee wuz little, helpin' with Pasty-Pronto? Wuz tha' ut? She wuz feelin' guilty about her own skills as a mother. Then again, she reckoned she'd done a good job – 'specially when she compared herself to the all young mums up on Trelawny. They didn' give a shit about their kids: pumped um out, and let um loose – t'slice the tops of roses, an' got on makin' the new one with another new bloak. Ally wudn' like tha' t'all. She lived fur Anthony an' Megan – not that this crowd in here knawed ut. Wuz they judgin' um? Wuz ut because they wuz from Trelawny? They hadn' said anything but sometimes, you cud tell by the way they looked an' tha'.

'Sorry,' went Ally.

Neil tried to stop her.

'No,' she whispered. 'I've got t'say somethun'...'

Her voice got louder; more combative.

'I've had enough ov this... All of you... you don't understand Anthony.'

She started to cry. Neil knew the kind of tears she was crying. Ee'd heard them on the road, a mobile-phone conversation from Luxembourg – or wherever else they happened to be playing.

'Mrs Davey,' went Geoff Hawkins, trying to be sympathetic. 'We all have the best interests of Anthony at heart... We know how stressful all of this has been for you both...'

'Do you though?' went Ally, in fur the kill. 'I don't think you do. You want a quick solution and... I don't think that's possible... He's my son an' I just want the best fur'n...'

She wuz sobbin' an' Neil wuz doin' is best t'comfort her.

'She's upset,' went Neil, stating the obvious, but having to defend her. 'We don't want to be here... to have your kid examined like this... it unnerves you... makes you feel rubbish as a parent...'

Voodoo Pilchard

It wuz a passionate speech, and the ADHD and Aspergers Support workers collectively leapt to the Davey's defence.

'Can we give Mr and Mrs Davey a bit of space please... fur a minute...'

Hawkins, their doctor, Mrs Evans an' the rest ov um stood up an' shuffled out ov the room.

'They're goin' t'take un away ent' um?' cried Ally.

Neil an' Ally looked across through the safety glass of another adjoining room. Anthony had been in there with another support worker. Anthony had his head pressed against the glass with his hands next to his mouth. Ee was watchin' 'is ma sobbing her heart out. In 'is hand was a Lego ARC fighter from the Clone Wars. Technical models like tha' ee could build in about ten minutes flat without any help. Then 'twud take un two days t'write one sentence in Literacy lessons.

When ee saw Neil holding Ally so tightly, that ee knew 'twas ee who they wuz talkin' 'bout, ee smashed ut against the door breakin' ut into several fragments. The social worker made a move fur'n to try to stop him damaging the door or himself any further. Ee ran away from her, s'she'd used a bit ov a rugby tackle on un: 'reasonable force' they called ut. Y'cud hear Anthony crying, an' the social worker trying t'calm un down.

'I think it's best we take un home dun't you?' went Neil.

Everyone wanted t'say sorry, but no-one could.

'We'll meet again next week shall we?' went Geoff Hawkins, like 'twas all fine. But 'twudn'. 'Twudn' fine t'all.

Headönizm Two Shampoo – Wash in squeaky-clean sea-salt freshness.
Deep Cleansing
• Removes dulling build-up – Thoroughly cleanses styling and finishing products form the surface of hair
• Helps add body, fullness and shine – Formulated with Atlantic sea-salt and our Activated Shine Blend
• Leaves hair super clean and fresh – Deep cleansing for oily hair with an Atlantic freshness

'Aw hell...' went Charlie. 'I wuz opin' ut might go better than tha'... Sorry t'hear tha'...'

Charlie wuz out in the garden chatting Neil on 'is mobile.

Things edn' gone well with the social workers an' tha. Ally wuz right shook up 'bout ut.

'I'll take un off yer hands fur a bit if ut helps,' went Charlie. 'Ee'll be a'right with me like, wun't a?'

"Course,' went Neil. "Ee likes you Charlie. You an' ee – well, you talk about Star Wars dun't ee?'

'I'n take un football if y'like. 'Spect da can wangle us a couple of free tickets fur tonight's friendly...'

'That'd be great Charlie. Give me a bit ov time with Ally an' Megan like...'

Shit. Charlie hated football. Ut seemed some bloaks seemed t'live by ut. Ee never quite got tha' in Cornwall – where the nearest decent football team seemed half a country away. Charlie cud understand why people got excited about their countries an' tha' in big championship competitions. But Cornwall wuz fucked tha' way too. You wuz shafted coz y'didn' really want t'support England. Yer nearest other bet wuz prob'bly Wales, who never got inta' the European Cup or the World Cup anyway, or somebody like Australia (where half the country wuz founded by the Cornish) who normally got through, but never did very well anyway. Still, ee wudn' doin' ov ut fur thaa'. Ee wuz doin' ut t'give Neil an' Ally some space, t'try to work through the shite with Anthony tha' they'd had t'deal with.

Charlie went down t'pick un up down Portreath. Y'cud tell ee wuz a strange little kid. Moast Cornish kids ov 'is age wud have their surf 'n' skate style clothes all untucked an' that. Well, not Anthony. Ee wuz standing there like a proper gimp with his top button all done up, an' shiny new shoes on. Neil wuz there, with his hands on his shoulders. Neil cud tell Charlie nawticed his clothes.

'Dun't say anything,' Neil went. "Ee likes ut tha' way...'

'A'right. Naw probs...' said Charlie. 'We'll have a good time wun't us boy...'

Anthony didn't say nothun'. Ee just stared forward, until Charlie opened the door fur'n.

'Like music do a?' enquired Charlie.

'Yes,' answered Neil. Ee gived Anthony a prod.

'I like Metallica. The Black Album. Track number 4.'

'Track number 4 it is then...'

'Charlie...' went Neil, with a warning tone in his voice. 'Dun't move ut on t'track 5... Thaas' next week's track...'

Charlie looked at Neil an' then at Anthony.

'I know all the lyrics,' went Anthony.

'Really?' asked Charlie.

'Have fun,' said a relieved-looking Neil.

'I shall recite them for you...:

NEW BLOOD JOINS THE EARTH
AND QUICKLY HE'S SUBDUED.
THROUGH CONSTANT PAIN DISGRACE
THE YOUNG BOY LEARNS THE RULES.

WITH TIME THE CHILD DRAWS IN
THIS WHIPPING BOY DONE WRONG
DEPRIVED OF ALL HIS THOUGHTS
THE YOUNG MAN STRUGGLES ON AND ON.'

Thaas' wha' the little cunt did fur the next ten minutes. Charlie'd heard nothun' like it before. Ee wuz like James Hetfield on speed. Either tha' or ee wuz Billy fuckin' Shakespeare. The way ee said ut wuz like ee wuz convinced of the song's meaning. Charlie hadn't heard anything like ut.

'How do ee learn them?' went Charlie. 'I wish I could remember lyrics as well as you can...'

'I just can,' went Anthony.

Track 4 on the album – which as anyone can tell you – was 'The Unforgiven' – was just about comin' t'a finish as Charlie pulled out onta' the A30. The CD went onta' 'Wherever I May Roam'. Anthony gived un' a bit ov a look. Charlie clicked the rewind button an' the song played again.

'Like this one do ee?' asked Charlie.

'Yes,' went Anthony.

So the song played over an' over again. Charlie tried a new tactic.

'Who's your favourite Star Wars character?'

'Obi Wan Kenobi,' went Anthony.

'Mine too,' said Charlie.

'Who's got the best light sabre?'

'Obi Wan Kenobi,' went Anthony.

'Who would win out of a duel between Mace Windu and Obi Wan Kenobi?'

'Obi Wan,' he went.

Fuckin' hell, this wuz some Obi Wan Kenobi fixation.

'Like the Ewoks do ee?'

'No. I only like Obi Wan Kenobi...'

Charlie'd got the message by now. Obi Wan Kenobi wuz the main man.

'Can we stop?' went Anthony.

'What for? Do you need the loo?'

'No,' went Anthony. 'I need to take my tablet...'

Aw fuck. Neil might've said somethun'.

'I dun't knaw where ut is...'

Ah shit. This wuz getting' better an' better.

'Anthony – what happens if you dun't take yer tablet?'

Anthony give Charlie a lot. Ut wuz a 'you wouldn' like me if I don't take my tablet' kind ov look.

'Did dad give it to you?'

'I can't remember.'

Fuck. Charlie needed t'find his tablet an' find ut quick – or ee cud see Anthony leaping over the barrier of the A30 an' like some kind ov' mini-Incredible Hulk, turnin' over a few emmet caravans fur fun.

'I have an addictive personality,' went Anthony, soundin' like ee wuz Nikki Sizz or Vince Neil outta Mötley Crüe. Or come t'think ov ut, Yak.

Charlie looked over at un. Ee looked s'little there. Y'wudn' believe that so much hassle cud come out ov somethun' s'small.

The last time Charlie had t'deal with somethun' like this wuz when Yak went inta' Treliske with a blood clot after a bit too much ov 'is 'medicine'. This wuz creepily similar somehow.

'Daddy sometimes puts ut in my pocket,' went Anthony.

'Which one?'

'This one.'

Anthony tapped his left-hand trouser pocket.

'You left-handed?' went Charlie.

'Yes.'

'Can you look fur ut then?'

Charlie seen un take out a few blocks ov Lego from his pockets, then ee produced a plastic bubble containing a pill.

'That ut?' asked Charlie.

'Yes. That is it,' said Anthony.

There wuz a pause. The tacker wudn' doin' anything with ut.

'Can we have track 4 on again please?' went Anthony.

'Yeah, course,' said Charlie, 'but then can you take your pill?'

'Yes.'

Charlie whacked on the stereo again. Anthony stared forward an' took the pill.

'Do you need water? I got some coke here somewhere'.

Charlie searched around for a warm, near empty bottle of Diet Coke he'd bought down garage a few days ago.

'I don't need it,' said Anthony.

'Gone?' asked Charlie.

Anthony turned an' stuck his tongue out like Gene Simmons of Kiss. There wuz the proof. It had, indeed, gone.

'Can we go to football now?' asked Anthony.

The little cunt seemed a'right again now. Charlie'd nearly 'bout had a panic attack tryin' t'deal with this tacker and 'is drugs. Ee'd stood before ten thousand people at some of the festivals they'd done in Europe, and not felt s'nervous.

'You a'right Charlie?' asked Anthony.

'Yeah, fine,' went Charlie, lying.

Fuck, if kids were this much stress, ee wuz never goin' t'ave any. 'Twudn' even on the horizon anyway. Thank fuck.

Charlie pulled out of the lay-by and they headed up t'Chiverton Cross. Ee tried again.

'What ee think ov Boba Fett? Like ee do ee?

Charlie looked over fur a response from the tacker. Ee knew wha' wuz comin'.

'Obi Wan,' they both said at the same time, Charlie confirming Anthony's answer.

Okay, now ee wuz beginning t'understand a bit more 'bout why Neil needed t'go home from Prestatyn.

In the Treyew Road ground in Trura, Charlie's da wuz already there. This wuz a friendly between the White Tigers an' Exeter City's B team. There wuz still a fair ol' crowd in.

'Who's the kid?' went Charlie's da.

Charlie gave un a look. Ut wuz like ee wuz askin' ut as if it was some long lost one from Charlie's past.

'Neil an' Ally's...'

'Wha' - thaas' Anthony is ut?'

'Yeah.'

'Pleased t'meet you Mr Curnow,' said Anthony politely.

Charlie's da leaned in t'un.

'Bit fuckin' strange idn' a?' ee whispered. 'Geeky as fuck b'the look ob'm...'

'Ee's a'right,' said Charlie. 'Neil an' Ally need a bit ov a break tonight... so I brought un along t'watch the game...'

'Well, fair enough like.... I got ee some tickets in the stand you... Cen't stay... We got a finance meetun' tonight...'

Aw shit. If his da wuz involved in the finances of the club, then sure enough, 'twas bound t'go pear-shaped. Still, that wudn' 'is concern now.

They made their way inta' the stand. A few boys from the old Trura' gig circuit recognised Charlie.

'Hey Curnow... got any gigs comin' up?' one of the shouted.

'Nothun' doin' at the moment,' shouted Charlie. 'Be out there soon though. Concentratin' on the songs...'

'Excuse me,' went Anthony, 'what is a gig?'

Charlie stopped in his tracks.

'A gig?'

'Yes. I haven't heard that word before.'

Shit. This wuz an intelligent kind of tacker, the sort you didn' meet much up Trelawny. Why the hell cudn' the school deal widn'?

'It's... a... a concert,' said Charlie, 'where bands play.'

'I see... Like what daddy does...'

'Yes... that's it. Like what me an' your daddy do...'

Charlie corrected hisself, '...or used t'do...'

They sat down in the stand. Kick-off wuz about five minutes away.

'You're brainy,' went Charlie.

'Mummy says tha',' said Anthony.

It wuz hard considering Ally giving out advice, tellin' this little kid ee wuz bright. Charlie cud only think back t'the way all the bloaks lusted after Ally a few years back. 'Twas weird how stuff panned out.

'She's told me I must eat lots of fish...'

That seemed quite a random thing fur this kid t'say – but then, right now, nothun' wuz surprisin' Charlie, given the way his evenin' wuz goin'.

'Why's tha'?' ee eventually asked.

'The fish – they have lots of Omega 3 fatty acids. It's good for my attention deficit and hyperactivity disorder.'

'Oh right…' went Charlie.

For one thing Charlie wuz quite glad ov the game startin'. Ut might stop Anthony from chitterin' on quite s'much. As usual, the back three ov the White Tigers were fairly shite, an' their midfield not much better. There wuz a few chances about twenty minutes in, but the first half wudn' nothun' tearin' t'watch.

'That man, he got the angle wrong,' said Anthony. 'It needed to be 15 degrees more to the left…'

Anthony wuz talking about one of City's strikers – a boy by the name ov Steve Pritchard – who wuz one of the few actual Cornishmen in the squad right now. Ee'd spent a few years up St Blazey, but City ud given un a good offer to come an' join them. How the fuck did a work tha' out?

'You got an amazin' brain Anthony,' said Charlie.

'The doctor told me it was magic sometimes,' said Anthony. They watched the match a bit more.

'I like Jimi Hendrix…' said Anthony.

This conversation wuz gettin' weirder. 'Twas like the little cunt had secret powers or somethun'. Charlie wuz beginning t'see how Ally wuz being driven t'destraction. Maybe the problem wudn' tha' ee had some syndrome or anything. Maybe ee wuz just bright. Perhaps ee got stuff quickly, needed more challenges than they were offerin' at school. 'Mean, despite everything, despite all the knobbers in their class, and the disruption their class caused, Neil an' Ally did pretty well at school. Perhaps 'twas in his genes.

'My favourite song is Voodoo Chile.'

It wuz one of Charlie's favourites too.

'How do you know tha'?'

'Da plays it to me…'

The first half wuz comin' t'an end.

'Come on… I'll buy ee a doughnut…'

'I'm not allowed,' went Anthony.

Charlie gave un a look ov surprise.

'Da says that kind of sugar is no good fur me…'

'Ah…' went Charlie.

Ee understood. Ee wudn' about t'buy un anything that might send un on a tacker attack which might take out half the stand in one go.

Just as Charlie wuz havin' this conversation with Anthony, out of the corner ov his eye, ee nawticed a few figures walkin' t'the managers' dug-outs. The way they were walkin' wuz unmistakable. They walked with confidence, like they knew everything there wuz to know about everything, an' that nothun' wuz goin' t'stop um. Aw 'es, tha' wuz the unmistakable fist ov Markie Phillips goin' out to shake hands with the Trura City manager, Dave Metters. Everything wuz looking like a load've smiles and photographic opportunities. Markie wuz standin' there like a right cunt, all dressed up in an M&S suit, a bit fatter these days, obviously livin' the good life.

'Who's that?' went Anthony, noticing Charlie's gaze.

'Ah nawbody,' said Charlie. 'Come on – come down the kiosk with me an' we'll find somethun' you're allowed to have…'

'Thank you,' went Anthony.

When ee wuz polite like this, you cudn' believe ee put half ov the infant class from Portreath Primary School inta' Treliske, but then when y'looked down on Markie Phillips being the 'big I am' on the touchline of Trura City, you wudn' believe half the stuff ee wuz capable ov either.

The second half wudn' much good. The Exeter City right back fouled Pritchard though, an' got sent off. That allowed Trura t'have a penalty which they scored. So tha' wuz ov ut: one nil t'the Tigers.

'What ee think ov tha' then Anthony?' went Charlie, hopeful fur a response.

'It was alright,' he said, 'but I think I prefer watching Clone Wars…'

'How many times have y'seen ut?'

'Seven hundred and thirty seven times…'

'You knaw precisely?'

'Of course. I keep count…'

''Course,' said Charlie. 'So do I…'

When Charlie got back from droppin' off Anthony, ee nawticed that just as ee'd said, Micky had sawn through the hoarding and taken out the square of street art made by the

Pilchard. Inside, you could just about see tha' Headönizm was takin' shape. The shopfitters were comin' on apparently. The current hold up wuz with the plumbing. Jess wudn' too happy; there just wudn' enough pressure. The old pipe comin' in from the mains would need t'be replaced. An' then all the sewerage wuz connected somehow t'the Trelawny Adit. Ut wuz a shitter because tha' wuz goin' t'delay their opening.

Charlie comed in the door. Only his ma wuz in.

'Da's still up there. Ee'll be back later... Some meetun' or somethun'...'

'Estate agents phoned earlier,' she went. 'You'n pick up the key tomorra' they said...'

Charlie's ma wuz excited fur'n. She gived un a kiss.

Shit. Charlie Curnow: homeowner. The rock 'n' roll dream had come to an end.

'What you been up to?'

'Took Anthony football,' went Charlie.

'How is a these days?'

'Weird,' went Charlie. That wuz honestly wha' ee wuz like.

'Bless...' went his ma.

'Na... ee's proper weird,' said Charlie. 'I'n see why they got troubles widn'...'

There wuz one of his ma's well-timed, evil kind of pauses, These days they wuz seemingly infested with the power ov her literature an' gender section of her *Voices and Texts* course.

'Well, be nice if my children might give me some grandchildren one day...'

She said ut like 'twas some kind of item you picked up in Morrisons over Pool.

'Jess dun't seem bothered... and you... well, you ent even with anyone...'

Aw es. Here it comed: the usual relationship counselling, goin' on like she was Oprah-fucking-Winfrey or Jeremy Kyle. She'd be sittin' on a step next, and lookin' on, all sympathetic like.

'That Bev... she wuz some nice... I dunnaw why you stopped seein' her...'

Charlie wudn' goin' t'argue with her. Ee cud've tried telling her 'bout the impermanence of adult relationships – and perhaps a bit more now about the permanence an' wonder of children, especially children like Anthony – but ee wudn' goin' t'bother.

Still, ee thought ut might be useful t'have a geek on what Anthony'd been sayin' about Omega 3 fatty acids. He switched on his laptop and clicked on Internet Explorer, then googled ut. Holy shit, there wuz a ton on there about how high quantities ov Omega 3 could helps kids with ADHD. Not much on there about Asperger Syndrome, but apparently these kind of fatty acids were good fur'n. Next time ee'd see Neil an' Ally ee'd have a yap with um 'bout ut. Maybe then Ally wudn' jus' think of him as the person who took Neil away from her an' their kids.

Yeah – turned out the best plaace t'get Omega 3 wuz from oily fish like pilchards or sardines: in Latin, the common or garden *Sardina pilchardus*. Charlie clicked around a bit more. Ee found a few pictures of hogsheads from years back in Cornwall. These were hug barrels in which the pilchards were packed in nice an' tight, layer by layer. Somethun' ee didn't knaw wuz tha' if the fish was smaller than four inches, it wuz classed as a sardine, but if it wuz any larger than tha', then 'twas a pilchard. See, you learned somethun' new every day. Tha' be handy next time they'd do a quiz night down Grenville. Apparently, in Cornwall, the industry wuz at its height between the years 1750 t'1880, after which it went tits up – or rather fins up. Ee stopped reading and instead clicked on Facebook.

The message wuz still there from Bev. Ee wrote her a message back an' then ee deleted ut. That ud gone wrong a long time ago – an' Charlie didn' want it goin' inta' terminal decline any further. Best wait ee reckoned, 'til they met up somewhere – crammed in, well - like sardines - at a gig or somethun'. Tha' way maybe, they could talk properly. Ee clicked back on Google. Readin' up on the life-cycle of the pilchard wuz like fuckin' Walt Disney an' Elton John had walked in. This wuz the circle ov life.

Shittin' hell, tomorra' mornin' ee wuz pickun' up the key t'his new house. How mad wuz tha'?

Gillyflower Rinse - Rises in moisture and shine.
Lightweight detangling conditioner
• Instant detangling – Gillyflower derived conditioners

help provide excellent wet and dry combing with a soft silky feel
• Lightweight moisture – Essential amino acids and apple derived conditioners help provide hydration without added weight
• Reduces static – Special conditioning agents help reduce static fly-way hair

The next morning, Charlie's ma looked proper depressed. She wuz outside the kitchen havin' a fag. She'd been tryin' t'give up fur a few weeks now, but 'adn' 'ad a lot ov success. The stress tended t'kick in every time she had t'submit an assignment fur her university course. The first one wuz on women's voices, so she'd said. She 'ad t'start writin' ut pretty soon. 1500 words on diversity and difference.

'Whaas' up?' went Charlie.

'Oh y'knaw...'

'Knaw wha'?'

'All these years, I didn' knaw wha' t'do 'bout everythun'... but now, well, now, I'm a feminist...'

Fuck. There must be another eclipse, or a fuckin' comet passing close by the earth. 'Is ma wuz self-declarin' as a feminist. Had she just got outta' bed the wrong side, or wuz ut somethun' more permanent?

'I's depressin',' she went, talkin' 'bout her epiphany. 'If I knawed what I knaw now twenty years ago, I wudn' be livin' 'ere on Trelawny... I'd have done things a lot different. My mother see, she' didn' knaw anything about the rights ov women. In fact, she wudn' even get on a Western National bus, if a woman wuz driving ut...'

Well, she might have a point, if literary feminism determined where you wuz going' t'end up spending the rest ov yer life. Charlie knawed wha' 'is gran wuz like – from wha' he cud remember ov her. She wuz dead now course, but Methodist as fuck, an' stuck in 1950. Well, prob'ly nearer 1850.

"Ave ee told da?' asked Charlie.

'Yeah – I told un lass' night when ee comed in from football...'

'What a say?'

'Not a lot...'

Charlie took a slurp of 'is coffee.

'You understand though Charlie, dun't ee?'

''Course,' went Charlie.

Charlie reckoned you cudn' possibly have any chance with the opposite sex in the early twenty-first century without an understanding of the feminist movement. Be a sexist twat, an' you guaranteed yerself a kick in the balls (that wuz except that big maid up football club with a tongue like a Komodo dragon, who didn' seem t'care what y'thought).

'Sometimes ut idn' the men though us ut?'

Shit. His mum wuz being like Germaine Greer this morning. She'd been readin' Hermione Lee of late – so perhaps tha' wuz ut.

'What ee mean?'

'Well, 'tis the women sometimes... They accept ut too easy dun't um? Sometimes, we'm our own wurst enemies...'

Charlie had a think about all the women ee knawed. Yeah – 'is ma 'ad a point. Then again, some ov um knawed what they wuz doin'.

'At the weekend Charlie, I'm thinkin' ov goin' down St Ives... Have a stroll around an' see Talland House an' tha'... Treat meself t'a bit ov a day out...'

'Ideal,' went Charlie.

She deserved ut. 'Is ma had been workin' non-stop fur ee an' Jess ov late.

'Da'll go with ee... wun't a?'

His ma gived un a look.

'Dun't 'spect so... Got football on ebm' a?'

Charlie knawed how ut wuz ov late. Watchin' kicking a ball around 'ad replaced un watchin' hot MILFs cavortin' around Carn Brea.

His ma stamped out her fag on the wall ov their mundic-blok shed, and comed inside. She gave a quick geek outside t'see some Cormac contractors pull inta' the estate.

Charlie had nawticed them too.

'Wozon with they?'

'Aw – we had a letter come round a couple weeks back. They'm doin' some exploratory work on one of the old adits... Disruption for the next month or so...'

His ma put the kettle on again fur er second cuppa' ov the day, and started t'get ready fur work.

Voodoo Pilchard

'Still, never mind all ov tha' eh? Today's the day idn' ut? Micky's ready with 'is van t'give ee hand t'move in...'

Charlie realised the momentousness ov what she just said. There wuz still time yet t'get down the Estate Agents.

His da comed down the stairs an' entered the kitchen.

'Kettle boiled es ut? Make us a cup love will ee...?'

His da looked wrecked.

'Did you have a few last night?' asked Charlie. 'After the game?'

'Na... Didn't sleep very well...'

'Why not?'

'Worried 'bout the Tigers...'

'You an' the bleddy Tigers Tommy... Betterfit you spent a bit more time helpin' your son an' daughter...' went 'is ma.

'Yeah – well, I'n give Charlie a hand this mornin'. I'm on af'noons this week... Jess's a'right though ent she? I heard um go down shop early this mornin'.'

His da scratched his gut an' sat down at the breakfast table.

''Ave ee heard?' he went, pickin' up yesterday's copy ov *The Sun*, ' – yer mother's turned inta' a feminist...'

'Thaas' a'right idn' ut?' said Charlie.

'Dunnaw,' he went, with all seriousness in his voice. 'I dun't like the sound ov ut... Down mine, you'n sense when things ent right. This is somthun' like tha'...'

'Well, things might change a bit round here now...' his ma went, like 'twas a full declaration of war.

His da turned onta' page three an' tried not t'ave a gake at the eighteen-year-old beauty in there, with her kit off. Jeez, thought Charlie. The tool 'ad learned nothun' had a?

'Dun't you be lookin' at tha' Tommy Curnow...'

'Nothun' wrong weth ut...'

'Pornography is the exploitation ov women...' his ma went, putting on her Homebase bib.

She 'ad a point. Problem wuz, the more combative his ma got, the more Charlie knawed wha' would 'appen. Ee'd seen the cunt ov late, an' ee knew ee wuz lookin' after Karen. The last few years peace negotiations between them had been goin' along steady – but this new feminist jag his ma wuz on, wuz tha' goin' t'push Tommy over the edge, an' make un go back there fur a few creature comforts? 'Twas a fine balance, Charlie

knew, an' 'is da wuz weaker than piss when ut comed down to
ut. Either ee 'ad t'accept the new Sally Curnow – or 'twas goin'
t'go back t'the old times with her 'eavin' out all his gear in bin
bags onta' the drive, an' goin' down Ursula's fur some comfort
an' chat. An' fuck, tha' wudn' naw good either, now tha'
Ursula'd gone Spain fur half the year.

'Gotta' go,' went his ma. She checked her watch. The discussion had made her a few minutes late. She had a stock-take on
t'day too.

Charlie sat down with his da.

'I knaw you'm seein' ov Karen a bit,' went Charlie.

'Who told ee tha'?'

'Dun matter who told me,' said Charlie.

''Tidn' wha' you think...' said his da defensively.

'Maybe... but 'tidn' wha' I think tha' d'matter do ut?'

His da nodded.

'I'm just makin' sure she's a'right thaas' all... We ent shaggin' or nothun'.'

'Yeah, well, make sure ma's a'right too wun't ee? She's want
t'go down St Ives on Saturday. You should go with er... She'd
like ut if you took a bit ov interest in what she's doin' ov...'

'Virginia Woolf us ut?'

'Yeah. Cen't ee miss football fur one week like?'

Charlie cud hear the gears ov his da's brain slowly workin',

'A'right – I'll take er...'

Prob'ly this wuz shapin' up t'be the wurst experience in the
world fur Charlie's da. Not only wud a 'ave t'put up with his ma
yippin' on about the wonders of Virginia Woolf, ee'd also have
t'be dodgin' fuckin' posh emmets aplenty (all boobed with
their Tate stickers) in the streets and opeways of St Ives. To be
honest there wudn' anything much worse ee cud think ov - but
still, if ut pleased Sally then ee'd do ut.

Outside, the postman wuz makin' his way t' 38 Trelawny
Gardens. The Post Office had given un reinforced Kevlar
trousers t'withstand all the dog an' tacker attacks. Ee always
wore gloves too – just in case of anything dangerous lurkin'
behind the letterbox. 'Twas a surprise really that ee didn' wear
a hard hat. A small parcel comed in through the letterbox.

Charlie's da looked animated.

'That'll be me order,' ee went.

Voodoo Pilchard

Fur a cunt who up until a few years ago, 'ad resisted every kind of computer goin', post-Club Rhino, ee seemed t'be makin' up fur lost time. This wuz another one of 'is orders off Amazon.

'Is da went to the front door an' picked up the parcel.

'Classic,' ee went, openin' ov ut up.

Charlie wuz still tryin' t' talk to un 'bout his ma, but the bugger didn' seem too interested.

'Wha' is ut?' asked Charlie.

'Whitesnake, *1987* – anniversary edition... Bonus tracks and a DVD...'

Charlie knawed ov ut. Whitesnake during tha' phase wuz all big perms and expensive videos fur MTV – Tawny Kitaen (in titillating white lingerie) rolling around on the bonnets ov Jaguar cars an' Coverdale boobed up like a maid, lookin' a bit lost an' soulful. This wuz his da's idea of rock music: glamour, sex and huge riffs. Shame the cunt looked about as unglamorous and as unsexy as y'cud. Still, ee wuz already in the living room pumpin' out the huge riffs and air-guitarin' an' singin' like the twat ee wuz:

NO, I DON'T KNOW WHERE I'M GOING
BUT I SURE KNOW WHERE I'VE BEEN
HANGING ON THE PROMISES
IN SONGS OF YESTERDAY
AN' I'VE MADE UP MY MIND
I AIN'T WASTING NO MORE TIME
HERE I GO AGAIN

'Can ee turn ut down a bit da?' went Charlie.

His da turned ut down slightly. Yeah – 'is da didn' really have much ov a clue where ee wuz goin'. Perhaps if ee listened t'the wisdom of Coverdale, ee might not be such a tool all the time.

'So you'm on with ma on Saturday?'

''Course... yeah...'

'Dun't let her down mind.'

'I wun't...'

The twat wuz doin' microphone twirls with a hoover pipe and fist pumps. How cud a possibly bring someone like Bev back ere these days – with the tool up t'these kind ov antics? Ee

83

wuz tryin' t'headbang but his baldin' mullet wudn' doin' a lot ov good. Thank Christ Charlie wuz movin' out.

'This'll go good down mine,' ee went.

Apparently, classic rock wuz the constant soundtrack down there these days.

'I gotta' go,' said Charlie.

Charlie's da gived un a puzzled look.

'Fetchin' the key t'day...'

'Aw 'es... bewdie...'

Charlie grabbed 'is key an' wallet. In ut ee found the tickets fur ee an' Anthony from lass' night's match. Charlie 'ad t'ask un.

'Da...?'

The twat had one foot up on the settee like he wuz John Sykes playin' his Gibson Les Paul. Charlie went over to the stereo an' turned ut down.

'Da? Whas' the deal with Markie Phillips over City then?'

'Who?'

'Markie Phillips – over Trura City – lass' night...'

'Ah well, I cen't say anything 'bout anything at the moment...'

'Wha' ee mean?'

'Well, we'm in negotiations... contractual negotiations...'

The tool wuz soundin' like some football agent, or maybe José Mourinho. His da wudn' the 'special one' though, even though ee wuz chitterin' on like ut.

'With him?'

'Yeah... well... nothun's sorted... not yet anyway... Our people are talkin' t'his people... but thaas' all at the moment... I cen't comment upon any further speculation at this point in time.'

Charlie didn' see ut comin' – but then, nothun' surprised un' 'bout boy Phillips. Tha' wuz 'is way wudn' ut? Wheedle is way in no matter wha' – however many people ee hurts along the way.

'Got two words fur ee,' went Charlie.

'Wha'?'

'Straight for the Heart' wuz comin' on the stereo but his da turned ut down.

'Clifford Mellow...'

Charlie's da went stock still.

'You d'knaw as well as I do wha' ee can do...'

'Well, 'tes hard Charlie... I be caught between a rock an' a hard plaace like...'

Charlie started t'leave.

'We need backin' see – if we'm goin' t'go fur the League... an' well, the state of Cornwall at the moment like, there idn' too many others offerin' t'write cheques with lots ov zeros on ut...'

'See ee later,' went Charlie, wantin' this conversation to end. He went out the back door and opened the door ov his battered Peugeot 306. He reversed out and indicated to pass the Cormac crew, who'd started t'dig up the road surface lookin' fur the problem adit. Ee waved t' a few ov them ee knew.

Charlie's da wuz left there listening t' 'Is this Love?' He reckoned there wudn' much there at the moment.

Lite Burcombe Detangler – Make tangles yesterday's news with this light leave-in conditioner.

Lightweight detangling spray

• Detangling – Mild leave-in formular aids in both wet and dry combing

• Enhances body and shine – Lightweight Burcombe cherries help leave hair full of volume with added shine

• Fragrance free – Excellent for clients sensitive to fragrance

The MP fur St Ives, Andrew George, was on the radio as Charlie drove down past Troon cemetery an' on inta' Beacon. Ee wuz sayin' how Cornwall wuz sufferin' from a lack ov affordable housin' fur young people, an' how 'twas causin' problems in communities such as St Ives.

'Blame Virginia Woolf,' mouthed Charlie at the radio.

Like the MP wuz sayin' though, ut wuz only goin' t'get worse fur future generations. Charlie's mind went t'Anthony and Megan – how the hell wuz they goin' t' cope in the future, when there wudn' enough houses now. The second problem wuz tha' there wudn' many sustainable jobs either. If y'didn' have the jobs. an' y'didn' have the houses, then the Cornish had naw choice. They'd have t'fuck off somewhere else. 'Course, years back that wud've been okay – cud've landed a gig somewhere across the globe, but now, well, all tha' 'ad gone too.

Charlie didn' feel smug about pickin' up the key t'his house. In fact, ee felt guilty, like ee wuz doin' somethun' wrong. In fact, the whole thing wuz like an out of body experience, as if it wudn' real. Maybe when ee got in there, and laid down on the carpet, ut might become a bit more believable.

The news comed on. Ee ignored the news fur the moast part. Moast of ut wuz just depressin' shit about the Council, or the 'bout the occasional Cornish nut who wuz tryin' t'row single-handed 'cross the Atlantic. Not today though. The headline wuz about another cashpoint robbery up Carharrack Spar Shop. Na messin' this time. The same gang, the police d'reckon. They'd gone in there in the daytime this mornin'. Backed up a JCB an' scooped the cashpoint out in one go. Some old maid wuz yippin' up 'bout ut. The owner ov the Spar Shop had been rushed over Treliske with a suspected heart attack.

'I cudn' believe ut,' she wuz goin'. 'The driver wuz wearin' a balaclava – and keen as y'like, they just dug un out of the wall, like 'twas a scoop ov sand...'

The license plates wudn' on ut or nothun' so it cudn' be identified in tha' way. This time, they d'reckon they drove the JCB inta' the back ov an' artic an' drove off with ut inside. Sebenty grand gone, so they said.

'Ah fuck,' Charlie mouthed t'hisself.

This whole JCB thing wuz gettin' out ov hand. The coppers wuz tryin' t'track down every registered JCB in Cornwall, to see if it wud give um a lead. Knawin' this crowd, they might get an excavator from over Crofty and do a bit ov demolition on Camborne Police Station.

By now, ee wuz down in Camborne, goin' past the Railway Inn. Ahead ov un wuz Trevithick's statue, lookin' grand. All around a lot ov the old buildings were being gutted an' done up. All fur offices or fur designer pads no cunt cud afford. Charlie went down Cross Street an' pulled in on the left, parking opposite the Indian there. Ee got out, an' stroathed down the pavement towards the Estate Agents: Miller & Son. As ee walked Charlie checked 'is phone fur any messages. One from Neil thankun' un fur lass night. Another from Jess, sayin the shop wuz nearly finished. Did a want the first haircut there?

Voodoo Pilchard

Not fuckin' likely, Charlie reckoned. Ee'd made a point of not lettun' his sister touch 'is hair since the days of Balance.

'Course, Charlie 'ad 'is head down didn' a? Thaas' why ee ended up bumpin' inta' Yelland. Normally, Charlie wud've done anythin' t'avoid the wanker, but this time ee cudn' do nothun'. Ee wuz cornered.

'Charlie Curnow...' went Yelland. 'Back from another world tour I see...'

Sarcastic twat.

'You a'right Yelland?' went Charlie, but ee didn' mean ut.

'Yeah – not bad. Getting' on me feet again...'

Charlie knew he'd had a suspended sentence fur his little bit of benefit fraud.

'Whaas' on with you then?' went Yelland.

'Well,' went Charlie, 'on me way t'the Estate Agents...'

'Lookin' fur somewhere t'rent are ee?'

'Na. Just bought somewhere...'

Fuck. Tha' nearly floored Yelland. Wuz this the same cunt who'd comed in the Job Centre a few years back?

'...Goin' t'pick up the key.'

Curnow – a fuckin' homeowner. Ah, the world wuz getting' more twisted by the moment fur Yelland.

For a moment, ee didn' knaw what t'say or do. 'Twas a sweet moment Charlie reckoned. Sheer karma.

'Well, you've come a long way...' said Yelland, nearly chokin' on the information.

Ee said ut like as if Trelawny wuz the last plaace on earth you'd ever want t'graw up in.

'You workin' at the moment?'

'Na... not at the moment...'

Lovely, thought Charlie.

'I hear they might be takin' on a few boys over Crofty again...'

Yelland looked horrified. Ee wuz pure white collar. There wuz no way ee wuz goin' underground.

'Not bad pay,' said Charlie.

'Well, I'm lookin' fur somethun' up-country...'

'Up the line like? Well, best ov luck,' went Charlie. 'Gotta' go...'

In his heart Charlie actually felt sorry fur the cunt. Ee'd been shafted by the system same as the rest obm'. Ee'd have liked Yak an' Neil t'have witnessed this moment though, just fur old time's sake. 'Twas true, revenge wuz a meal best served cold.

Ut made Charlie laugh when ee went inta' Miller & Son. Some of the maids workin' there knew ee wuz a bit ov a singer. Like moast days, at the moment, the housin' market wuz a bit slow.

One ov um went, 'The rock star's here look... t'collect 'is keys...'

She'd heard of Charlie – ee'd gone on *X-Factor* hadn' a?

She wuz being sarcastic, but Charlie didn' mind. Nothun' wuz goin' t'ruin his day.

'There you go Mr Curnow,' went the manager. 'We hope you will be very happy there... All the bank details are confirmed. Your mortgage is all in place. Do let us know if there is any more assistance we can give. You have the developer's number now don't you – just in case anything isn't right?'

'Thanks,' went Charlie. 'Yeah – got ut all.'

Tha' wuz ut then. The dream wuz over. Now ee 'ad t'be responsible.

Naw more sex.

Naw more drugs.

And definitely naw more rock 'n' roll.

Road lesson No. 2, wudn' ut? Be success savy.

Charlie decided t'walk back up Cross Street t'have a gake at Trevithick's statue. Even after all this time, his presence still dominated Obby Stanker Country like some kind of colossus. Fur some, Trevithick wuz like a God, a supernatural Deity beyond normal life. Ee wuz both transformation and protection, mandrake an' healing. Charlie went there t'give an offerin' – maybe t'thank un fur the world around un. Where wud his da an' Crofty be without un?

In his pocket, wuz the key to his house on School Lane. It wuz a talisman, a tiny piece ov his future. Charlie liked the statue – with him holding the cute little train in his hand: one of his small-scale models. Charlie remembered when Balance had played Trevithick Day a few years back. Then, afterward tha' fuck up ov a gig down the Pirate in Falmouth with Break the System. Back down Centenary Street towards the Weslyan Chapel, ee cud hear the Holman Climax Male Voice Choir, conducted t'perfection by Jimmy Pengelly. Perhaps 'twas as

Jimmy'd predicted, time t'take his place with um. Not just yet though...

Then, WTF?

Charlie did a double-take.

On the base ov the statue of boy Trevithick facing Trevu Road wuz somethun' Charlie hadn't expected. There ut wuz: Voodoo Pilchard - the usual street art; the stencilled letterin' an' the fish. Charlie cudn' believe ut. Now ee understood why the Minister back Centenary wudn' too happy. Trevithick's statue? Thaa' wuz fuckin' sacrilege wudn' ut? 'Twas worse than say, drawing an anarchy symbol on the Jedi Temple. Who the fuck 'ad done tha'?

Charlie looked at ut a bit more closely.

'Na,' Charlie said t'hisself. 'This ent right...'

An' ut wun't right – because this piece of street art wudn' nowhere near as good as the stuff elsewhere – up Centenary an' on the new premises ov Headönizm. Fur certain, the stencil ov ut had been copied like, but 'twudn' as sharp or sophisticated. 'Twas like comparin' Queen's 'Bohemian Rhapsody' with any other boy-band cover version ov ut. Na – this wudn' the Pilchard t'all. This wuz some other gobshite copyin' ov ut. Y'cud tell. The Pilchard always did 'is in a kind of blue or black paint. This artist wuz using red an' orange. The pilchard wudn' right either. 'Twudn' big enough. In fact, 'twas lookin' like more of a pathetic sardine to be honest.

Charlie gaked at ut. An old man walked past.

'Disgustin' idn' ut pard?' ee went.

'Yeah, terrible,' said Charlie. 'Kids these days...'

The old man nodded. Ee nodded back.

'The council need t'get ut cleaned off...'

Charlie touched the paint. Part ov ut wuz still wet. The artist 'adn' long been gone.

Fur a bit, Charlie forgot about his new house, an' instead, 'ad a drive 'round Camborne. Sadly, 'twas as ee thought. There were more red an' orange voodoo pilchards around. One wuz on the black litter bin by the bus-stop outside the Church of St Martin and St Meriadoc. Another wuz on the wall at Tyacks Hotel. Ee found two more down Rosewarne Road, one on the gents' toilets by the car park an' another on a garage door. Fuck, ut seemed they were multiplying like rabbits. Up near Tesco, ee found one on the old Holman's building, an' another on one of the trolley collection points in the car park.

His phone beeped. A text message comed through. It wuz from Micky asking where he was? 'Course, Micky wuz due t'be helpin' un move this morning. Charlie phoned un an' told un ee wuz on his way back Troon. Charlie told un 'bout seeing Yelland, which made Micky's day – but ee didn' say anything yet about the new Pilchard on the block.

Jus' t'add insult t'injury, ee'd gone back the Trevu Road way adn' a? An' as the crossing barrier went down t'let the 10.09 from Penzance go through, there 'twas - bang in the middle of one ov the gates: voodoo pilchard. Shittin' hell – they wuz comin' at un from all angles now. Y'cudn' escape ut – so fur five minutes, ee sat there gazing at the words.

'Time Charlie got back, Micky wuz pretty pissed off.

'Thought you said half-nine,' ee went.

'Yeah – well, I got delayed didn't I?'

'Yer da helpin'?'

'S'paused t'be...'

When they got t'his ma and da's house, his da wuz upstairs havin' a shave, although the Whitesnake wuz still blarin' out. Ee wuz up there singin' along to 'Still of the Night'. The kids comin' in an' ov the mephedrone house opposite were tryin' to make out wha' 'twas, but as they wuz high as fuck already, they remained clueless. Up Arnie's garden, the roses still looked pathetic. Fur safety's sake, the coppers had boarded up 'is windows.

Loadin' Charlie's gear inta' Micky's van took nearnly 'bout all morning after tha'. There were endless trumps up an' down the staircase from his room. A lot ov crap that prob'ly didn' need to go went – and then there wuz all the stuff that had been accumulatin' in the kitchen that 'is ma had brought home from Homebase fur'n. Fuck, 'twas hard t'knaw where ut 'ad all comed from. Then down garages, a lot ov the main furniture that wuz goin' in – needed t'be picked up. Tha' would take another van.

'You'd better hurry up cuz I'm on af'noons... I wun't be able t'help ee after one o'clockish...'

'I's a'right,' went Charlie. Yak's comin' over then.

The Cormac crew were cuttin' a trench though the garages.

'Twas quite a deep fucker by the look obm'.

'Through t'Australia yet are ee?' joked 'is da...

They all knawed ee worked over Crofty.

'Wozon with ut?' his da enquired.

'Some people have lost their water down the road... They reckon the Trelawny adit's t'blame... ruptured the pipes somewhere.'

'Fuck,' went his da, knawin' a little bit 'bout the old world below their feet.

'Fill un in then?'

''Es – tha' should sort ut out. South West Water'll need t'put new pipes in though. 'Twill take um a day or two mind...'

By this, tha' meant a month or two.

'Leave ee to ut,' went his da. 'Me boy's movin' house – so best make 'iss...'

'Tis an amazin' moment t'open the door ov your own house.

Charlie wanted Emerson, Lake and Palmer's 'Fanfare to the Common Man' t'be playing. Micky wuz reversing in the van, but Charlie 'ad already got out an' 'ad put the key inta' the lock. Ee felt like Frodo Baggins putting the ring on. 'Twas magical, unreal, like as if 'twas somebody else doin ov ut. Ee'd already had a good look at what ee wuz buyin' when the developers wuz finishin' ov ut off. Nothun' wuz a lash up. Everything wuz clean and new – all the walls decked out in bright Magnolia. No stains or marks on the carpets. No fuckin' crazy bits of DIY like wha' his da sometimes ended up doing back on Trelawny. As well as tha', ee'd escaped: got out of Trelawny. Well, 'twas half a mile down the road, but at least ut wudn' there anymore. Charlie wuz thankin' Chakira an' her management fur coverin' his song. If 'twudn' fur they – well none ov this would be happenin' would ut? Unlike the Co-Op down the road, which at the moment wuz lookin' like ut had just been hit by a air-to-surface missile, this wuz looking amazing.

Charlie stood there, turning his feet, facing each of the walls in the living room, as if he wuz inside some kind of cosmic egg. 'Twudn' nothun' like tha' really. In fact, 'twas a small starter home. But never mind, this wud be the next stage ov his dream. Ee climbed the staircase, an' looked in the master bedroom. Big enough yeah... But then ut wuz the other third room, ee 'ad 'is eye on. That would be the studio. A lot you could do these days with Pro-Tools. Yeah – ut would need soundproofing an' so on, but the thing would be ideal. Then there wuz the bathroom. Ut looked clean an so white – so different from the one back at his ma an' da's – the fuckin' horrible 70s' colour olive-green suite, with the mould growin' around the tiles. Charlie told hisself ee'd keep ut like this forever. Now ee wuz startin' t'knaw what Neil felt like when ee wuz away on tour fur such a long time. Y'wanted yer own bathroom, bedroom an' sheets. Y'wanted t'be able t'sit in your living room bollock-naked ov a morning with a bowl of Crunchy Nut cornflakes, enjoying the witty banter between Holly Willougby and Phililp Schofield on *This Morning*.

'Where d' ee want this?' came a voice.

It wuz Micky, strugglin' in with his Marshall cabinet.

In terms of stress, moving house is supposedly only second down the list from getting divorced. It certainly felt like tha'. 'Course, Charlie bein' a knobber, didn' label his boxes fur which room, so everything ended up in a g'eat heap in the middle ov the living room. It didn't take more than around twenty minutes fur the pile t'look like a rubbish tip over United Downs, and then fur Micky t'chip the paint in the hallway, while bringin' in Charlie's computer desk.

'Sorry mate,' ee went.

Charlie wanted t'call un a dickhead but ee didn'. 'Least the cunt wuz helpin' un out. 'Is da 'ad fucked off work, an' there'd been no sign of Yak yet.

'Not a bad pad,' went Micky. This, from ee, who'd spent moast of his youth, livin' over United Downs in a van. 'I reckon you'll be getting' some chick action here mate...'

'Y'reckon?'

'Ah yeah... definitely...'

Ut wuz weird talkin' t'Micky about women, because the cunt wuz goin' out with 'is sister. It just didn' seem right somehow.

Charlie looked around the house. Ee wondered wha' would transpire there. His mind raced. Ee thought about some ov the hard slog ee'd put in over the past three years. When ee thought about ut, ee s'paused this wuz what 'twas all about really. Yeah, there wuz fame, glory, groupies, drugs, diversions an' ego, but the bottom line wuz this: somewhere tha' wuz home. Talk t'any rock star, an' on the road, thaas' wha' they really wanted. Not t'live out of a suitcase an' yer laptop any-more.

Be fixed.

Be stable.

Be sorted.

Micky cud think wha' ee wanted. Girls. Na, tha' wudn' the reason fur this t'all.

Fur the rest ov the afternoon, they loaded in an' out of the van the rest ov the furniture from down garages. 'Twas knack-erin' work mind.

'You'n help me an' Jess with the salon tomorra'?'

'Yeah – course,' said Charlie. 'No probs...'

On her way back 'ome from work, Charlie's ma comed in. She went around the rooms just like Charlie did, touching the paintwork and breathin' in the newness of ut all.

'Aw... they've finished it off some nice...' she wuz goin'. 'They curtains'll work well there Charlie. I'm glad we got them...'

She wuz soon off on one – tellin' Charlie where ee should put stuff. Charlie let er do ut. There wudn' many moment like this in her life. 'Twas the sort ov thing she spent her days think-in' about over Homebase.

'Da's goin' t'go with ee on Saturday,' said Charlie, 'down St Ives...'

She stopped wha' she wuz doin' ov.

'Wha' – an' not go football?'

'Yeah, ee told me...'

'Well... Perhaps ee bin listenin' to what I've bin sayin'.'

Unlikely Charlie reckoned. Perhaps the tool had been listen-in' t'what Charlie had t'say to un though.

'Forecast's good...' said Charlie.

Ee knew is da would prob'ly fuck ut up.

'Heard ov ee? They dun the Spar over Carharrack – that crowd with the JCB...

'Heard ut,' said Charlie, 'on the radio'.

'Ebm' got naw one fur ut yet...' said his ma.

'Terrible idn' ut?' went Micky.

'Well, you dun't think ov ut happenin' here do ee?'

Charlie didn't answer. The fact wuz ee knew 'twas 'zactly the sort of thing that happened here - even if the police in Exeter didn't think it wud. Ee reckoned ee knew intimately who the trail might lead to. Road lesson No.10, wudn' ut? Know your enemy. Wha' did um say? Keep yer friends close an' yer enemies even closer.

'Eh... Mrs Curnow,' went Micky. 'I reckon you should get a tattoo done...'

Now hear ov un. The cunt wuz toutin' fur business already. Ee wuz shinin' up t'er some crafty like.

'Wha' me?'

'Well, a lotta' older...ahem... more mature women are getting' tattoos done these days...'

Shite, thought Charlie.

'It can look very attractive on mature skin...'

'I dunnaw,' went his ma.

Charlie knawed wha' she wuz thinkin'. She wuz thinkin' about the crappy tattoos his da had on his forearms, that she always tried t'get un t'hide at weddings an' that.

'The bottom of the back,' went Micky. 'Above the ass... ah - rear. It's very trendy at the moment... Have somethun' tribal dun, t'show yer true Celtic heritage...'

'Tribal?' asked his ma. 'Celtic... wha' do ee mean?'

'Lot of feminists have them... a sort of statement... tha' they wun't be controlled by a man...'

'Aw really?' went his ma, a bit more interested.

'I dun't think Virginia Woolf had ass antlers ma...' went Charlie. 'Now, shallus drop ee back home?'

Charlie shook his head at Micky. Dun't push ut, ee wuz indicating. Micky eased off, and took another direction.

'So Charlie, when's yer house warming party? I'll get me decks set up shall I?'

Charlie's mind went back t'some of the parties on the estate – they wuz sometimes house-warmers. Right enough, as they usually culminated in a bit of pyromaniac activity. Charlie didn't want any ov tha' shit happenin' here.

'I'm not havin' one,' said Charlie.

'Not havin' wha'?' came a voice from outside. 'Y'gotta' have a party Charlie... I mean, this, this is stonkin' idn' ut?'

Yak stuck his head round the door.

'Where you been?' asked Charlie. 'You wuz meant t'be here hours ago – t'help with the move...'

'Down Newlyn. Sorry. I got delayed...'

'Newlyn? Wha' ee doin' down there?'

Yak seemed nervous, edgy, then ee comed out with, 'Just seein' 'bout a gig... er... bit ov jazz like...'

'Bullshit,' went Micky. Charlie wudn' far behind un. Yak wuz about as keen on playin' jazz as Charlie wuz on dance music, or Trescothick wuz on the English folk tradition. Yeah – 'English *fuck* music' ee called ut.

'Yer da around?' asked Yak. 'I wanna' word widn'...'

'Not here m'andsome,' shouted in Charlie's ma. 'Ee's on af'noons this week.'

'Okay, I'll wait,' said Yak, who walked inta' the living room an' whacked on the telly. Ee kicked off 'is shoes an' made hisself at home.

'Put the kettle on Charlie. Mine's a coffee: white, two sugars... Bring in the HobNobs if y'like too...'

The Treslothan Masque – Transforms troubled hair into healthy hair with this weekly deep treatment.
Intensive conditioning treatment
• Improves elasticity - Natural oils, vitamin E and wheat proteins help enhance elasticity
• Strengthens and protects – Natural mosses and lichen ingredients help provide strength, moisture and added protection
• Suitable for chemically treated hair – A conditioning complex helps to mend and stabilize the hair

Nawbody got invited t'any party t'all. The thing just happened. Fuck, Charlie wuz soundin' like Mick Jagger an' Keith Richards talking about the somewhat extra-curricular parties they 'ad while recording 'Exile on Main Street'.

But wha' ee said wuz true. People just assumed tha' because ee'd moved inta' a new house, that there'd be a bit ov a bash. Well, on Trelawny, 'twas 'tradition wudn' ut? An' fur the Cornish, well, tradition in the community wuz everything wudn' ut? Feasten and Saints' days an' tha'. Basically, any chance of a piss up an' they wuz on ut. Perhaps tha' wuz the reason Cornwall seemed t'have a fuckin' festival every week these days. If 'twudn' Bodmin Riding then 'twas the Oyster

Alan M. Kent

Festival down Falmouth, an' if ut wudn' tha', 'twas Lafrowda
Day down St Just or maybe Mabe Shindig.

'Tidn' on Trelawny though,' went Charlie t'everyone.

'Yeah, but, near nuff...' everyone said.

Disturbingly, Yak 'adn't really gone away. The first night,
ee'd pegged out on the living room floor, overdosed on
HobNobs an' too many cups ov coffee, an' then the second
night, ee got so canned, ee cudn' move again either. Ee wuz
sprawled on out on Charlie's new carpet, occasionally makin' a
groanin' sound like a g'eat bear during hibernation. There'ud
been delays on Headönizm because of the problem with the
plumbng an' water supply, brought on by difficulties with the
Trelawny Adit, so Micky an' Jess wuz up fur ut too. A few
Twitters an' text messages later, an' what felt like half ov West
Cornwall turned up in School Lane. There wuz cars everywhere,
blockin' the pavements an' annoying the neighbours, who'd
moved 'ere t'escape jus' tha' kind of thing. Charlie cudn' really
enjoy hisself. Ee wuz constantly monitoring the plaace, so no-
one kicked over glasses ov red wine, or that no other 'illegal' or
sexual activities were taking place. The issue of vomit wuz also
requirin' close scrutiny in the bathroom. Ee felt like one ov
they artists who does plate spinning on the top of poles. Set
one goin', an' soon, another catastrophe seemed near to be
occurring.

The party went on s'long tha' some people had two cracks at
ut. Tommy, fur example, came the first night, went home, had
a sleep, put in an afternoon's work over Crofty, an' comed back
again t'carry on where ee'd left off. His ma seemed t'be makin'
a constant supply ov grub fur um all, and every whip and
wham Charlie wuz down the Co-Op (which wuz now under
major structural repair, but still tryin' t'trade as normal) fur
what seemed like vast quantities of snack foods.

Kelv and Mel wuz the same. They went work an' came back.
Bluett just stayed fur wha' seemed like an eternity. 'Course, ee
had news too. The stupid cunt 'ad only 'ad all his hair cut off,
an' wuz about t'join the army. This seemed t'be 'is last blaw out.
Well, fur a tool who'd spent the last ten years ov his life in his
bedroom doing the following: playing video games/listening to
extreme death metal/having a daily wank/watching porn/
watching any sad and geeky Sci-Fi series (delete or insert as

appropriate), that wuz quite a move. 'Twas nearnly 'bout as monumental as Charlie buying a house.

'Gotta' do somethun' ebm' I Charlie?' wuz 'is take on ut.

'Why the army though?' Yak asked. 'In tha', you'm moast likely t'get blawn up surely?'

'I'd do the Navy meself,' went Micky. Like ever.

'Well, I reckon I got a lotta' shootin' practice through video games,' went Bluett, which was as much ov a half-baked, cakey kind ov answer you cud expect from un. Ee and Trescothick wud make a fine pair. And did. They got pissed together on bottles ov Strongbow. 'Twas lookin' like they wuz makin' plans too.

Amongst the chaos ov the second day, Charlie cud hear a knock on the front door. This wuz ut ee reckoned. This wuz when the coppers shawed up an' told um somebody'd been complainun' 'bout the row. But na, standin' there with a palmtop wuz fuckin' Spryer, with a big smile on his face.

'My boys,' ee went. Cunt.

By now, Yak an' Neil wuz there in hallway, slightly in shock that Spryer wuz in front ov um.

'My boys,' ee went again. Cunt. 'Pack yer bags. Get them guitars. I got Purple Haze an American tour...'

The tool walked in, still jottin' stuff down on his palm-top. Yeah, ee wuz Peter Grant an' Sharon Osbourne rolled inta' one. These days Spryer wuz reckonin' ee'd be runnin' Download or Sonisphere soon enough. In his own little world, ee thought ee wuz a combination of Harvey Goldsmith an' Rod Smallwood. In reality, ee wuz just a cocky little fuck who'd got lucky. Perhaps that' wuz everyone in rock 'n' roll management really. Ee went straight inta' the kitchen helped hisself t'a cold beer from the fridge, then from his pocket, ee produced a small bag ov coke, lined ut up with a B&Q loyalty card, then in one go, sniffed the lot ov ut up his left nostril.

'Aaaaahhhh,' ee went. 'Thaas better. Nice house Charlie. Now where wuz I? Yeah – American tour. 40 dates. 40 cities – part of a 60s' Psychedelia tour. We start New Orleans an' Louisiana, up t'New York and Chicago, then all the way out to San Francisco... A lotta' money boys... You want in?'

Charlie's jaw nearnly 'bout hit the floor. This wuz a proper Cousin Jacker this one.

'I've bin tryin' t' phone you cunts... Where've y'bin? 'Tis like y'disappeared off the earth...'

'Troon,' went Charlie.

'Portreath,' went Neil.

'Newlyn,' went Yak.

'We got a triple biller: Jefferson Airplane tribute, a Grateful Dead tribute and you boys... Fuckin' way t'go... Straight outta Camborne t' New fuckin' Orleans...'

Voodoo pilchard more like.

There wudn' much response from any ov um.

'Whaas' up?'

Charlie wuz the first t'speak.

'We en't doin' ov ut naw more...'

'Wha the fuck?' went Spryer. 'That was not what we agreed at Prestatyn at all...'

'It was,' went Neil.

'Shut the fuck up Davey...' said Spryer, getting stressed. 'Okay – I mean, I know you've had problems with yer psycho-kid and that. But we agreed boys? A bit of time off, and then back to it again...'

'Na,' said Charlie. 'None ov us agreed t'anything... We told you. We wanted out.'

'No, no, no...' went Spryer, shakin' 'is head, an' now undo-ing his tie.

Micky an' Jess wuz overhearin' the conversation.

'Look's like you'm shafted Spryer,' went Micky, enjoyin' the moment.

'Who asked you y'loser?' said Spryer.

'Well, clearly, the band have made ut quite clear tha' they dun't want t'do ut...'

'The band?'

'Yeah – all three ov um...'

'Twas startun' t'get a bit heated.

Spryer went inta' the living room an' had a gake at Charlie's CD collection. Ee'd come a long way 'ad Spryer, from his hard-core punk past. Ee scanned along Charlie's collection. Some Bad Religion. The usual Hüsker Dü and Black Flag. The cunt Curnow still had a bit ov taste then.

'Fuck you, you fuckin' fuckers,' ee went. 'A'right... so I'll get another Purple Haze ready fur ut yeah?'

'Explain...' asked Charlie.

'Well, if you cunts ent up fur ut, well, I'll find some other 'musos' who are... Hendrix's stuff ain't that difficult....'

'Have you tried playin' ut?' yipped up Neil.

'Shut up Davey.'

'So you'll just replace us?' asked Yak.

'Yeah – don't see why not. If Kiss can do ut with their members, why can't we?'

Ee wuz still speakin' collectively, like they were all in ut together.

'Okay,' went Spryer. Ee wuz makin' notes on his palm-top as he wuz contemplating the deal ee'd already made with the booking agents an' promoters in the US. As Spryer did 'is thing, Charlie wuz almost thinkin' they'd made a bad move. Shittin' hell, a trip t'the States sounded great.

Then came the question they'd all been expectin' from the moment Spryer walked in.

'So I'n have the costumes then?'

Where wuz the fuckin' Pilchard when y'needed un?

'We ebm' got um naw more,' offered Yak.

Spryer turned, an' gave un a look like ee wuz about t'take Yak out with a light-sabre, an' cut un inta' two: in the style of Obi Wan Kenobi versus Darth Maul.

'Where are they then?'

'Burnt,' went Neil. 'We burned um – up on Carn Brea... the whole fuckin' lot...'

Yak laughed.

'Aw – this gets better an' better,' went Spryer, shakin' 'is 'ead.

'Spryer mate...' went Charlie. 'Listen will ee? We're just burnt out from the Hendrix stuff... We just can't do it naw more. All ov us... we want t'get back to doin' our own music. Thaas' wha' I'm goin' do here. My own studio. New music... back t'more like we wuz doin' with Balance...'

'Thaa' shite?' asked Spryer.

'Yeah – ut might be shite, but at least ut's our shite...' Charlie responded.

Spryer looked like ee needed another line of coke t'pick un up a bit. Ee 'ad t'settle fur a couple ov cheese an' chilli tortilla chips.

'So, is this a parting of the ways, so to speak?' said Spryer, sounding all philosophical.

'Maybe,' said Charlie.

Yak whacked the stereo up t'full volume again. Ee 'ad Them Crooked Vultures on – Dave Grohl an' John Paul Jones' side-project.

Spryer went over t'speak t'Jess. Ee'd always fancied her a bit. Not that ee cud do anything now.

'You a'right?' he said.

'Yeah – good,' said Jess. 'Hair's lookin' good...'

'Really?' said Spryer.

'Yeah – cud do with yer highlights... well, highlighted a bit...'

'You reckon?'

'Yeah – come in the salon – an' I'll do um fur ee...'

Jess gave un one of er newly-printed business cards.

'Headönizm,' it read. 'Head over for the best in hair and beauty.'

What was happening here in Troon? No more anarchy of the kind ee wuz used to. Cunts were turning down gigs like there wuz naw tomorra' an' Jess Curnow wuz givin' un hair and styling advice - like she knawed jack shit. Bluett joinin'up? an' Yak newly focused. The next thing you'd knaw wuz tha' the tackers were behaving themselves and stayin' at home, watching Dick an' Dom.

Someone or somethun' must've been using some magic on um. If these tools wuz the puppets though, then who wuz the puppet-master?

Trelawny Baby Don't Cry Shampoo – Keeps bath time a fun time.
Gentle tearless Cleanser
• Gentle – Mild cleansers and a pH the same level as children's tear creates this tearless formula
• Soothes – Cornish-grown chamomile extract to calm and soothe the skin and scalp
• Excellent baby wash – A unique blend of extracts helps replace and prevent the disruption of naturally occurring moisture on the skin

The last few days ov decent partying over Charlie's 'ad given Tommy a stankin' hangover. Never mind though. Nothun' like

Voodoo Pilchard

the sound of hard-rock drill t'cure tha'. There wuz a big mee-tun' over mine. Management wanted all the cores in on ut. So if you 'ad time off in *lieu* or wuz on a rest day, they'd pay ee t'be in there. Not bad eh? Tommy knew the kind ov meetun' tha' wuz on. 'Twas like ut wuz a few years back when the former management had t'unfortunately announce redundancies or the closure ov part ov the operation. Ut 'ad the feel ov tha', although nothun' goin' on in the mine or the share price seemed t'indicate tha'. In fact, all the signs were tha' things wuz goin' 'long pretty good.

Get all the shift cores in an' you could guarantee everyone wuz goin' t'have a good ol' yap. Moast of the time 'twas about stupid shit tha' happened underground years ago – when, well, health an' safety wudn' s'rigorous, an' y'cud have a bit ov a laugh, but then, some of ut wuz about wha' wuz happenin' now. T'be 'onest, a few bloaks in there wudn' lookin' too happy you. They wuz thinkin' 'twas a case ov 'Here we go again'. Mining in Cornwall cud sometimes be like a fuckin' mass Hokey Cokey conducted with hard-rock drills. In and out, in an' out through the centuries. The younger fuckers still there wuz openin' an' prayin' 'twudn' a case of 'out' – well, wha' the fuck wud um do if tha' happened again? The old boys wudn' s'bothered you s'paused, because they'd seen ut and dun ut before.

The meetun' wuz t'be held in the canteen. Everyone wuz in there with their crowst bags an' flasks yippin' a way on. There wuz a lot of rumours goin' on too. Some of ut wuz ludicrous you. A few boys had been sayin' the RDA wuz sick of dicking around with the land around the mine, an' that the wuz goin' t'bring in the big guns from the government to stop any further development ov Crofty. Basically, 'twas simple enough – they'd revoke their mining licence an' then, well, the shafts below ground – would… er… be shafted. There wuz always a sense too, tha' Cornwall Council wudn' really behind what Crofty wuz doin'. The buggers on there didn't really want their tourist-friendly Cornwall ov eco-bed an' breakfasts an' shoulder-season festivals buggered up by a bit ov heavy industry any more. Aw 'es – the romance of ut in the past wuz all very nice. Felt-hatted miners and bal-maidens in sepia photographs wuz wha' they wanted all over the shop. In fact, bleddy hundreds of millions ov pounds ov course 'ad been put inta' preservin' what wuz left as a World Heritage Site. Shame they didn't put s'much inta' the real, livin' operation. See, fur they, Crofty wuz a like a kind ov running sore in the middle ov Pool – worse even than Club Rhino – an' in their mind, the best thing wud be t'get rid ov ut altogether. T'their credit, the management of Crofty continually gave they the middle finger at every opportunity. Nice one.

Y'cud tell wha' Tommy wuz like in this kind ov situation. Ee wuz the 'special one' here. First-class knobber at 'ome, an' failed shag machine ee might be, but 'ere, ee wuz a legend. Ef you wuz on his core, well, you wuz made. Tommy'd look after ee no matter wha'. Not only tha', but the cunt 'ad the gift-ov-the-gab didn' a? Ee cud always speak his mind t'management, and they took nawtice ov un. Thaas' cuz ee 'ad respect underground. His activities outside ov Crofty didn' detract from un at all. In fact, ut enhanced his reputation. Underground, Tommy comed from a fine tradition of mining cap'ns that stretched back inta' industrial history in time immemorial. Everyone knew 'bout Charlie too – an' although initially they reckoned ee wuz a bit ov a gay boy prick fur dressin' up in Hendrix gear an' tha', y'had t' hand ut to un – 'least, ee wudn' down mine like they were. Even better if ee'd made a few quid, which apparently ee 'ad. An' the fact tha' Tommy wuz still with Sally Curnow – said ut all, didn't ut? 'Mean, Sally Curnow wuz tasty as fuck – a hornier MILF you wudn' find from here t'Stithians an' back again.

Anyways, management wuz comin' in t'stand behind a table up the front end. There wuz a bit of buggering around with the projector an' their laptop, but soon enough, 'twas ready.

''Ere we fuckin' go,' went Tommy to a few around un. 'More bullshit 'bout maximising the yield...'

Gerald Matta, who wuz the chief operating officer, wuz up out ov his seat. Ee took a swig of water before ee beginned.

'Good morning everyone. Thank you for attending this meeting today. I know some of you have had to come in off your rest days, and for that we are grateful. At this stage in the proceedings I think it important that everyone connected with the mine hears the same message at the same time...'

Matta wudn' a bad ol'boy really. Bit fuckin' snobby at times, but he knawed his stuff. Trained at the School of Mines, an' 'ad had fifteen year out in South Africee doin' diamonds.

'As you know, tin production is up, and given the current share price, we see no reason why, over the next three years, expansion of this part of our operation should continue expendentially...'

Tommy didn't knaw wha' expendentially meant, but it sounded a'right.

Boy Matta seemed t'back ut up with a bunch of graphs on the powerpoint. The slides had graphs on ut looking like 'twas goin' up rather than down. Ee wuz clickun' around with the mouse, an' showing all the levels offerin' the best yield. Future production wuz also shown and predicted.

There wuz a collective sigh ov relief around the room. Nawone wud be havin' t' take the furniture they'd bought on 0% finance back t'Furniture World, or more importantly, stop goin' out on the piss on Saturday nights down Rose Cottage or Institute.

'You'll get all this shortly,' ee went, 'in our new development plan...'

Well, if tha' wuz a'right then, why the fuck did um want um all in 'ere today?

'Now, some of you know that we have been prospecting in some older areas of the mine again...'

That wuz true. Tommy an' 'is core had shown around some scientists an' mining engineers a few months back. They'd been sample drilling, and computer mapping the mine's resources. A 3D map of the mine wuz put up showing potential yields. 'Twas amazing what you could find out these days with all tha' bleddy geo-physics. Samples had been sent up to the lab, and then there'd been some discussion about refining methods: adapting existing gear.

'The bottom line of this is that we have found traces of gold and are identifying gold targts...'

Matta looked up at the other directors an' then at the boys. Ee continued.

'We have already found it at a commercial-level grade. So far, the results have been very encouraging...'

There wuz a collective gasp ov amazement, although this wuz wha' one or two ov them 'ad been sayin' ov late.

Tommy cudn' help ut. Like a twat, ee stood up an' shouted, 'There's gold in them thar hills...' as if he wuz some bushy-bearded prospector in the middle of Arizona.

'Well, Tommy,' went Matta, 'you may well be right. Now, before anyone here thinks we're going to strike big, I have to inform you that currently, each tonne of rock found contains only 1.6 grams of gold. However, given the current gold price, this does make it viable to extract. In this way then, we will be able to expand the mine, and continue to find new metals. Some of you out there will be considering the response of the RDA to this news, who as you know, wish to see the cessation of mining in this particular area of Pool. We have obviously, informed them of this matter and are desirous that they continue to grant us our extraction licence.'

Tommy knew ut wuz good news. Gold. 'Always believe in your soul. You've got the power to know. You're industructable...' Spandau Ballet wuz goin' through 'is head.

'We shortly intend to have some trial cores working on gold extraction... Now, it perhaps goes without sayin' tha' we do not want a media frenzy about this discovery. We wish to present this development in a measured way, so I would be grateful if at present, we could keep this within the South Crofty community. Meanwhile we have prepared a low-key statement about the development for the media...'

Well, y'knaw the way 'tis today. Y'only got t'say somethun' t'somebody an' the next thing 'tis on You tube an' then Sky News. Thaas' wha' happened. Ut only took some cunt t'phone a mate an' fur tha' mate to phone somebody else, before what looked like all the world media descended on Crofty. Still, 'least 'twas on a positive note. Visually, there wuz lots of juxtaposin' goin' on, with shots of Wheal Coates out St Agnes an' the Crowns engine houses down Botallack compared to the wheels ov Crofty's head frame turning. The reporters were taking the tone of 'A once dead industry now has the hope of revival...' The usual shite then. Matta didn't particularly want t'go on camera, but there ee wuz, more or less sayin' the same thing as ee'd told the workforce at the meetun'. With the BBC pointin' a microphone at un, ee wuz lookin' a bit more flustered, but managed t'say the right thing.

An' gold, well, gold got a power like no other metal 'adn' ut?

Voodoo Pilchard

'Twas also the sort of good news story about Cornwall all the English newspapers liked. Normally, they wuz calling anyone west of the Tamar 'pasty-munchers' or 'Cornish nasties' (if ever it involved a bit ov nationalism), an' beginning every story with 'Oo-ar!' Cunts. Save tha' fur Somerset an' Bristol will ee? Well, now Tommy's cry about 'them thar' hills wuz the head-lines all over the shop, an' for once, somethun' positive wuz being reported. Fur all the local papers, it made a change from JCBs an' cash points. Now they cud talk about digging up gold instead ov digging out ATMs. So it went round the world didn' ut? Images of electric pastyland: looking north east with the Roskear shaft, then New Cooks Kitchen on the right, the Robinsons and Taylor's shafts more distant. Their reporting wuz voiced over images of the two winders: the man-riding cages an' then the ore-hoistin' skips. In between this, you got head-shots of a "Cornish miner" (like 'twas some kind ov' near extinct species) talkin' about the gold discovery, alongside his shift workin' an air leg drill.

'In the honeycombed depths of the mine here at South Crofty - covering an area two and a half miles long and half a mile wide - the Cornish miners are no longer just seeking tin. Instead, the new objective for them is that most ancient of pre-cious metals... gold...'

Moast of um wuz fuckin' clueless. If they'd dun any research t'all they'd have knawn that tin was about one of the oldest mined metals in the world: Joseph ov Arimathea an' Solomon's Temple an' all. The whole thing wudn' really helped by them addin' in the music from the Bond film *Goldfinger* an' using any pun on El Dorado at every opportunity. El Kernow wuz the lat-est in a long line.

Anyone who knawed Cornwall knawed this wudn' nothun' knew. Thousands ov boys from round Obby Stanker County had heard the call before, an' 'ad headed t'plaaces all over the world t'search for gold. Y'only had t'look on the internet: Waihi gold mine in New Zealand was begun by Cousin Jacks; same with the Empire Mine in Grass Valley. Gold wuz like a kind of Holy Grail fur the average Cornish miner. Y'had t'pursue ut. No doubt some stupid cunts wud be on the fringes of Crofty dig-gin' trenches, an' some might even be out there panning some of the streams from the adits. 'Twud all come, naw doubt.

Behind all the satellite trucks, the sexy young female reporters an' where the now faded graffiti of 'Cornish lads are fishermen and Cornish lads are miners too, but when the fish and tin are gone what are Cornish boys to do?' wuz a small, but new and significant piece ov street art. The shape of the fish was unmistakable. Voodoo pilchard, it read, in blue-black ink. Nawbody took any nawtice fur the now, but one day, they wud. Es – the Pilchard wuz watchin' – filled with the spirit of Voodoo.

Meanwhile in the Crofty workforce, this finding ov the element *Au* opened up a whole new can of worms. If y'found a nugget in a stope, what did' ee do with ut? Pop in in yer pocket and take ut t'grass, or did ee declare un t'yer shift cap'n. In Africa, the miners in the gold and diamond mines were more or less strip searched after a shift. Get up from the shaft an' you'd go through a detector ov some kind. Na, ut wudn' come t'tha' surely wud ut? Na, Tommy reckoned. The kind of gold they wuz goin' t'find wudn' be in nuggets t'all. Y'wuz talkin' trace elements compared t'they kind ov finds. 'Twas all in the refinin' process, not the extraction. Any boy who reckoned on findin' a lump ov gold – enough t'pay off their mortgage an' retire on – well, they wuz mazed. Dare say though, tha' anyone walkin' the network ov drives, declines or raises had their eye a little bit more on the ground they wuz walkun' on than usual, after Matta's announcement.

Fairings Taming Spray – Bring on shine and bouncy body. Leave-in, detangling conditioner
• Spray on and leave in – Provides easy detangling on dry or damp hair
• Fast acting – A gentle ginger compound penetrates quickly leaving hair fresh and full of body
• Happy kids – Excellent for use on children's 'morning hair'

Back Trelawny another kind ov gold rush wuz on. Some marketing cunts had worked out tha' the plaace t'do good business wuz on the poorer an' moast disadvantaged estates ov Cornwall. So, there wuz heavy tv rotation ov adverts on ITV1 and the shopping channels, an' a postal campaign by

Cash4Gold UK. This wuz apparently the trusted industry leader, who paid out 60% more than its competitors. What wuz ut? Well, they offered desperate tools the chance t'turn old gold jewellery inta' cash didn' um? 'Twas easy apparently – bit too easy if you wuz in the knaw. All you had t'do wuz put yer fuckin' old earrings or chains or whatever inta' the freepost jewellery return pack. 'Getting cash fur gold has never been easier,' so ut said.

There wuz testimonials wudn' there:

'I had a pile of unwanted jewellery I never wore. I sent it off to Cash4Gold UK and I got £424.'

'I got divorced. I didn't know what to do with my wedding ring, so I sent it off to Cash4Gold and the gave me a cheque for ninety quid. Fantastic!'

The way 'twas, then you could sit back and relax and they'd send ee yer payment within 24 hours of having your jewellery evaluated. If you wudn' completely satisfied with what they wuz offerin' then, well, you could get your jewellery back. Ut sounded good t' a lot ov the struggling fuckers on Trelawny – so in this gold rush – they wuz parcellin' up every bit ov crap they had: Pool Market stuff as well as anything from H. Samuels. Problem wuz though, well, y'might ov thought tha' yer earrings might ov made a few quid, but not really. 'Twas a buyer's market see, an' they cunts at Cash4Gold UK could offer whatever the fuck they wanted. In a way, 'twas 'zactly the same as the loan sharks who handed out leaflets down Trelawny jus' before Christmas – when things wuz a bit tight. Thaa' wuz when all the single mums signed up fur a two hundred quid loan – so they cud buy their Beyonce Trebilcock or Shanice Penhallurick a Nintendo DS, an' neglected t'see the small print ov what they'd be payin' back.

Still if you'n desperate enough fur money, you'll do ut wun't ee? Thaas' why down the Post Office the postman (in his Kevlar trousers) nearnly 'bout broke his back tryin' t'lift the postal sacks one mornin'. 'Twas either tha' fur some ov um – or go on the game – just like Mel's ma. An when y'had the choice of gettin' inta' some bloak's car over Beacon fur a quickie blaw-job, or getting' a few quid in from Cash4Gold UK, you knawed wha' you wuz goin' t'do. In Mel's ma's case, she'd prob'ly do both, an' see wha' cheap gold she cud pick up on the hoof

down Hayle car boot too. See, this wuz how the world economic situation affected the streets of Obby Stanker Country.

So there 'twas: the Trelawny Gold rush – miner forty-niners
again. Some cunts was goin' cash fur gold an' others wuz goin'
gold fur cash. Always the way though edn' ut?

Surfer's Colour Protect Daily Shampoo – Jeans may fade,
but hair colour doesn't have to.
Gentle care for colour-treated hair
• Cares – Gently cleanses whilst helping to add strength,
elasticity and body
• Extends – High-powered sun screen helps extend life or
hair colour
• Moisturizes and adds shine – Activated Moisturizing and
Shine Blends help provide ample moisture and intensified
shine

Elsewhere, other cash-fur-gold/gold-fur-cash type deals were
goin' on. Yak 'ad finally agreed t'meet up with Tommy Curnow
– or rather Tommy'd finally got around t'getting 'is arse in gear.
Both ov um got too hammered at Charlie's house t'make any
kind ov sensible conversation. Usually, they got onta' the top
of the world's greatest rock drummers. Yak wuz pushin' fur Neil
Peart an' John Bonham, while Tommy wuz goin' fur Cozy
Powell an' Keith Moon. Tha' wuz before both ov um crashed
out.

At tha' stage ov the proceedings, it wuz top secret. Yak didn'
want naw-one knawin' 'bout 'is plans. Yeah – Charlie, Jess,
Micky – they 'ad plans, but so did ee now. 'Twud come out in
the end – ut always wud on Trelawny. You cudn' keep nothun'
secret. But ee'd 'ave a go.

Tommy's fuckin' old Capri wuz just about still goin'. These
days ee'd resigned hisself t'the fact that ee cudn' use ut fur
work. Fur ut t'continue as any kind of working automobile,
'twas shortly goin' t'need some serious body work an' prob'ly a
whole new engine. The scrapy over United Downs wuz keepin'
his eye out fur'n.

'They'm proper in boy… See um bein' used on telly all the
time… All they retro cop shows, yeah?'

'Bewdie, yeah, bewdie,' went Yak, over an' over again, as

Tommy wuz yippin' on 'bout the difficulties ov finding car parts these days; Yak soundin' like ee 'ad the same level ov Asparagus Syndrome as Anthony Davey.

This looked the kind of deal where Yak didn't want naw prying eyes – so Tommy drove north out towards Reskajeage Downs an' they pulled inta' a layby there above the cliffs at Deadman's Cove. 'Twas the sort ov plaace y'come fur a shag ov a Saturday night; so hence the quantity of used condoms hangin' off the gorse out there. As ever, Tommy'd not gone fur his new Whitesnake CD, but had a bit ov Rainbow blastin' out:

COME DOWN WITH FIRE
LIFT MY SPIRIT HIGHER
SOMEONE'S SCREAMING MY NAME
COME AND MAKE ME HOLY AGAIN
I'M THE MAN ON THE SILVER MOUNTAIN

The genteel middle classes (newly moved in from England) were out walking with their OS maps, shootin' sticks, rucksacks an' walking boots, an' lookin' mightily pissed off with the row comin' blastin' out of the Capri's rear speakers. Tommy an' Yak rolled some fags an' had a smoak. Tommy wuz by now beginning t'get a sense of wha' boy Yak wuz after.

'So tell me Yak? What 'zactly 'ave ee got in mind fur ut?

Ee turned down Dio's vocals an' Blackmore's gargantuan riffs.

'I wanna' run a club there…'

'Wha' like Twilight?'

'Na… not tha' kind of shit…'

'Wha' strip plaace – like Rhino?'

'Na… ut'll be like CBGBs…'

Tommy wuz lost. Ee didn' have a fuckin' clue 'bout CBGBs…'

His sense of rock 'n' roll history wuz limited t' bullet belts, studded wrist bands and bandanas. NFC see? Normal fur Camborne.

'What ee say? EBGBs?'

Yak cudn' be bothered t'explain.

'The idea of ut is like a proper rock venue fur Cornwall – fur bands an' tha'… It'll be like plaaces Purple Haze played…'

Well, tha' wudn' quite true. Purple Haze hadn' always got booked inta' the moast cutting edge venues across Europe.

Tommy nodded his head.

The last thing ee really wanted t'see wuz Rhino demolished. Yak's idea might work. 'Mean, Tommy knew the cunt for years, an' ee wuz a total tool, more or less, but this, well, this might jus' work.

'So you wanna' buy the lease? Tha' right?'

'Yeah.'

'Well, I d'still own the lease... but following the past difficulties I 'ad with ut... I ent' allowed t'do anything with ut at present...'

Tommy recalled his appearances before the court an' licensing authorities.

'So - you'n sell ut t'me?'

'Yeah. S'pause so.'

Tommy wuz seein' lots of possibilities here. Maybe this, along with the gold strike at Crofty, might give un enough money to make the move outta' Trelawny, so easin' all possible nightmare scenarios with Sally an' thus gainin' ten – or maybe twenty years - ov trouble-free existence. Enough t'take un t're-tirement which in 'is view, ee'd be spendun' sittin' in one of the director's boxes at Treyew Road, as they took on the mighty Newcastle United in a one-end-of-the-island-t'-the-other semi-final grudge match.

'Hang on a minute though,' ee went. 'How've you got the money fur tha'?'

This wuz Yak ee wuz speakun' too: a cunt ov the first order, who'd ee'd seen flaked out on 'substances' at just about every estate party in the last ten years. Charlie'd had t'lock un in Jimmy Pengelly's shed a few years back t'get un off drugs. Any money ee'd ever had ee' squandered on wine, women, song an' illegal substances.

'I got a deal on,' whispered Yak.

'A deal?'

'A deal that'll sort out the cash... an' set me up...'

Tommy didn' really want t'ask wha' kind of a deal. Ee knew wha' ut might involve.

'Drum lessons es ut?' Tommy joked.

'Yeah...' winked Yak. 'Expensive ones...'

Tommy knawed how stuff worked in Cornwall. You didn' ask too many questions. Hear naw evil, speak naw evil, see naw evil.

'Well boy, if you'n get me the money, then the club's yours... Mind you I'm s'paused t'charge ee fur fixtures an' fittin's too like...'

Shit. Yak hadn' calculated on tha'. Ee'd need all tha' t'make ut happen.

'Is there any kind ov sweetener I can offer ee?' went Yak, tryin' t'negotiate a further deal.

'Whaddee' mean?'

'Well, I got contacts...;

'What sort ov contacts?'

'Good ones. They'n get ee anything y'need?'

Tommy 'ad a good ol' think. Ee didn' need much really. T'be honest, ee wuz quite glad boy Yak wuz finally takin' the white elephant that wuz Club Rhino off 'is hands. A few debts might be settled then.

'How be doin' in the bedroom department these days? went Yak.

Hear ov un yippin' up to un.

'Wha' the fuck d'mean?'

'Well – a man of your age Tommy. Things start t'go downhill a bit dun't um?'

'Not me boy. Not me,' went Tommy defensively. 'Sally ebm' got nothun' t'complain about... dun't you worry...'

Yak wuz beginning t'think this wuz too much information, but if ee wuz in fur a penny, then ee wuz in fur a pound

'See – I'n get gear... little blue tablets...'

Tommy realised wha' he meant. When ee thought about ut, 'is pecker 'adn't 'zactly had the poke an' hardness of a hard-rock drill lately. All told, 'twuz a bit flaccid really. Sally 'adn' complained or nothun', but now she wuz a feminist, maybe she'd be expectin' a bit more ov un. The Germaine Greer book ee'd been lookin' at on her desk, wuz explainin' the high importance ov the G spot t'a woman – plateaus before orgasm etc.

'Are we talkin' Viagra?' said Tommy, windin' up the window, so no cunt could hear.

'Yeah – extra, extra strong...'

'How much?'

'Lifetime's supply if y'want ut... Imported from Mexico... real 'loco' stuff...'

'Sounds good. You'n sort tha' fur me...?'

''Course.'

'Well, now you'm talkin'...'

'I wun't say anything. Strictly between us, yeah?'

'Right – so you'n have the fixtures an' fittun's too...'

'Proper,' went Yak an' they shook hands.

A quick call t'his man down Newlyn an' 'twud all be sorted. Yeah, 'twudn' be a problem. When they made the drop, the pile ov Viagra'd be on top of the coke. Wuz tha' a'right? Yeah, bewdie.

Tommy wuz feelin' good. Shit – extra, extra strong Viagra must catapult un back t'the stud ee wuz in his youth. With tha' on board, well, ee'd be an unstoppable sex machine. Drilling machine by day and sex machine by night. Whoopee do.

'Want me t'take ee back Troon?' asked Tommy.

'Proper job,' went Yak.

Now wha' wuz ut tha' Tommy'd called ut? EBGBs?

With all this weird voodoo shit goin' on round Camborne, tha' sounded perfect.

A club tha' wud give ee the 'ee bee g bees'. Just right fur an alternative rock venue. Catchy as fuck too. Tommy Curnow – tosser, wanker, tool – but na ordinary fool. All tha' wuz needed now wuz fur his man with the plan down Newlyn t'do 'is bit ov fixin'. Yeah – fur once, Yak may not've been strikin' gold like everyone in Crofty an' Trelawny, but ee wuz now the man on the silver mountain.

Tommy an' Yak whacked on the Rainbow again an' went up through Illogan makin' the devil's horns, an' scarin' moast of the grannies who'd comed out ov Knit an' Natter club.

Tea Treat Colour Protect Daily Conditioner – Harnesses the power of tea extract for longer-lasting hair colour. Detangles and helps repair colour-treated hair

• Detangles – instantly detangles and helps smooth the hair to provide a light silky feel

• Repairs – Tea leaf and panthenol help strengthen and moisturize

• Moisturizes and adds shine – Activated Moisturizing and

Shine Blends help provide ample moisture and intensified shine

Ut took Charlie nearly a week to recover from the house-warming and prob'ly another fortnight before his house wuz lookin' somethun' like ut again. At one point, ee'd nearnly considered getting in the builders again. The wreckage from the party ensured that the bin bags outside his house wuz approachin' Mount Everest proportions. Ee'd nawticed quite a lot at the party: Yak (who somehow had now progressed inta' one of the spare rooms with a sleeping bag) 'ad been yippin' on with 'is da fur a fair bit. They'd 'ad their usual debate about drummers and so on, but somethun' else wuz goin' on. Ee cud sense ut. Just a feeling perhaps. Intuition maybe. Sixth Sense? Magic? Perhaps.

Between the chaos, Charlie'd felt alone. Thaas' when we d'become weak. Road lesson No.1: Always fight yer Demons. But ut wudn' workin'. Thaas' when our guard 'is down. So yeah, while everyone wrecked 'is 'ouse, once his broadband 'ad been sorted, ee contacted Bev didn' a? Ut wuz somethun' ee'd pondered about fur a few days. Sometimes 'twas best t'just leave ut. Thaas' the way ee'd felt when Yeugen an' Bev wuz both inta' un at the same time. When Charlie thought back t' the heartache of that down the Pavilions, ut nearly 'bout gived un a cold sweat. And now, ee wuz e-mailing her, gradually increasin' the amount of texts ee wuz sending. Ee wuz trying not to flirt with er, but you d'knaw how 'tis – you cen't stop yerself. You need it t'make moments ov yer day special. Mainly, Bev wuz being very impressed with Charlie as home-owner. She wuz still in postgraduate student mode, so t'imagine having your own plaace, well, that wuz somethun' t'be admired.

After they'd met up in Bierkeller in Bristol, Charlie'd got the same feelings back. And then, well, 'twudn' the same with Yeugen naw more. Yeugen an' ee 'ad hung out a bit when ee wuz back home fur Christmas, but ut was more goin' through the motions in Charlie's view. She'd carried on working down Tescos fur a bit an' then started a degree course here in Cornwall. Ut didn' last though. Last time ee saw the Polish boys, the work wuz dryin' up in Cornwall, and they wuz thinkin' ov makin' ut back t'Poland. Apparently, the economy wuz doin' a bit better there now. So she went, but as far as Charlie knawed, she'd always thought of returning at some point. She wanted t'stay in touch with un – even if things hadn't worked out. Charlie reckoned tha' 'is exotic phase ov relationships wuz over now. Nice while ut lasted but 'twas never goin' t'go the full distance. Latterly, there'd always been a bit of tension there between um. Yeugen didn' seem t'mind yippin' up t'Markie Phillips when she wuz out anywhere. 'Twas all connected see, because Markie – the flash bastard - started employing a few ov the Polish boys remaining. Ee 'ad um on the jobs no other fucker wanted t'do, down Stithians abattoir. This wuz mainly cleaning up offal an' disinfecting the boners. Piotr'd stayed fur a bit – but eventually when the waste t'energy plan fur West Cornwall went tits up – after a planning row – ee cut is losses too, an' headed back t'Quidzin. They just wudn' quids in anymore.

There 'adn' been anyone on tour fur Charlie. 'Mean, a few maids liked un an' tha'. You cud tell. But see, there wudn' the time anywhere really. Do one gig an' you wuz back in the van again – with three other cunts. 'Twudn' right. Yeah – there'd been some fanciable women on the road. But that wuz one of the road rules wudn' ut? – No.5 again – beware ov groupies. If Charlie took good nawtice ov tha' rule, Yak didn' care much. Christ knawed what interesting infections he'd picked up along the way. If 'twas on offer, ee'd accept ut without any conditions. Spryer wuz about the same – but the way ee wuz goin' on, 'twas more the owners ov the venues ee wuz after: the MILFs an' Cougars of half of Western Europe's gigging circuit. Give un due – Spryer could put on the charm if ee wanted to. Ee seemed t'like the older ones. Charlie laughed to hisself. Despite Spryer's shock at them not wanting to take up his offer, they had done well together. At the party the other night, ee'd been all 'I shall rip up your contracts' an' 'You'll never gig again' – which wuz fair enough. Ee cud sue them, if 'ee wanted to, but they all knew ee wudn' bother. Maybe Spryer would be back in again – when the new direction 'ad been decided. Until then, well, ut had t'be a bit voodoo pilchard fur a bit.

But Bev?

Beverly Bennetts. Ee'd say er name over an' over again as ee sat bollock- naked in the living room watching *Come Dine with Me*.

What should a do?

Well, ee could take er out again – but that would be weird. Some restaurant and them two, sat there, like a couple of lemons. Ee'd even thought of suggesting the Meadery in Redruth – fur old times sake. Then there wuz Jamie Oliver's *15* up at Watergate Bay. Tha' seemed the kind of plaace she might appreciate these days. Plenty of fancy plaaces down Falmouth too. But na – it wudn' right.

As ee wuz decidin' how to proceed, ee went upstairs and put some boxers on. Yak heard un.

'Wha' time us ut?' ee groaned. His room stunk of beer, bad breath an' farts.

Yak looked more wrecked now than ee ever did on tour.

'Twelve,' went Charlie.

'Fuck,' said Yak, leaping up. 'I gotta' a meeting down Newlyn at one o'clock...'

'Better get yer ass in gear then, 'adn' ee?'

'Fuckin' right... Cheers Charlie...'

Charlie'd come t'a decision. Yeah, ee'd cook a meal for Bev here. Invite her over. Show er tha' people from Troon could be as sophisticated as her family from down Malpas.

'I dun't want you here tonight,' said Charlie.

'Wha'?'

'You heard... I want the plaace to meself tonight...'

'But...'

'But wha'?'

'I thought we wuz shapin' up here like...'

'Yak – you ent movin' in here...'

Yak looked crest-fallen.

'I's nothun' personal like,' went Charlie. 'I just need me own space...'

'I see,' ee went, sounding like ee wuz eight years old.

'What if we sort out some rent an' tha'...'

The prospect ov some rent an' tha' sounded interesting. What else wuz Yak going to provide?

'Anyways, why do ee want me gone tonight?'

The cheek ov the cunt.

'Got plans ebm' I?'

'Ah... fuckin' 'ell. Charlie's back on... Who es ut?'

'None of yer business...'

Alan M. Kent

'Ah, Micky reckoned you'd be havin' loads of chicks back here...'

''Tis nothun' like tha'' went Charlie.

Yak gived un a wink, 'eaved on his clothes and went out the door.

Charlie phoned Bev. Ee knew she'd be free, almost as if she wuz waitun' fur 'is call. They'd spoken before, but she seemed enthusiastic to hear from him. Charlie remembered those first few conversations they'd 'ad on the phone years ago. Ee smiled. Ee knew the way her dad thought ov un. Still, from what ee knawed, ee seemed to like Charlie a bit better than her ex – goth-punk boy Mike, so ee'd learned, when ee saw un a while back down the Piazza in Trura. Her da wuz a bit ov a Trura City fan too. Best not tell his da tha' – not fur now at least.

So, they agreed, she'd be comin' over fur 7.30pm.

Charlie needed t'go t'Tescos. This had to be fuckin' the business. Nothun' less than the best fur her would do. Yeah – an' the atmosphere wuz important too. None of yer fuckin' cheese either. Ut 'ad t'be classy.

Charlie stepped over the heap of bin bags outside ov 'is house. 'Twas now looking very Trelawny-like in its sense of environmental chaos, like a kind of demonic and plastic Carn Brea. All ut needed now wuz a scabby old mattress an' a broken telly. Fuck, Charlie wuz 'opin' ee wuz escapin' tha' lot; not recreating ut on a new scale. There didn't look like much progress on the rebuilding of the Co-Op. As ee went past, ee seen Jimmy Pengelly comin' out the shop carrying a frail with some cabbage and carrots in ut. Ee adn't see ov un fur a bit – prob'ly because ee wuz down 'is Treslothan allotment grawin' 'is apples an' cherries. Charlie tooted his horn and jammed on 'is brakes.

'Alright boy?' went Charlie.

'Charlie Curnow – you old bugger... Keepin' alright are ee?'

'Fine Jimmy. Doing well.'

'See you bought one of they new houses up School Lane?'

'Yeah – it's going good Jimmy...'

Jimmy leaned in a bit more.

'Now, you missed a good night down Centenary...'

'Fisherman's Friends wudn' ut?'

'Bleddy lovely,' went Jimmy, 'Some good – they old shanty tunes... Better than tha' row you lot d'play...'

'Eh, come on,' went Charlie. 'We'm getting' quite musical these days...'

'Well, we got auditions on, you, at the moment... Lookin' fur new singers... I told feyther ee should try out...'

Charlie knawed his dad wuz more inta' listening to Rainbow and Whitesnake than being in the choir with a lot ov retired ol' boys weth nothun' better t'do. Had gold on 'is mind too now tha' the Great Crofty Rush wuz on.

'Now you'm back, you'n join too cen't ee boy?'

Maybe Jimmy 'ad a point. Ee'd never have thought tha' a few years back, but ef ee wanted some good vocal work-outs, then prob'ly the Choir wuz the natural plaace fur'n.

'I'll think about ut,' went Charlie. 'Gotta' go...'

Jimmy watched un speed off, and then 'ad a gake behind un' at the mess of the cashpoint crime. The world wuz in some state, Jimmy reckoned. Good job there wuz young buggers like Charlie out there.

Charlie pushed on pretty sharpish down through Beacon, an' over the roundabout. The graffiti wuz still written on Boy Trevithick's podium. He turned right, an' headed up Centenary Street towards Tescos.

There wuz decisions t'be made. What wuz ut goin' t'be? Tesco had a very nice Finest range, which wuz basically ping meals made t'look somethun' special. Not bad prices mind, but na, wha' ee needed wuz somethun' a bit more sophisticated. Charlie wuz goin' t' impress the pants off her. Ee checked himself. Ee knew how fuckin' sad tha' sounded. Right, ee wuz just goin' t'impress her. Nothun' else. The years on the road had honed Charlie's ability to cook quite nicely. Yeah – cookin': thaa' wuz the new rock 'n' roll wudn' ut? Suddenly Charlie wuz fancyin' hisself in a Levi Rootes kind of a way. If he cud bring the soul inta' the food, maybe ee could bring the soul inta' ee an' Bev once again. Charlie wuz goin' organic, fresh vegetables, carrots, lentils ore-fuckin'-gano, salads. Ee didn't really have much ov a plan. Ee wuz just buyin' ingredients ee'd heard television chefs use. How sad wuz tha'? Still, ut seemed t'be workin'. The trolley wuz filling up an' people watchin' un, seemed t'be impressed.

Charlie imagined how hard ut might be t'do this kind of thing ef you wuz actually a famous rock star. Ee reckoned you'd

Alan M. Kent

need a few flunkies t'go out an' get this kind of stuff, if y'had tha' 'rock 'n' roll royalty' kind of status. No matter, ee didn' have t'contemplate tha' these days. Still, tha' wuz one of the rules ov the road wudn' ut? Stay healthy. Ef y'didn' do tha', then y'd suffer. Tha' wuz when y'picked up vocal infections and when you got sick. Long term – if you ate too much dairy or other crap – you'd get nodules on your throat. So this, this food fur Bev wud be rock 'n' roll too. It would be infused with all the touring ee'd ever done. Charlie wuz just about reachin' this point ov ecstasy in the frozen food aisle, when ee heard a voice.

'You a'right Charlie? What ee lookin' fur?'

Charlie turned round. Ut wuz Neil.

'You workin' here again?'

'Yeah – well, had to come back didn't I? I's not management naw more – but I know me way around like... so they offered ut to me...'

Ah fuck. Y'didn't need a fucking Ph.D t'realise tha' wuz what Neil'd prob'ly do. Charlie might have seen ut comin'.

'Need the money dun't us?' ee went. 'Fur Anthony...'

'Eh? Nice trolley-full. Stockin' up again after the party are ee?'

'Sort ov,' went Charlie.

Neil had a gake at his trolley. 'Twas full of the sorta' crazy unedible shit bloaks buy when they'm cookin' a meal fur a maid.

Neil wuz more circumspect than Yak though. Ee didn' say a pile.

'How's the boy anyway?'

Neil dropped his new price tagging machine a little.

'Not good,' ee went. 'We 'ad another meeting. Looks like ee might be goin' t'a special school in Trura fur a bit... They think they'n manage un a bit better there...'

Charlie nodded. Ee knew this wudn' want they wanted.

'We want t'give un a bit more independence...' said Neil. 'But Ally's findin' ut hard... Ee might go residential fur a bit.'

Their conversation came to a pause. This wuz tricky stuff, the kind ov stuff you never think you'll be dealing with. This wuz the crazy shit that happened to other people, not they.

'Eh?' went Neil. 'Y'knaw tha' Voodoo Pilchard graffiti... You an' Micky wuz talkin' 'bout ut... have a gake up Foundry

Voodoo Pilchard

Road... Fuckin' hell, Charlie – you never seen nothun' like ut...'

Charlie swallowed. Ah hell. More of ut? Charlie didn' right-ly believe ut at first, but after he said goodbye t'Neil, gone through the check-out an' loaded the food inta' the back of his car, ee 'ad a look.

Shit. 'Twas now officially out ov control. All the way along Foundry Road wuz a set of hoardings, purple-coloured and filled with politically-correct information about the redevelop-ment of Holmans, all intended to persuade the public ov the RDA's good intentions. All the way up through, an' over the purple hoardings – up t'the railway bridge, where the road turned inta' Park Lane an' Carn Avenue were hundreds of red-and-orange Voodoo Pilchard symbols. 'Twas the sort of epic piece of artwork tha' would take anyone days to do. Someone must've been workin' at night – maybe with a full-scale spray-ing team in there. This wudn' just a tiny bit of taggin' now; this wuz a full-scale assault on the senses. Charlie got out and scratched his head. Nothun' wuz makin' much sense anymore. Each one wuz neatly inscribed, and placed in tessellation with the next. 'Twas the Terracotta Army – only weth pilchards. Wha' the fuck wuz going on?

This wuz gettin' weird. Some magic wuz goin' down on a hitherto unimagined scale, and Charlie wuz inside ov ut, spin-ning around like ee didn't knaw wha' wuz on anymore. Somebody, somewhere, had a doll, an' they wuz stickin' more an' more pins inta' ut on a daily basis.

Gold Mine Platinum Blonde Shampoo – Brings out super-star shine and re-discover glamour.
Brightening shampoo
• Brightens – Cool real gold micro-fragments help to brighten and enhance blonde, grey or white hair while neutralizing yellow tones
• Hydrates and adds shine – A powerful combination of conditioning agents and extracts provide ample moisture and intensified shine
• Gently cleanses – Mild ingredients cleanse whilst retain-ing moisture and softening the hair

Bev wuz a veggie. A *Zippy*'s–style burger ov mechanically-recovered meat you could find on the road somewhere between Rose Cottage an' the Twilight about 1.30am in the mornin' wudn' goin' t'do it.

Na. Charlie 'ad a plan:

2 teaspoons olive oil.
1 medium onion, chopped.
3 medium carrots, diced.
3 garlic cloves, finely chopped.
5 teaspoons mild chilli powder.
4 teaspoons ground cumin.
1 teaspoon dried oregano.
1 litre vegetable stock made without salt.
150g brown lentils, picked over and rinsed.
2 x 400g cans chopped tomatoes (undrained).
2 x 400g cans red kidney beans, drained and rinsed.
Freshly ground black pepper to taste.

His phone rang. Ut wuz his ma.

'What ee doin' ov?'

'Lentil an' bean chilli,' ee went.

'Well, I 'ope she' d'like ut, whoever she is...'

'She'll like ut,' went Charlie. 'Got a butternut squash soup fur starters...'

Right then, ee wuz thankin' his ma fur all the utensils she'd got fur'n from Homebase. Ee seemed t'have gone through all ov um in the last half-an-hour.

'Da still on fur t'morra'?'

'Yeah – says ee is. We'll see if we get there... Aw – forgot t'tell ee. The water've been sorted over Headönizm... The Adit an' tha's fixed.'

'Gotta' go ma,' went Charlie.

'They'll be openin' ut up next week...'

'Proper...'

'Here... 'tidn' Bev... us ut?'

'I'm goin'. See ee later...'

Nosy cow Charlie thought. Feminist or naw, sometimes she cud push ut. Thaas' when ee understood his da, and why his da needed to belt out Whitesnake from time t'time.

Charlie'd pulled out all the stops in the dining area of his new plaace. Ee wuz goin' fur candles – but nothun' too cheesy. Ee just wanted t'create some light an' shade. Then again, ee realised ee knew Bev – or thought ee knew the Bev ov old. Ee knew what she liked and what she disliked. Fuck – ut worried un. Maybe she'd altered. People do. They don't stay the same. Why should she? They were, after all, kids back then.

Ee did the bulk ov the first round of dishes, an' 'ad a hurried tidy up. He found hisself doin' weird shit – like plumping up cushions an' wiping marks off the wall of the hallway. Rock star t'home-maker in a day.

The door-bell went. Ee opened ut, and standing there wuz Bev. She'd driven over in her nearnly new Fiesta – birthday present from her da apparently. Fur a second or two, neither ov um spoke. There wuz still the old energy there – or at least, Charlie felt it. Eventually, after checking each other out, they embraced.

'Good to see you Charlie! I brought this for you.'

It was a quality bottle of Pinot Grigio. None ov yer Co-Op 3-fur-1 deal shite.

'And you... You look amazing...'

That wuz the wrong thing t'say prob'ly – but ee cudn' help ut. She did look amazing, in the way that women you always want to go out with always do.

The thing about Bev these days wuz her naturalness. There wuz nothun' feigned. See, instead of the dreadlocks and corn rows, her hair was back to her own brunette colour, and worn long, hanging down to her shoulders. Charlie could smell ut from where ee stood. Ee wanted t'be touching it again. Fuck, ee felt like a right ol' perv.

She had a white sleeveless blouse on – dainty, with a row of buttons up the front, and then a kind of tartan black and pink skirt on. It was her style precisely, the way you imagine some-one to be. Her legs were long and brown, heading down to some Egyptian-style sandals that made her look like she'd just stepped off a barge going down the River Nile.

'So, this is your pad? It's so cool... and all on the money from Chakira... Way to go! When I told my friends down Falmouth, they couldn't believe it?'

'I's... It's...'

Charlie corrected himself. He always tried to speak proper

when Bev wuz about.

'It's okay isn't it? I mean, it's what I could afford...'

'Oh. I'd love my own place. I really would. Won't be for a while yet though...'

'Good to have you here Bev... It really is,' said Charlie.

'And to be here... back in Troon...' she giggled. 'So, what's the latest?'

'Phew... Hard to know where to begin... Some of it you knaw already... Jus' the same really I suppose... Look, I've wine... red or white...'

Charlie had steered her inta' his kitchen. She wuz havin' a good gake at the plaace. Even though Charlie'd done a huge tidy up that afternoon as well – ee cud still smell Yak's feet somehow. Fuck, ut stunk. Ee knew tha' smell anywhere.

'A red please...'

This wuz fuckin' weird Charlie wuz thinkin' to hisself. Here ee wuz: the host with the most, when only a few days ago, the plaace wuz proper trashed thanks to Trelawny tradition.

'What are you cooking? It smells good...'

'Surprise...' went Charlie. 'You'll have to wait an' see.'

'Twas soul-food hopefully.

So wha' did um do? Well, like you do. You shoot the shit. You eat. You talk, an' you forget how much you're drinkin', so you say stuff you didn't really mean, and don't say the stuff you really want to. So you dance around topics like they aren't really there, and try to wipe out your history and past. But y'can't do tha'. Not really. Anyone who lived in electric pastyland could tell ee tha'. So when the question comes, you have t'gulp and take in extra oxygen, and fur a while, y'sit there mute and with a dry taste inside your mouth.

'So – you and Yeugen then, it didn't work out? I mean... give me all the gory details...'

Charlie took another sip of Pinot Grigio to try to moisten his mouth. The only effect ut had wuz to just dry it out further.

'No. It didn' work out... Fur the best really,' said Charlie. 'I mean, if... you and I... well... you know... down Falmouth tha' night...'

There wuz a pause in the conversation, like both ov them needed to absorb wha' Charlie had just said.

'And you an' Mike? I mean, do you hear from un?'

Voodoo Pilchard

'No. We're over. I mean, I hear what he's up and so on...
Doing a Management course I last heard at the University of
the West of England... He's no punk anymore...'

Charlie wanted to say he didn' knaw what she saw in un.
Looked an utter tool. Pretend Punk wudn' a? Charlie wuz a
rocker by nature, but ee reckoned ee wuz more punk than ee
was. But ee didn' say anything. The old Charlie wud've been
more honest, but not this one. The new one wuz more circumspect, more thoughtful.

'So no-one special?' Bev asked, giving him a big smile.

'Nawbody,' went Charlie, 'well, except Yak...'

She laughed, and wanted t'knaw about the rest ov the band
and crew and what they were up to. Charlie told her as much
as ee knew. They spent ages talking about Neil and Ally, Boy
Bluett, Kelvin an' Mel, and then what had happened to
Clifford. She knew moast of ut pretty well, but Charlie put her
right on a few aspects of ut. Ee didn't tell her about Gwennap
Pit an' Trescothick though. One of these days maybe, but not
right now. The butternut squash soup had gone down well.
Charlie carefully dished out the chilli. Ee'd invested ut with his
whole soul.

Ee'd asked her earlier on, 'Did you come up through
Stithians?'

'Yeah,' she'd answered. Then Charlie knew she'd gone past
the abattoir. Tha' chilled him – t'knaw tha' Bev – this beautiful
woman in his house – had come tha' close to evil. Tha' close to
offal. Tha' close to blood. Tha' close to fryin' pans. Because of
tha' though, Charlie wanted to hold her, protect her, show her
how he felt.

Later, ss they ate 'is Strawberry Frozen yoghurt, drizzled with
mixed berry coulis, Charlie could feel himself melting. In
moments like this normally, ee'd check himself, stand up and
ask if the girl he wuz with might fancy listening t'the latest
album from thrash legends Slayer or somebody (which actually
Bev might appreciate) but tonight wuz different. Charlie cud
sense ut and ee wuz hopin' Bev wuz sensing it too.

'Mmmm.... That wuz love-el-y...' said Bev, making a face at
him.

'Stop making faces,' said Charlie in response.

They both laughed at the old Balance lyric.

Alan M. Kent

'Why did you sell all your gear?' asked Charlie. 'I mean, you were...'

'I was what?'

'You were good... Better than me... You're an accomplished bass player... I just dabble...'

'Not your thing though was it Charlie?'

She didn' have to say anymore. She knew him better than anyone. Charlie shot her a shy glance over the table.

'I only said I was thinking of selling it. I've still got it... Can't get rid of me that easily Boy Curnow.'

Charlie loved the way she said his surname. It was posh – certainly all Trura private school – but underneath it was somethun' darker, deeper, Celtic – knotwork an' lichen being fused together. Ee cud feel ut.

'So, new band then – on the horizon – is there?' she asked.

'No.'

'No? You surprise me... You were never one to give up Charlie...'

'Well, maybe I'm too old to rock 'n' roll anymore. I mean – all the bands making ut now – on the cover ov *Kerrang!* an' tha' – half ov um ent even left school... I reckon it's a young man's game...'

'Wha' – an' you already ancient?'

'Na – but ut gets harder dun't ut? I mean there's a golden age ent there – when you've got the drive and the ambition to get there, and then, well, get a few knock-backs an' thaas' ut... I's even harder now in the age of the download...'

Both of them simultaneously thought back to the record deal and contract they'd been offered over Newquay.

'You did the right thing,' went Charlie. 'I mean... you had some fun... we all did... but you, well, you studied, worked hard – and you'll have a good career... Me – I'm kind of washed up. What if Purple Haze wuz ut? My shot...'

Shit. This wuz Voodoo Pilchard territory. He wuz maudlin' on an' she musn't hear tha'. She'd be thinkun' ee wuz a manic depressive or somethun'. Ee changed the subject.

'So tell me about your course?'

She explained how well it wuz going and how cool it was to be back in Cornwall. They spent half an' hour on Early Modern Witchcraft. Fuck, there wuz a lot ov ut in Cornwall. Some real

Voodoo-type shit like. Bev wuz thinkin' ov goin' inta' lecturin' in higher education. Well, tha' wuz her plan – but then, she wanted t'see a bit ov the world too. America maybe? Charlie thought ut best not to tell her about the deal from Spryer they'd just thrown away.

'Do you remember?' Charlie went. 'When we first came down your parents house?'

Bev an' Charlie laughed.

'They thought you were some kind ov zombie from the back woods or somethun'...'

'I know,' went Charlie. 'I wuz tryin' me luck with a bit of posh from Trura...'

They stopped laughing. It seemed amazing that all that time had passed, and that their lives had run in completely different directions.

'Cheese?' asked Charlie. 'Got some real nice stuff out there...'

Bev nodded.

As Charlie went inta' his kitchen Bev glanced around Charlie's plaace. She saw the photos, the vast CD collection, his Marshall amp in the corner. She picked up a little knockie figure on the shelf, holding a tiny pasty. 'Pasty-pronto' it read. She looked down an' saw his bookshelf: all his media production course books, John Harris, George Lucas and Mötley Crüe's autobiography, *The Dirt*. Charlie wuz brave really. No-one else had the bollocks fur things like ee did. Thaas' why she'd always have time for un. Charlie wuz the umlaut over the o, the devil's horn, the one she...

Charlie comed back in with a cheese-board. It looked delicious. Ee fed her some smoked cheese an' a grape.

'Will you come down sometime?' she asked.

'What – down Falmouth?'

'Yes – my place. I'll cook fur you. Try bakin' you a pasty... My mum did show me you know...'

She looked over at the Pasty-Pronto plastic knockie.

Ut wuz gettin' late. Bev hadn' been too bothered about puttin' away some of the wine Charlie had in. In fact, when ee looked in the kitchen, they'd polished off almost four bottles. She wuz either goin' t'be getting' a taxi home or stayin' over. Charlie wuz hopin' ut wuz goin' t'be the latter.

'I missed you Charlie,' she said.

Charlie stood still. Ee didn't knaw what t'do fur the best. Like a lot ov bloaks in the same situation, ee wudn' sure what t'say. Say the wrong thing an' y'cud blaw ut. Say somethun' cheesy an' that wuz even worse.

What comed out made un sound like a fuckin' *The Sun*-style 'pasty muncher'.'I knaw,' ee went.

'Hold me,' she said.

So ee did. They lay down on the floor an' held each other. Neither of them kissed or did anything else. They just held each other and listened to each other breathing. It wuz a beautiful moment – prob'ly, one day, worth writing a song about. Down Godrevy, the tide came in and went out, washing over the seaweed on Magow Rocks. The seal calves at Mutton Cove snuggled into their mothers and watched the moon up the coast, over Carn Gowla. The earth didn' move, but ut didn't need to anymore. In Bev, Charlie knew he'd found his solace in the Celtic West. Whatever other weird Cornish-style voodoo shit wuz happenin', she wuz his protector now. In the same moonlight tha' fell through his new curtains on School Lane, ee woke an' saw how wondrous she was. Gently, ee pulled her close. The ultimate job, Charlie Curnow...

St Meriasek Extra-Body Daily Shampoo – Super bodybuilder for improved manageability.
Thickens fine and normal hair
• Extra-body – Effectively cleanses the hair while panthenol and thickening conditioners help increase volume and and improve both wet and dry combing
• Thicken and repairs – Panthenol penetrates deep into the hair and attaches to the surface to add volume, increase body and help repair damage on the cuticle
• Adds shine – Activated Shine Blend of Cornish chamomile, henna, rosemary and aloe vera help create brilliant shine and reflection

Like Charlie 'is da wuz plannin' the ultimate day of romance. Ut wuz one of they rare kind ov moments. Yeah, although ut wuz like a sharp stake goin' through his heart, ee'd agreed to go with Charlie's ma down t'St Ives.

Voodoo Pilchard

'The parkin's a right rip off down there... Fuckin' miles t' walk... all up hill on the way back too...'

St Ives see. An even bettermoast class ov people. Like Trura, but even fuckin' snobbier. The plaace wuz fulla' cunts seekin' the light, and gakin' at Alfred Wallis and Ben Nicholson paintun's. A few years ago, 'twas crammed with tacky old tourist shit – red an' green pixies sat on the tops of shells tha'd had St Ives written on them – prob'ly made in Taiwan. or snow-globes with Godrevy Lighthouse in um – tha' didn' look anything like Godrevy. These days the plaace wuz filled with designer restaurants an' surf shops. 'Twas hard t'find tack anywhere. Along the front, you had the usual trendy cunts readin' papers and checkin' their stocks an' shares from their pad in St Ives, an' sippin' on Lattes an' Cappuccinos in cafés tha' once used t'be fish cellars. These were the kind ov plaaces where pilchards once got smoked and barrelled up. Then there wuz the usual neo-pagan shops downalong, with their fuckin' stupid crystals, pendants, new-age books an' Celtic crosses. There, you read anything y'liked about quoits an' standin' stones. Y'cud see how ut all inspired past post-modernist buggers like Barbara Hepworth and Terry Frost.

After wha' seemed like an endless time of lookin' at the walls an' garden ov Talland House (trying to pick up on the spirit ov Virginia), Tommy an' Sally went out onta' the Island fur a picnic. Sally cudn' really believe ut. Years ago, when Tommy'd first been wooing her, this wuz the kind of thing they did. Ah yeah, back in the glorious 80s this wuz how ee wuz a smooth operator. But now ee'd brought a blanket from the car, an' they were just sitting there, gazing out over St Ives Bay. This wuz as ut should be, Sally thought. Perhaps, perhaps her Tommy wudn' s'bad as she made out. Right there an' then, she wanted Tommy t'kiss her, start rippin' off her clothes, passionate-like, an' make love t'her. Whoops. She 'ad better control herself. When she thought about ut, she didn't really think thaas' what she should be wishin' fur if she wuz now a feminist. Still, ut wuz the combination of factors. Boy Kelvin an' Mel had been up St Agnes being extras in the latest Rosamunde Pilcher novel t'be adapted fur German tv, an' she'd been thinking of that too: romance, return, an' a revival in her love life. Tommy wuz doin' his best t'act cool. 'Twas pretty tricky fur'n really, since all day ee'd 'ad t'look interested in art, literature an' the light. Now they wuz looking up the coast, over to Gwithian, across to Godrevy an' further up all the way to St Agnes.

Ee'd brought a small radio weth un, in the car, just in case ee might be able t'listen t'the Trura City game, while havin' the picnic, but naw, naw chance ov ut really. Do tha' an' ee'd have blawn ut. Sally wuz now readin' sections of *To the Lighthouse* to un, but 'is mind wuz on other stuff. Well, there wuz the gold down Crofty, then there wuz workin' out how best to move Trura City forward, sellin' the lease ov Club Rhino and then, well, there wuz the extra, extra strong Viagra. Maybe, just maybe Sally wuz wishin' fur a bit of tha' kind ov action right now. Tommy wudn' daft though. As well as goin' on Amazon, ee'd done his homework. From his jacket, ee fetched a parcel.

'Got this fur ee Sal,' ee went.

Sally looked surprised. The tool normally didn' bother t'get her anything fur her birthday an' Christmas, so wha' wuz this?

The parcel wuz wrapped in quality wrapping paper – not the kind ov cheap stuff you got over Pool Market.

'Lovely wrappin' Tommy,' she said.

'Open ut...'

She did.

Sally let out a little gleeful laugh.

'Like ut?' asked Tommy.

It wuz a book.

'I's wonderful.'

Sally read out the title: '*Virginia Woolf: A Critical Study*'.

'I'm tryin',' went Tommy.

Sally kissed him, an' they fell onta' the blacket just like somethun' out of Rosamunde Pilcher novel. Suddenly the world of Obby Stanker Country wuz a million miles away.

Tommy tried t'get ut up – but well, 'twudn' go anything like a Godrevy Lighthouse in his kaks these days. Thank fuck Yak wuz goin' t'sort un out in tha' department very soon. So there 'twas: a bit ov Pilcher and Pilchard, an' Tommy's knob flatter now than Gwithian Sands at low tide.

Trevithick Extra-Body Daily Rinse - Max out style with thicker, shinier hair.
Thickens and conditions fine and normal hair

• Detangles and adds shine – Smooth, lightweight conditioners blended with the Activated Shine blend of
Trevithick Garden Herbs, providing easy detangling and
intense shine
• Thickens and repairs – Panthenol penetrates deep into
the hair shaft and attaches to the surface to add volume,
increase body and help repair damage to the cuticle
• Prevents damage – A special combination of herbs help
prevent damage caused by blow-drying and styling, and
adds thickness and volume while still leaving the hair
feeling light and silky

Proudly, Jess looked at the shiny new surfaces of Headönizm.
She spun in the middle of the newly-converted salon. The smell
was incredible to her. The tasteful oak-style wooden flooring
mingled with the host of styling products she'd tested and
squirted, sprayed and combed into her own hair, let alone anyone else's. In the rear of the salon, were four, white backwash
sinks to wash hair. These were the specially designed ones
where clients placed their necks in to have their hair washed
and conditioned, and their scalp massaged. In front of them
were black, angular seats. One of them was a vibro-chair to provide a back massage while the client's hair was being washed,
fur tha' extra special experience. Along the walls were all the
trendy-looking mirrors and styling units (Jess has gone fur wha'
wuz called the Zulu-style: shield-looking ones), placed purpose-
ly at angles, and than all the service blocks containing hair dryers, trimmers, brushes, clips, curlers, chemicals and straighteners. There 'ad been all the tongs, sterilizers, trays, and hand mirrors to sort out. Next to all of this equipment were the Easyfoil
dispensers and workstations holding the colouring trays – each
positioned beside the chairs in which her clients would sit.

Jess had a clear vision of what she wanted. She'd begin small,
but once business picked up, she'd appoint more staff. They
would all be asked to wear black. She didn't mind what style or
type of clothing they wore as long as it was black. She'd already
purchased scissor pouches for them to clip onto their trousers
or belts. Jess wanted the services offered at Headönizm to not
only be a haircut, but an 'experience' - not a Jimi Hendrix
Experience - but something people would tell their friends

about. She 'ad bigger plans fur the future too – her own brand
ov Headönizm beauty an' hair products, incorporating real
Cornish ingredients. This wuz just the start.

Jess got Mel in didn' she? Well, Mel had progressed on a lot
from her blaw-job days - t'blaw dryer days - and wuz now
lordin' ut up in Troon thanks t'be being third woman on the
left at the party they'd been filming as part of the Rosamunde
Pilcher novel. Kelv 'ad been good fur her. Ee wuz the one who
suggested t'Mel she should give Jess a ring about the salon, an'
see if there wuz any work goin'. Jess 'ad accepted, on condition
tha' Mel signed up fur a part-time advanced hairdressing course
down Cornwall College. So, there was Mel, ready to go, and
then there was another stylist whom Jess knew, called Kayleigh
who she'd poached off a salon over Pool.

'Yeah,' she'd gone at the interview, 'I was named after the
Marillion song...'

She wuz a good-lookin' maid who looked like a few male
punters might like er fondlin' their locks.

Beyond the sinks wuz the tanning booth and the nail bar. In
another room, a massage table for that purpose, as well as other
beauty treatments: hot pebbles, mud packs and exfoliation.
One day, Jess dreamed, in her next store, she'd be offering spa
treatments too. To the side of these was a kitchen area (she'd
got the units cheap up Homebase – quality stuff mind). In
there, were tea and coffee-making facilities for both staff and
clients; trays of small, foil-wrapped biscuits, and chocolates too.
Pampering – thaas' wha' 'twas all about. As well as this, there
were a couple of industrial-strength washing machines and a
tumble dryer, to keep a fresh supply of towels ready for the
clients. The black towels matched the colouring of the chairs
and the capes clients would wear. Likewise, the couple of hood
blaw dryers she had invested in were black in colour. The trol-
leys and stools also matched these. Naw tack with this lot.

Jess walked through the salon, pretending that instead of
just the three of them that there wuz an army of stylists in that
day. She wuz giving out advice to everyone on the detail of the
cuts being completed and how long colours ought to stay in.
She wuz the boss. Everyone *kow-towed* to her at Headönizm. She
made her way to the front of the salon. There stood the illumi-
nated reception desk, the till, the debit and credit card machine

and the bookings ledger. She reorganised the desk slightly, moving a potted plant and making the phone more accessible to whoever was sat behind it. She imagined it ringing; fussy clients wanting particular stylists. Well, they had an event on at the weekend. A board above the desk outlined the services available, as well as their prices. Some people in Troon would prob'ly think ut dear, but if y'aimed to be the best in the area, you had to 'up' the prices. Y'don't get somethun' fur nothun'. Just across from the desk sat two waiting area sofas – both in luminescent pink t'offset the black ov everywhere else. She'd already tested them several times.

Out of the half-frosted window, with Headönizm etched into it, she peered out onto Troon. She knew it intimately, of course: the same tiny miner's cottages, which people had tried to do up with endless extensions and porches; the same youngsters going up and down the street on shitty little mopeds, and the usual oozing Troon mizzle. Never mind, she thought. This is where it begins. This was the start of her beauty and style empire. Charlie'd 'ad 'is crack at success. This was her turn now. Jess though, had a different attitude to her roots than Charlie. Ever since she could remember, she'd wanted to get out and see a bit of the world. Cornwall – yeah – nice fur two weeks in summer: rest of the time a bleddy dump. Thaas' why she an' Micky'd gone out and travelled the world. She reckoned ut wuz the best thing she could have done: travelling a bit, earning money, saving for this. While the rest of her peers were already pumping out their third kid, and hoping and praying for a plaace down Pengegon, she was doing this – an Alan Sugar-style young business-woman with a wise head on her young shoulders. She wudn' goin' to have the same life as her mother. Oh naw. She might be a feminist naw, but she'd had t'put up with twenty years ov crap.

Upstairs, Micky wuz at work. The tattoo and piercing studio wuz designed in the same style. It wuz none of your dodgy-looking plaaces y'found in the back streets ov Redruth or Penzance, run by some rough-bearded old biker with no teeth. No. Micky's plaace wuz classy and sophisticated. Fur a start, there weren't the same old cheesy flashes of tattoo designs decorating the wall. Instead, the emphasis was on steel and black colours working together. They'd both wanted it pristine-looking, so the emphasis was on cleanliness, and so that it at least looked organised. Micky 'ad a couple of two-person black leather settees in the front half of the studio, and then a coffee table between them. Here wuz where clients could browse through his bespoke designs. So it wudn' the kind of plaace where Micky wuz goin' to do throat swallows, hearts-with-mum-written-on-them, or the names of girlfriends under roses. Na – the feel was going to be modern primitive: tribal, gothic, Celtic – in vivid colours. He wanted to work with clients and help them create the ultimate tattoos for their shape, size and personality. Micky had the patience and the commitment to do this. 'Course, there wuz a good sound system set up. You cudn' run any kind of tattooing business without tha'. Today it wuz pumping out some industrial style rave – the typical kind of thing Micky liked, an' wished Balance had done more ov.

In the studio area was also a booth and room for piercing work. In there wuz all the Studex piercing equipment. Holes could be made in 1/10th of a second through whatever part of your body you wanted done. The piercing gun was easy to load and simple to keep clean. In there too, were the steel ring opening pliers, forceps, and the ring closing pliers. Micky had become trained up in this field, gaining all the necessary licences he needed. The booth was more hospital-like than the rest of the studio, but that was what ee'd wanted: fur ut to be clinical an' safe fur clients. This sanitized environment matched the electric tattooing machine itself which sat alongside the sterilizing autoclave machine. Next to ut all his needles, inks and disinfectants. Ee peered over the autoclave (one of the new ultrasonic types) then back across to the couch and where the arm rest was located. Micky knawed the scene inside out. Ee'd gone for the Exel Steel and Iron Master colouring and shading machines. In and out of the skin 150 times a second.

He had a large supply of Kubuki black ink for outlining, as well as lots of shading inks. His Skin Candy colouring inks were located on a shelf above the autoclave. He repositioned the ink pot holders and ink caps so they were tidier than before. In the cabinets were the needles. He had a range from Premier: outliners, colouring, and shading ones. By them, plenty ov disposable tips and grips, and nitrile gloves. Obvious gear like spray bottles and needle disposal bins he'd also bought in. He double-checked the two roll dispensers on the wall, and opened a couple of packets of tattooist's green soap, ready to go. Next to the waiting area were the tattoo after-care items – in Micky's case, some wipes and tins of Tattoo Goo treatment oil. By them, all the warning signs about clients needing to be over eighteen years of age, and a pad of disclaimers.

'Course, Micky wuz the kind of bloak who loved going to tattoo conventions, or watching shows like *Miami Ink*. So this wuz 'is version of ut: *Camborne Ink*. Yeah. Ut didn't have quite the same ring to it, but once his reputation was up and running, he reckoned he'd clean up. Recession or naw recession, people in plaaces like Camborne still wanted tattoos done. 'Twudn' just people on the estates ee wuz targeting though, Aw naw, it wuz the middle-classes, they who wanted to look a bit cool, a bit edgy – inked up - with a tattoo somewhere private: the revolution lurking under the three piece suit. Thaas' the kind of client he wuz after. Micky was under no illusions though. 'Twud take work an' time to build things up.

Headönizm had a website. Tha' 'ad lots of great pictures of the premises and the kind of services offered. Then Jess and Micky'd been working hard on a mass advertising campaign. They'd been out leafleting in the streets of Camborne, Pool and Redruth. There had been mail drops in Beacon, Troon and Four Lanes. Pool Market wuz next. Wretched hive ov scum and villainy ut might be – but if buggers would come over t'Troon fur some styling and a tattoo, then ut didn't matter. While over there, Micky and Jess checked out the competition. It wudn' nothun' special – stalls in there cutting hair, but next to plaaces tha' sold dog food and Country and Western CDs. The cut hair fell onta' the concrete floor. Bet tha' must make ee feel good. Micky knew ut well of course. If Curnow hadn' come in looking fur bootleg recordings, ee'd never have met Jess. Ut wuz where ee'd started – but ee'd moved on, progressed up the ladder a bit. All ov ut reminded Micky of the old days with Balance. This time though, there wuz no fly-postering. They'd even gone for some radio advertising on Pirate FM. The aim of the campaign was directed at the 16-30 age group. This wuz the clientele they were trying to get in. But y'needed word ov mouth too. Y'needed a crew over Cornwall College to get some trendy-looking cut done, and then spread the word. If y'did

tha' then people would come. It wuz the same with the tattoos.
So Jess an' Micky were prepared to do a few freebies to get
things rolling.

So the grand opening came. The salon wuz packed out. It
was on the Saturday after Tommy and Sally Curnow had been
down to St Ives. On a Saturday, y'cud at least let ut run through
moast of the day, an' give everyone a chance to come along
whenever they wanted. Not that you cud get yer hair done – or
even have a tattoo. Na, y'd get a chance to do that later. Fur
now, this wuz about Micky and Jess shawin' off what they'd
achieved. Jess' ma an' da had treated them to some nice
canapés and champagne t'see ut opened in style. They'd even
fuckin' asked Ursula to come back an' cut the ribbon fur um.
She wuz pleased t'do tha' – but didn' knaw wha' t'think of the
piercin' studio upstairs.

'I'n do your tongue if y'like...' went Micky.

'Some nice,' Jess' ma wuz goin'. 'Aw! I cen't wait t'have me
hair done here...'

Tommy Curnow wuz lookin' at all the gear they'd invested
in. Some money you. Ee wuz just opin' an' prayin' there'd be
enough custom fur um. Then ee looked in one of the Zulu-
shield style mirrors and wondered if he should get extensions
or even a weave – like his hero, guitarist Ritchie Blackmore. He
touched his hair – a few flakes of tin dust fell in the sink.

Charlie wuz amazed at what Jess had accomplished. He
arrived with Bev, which got all ov um there talkin' – an'
Charlie's ma cooing over her.

'Some nice t'see ee again maid,' she wuz goin'.

'A'right maid?' went Tommy. 'Heard you wuz back...'

Bluett wuz there too. Jess 'ad styled up 'is buzz-cut a bit.
Bluett wuz looking in the mirror, eatin' ov a canapé and struggling t'knaw who he wuz anymore. Wuz ee the same tool
who'd only a few yeas back filmed Mel and Kelv in action? Yeah
– ee wuz, but things were different now. Soon, ee'd be leavin'
this all behind. Yak – whose idea of hairdressin' – wuz t'avoid it
and them as much as possible – wuz havin' a yap with un, an'
quite gutted tha' ee wudn' be able t'help un with his planned
EBGBs Club. Still, there wuz free grub an' booze wudn' there –
so they wuz delving inta' ut.

Bev wuz also catchin' up with Neil an' Ally, who were there

with both Anthony and Megan. Charlie stood watchin' ov ut all. Fuck, at one point, the line-up ov Balance just crossed in front ov un. How different they all were now? How had the fuckin' universe brought um all back together in a hairdressin' salon in, of all plaaces, Troon. Anthony had started some new treatment apparently. T'calm un down, Ally and Neil had bought un a cheap Clone Wars small Lego toy, an' ee wuz playin' with tha' on one of the chairs close t'the dials on the tanning booth. Megan stood close to Ally, holdin' her hand and lookin' up at all the big people around her. Charlie felt sorry fur her, now that Anthony had the lion's share ov everyone's attention. Jess took Megan around the salon to show her all the new equipment. When the party headed upstairs to look at the tattoo studio, Charlie went over t'Anthony.

'A'right Obi Wan?' ee said to Anthony.

'I am not Obi Wan,' said Anthony. 'I am Anthony...'

''Course,' went Charlie. 'How's school?'

'It is fine,' Anthony went. 'We are doing simultaneous equations...'

Fuck, reckoned Charlie. This was the kind of stuff they were doing in Primary Schools these days.

'I'm good at Maths...' went Anthony.

'This is Bev,' said Charlie. He reached out for Bev's hand and introduced her. Bev knew the background.

Anthony looked her up and down.

'She is pretty Charlie. Is she your girlfriend?'

Bev laughed.

'Yeah,' said Charlie, looking at her, and smiling. 'She is my girlfriend – I think...'

'I have a girlfriend,' said Anthony. 'At school... She's called Charlotte.'

'That's good,' said Charlie.

'No. It isn't.' said Anthony, re-assembling the Lego. 'She annoys me...'

'Why's tha'?'

'She always wants to kiss me.'

Bev and Charlie looked at each other.

'That's what people do when they like each other...'

'Well, I don't like ut...' said Anthony, and then changing the subject, 'Where is everyone?'

'Upstairs…'

'Can I go up there?'

''Course,' went Charlie.

Anthony wriggled out of the chair he was in, and went out into the lobby of the shop, to climb upstairs.

Charlie an' Bev smiled at each other.

'I always want to kiss you Mr Curnow,' whispered Bev.

Charlie wuz feelin' the same way. As much as ee wuz tryin' to control 'is emotions, ee cud feel them takin' over him. Because of tha', ee'd been songwriting all week. There'd been an outpouring of lyrics, and some inspirational ideas for riffs and chord sequences, which he'd shared with Neil. Some ov them were stonkin' – real chest-rattling anthems. Everytime ee kept tellin' himself to calm down, not rush inta' things with Bev, play ut cool, seem a bit distant – he cudn't. Ee'd find his-self texting her, or wantin' to e-mail a quick message to her. In moments of madness, ee'd even wondered if ee an' Bev might write more music together again. In the middle of Jess' new salon, they embraced and kissed. Fur Bev, there wuz somethun' wonderful about being back here with this crowd. Wha' wuz ut about them? Spirit, she reckoned. Yes, Charlie and the rest ov the Obby Stankers. Ultimately, thaas' what they had: spirit.

'Stop it,' came a voice. It was Anthony, peering at them from the bottom of the stairs. 'Charlie, come and see. I want a tat-too…'

Shit, throught Charlie. Thaas' all Ally an' Neil needed now – a six year old who wanted a tattoo done.

At the opening, Jess had issued out several cheap an' cheer-ful offers. On Monday morning, she wished she hadn'. Ut seemed every fuckin' pensioner in Troon, Beacon an' Camborne wuz phonin' up fur the over 60s deal. Come ten o'clock in the mornin' an' the old women of the area were just about queuing out the door. Well, maid Curnow wuz doin' ut cheaper than down town. They'd save on bus fare too – an' there was a cup tea an' a chocolate. By the end ov the day, Mel, Kayleigh and Jess wuz completely knacked from endlessly doin' perms and blue rinses for old maids. This cudn' be ut cud ut? This crowd every fuckin' week wud do their heads in. Y' had Mrs Rodda in, moanin' on about her dogs an' cats, and then the smelly old woman who lived next to Mrs Freethy, chitterin' on and then Trevor Hoskin's sister – who'd comed all the way from Praze-an-Beeble just t'take a gake and decide she wanted a perm. All ov um wuz askin' if the deal wuz still on. Yes, 'twas still on – if they'd like t'take a seat.

Getting' in the older men ov the village wuz just as easy. Well, nawticin' that the three maids who worked there were a bit purty, an' tight in all the right places encouraged they t'get in there an' have a quick trim. As Kayleigh nawticed, 'twudn' 'zactly stylin' to be honest. Half ov um didn' have much on top anyway. The remaining Polish comed in too – not that they said much. Just a quick in and out, before zippin' off back down Stithians abattoir fur a shift or t'the Polish Shop in town. There were a few youngsters too – young kids who squealed all the way through havin' their first trim – an' they started to pick up the teenagers. At least, there you cud develop some cool styles. Other than tha' though, 'twas provin' harder to get in the clients they really wanted. Still beggars cudn' be choosers – not fust ov all, at least.

Even Yelland comed up to check ut out, an' get the grey sorted.

'Got an interview Monday... up the line,' ee'd gone, 'an' I want um to think I'm young-lookin'...'

Took years off un, apparently.

Tommy went in – kept the mullet, but had ut styled a bit. Ee went out later, with a bit more ov an eye than usual on the MILFs over Institute.

Jess' ma comed in and wuz treated like royalty. She'd be given the lot – hot pebbles, pedicure, colourin' and a bit of a trim.

Yak comed in, looked at the prices, an' walked out.

Ally went in. She didn' need anything doing but had her hair trimmed and straightened. She looked even more ov a goddess than ever. Ut made her feel better though, and sometimes, tha' wuz the point.

Kelv went in. Went fur an emo straightened look.

The owner ov the Co-Op comed in. He wanted a grade 1 all over. The stress ov the rebuild wuz getting' to un.

Bluett comed back in. Tha' wuz cuz ee fancied Kayleigh.

Jess did Mel's hair. Put some purple highlights in.

Some tackers comed in an' asked if they had any more old mirrors they cud smash up.

Alan M. Kent

Constable Combellack comed in and introduced himself as part of the Community Business Alliance, which looked after businesses in the area. He offered his services in terms of advising them about security. Mel cleaned out the gnarly black hairs in his ears fur'n.

This wuz the way ut went on downstairs.

Upstairs, things took an interesting turn. On their way out from having their blue rinses, Micky'd been chattin' to the old ladies about tattoos. Ee wuz goin' how 'twas the latest thing fur pensioners. Well, ee never thought ut wud work, but one day old Mrs Nancarrow comed in, and said she wanted somethun' on her shoulder. Well, after all, 'twas her eightieth birthday. Now, old Mrs Nancarrow – wudn' a bad lookin' old maid t'tell the truth. She set the pulses risin' ov some ov the horny old boys down the Day Centre. Years ago, she wud have been very good lookin'.

'What've ee got?' she went.

'I'll design ut fur ee,' said Micky, shoutin' because she wuz a bit deaf.

''Ave ee got any dolphins?'

'Dolphins.'

'Es. Stella over Institute got a dolphin an' I always fancied one ov they...'

'A dolphin ut is then,' went Micky.

When 'twas finished, she wuz proper tickled.

'I'll be shawin' um all down the Day Centre,' she went.

Prob'ly, some of the old boys down there might nawtice a rise in their blood pressure some time soon, if she started stripping off.

Well, tha' let the floodgates open. Every whip and wham, some bleddy ancient old git comed in fur a tattoo at the shop. Wha' wuz on with um? Mrs Nancarrow'd started a new trend. A seventy-seven year old comed in fur some paisley-style tramp stamps on her lower back.

Next thing ee knawed, even Jimmy Pengelly comed in fur a look around. Ee didn't have anything done – but wuz thinking about havin' somethun' t'do with the Holman Climax Male Voice Choir on his back.

But then, one day, when there didn't seem much on, in walked Georgie Angov. Ee wuz boy Arnie's mate – who got t' the point ov takin' naw prisoners down Trelawny. Basically, Georgie an' the rest ov um wuz takin' on the role ov a Vigilante Squad on the estate, Operation Goodnight or naw Operation Goodnight. Arnie Crago and tools on Mephedrone had been their inspiration.

'I wun't tha' done, went Angov. 'On me shoulder...'

It was a picture of a chainsaw in a circle.

'They letters too...' he said.

Micky read ut: TCC.

'Trelawny Chainsaw Crew.'

Micky nodded.

'Well, we've had enough' argued boy Angov. 'The police dun't do shit do um?'

That they didn' - or cudn'. True 'nough.

Cakey Trade Finishing Spray – Creating a style that lasts all day long just got easier.
Finishing Spray
• Rapid Drying – A unique blend of styling agents reduces the dry time
• Strong Hold – Powerful, flexible polymers help provide strong, long-lasting hold
• Clean hold – Spray can be layered onto hair without stiffness or dulling build-up while conditioners and shine enhancers help impart high gloss and reduce static

Because ee wuz a tool, Trescothick comed inta' Headönizm t'check ut out, an' see tha' 'twas Cornish enough fur'n. Ee looked a fuckin' right state. Nothun' much new there then. The style ee wuz modelin' wuz more or less whatever you cud get in the old man's barbers down town fur a couple ov quid. Then ee had a fuckin' black beret on. T'be frank, there were eighty-year old pensioners who comed in who looked more suave in the hair department. Ee looked all wrong. In fact, Trescothick looked like a lot of Cornishmen who hadn't got their shit together in terms ov attracting the opposite sex. Still, you cudn' blame the cunt. Ee wuz more inta' the forthcoming glorious revolution and the imminent òverthrow of English imperialism than looking good. Challenge un on ut, and ee'd probly say somethun' like 'You never seened Che Guevara looking like a fashion item…' Then when ee comed t'think ov ut, considerin' y'cud buy his face on many a t-shirt now sold at Top Man, Che Guevara was a bit of a fashion item t'be honest.

'A'right Jess?' ee went.

'Hello Tres…'

She always called un Tres, which ee liked. It sort ov rhymed with Jess, which ee found amusing, an' ee wuz also looking forward t'a twenty-three year old getting' a bit close to un with her body.

'I d'fancy a bit of an image overhaul…'

'What, hair?'

'Hair, body, nails…' he went, 'everything…'

Fuck. This wuz Gok Wan gone mental. How many times did a geeky nationalist like ee come in an' say that in yer nearest hairdressers?

'Do you want the tannin' too?'

'Tannin'?'

'You know… spray tan…'

Clifford wuz sizin' ov ut up, He'd read something about the Index of Nigrescence in Britain an' Ireland. All the true Celts were meant t'be dark-skinned. If ee cud be related t'the "brothers" then ee wuz goin' fur ut.

'Bewdie. Yeah – I'll have one ov they too…'

'Mel…' called Jess. 'Can you give Mr Trescothick's hair a wash? Plenty of that silky smooth conditioner…'

Mr Trescothick spent all afternoon in there. Jess cut his hair stylishly, goin' fur a longish style with GHD power straighteners sorting out the frizz.

'Ee's lookin' well-emo…' went Mel.

'Well, ee is a terrorist…' said Jess. 'Ee got high emotions ebm' a?'

'D'y'like ut?' asked Jess.

Trescothick looked in the mirror, turning his head from side to side, one day seeing his own fizzog on every t-shirt made in Cornwall. Jess held up a hand mirror to show him the back. He nodded. It made him look mean an' moody – just the way ee felt about the centralised UK government and the fascist English state.

'Ready fur your tan now Tres…'

'What do I have to do?'

Voodoo Pilchard

'You need to put these on first of all...'

They were small black glasses to cover his eyes. Y'had to scrunch yer eyes together fur them to stay there.

'Just go into the booth, and undress. You'll need t'get naked. Put your clothes in the locker inside. Then when you're ready, give me a shout... I press the button and the tan coats your body... nice and easy. It takes about thirty seconds. Turn around and it'll then do the back of you...'

T' be honest, this wuz prob'ly only 'bout the second time Jess and Mel had used the tanning booth inside Headönizm. The first time wuz when the Rep was there last week, to explain how it all worked. There shudn' be any problem though – Jess had used um all the time in other salons 'round Cornwall.

Upstairs, you could hear the buzz of Micky's tattooing at work. Ee 'ad another old dear in again – with some saucy message fur her fancy man. You cud also hear Trescothick in the booth, fartin' around and gruntin' and groanin' like a stuck boar. Neither Mel nor Jess really wanted t'think 'bout what 'twas lookin' like in there. It seemed like Trescothick would be scarily milk bottle white underneath all his clothes, an' hairy in all the wrong plaaces.

'Ready!' ee shouted.

'Are all your clothes in the locker?'

'Yeah...'

'Okay – here we go... Make sure you stand up straight...'

Jess pressed the Start button, and the spray tan booth buzzed into life. Y'cud hear the mist of the spray passing out of the fine nozzles an' falling on Trescothick's body. Inside there, ee wuz quiet as a Teddy Bear, like the man 'ad never even owned a surface-to-air missile. As ee wuz being sprayed, Jess checked on old Mrs Bosanko's perm. When the first pass up and down his front was finished, Jess shouted in.

'You alright Tres?'

'I d'reckon so... It've gone on a bit thick mind...'

'Thick?' Jess asked worriedly. Then she realised, it always felt like that on the first session. Much of the spray would soon evaporate as the drying process kicked in.

'You'll be fine...'

'I'm turning around now...' went the Kernewek Jihadist tanseeker.

'Okay. Pressing start again now...' said Mel.

Jess wuz listening intensely. Over in the dryer, Mrs Bosanko wuz tryin' to engage her in conversation over a particularly juicy article about Cheryl Cole's love life, but Jess's face wuz lookin' increasingly worried. The cycle seemed to go on too long.

'Can y'open the door?' she asked Mel.

Mel tried it.

'Naw. I's still locked... Still spraying...'

'Ee idn' goin' t'be happy,' said Jess.

'Ee wun't mind. It'll look like ee've been out the Med fur six weeks... or down Porthcurno fur six months...'

Eventually the tanning booth stopped itself and the door went to 'Unlocked'.

Inside, Mel an' Jess cud hear the sound of Trescothick stumbling around, obviously putting back on his clothes.

'You okay Tres?' Jess asked worriedly.

There wuz no answer.

She cudn' stand ut any longer.

She opened the door to the booth, and hoped tha' Trescothick was at least partially dressed, otherwise Mrs Bosanko might have a bit ov a surprise if she geeked in the mirror in front ov her an' saw wha's wuz goin' on in the reflection.

Trescothick stood there in a pair of green grape smugglers. The green ov they wuz offsettin' nicely the colour ov his bright new orange body. You cud only describe un as lookin' like an Oompa Lumpa with nationalist tendencies.

Trescothick seemed t'like the fact tha' Jess an' Mel wuz oglin' un.

'I like ut,' ee went. 'I feel some cool... Why didn' I get this dun before?'

'Us ut too... dark fur ee?' asked Mel. 'We might be able to...'

'This? Na – this is proper, I tell ee...'

As Trescothick put on the rest ov his clothes, Jess checked the spraying cylinders. The bleddy dial wuz up t'max – the level ov spraying only advised to those people with good tans already. Jess thought back to the opeing event. Maybe Neil an' Ally's kids had fiddled with ut. When Trescothick walked out inta' the lights of the salon ee wuz glowin' even more. In fact, ee looked properly luminescent. Na, that wudn' right. Ee wuz actually illuminatin' everything around un. If ee stood on a rock down Gwithian, ee'd look like another Godrevy - 'twas that bright you.

Still, the cunt didn' seem to mind.

'Hundred quid do will ut?' asked Trescothick. He'd noted the prices earlier.

'Fine.'

'A tenner tip fur ee both too... Buy a coupla' pints an' some chips over Institute...'

See, Trescothick had style. He had a fuckin' orange face an' hands. When they would see un down Park an Tansys they might think aliens had landed (if they didn' already!).

'Now – reckon I'm goin' upstairs t'see Micky... I be thinkin' on getting' a tattoo done...'

'Ah shit,' went Mel to herself, an' carried on brushing up the cut hair on the floor.

Now, because Trescothick wuz a tool, an' cud never keep his mouth shut (which is why the original 'mother of all attacks' on the Tamar Bridge went wrong), ee cudn' stop his gob from running away weth itself. In fact, ee'd blurt on t'anyone who would listen to un about the evil plans of English Heritage or Natural England. Usually, they wud just about keel over on the spot, and wish they'd voted Mebyon Kernow fur once in their life. But Micky, well, Micky wudn' about to turn out a new customer: not like Trescothick at least. In fact, Micky wuz hopeful ee might want some extensive work done – the whole of his back covered with Celtic knotwork, or a huge Celtic cross goin' up his spine. The bugger cud stand pain. From wha' Charlie had told un, while ee an' Jess wuz away in Australia, ut 'ad took Charlie an' a tacker a fair few old BB pellets to take un out that time.

The glow that accompanied un when ee walked inta' Headönizm's upstairs tattoo studio wuz as if South Crofty had suddenly started mining radioactive elements. Fur certain, Micky wudn' be doing naw tattoo on un, while his skin wuz that colour. 'Twould fuck up the pigment good an' proper. Then ee nawticed Trescothick's new hair style – a Jess special, made fur knobbers like ee who didn't knaw nothun', but who might pull tha' off down Twilight ov a Saturday night. 'Cept without the beret.

143

'You a'right Trescothick?'

'In fer a tat or fancy some piercin'?'

Piercing wudn' really Trescothick's thing t'all. In fact, every since ee'd digested every single fact about the hanging, drawing and quartering of Michael Joseph An Gov in 1497, ee didn much care about metal objects being inserted anywhere in his body. With a boy like Trescothick, there wuz always the suspicion the English police state might do ut to someone like ee again.

'Tat...' went Trescothick.

'By the way... nice tan... What ee thinkun' ov?'

'A chough...'

'A chough?'

Thaa' wuz about as cool as a fuckin' night out up Zelah.

'The bird?'

'Yeah. It carries the spirit ov King Arthur...'

'Really?'

'When the Cornish ate them and made them extinct, they were actually eating themselves...'

Fuck. Trescothick wuz on one t'day, yippin' on about choughs an' cannibalism. The orange must've brought ut outta' un.

'Bespoke one?'

'Bespoke?'

'Well, shall I design it fur you? – or would you prefer something more off the shelf...'

Trescothick had enough money widn'. Ee'd have ut bespoke. Shit, ee'd be the only fucker in Kernewek Jihad with a bespoke chough.

'Chough's are so twentieth-century though idn' um Trescothick? I mean, every fucker back Crofty got tha' or a St Piran's cross on their upper arm?'

Trescothick wuz lookin' at all ov Micky's designs on the coffee table. Ee then stared up at the piece ov hoarding with Voodoo Pilchard written on ut, but didn' say anything.

'Thaas' an original thaa',' said Micky. 'None ov your orange an' red shit...'

Micky looked at un. Ee wuz exuding opulent orange. In fact, his fingers even looked a bit red.

'I mean... not one of they down Foundry Road.'

'What ee recommend then? I mean whaas' cool in the music scene? I mean, you an' Charlie... you knaw whas' in dun ee?'

'Well, you'm prob'ly talking sleeve tattoos there boy... covering the whole arm. Contrast ut with a clean white shirt, an you'm cool as fuck... Look at these look.'

Micky shawed un a few images on his laptop. All the bands like The Gaslight Anthem an' anything remotely Emo had um.

'Na... I knaw wha' I want,' said Trescothick confidently. 'I'll have the last words of Michael Joseph Angov on me arm...'

'What did a say?'

'I shall have a name perpetual and a fame permanent and immortal...'

That wuz clearly Trescothick's plan too.

'I wun't ut in Cornish though...'

'Can ee translate ut fur me an' write ut down?'

Ee gived Trescothick a pen and a pad. Trescothick scribbled away.

'Me am beth hanow heb dewath ha bry bisgwethack rag nevra...'

Having the kind of tool of a word like bisgwethack on yer forearm seemed mental t'Micky. But 'is wuz not to question the reason why; 'is wuz jus' t'ink and dye.

'Okay. I'll design ut up...'

'Na,' went the tool perpetual. 'Put ut on now...'

'But you got tha' tanning spray on yer arm right now...'

'Matter do ut?' said the knobber permanent and immortal.

'Well, ut might...'

'I'll take a chance... '

Well, Trescothick wuz the boy t'take a chance. Remember, ee had taken a missile across Cornwall in the back ov a Bedford van.

'Sign this then,' said Micky. 'I's a contract an' disclaimer fur the work and the lettering...'

Trescothick stuck out an orangey-red thumb an' forefinger and signed ut.

Micky took a deep breath. This wuz goin' t' be hard work. After Trescothick had chosen the lettering he liked (the tool wanted somethun' tha wudn' look amis on the torso of Tommy Lee or David Beckham), Micky set to work, cleaning the chosen position.

'Relax,' went Micky. 'It'll be done pretty quick...'

Trescothick gritted his teeth. If An Gov cud stand bein' drawn and quartered, this, well this, wud be a piece ov piss.

Micky wuz a good artist. Shite DJ, mixer an' wannabe rock icon maybe – but damned good tattooist. Ee took care with his art, so ee an' Orange Trescothick had plenty ov time to shoot the shit.

'So how's the revolution comin' on then really like?' asked Micky seriously. 'I mean MK did shit in the last elections didn' um?'

Trescothick cudn' deny ut, but ee 'ad the answer.

'English media see? BBC an' ITV - they wun't let um have any political broadcasts... Bias – thaas' wha' 'tis...'

'Dun't move. This may hurt a bit. Close to the bone here...'

'MK are too soft though,' continued Trescothick. 'We need somethun' better, more radical... shake ut up a bit...'

Trescothick leaned back an' took the pain.

'You'm doin' well,' went Micky.

'Are we alone?' asked Trescothick.

Micky gived un a puzzled look.

"Mean, naw spies or anything...?'

Micky had a gake over at the voodoo pilchard street art.

'I dun't think so...'

'Let me tell you about the next level...

Trescothick looked around and leaned inta' Micky.

'Black Panthers...' he said in a whisper and conspiratorially touched his nawse.

'Who?'

'Y'knaw... the Black Panthers...'

The way Trescothick wuz goin' on 'twas like ee might talking about the legendary wild cats up on Bodmin Moor.

'Wha'? The Beast?'

'Naw... Black Panthers wuz a left-wing African-American revolutionary organisation working fur the self-defence of black people... in the 1960s and 70s...'

Now, wuz Trescothick's new orange nigrescence takin' un in this direction? This wuz wha' Micky wuz thinking ov.

'Listen... They wuz formed in Oakland, California by Bobby Seale and Huey Newton on the 15th October, 1966, with the express plan calling fur the protection of African-American

Voodoo Pilchard

neighbourhoods form police brutality... but then on a wider level Micky – they wuz articulatin' the economic and political grievances ov black radicals and liberals...'

'Like Hendrix?'

''Course. Ee wuz one of their heroes...'

'So why you telling me this...?'

'Stop the tattoo machine a minute. Let me click on this website I've made...'

Trescothick sat up and leaned over to Micky's laptop.

'We're goin' t'have some Black Panther-type action here in Cornwall...'

'Wha'?'

'Well, I d'reckon the Cornish is ready fur the Cornish Tigers...'

'Ent tha' Trura City?'

'Naw – y'knobber. They'm the White Tigers. We'm the Cornish Tigers...'

The Cornish Tigers website loaded in. Fuck, this wuz radical stuff.

'I's secret...' went Trescothick.

Like fuck, thought Micky. Nothun' Trescothick ever said wuz secret.

'There's 'bout fifty ov us... fightin' fur freedom...'

On the screen came a shot of around fifty Cornish bloaks all dressed up with black berets. They wuz tryin' t'look hard as fuck – but failing.

'Why berets?' asked Micky. Ee wanted t'say ut looked a bit gay.

'Revolutionary idn' ut?' said Trescothick. 'Besides, the beret wuz the standard wear of the Cornish and Breton peasant...'

Micky reckoned these days ut wuz a chavvy pair ov tracksuit bottoms an' a cheap shirt from over Matalan – or as the Cornish put ut, 'Matterland'.

'I've adapted the ten point plan ov the Black Panthers... t'be the Cornish Ten Point Plan.'

Fuck, Micky thought. This wuz sounding like Maoist China rather than Kernow.

'Check this out,' went Trescothick, like wha' wuz there wuz undeniably cool.

Micky read ut:

Alan M. Kent

1. We want Freedom. We want power to determine the destiny of our Cornish and oppressed communities.
2. We want full employment for our people.
3. We want an end to the robbery by the capitalists and of Cornish and oppressed communities.
4. We want decent housing.
5. We want decent education for our people that exposes the true nature of this decadent English-based society.
6. We want completely free health care for all Cornish and oppressed people.
7. We want an end to police brutality and murder of Cornish people.
8. We want an immediate end to all wars of aggression.
9. We want freedom for all Cornish people accused of so-called crimes under the laws of England and the reinstatement of Stannary Law.
10. We want land, bread, housing, education, clothing, justice, peace and people's community control of modern technology.

Fuck, they wanted a lot.

They wudn' givers really, this Cornish Tiger crowd.

'What ee reckon?'

'Radical s'fuck...' went Micky. 'I's amazin' tha you an' the Black Panthers of the 1970s wanted the same thing...'

'Idn' ut,' went Trescothick nodding enthusiastically.

This wuz what Trescothick meant when ee'd said t'Charlie 'bout takin' ut up a level.

'This is the future, this,' said Orange Trescothick. 'This is only the beginning...'

Fur a second there, ee wuz standing like Trevithick's statue down Camborne addressing the Cornish masses, who all clearly wanted t'be liberated an' wear berets on a daily basis.

'I need t'finish tha' there bis... gweth... ack word,' said Micky.

Trescothick logged off, lay down again and stuck his left arm out again. What comed next, wudn' wha' Micky wuz expectin'.

'Eventually, the Tigers'll get tha' Markie Phillips too... fur wha' ee done...'

Voodoo Pilchard

Micky didn' answer. Sometimes... ahem... clients told un too much information. Markie eh? Up there on the same scale as the English. Proper villains see. Now there wuz a man with a name perpetual and a fame permanent and immortal. Micky finished Trescothick's tattoo an' hoped Phillips' boys wudn' be payin' Headönizm a visit. Considering Trescothick's attitude though, an' the way rumours went round Obby Stanker Country, Markie Phillips an' ee might be meetun' up pretty soon. There'd be no end t'wars ov aggression then.

> Not Dreckly Definer – Get ready for rapid curls and save valuable time.
> Liquid Curl Definer
> • Clean definition – Unique styling properties provide weightless detail to wavy or curly hair
> • Long-lasting bendable hold – Helps condition and protect curls while creating durable body and bounce
> • Reduces drying time – Specially formulated to help reduce drying time

Charlie wuz over Micky's studio, later that week.

Ee wuz doing a bit of thinking about Voodoo Pilchard, or the Pilchard, as Micky liked to call un. The Pilchard's work wuz gettin' outside of Camborne. Ut 'ad gone back to back an' end to end there, but you wuz startin' t'see ut up an' down the main A30, an' in other towns like Redruth, Trura, and Hayle. There were even backjumps now – quickly delivered calling card pieces that found themselves on buses an' other movin' objects (like Post and delivery vans) in Obby Stanker. These were originals in black an' blue ink.

The bite that had gone on though, was continuing. As well as the Pilchard himself, there seemed to be more and more orange and yellow copies being made. These full-scale bombs were happening around any piece of ground that wuz up fur development in Pool. Obviously, the authorities from Cornwall Council and the Highways Agency were starting to take nawtice. They'd even buffed over a few pieces, including a couple of originals.

'What ee really needs,' went Micky, who wuz in philosophical mode, 'is a few more burners...'

Charlie gave un a look that said please explain.

'Pieces that burn out ov walls or whatever... you knaw, t'completely dress up a wall or window or somethun'...'

Charlie nodded.

'The kids who are copyin' the Pilchard are doing dubs ov ut. You'n tell by the way the fills are being done...'

'Fills?' asked Charlie.

'Thaas' whas inside of it... y'knaw the way the fish is solid inside ut.'

Micky went back to sterilising a piece of gear in the autoclave.

'Look, what we need t'find is where 'is gallery is. All street artists have their gallery... it's their special place where you can see an extended run ov their work. It's normally secret – somewhere hidden from public view. Only the chosen few get to see ut...'

A Jedi temple then.

'What if ee's got no gallery?'

'Ee must do. Ee won't have spent the last few months getting up t'not have somewhere like tha'...'

'From what you're saying though Micky, ee needs a few more proper heaven spots...'

Charlie knew this was what street artists called those inaccessible but high-profile locations within the urban landscape which made sure everyone saw their work, but proved impossible for the authorities to move.

'Perhaps he's a single worker,' went Micky. 'Maybe he's afraid of heights... I dunno. Most people have help these days.'

'Well, his pieces are just throw ups an' stencils at the moment. I'm lookin' fur more ov his pieces now. There must be some stuff out there. We just gotta' keep looking. '

All this wuz giving Charlie food fur thought. Right now, the activities ov the Pilchard and those imitating the Pilchard were an interesting sub-genre of anarchic activity within Camborne. It seemed graffiti had come a long way from that which used to adorn the railway bridges over the main-line from Penzance to Paddington. where ut got about as exciting as ENGLISH GO HOME and KERNOW BYS VYKKEN.

'Eh?' went Micky. 'I had Trescothick in here fur a tattoo.'

And tha' wuz how Charlie comed to knaw about his latest mission.

Voodoo Pilchard

When Micky told un, ee might have said 'Get away with ee' or 'Naw...' but actually ee jus' sat there with 'is mouth abroad, and went, 'Jesus Christ...'

This wuz like the Second Coming.

Charlie realised the epic battle between good an' evil wuz goin' up a notch. Ee wuz beginnin' t'think ut might have been easier to have stayed on tour with Purple Haze. On the road, there wuz just simple stuff to deal with.

Dolcoath Spray Gel – Soft style, but no pushover.
Flexible styling spray-on gel
• Builds body and fullness – Light hold, flexible styling agents add volume and control
• Creates soft, natural looks – Conditioning and styling properties help provide a natural soft finish
• Adds rich shine – Activated shine blend of micro-particle tin helps create brilliant shine and reflection

When ee got home, an' sat down t'eat his tea ov a micro-waved curry, there wuz a piece on the local news about Cornwall pioneerin' environmentally-friendly power. Accordin' t'some experts on there, the territory wuz now the centre of eco-power across Europe (not that anyone in Troon had seemed t'nawtice). How this had come about wuz that some party had bought the rights t'develop Wave Hub energy off the coast near Hayle. The way it worked wuz that a socket had t'be constructed some 10 miles out inta' the Atlantic. These were fur wave energy converters of which there were four kinds under test. Just one hub might allow some 20 megawatts ov power to be fed inta' the local distribution network. Eventually, the plan wuz to connect ut to the national grid. The connection device on shore had now finished being built just down from where the now clean Red River flowed inta' the sea.

'This is clearly the future direction for Cornwall,' some posh boy from the RDA was going. 'We have a long tradition of innovative engineering here at Hayle, and we have great anticipation that eventually it will be a world leader in wave hub technology.'

Charlie reckoned tha' in reality, this wuz another sound-bite, just telling the Cornish what they should an' shouldn't be doing. The undertone ov ut wuz forget about gold down Crofty, an' forget convertin' all yer naff gold inta' cash. This wuz where the real gold wuz to be found. Maybe they had a point you. Perhaps considering the way the world wuz goin', maybe this wuz the way forward fur Cornwall. After all, ut helped being surrounded by the sea.

Then there wuz another interview with some director boy from WestWave. These boys were installing a device called a Pelamis. This turned out to be a semi-submerged articulated structure, made up of cylindrical sections that were linked together by joints. Every time they moved, they apparently caused other joints to move. These joints pushed into hydraulic rams which then pumped oil through hydraulic motors to make electricity. Simple really see – as long as you've got joints. The picture ov um on the telly looked like they wuz big buggers though – somethun' you wudn' want t'hit in a trawler ov a night-time. That' ud bugger ee up good an' proper, so not every cunt wuz happy 'bout ut. The fishermen ov St Ives an' Hayle wuz moaning on tha' their fishing grounds and industry had been ignored. They wuz expectin' further developments now off the Cornish coast, which would shaft they even further. Fuck, this wuz Cornwall all the time. Nawbody wuz ever happy you. Perhaps the Pilchard cud get out there an' do a bit of a piece on the Pelamis.

Charlie had been at work on his studio up in the second bedroom. This wuz a fair-sized room you. Ee 'ad a model fur ut from one of the promoters they'd met in Holland, who'd showed un his home studio. About the only thing that wud be hard t'record wud be a full drum kit, but as presently, Yak's kit wuz sat in his garage fur some reason, there might be possibilities there. Ee'd set about soundproofing ut an' giving it a kind of homely but workable feel. A carpet went down an' then he'd got the kind of Arabic-style rugs that the Black Crowes might record a new album with. Some booths that he'd custom-built with gear from up Homebase divided up the microphones he wuz goin' t'install from the roof. Dun right, this plaace cud serve him well. In the nearside corner, ee placed his mixing consol and his computer equipment. As fur Yak, ee'd been living there on an' off – which wuz a fuckin' pain in the arse. Ee 'ad a key now, which wuz even worse because Charlie wuz worried ee'd stumble in on Bev an' ee havin' some intimate moment. Regardless of tha' though, ee really wanted t'get down t'some recordin'. Charlie wuz formulatin' see, and ee wuz reckonin' that the best way forward wuz t'see if ee cud write some more hits. Then that might keep un in the style to which ee wuz now accustomed. Rock 'n' roll royalty yeah?

Pengegon Pommade – Smooth it out and shine it up.
Multi-texture smooth polish
• Smooth control – Excellent for smoothing and light control on textured hair
• Intense shine – Activated blends create brilliant shine and reflection
• Improves texture – Rich, clean natural oils help soften and condition

Micky wuz about t'lock up Headönizm for the night. Ut 'adn' been a bad day. The usual additional member of the TCC had come in to have his upper arm done. Ee'd had a few telephone enquiries from further a field in Cornwall which wuz encouragin'. Jess had already left, an' gone with Mel to pick up some more supplies down the wholesalers. Ee set the alarm and closed the door. As ee locked ut, in the window the reflection revealed a car that 'ad pulled up opposite the salon. The windows ov the BMW were darkened, but Micky noted whoever wuz inside, clearly had their eye on un. What did they wun't with ee?

As he began walking back down to Trelawny, the window slowly buzzed down.

'Micky, good to see you?' came a voice.

Micky peered down to the backseat of the BMW. Inside sat Markie Phillips. Next to him wuz a woman with long legs, but ee cudn' see her face properly due to the angle ee wuz standun'. Somethun' about her wuz familiar though.

'Markie Phillips,' went Micky. 'Long time – no see…'

'Heard you were off travelling the world…'

'Well, not any more. More back here now… with this… Got a studio upstairs see…'

'Very nice, very nice,' went Markie. 'Tattoos edn ut? I heard…'

'Yeah...'

'Mine are bit faded,' said Markie. 'Might need re-inking sometime...'

'No problem,' said Micky. 'Come in – any time...'

'Well, thaas' very kind ov you Micky. I won't forget tha'.'

Markie took a sip ov a glass ov Scotch. Ee has a bottle nestled between ee and the maid.

'We've all come along way from Trelawny ebm' us?'

Micky didn' knaw wha' t'say. Ee wuz just off down the Curnow's plaace again – so ee 'adn' really comed tha' far. But Markie – yeah – whatever ee wuz doin' wuz allowin' un a certain style of lifestyle an' a certain style ov woman.

'So... tell me... the band back are um?'

The vagueness of tha' wuz actually very specific. There wuz only one band: Purple Haze.

'Yeah... been back fur a bit now...'

Markie nodded.

'Neil back is a?'

Micky nodded. Ee knew the history there. Markie'd never got over Ally. Micky'd 'ad a yap with her the other day when she'd comed in the salon.

'They got troubles right now...'

'Troubles?'

Despite everything, despite being an evil fucker, Markie'd still do anything fur Ally. Ee knew ee'd walk over jagged glass an' burnin' coals jus' t' hold her hand again.

'Anthony – their son... well, ee's got Asperger syndrome an' tha'...'

Markie nodded meaningfully as if ee wuz sympathetic. Micky knew ee'd already said too much.

'Where are you off then Markie? Anything special on?'

Anything special on – might mean robbing cashpoints with a JCB or holding some cunt hostage somewhere.

'Football,' ee went. 'Trura City... Got bit ov a deal on... Hopefully 'twill see um be accepted inta' Football League Two this year s'long as the results hold...'

Micky knew the club wuz close to promotion from wha' Tommy'd said. They wuz top ov' the table.

'Well... best be gettin' off...' said Micky nervously.

'Yeah... well... good t'see you again... Wha' wuz the name ov tha' band you lot had again?'

'Balance.'

'Aw yeah – thaas' ut... Shame it got fucked up...'

'Yeah,' said Micky.

'Never mind. Plenty more fish to fry... eh, Micky?'

Markie gave a flick t'his driver an' the window buzzed up, with Micky's reflection peering inta' the glass. The BMW pulled off.

Ee turned the tone ov the conversation over in his mind. Now, the last thing ee needed wuz Markie Phillips steppin' inta' 'is studio. Next thing ee'd be wantin' wuz some protection money – or a regular cut like, ov dodgy clients put 'is way. Now ee wuz beginnin' t'understand where the boy Trescothick wuz comin' from.

Park an Tansys Soft Spray – Touchable hair is sexy hair. Light hold finishing spray

• Excellent working spray – Easy to brush through, reactivates with heat or water, perfect for smoothing irons

• Produces a natural, touchable finished – Soft, flexible styling ingredients for whatever your day brings

• Added protection – Helps protect against damage

Later tha' night Charlie went down t'Bev's plaace down Falmouth. She wuz sharin' a plaace down the top ov Trelawny Road, which they both found funny – a kind ov coincidental connection there, between two very different plaaces. This wuz student-central in the town, where over the years, thousands of those who'd come to study in Falmouth found digs. 'Twudn' a bad plaace, an' Bev's room airy and light, in the top of the house. If y'strained yer neck a bit, y'cud just about see the harbour. 'Twas in reality, a stone's throw from the old Pirate venue they'd played, now done up as some swanky restaurant near t'Events Square. Falmouth had altered a good bit. There wuz lots goin' on there – principally related to the expansion of the university over Penryn. The Pavilions, where Purple Haze, had played, seemed to be upping the profile of the kind of bands they were getting' in. No longer wuz ut just the tribute bands ov old, but also some performers – who though not 'zactly top flight in the world ov rock – had credibility. Put ut this way:

Charlie and the Trelawny crew had already seen people of late like Glenn Hughes (ex-Deep Purple bassist and funk legend), anarcho folk-punks New Model Army and space-stoners Hawkwind there. Yeah - 'twas *tha'* good.

Fur Charlie, ut felt a bit odd goin' back to this world ov student culture. Ee'd left tha' behind now. Havin' said tha', Bev's plaace wudn' like some of the dives ee'd encountered in the past. On many levels, the accommodation tha' Bev wuz in, made some of the housin' back Troon look proper third world. Well, come t'think ov ut, tha' wudn' too difficult, 'specially at the moment as the Trelawny Adit works wuz getting' bigger and bigger by the day.

Charlie wuz amazed. In Bev's room, she still had her bass, pedals and amp. Ut looked like she'd been using ut as well. The frets weren't dusty.

'Oh, I wuz just having a play around the other night,' she said. 'I was bored.'

'What were you playing?'

'Dunno. Just old stuff... Sabbath... Soundgarden... Pearl Jam...'

Charlie smiled. Ee wuz glad to hear tha'. Ee rated Bev.

Ee looked around her room. The plaace wuz packed with books and files. Some items ee recognised from her parents' plaace back in Trura. There wuz a photo of him too, on her desk, but Bev wudn' sentimental like Charlie though. She'd hadn' kept any of the flyers or posters from the old days like ee had. See, Charlie, well, ee always had tha' notion tha' one day, when obscure live albums were released ov 'is band ('Is band? What band?), that there'd be old ticket stubs an' posters on the booklet of the limited edition CD. Not Bev though. She wuz lookin' more to the future, obviously. Er vision ov the future wudn' quite rock 'n' roll any more though.

'I told my mum and dad about us,' she said.

'And?'

'They were really glad. Happy fur me.'

'Really?'

'Yes – they always liked you Charlie. They were dead impressed about you owning your own house... They'd like to come round an' see it sometime...'

''Course,' said Charlie.

Charlie wud definitely need t'make sure Yak wuz out ov there tha' day.

Although there wuz a shared kitchen in the property, Bev had organised her own small kitchen area up in her room. She was there making them both a coffee.

'So what's next fur you then?' she asked enthusiastically.

Charlie didn' quite knaw wha' she wuz getting' at.

'What ee mean?'

'Well, knowing you, Charlie Curnow, you've usually got something up your sleeve...'

'Just writing really,' said Charlie. 'I need to craft better songs. If the songs are right, then everything else follows... I need to spend time on ut.'

Bev knew that.

'But work?'

'Well, somethun'll come up... I got enough t'live on fur now.'

Charlie didn' really knaw what ee wuz goin' to do. Ee 'ad about a year ov money t'sort hisself.

She passed him a cup ov coffee. Ee took a sip.

'Write with me,' said Charlie.

'Me?'

'Yeah...'

'No. In the old days, it wuz always you an Neil who had the ideas...'

'No. Not always. You always got ut. You know rock... You know what ut has to be like...'

Charlie indicated the rows of CDs Bev had.

'Always. You know. That's what wuz always great about you... Y'always had that great Smashing Pumpkins sort of vibe...'

Bev laughed.

'Yeah, but not really. I'm not like you Charlie. I'm just not good enough. I mean, I realised that early on. You, you're different. You are good enough...'

Charlie cud tell by the ways she was speaking - with such conviction - tha' she wudn' be up fur ut. Ee'd had hopes ov them crafting something together. If ee wuz good enough, then why wuz a not touring the world an' hangin' out down Micky's tattoo parlour in Troon, contemplating the significance of a local street artist?

'It's goin' t'happen fur you,' said Bev. 'You just have to be patient.'

Ee 'oped she wuz right. The thing about Charlie though, wuz tha' ee wudn' patient. Ee knew only too well tha' 'dreckly' wudn' a concept in 'is vocabulary.

Charlie stood up an' walked over to Bev's desk. Ee peered out over Falmouth harbour – just visible wuz the Maritime museum and some ocean-going liner that had put in. The cruise parties did a quick coach-ride up t'the Eden Project, an' then on their way again. Tha' wuz all Cornwall meant to people like they.

Bev could tell ee wuz thoughtful and meditative. She came and stood behind him, pushing her breasts inta' his back and wrapping her arms around his stomach. Ut felt good. Whatever might happen in the future, Charlie knew ee cud rely on this. Ee rolled 'is neck with pleasure an' 'is eyes gazed down to the notes on Bev's desk.

'What you been studying?' ee asked.

'Oh... nothun' much. Just some notes on ill-wishing... Folk beliefs...'

'Whaas' ut mean?'

'You know, when people ill-wished someone else. Supposed to be pretty powerful stuff years ago...'

Charlie picked up the copy of the book she was reading.

'That's Robert Hunt... He wrote a lot about it in Cornwall... See this, look....'

She showed Charlie the page.

'It says there wuz once a fisherman, who put to sea, and some times when he went out, an old woman used to wish him good luck. When tha' happened, ee'd never catch any fish. So the fisherman got to think that she wuz actually ill wishing him, so he went to see the local peller...'

'Peller?'

'That's a wise man... a kind of male witch. An' when the fisherman did tha' the old woman came an' begged his forgiveness...'

Wise men. Ee'd knawn a few: Druid Dave, Jimmy Pengelly – Clifford Mellow perhaps.

'So it wuz a kind ov curse?' went Charlie, in a kind ov pirate voice.

'Yeah... Look there are other examples here too. It was a kind of way of getting' revenge on somebody...'

'Do you believe in ut though?' asked Charlie.

'I dunno. That's why I'm researching it all. There's got to be something in it. There are lots of recorded examples – not just in Cornwall – but all over the world.'

Charlie contemplated what she'd said.

'So it's a bit like voodoo then?'

Bev thought fur a bit.

'Yeah... I don't really know that much about voodoo, but I suppose so... Thaas' Haiti an' plaaces like Louisiana isn't ut? New Orleans?'

Charlie nodded a yes.

There wuz a pause, while both of them thought over the implications of ill wishing. Were there buggers out there still doing it? It seemed to scare Bev a little.

'You'll stay tonight, won't you?' she asked sexily.

'Yeah.'

So they went to bed together, for the first time, in a long time.

At three in the morning, Charlie woke. He had a sip of water, and nawticed the strewn condom wrappers on the carpet of Bev's room. Ee cudn' get back to sleep. On his mind were inescapable pairings: Curnow and Bennetts, fisherman and curses, pilchards and voodoo.

Atlantic Super Clean Light – Natural beauty is always in style.

Light hold finishing spray

• Produces natural touchable hold – Soft, flexible styling ingredients blended with Atlantic waters help provide a natural finish

• Builds soft body and shine – Light aerosol mist provides even, dry applications to help build body and shine

• Added protection – Helps protect against sun damage

Everything wuz perfect. Yak 'ad organised the drop off t'the letter. His contact down Newlyn 'ad sorted the deal out fur'n. 'Twas a lot ov money ee'd handed over – his whole share of the the Chakira songwriting credit. But then, tha' wuz peanuts

compared t'what ee wuz goin' to make on sellun' the powder
tha' wuz comin' in. Ef ut all went t'plan, ee'd be made. Keep his
nawse clean, an' keep the coppers out of the deals ee wud make,
an' ee'd have enough t'buy Club Rhino – an' treat hisself t' a
few little extras. All ee needed now wuz a bit ov luck. Yak 'ad
t'face ut, just like Charlie did. The rock 'n' roll dream wuz over,
an' where wuz a? Now, ee wuz in 'is mid-twenties, well, y'needed t'be sorted, organised, in control. Thaas' wha' ee wuz tryin'
to do with 'is life.

Now, ee'd considered askin' ov a few others t'come in on the
deal with un – or at least, help un out a bit. Bluett wud've been
the obvious choice, but with ee now signed up fur the army, an'
prob'ly about t' go on anti-drugs missions around the world,
tha' didn' seem a particularly good move. Besides, ee wuz too
busy tryin' t'chat up Kayleigh. Micky wudn' opposed to such
medicinal items in his former life, but given tha' ee'd wuz now
tryin' t'become a tattooed millionaire up Troon, that didn'
seem right either. Neil an' Charlie were way off the list (as
both were complete health nuts anyway these days – all
straight edge an' tha' - almoast), as wuz Kelvin. There wuz only
Trescothick who might want t'be involved, but ee wuz too
mazed fur Yak, too out there. Na – ee'd be sole trader. 'Twas better that way.

So there ee wuz. Twelve o'clock at night, boobed up in a
Transit van down on Gwithian Sands. This wudn' by Riviera
Towans or even Upton. Na, ee'd managed t'get the van quite
close t'Strap Rocks, and wuz waitin' fur high tide. Here wuz the
deal: a transfer would be made from the tanker to a Newlyn-
based trawler. From the trawler, they'd load the freight inta' a
rigid-hulled inflatable boat an' bring ut straight inta' shore.
This time ov night, all the tourists 'ad gone 'ome, an' even
some ov the mad night-surfers wudn' stay out this late. Yak
took a pair of binoculars and scanned the ocean. Out there, ten
miles off the coast wuz all tha' Wave Hub crap, but ee wudn'
bothered about tha'. Ee wuz just countin' on the deal. To the
right, the light of Godrevy lit the blackness every ten seconds.
To the left, ee saw the street lights of Carbis Bay and St Ives
sparkling. There wuz a light rain, but nothun' tha' wuz goin'
t'stop un. Out there, somewhere in the Atlantic, they wuz seeing tha' light – knawin' tha' the drop had t'be made.

Voodoo Pilchard

Yak drummed the steering wheel. Ee wuz thinkin' of the beat ov Black Sabbath's 'Symptom of the Universe'. Some days, Yak cudn' be bothered t'play or rehearse, but tonight, well, ee wuz filled with energy, an' when ut got like tha', the only thing ee wanted t'do wuz drum. Right now though, there wuz nothun' ee cud do. Ee just had to wait.

The beach stretched out a long way west and east from where ee'd parked up. In more innocent times, 'is ma had taken un down here a lot in the summer holidays. This seemed to be the plaace where they always went to build sandcastles and paddle in the shallows. Ee pictured a memory of Charlie an' ee playin' in the dunes, sliding down a run of soft sand on boogie boards. Then ee remembered a gig Purple Haze had done on a beach in Brittany. There, they had the same kind of sand; him peering out over the same vast ocean, as ee played the gig. They were on fire then. Tha' wuz the early days of Purple Haze still. It wuz only later on tha' things become more difficult. Yak completely understood why drummers went off the deep end sometimes. Ee wuz 'zactly the same. Ee reckoned 'twas somethun' genetic in drummers – like Animal off the fuckin' Muppets.

Ee wondered how many other deals were being made around the Cornish coast tonight? A few ee reckoned, just the same as ut had always been. It wuz the Cornish way, wudn' ut? Y'had t'scrape along as best y'cud.

A text message came through:

Tide is not right yet.

Fuck. Ee took the number an' phoned back 'is man.

'They've transferred, but the currents are a problem.'

'But i's got to be tonight,' went Yak. 'You said.'

Yak had a good deal on tomorra', an' ee wanted t'sort Tommy out later.

'You'll have to be patient. Wait there. I'll phone or text with further instructions.'

Yak cud do jack shit. Ee wuz totally in their hands, an' ee didn' like tha' feelin' one bit. 'Twas worse than bein' controlled by Spryer.

With 'is binoculars, Yak took a look out again over the

ocean. There – wuz tha' a light or naw? Ee cudn' tell. The original plan wuz that they wuz goin' t'text un when they got inta' shore a bit. Then ee had t'flash the lights ov the van a couple ov times t'let them knaw where ee wuz. Yak wuz pissed off. 'Is man had set this up 'specially because the tide wuz meant t'be good fur 'zactly this sort of beach party. Wuz the cunt havin' un on? Ee did wonder. Ee wuz s'paused t'be reliable: a Camborne boy after all. Had they shafted un ee wuz wondering? After all, there wudn' naw written contract or disclaimer like there wuz fur Micky's tattoos.

Yak checked the tide times again. Yes – ut should be fine.

Another hour passed. 'Twas comin' around fur two o'clock in the morning now. Leave ut much longer an' the tide would be too far out. That wud prevent a landing because ut would be too shallow over the rocks. Finally, another text:

```
Approaching shore. Turn on lights.
```

Yak switched on and off his lights a couple of times. Ee stepped out of the van and scanned the ocean. Now ee cud see them. The rigid inflatable wuz comin' in just as 'is man 'ad said.

'Bewdie,' Yak said satisfyingly to hisself. Never mind wha' twats did the cocaine in the toilets ov posh clubs in Trura; just focus on gettin' the gear loaded. Tommy's Viagra too. The packets would prob'ly be on a pallet of some kind, so they'd need transferring manually inta' the back ov the van. 'Is man told un, tha' they should be able t'complete the transfer in less than five minutes. Ee got back in the van and switched on the engine.

Just as ee wuz about t'pull off, from over the eastern side ov the beach, travelling fast, ee saw another vehicle. Ut looked like a Landrover ov some kind. No lights on ut.

'Ah fuck!' went Yak t'hisself. 'Who's tha'?'

Like The Clash, ee didn' knaw whether t'stay or go. For all ee knew at tha' moment, ut cud well 'ave been the police. Ee reckoned somehow tha' they'd been monitoring the operation all along, and now they were goin' to make the sting: capture the smugglers an' the mule red-handed. The fuckers had timed ut well too. Just as they beached the rigid inflatable, they arrived with the Landrover. The party who wuz inside the

Landrover got out, and within seconds jumped on they in the inflatable, an' had um pinned t'floor. There were voices. There wuz shoutin'. Yak cudn' make out wha' wuz being said, but then ee nawticed that the cocaine wuz being neatly loaded inta' the back of the Landrover.

Hang on a minute, thought Yak. Thaa' wuz his fuggin' cocaine. Not theirs.

How d'fuck did they knaw tha' the landin' wuz goin' t'be made right then?

Yak's jaw dropped. Ee might as well have taken his money from Chakira an' scatter ut t'the wind up on Carn Brea.

'I'm screwed,' ee went t'hisself. 'Really, really screwed.'

One of the Landrover crowd gave the boys in the rigid inflatable a kick, an' looked like ee told um to start up the engine again. Ee also looked to be tellin' um t'stay down. The Landrover crowd had shotguns trained on um. Yak heard the inflatable engine start an' the boat headed away from shore. Now the Landrover crowd were lookin' up the beach towards where Yak's Transit was parked.

Yak wudn' sure what to do. Fur a second or two, ee peered down the beach. One of the crowd there wuz a woman, an' she wuz holdin' a fuck-off style handgun tha' looked like it might pack the kind ov munitions tha' wud split Yak's van in half. T'tell ee straight, Yak wuz nearnly 'bout shittin' hisself. But wha' cud a do? They wuz menacin' un now – waitin' fur'n t'go. If a pulled off, wud they follow un back 'ome? Wuz ut best t'get out now an' run inta' the dunes of Upton Towns?

Now, Yak was suddenly beginning t'understand wha' Charlie an' Micky'd been talkin' about with all tha' voodoo pilchard shit. It wuz naw choice, a kind ov paradox ov experience tha' left ee shafted: magic an' a stinkun' fish. They wuz holdin' all the cards from wha' Yak wuz feeling: a full on Voodoo deck ov um – Loa gods across the beach there. It wuz a tarot tha' wuz goin' t'change 'is life.

'This is why you d'need a gun,' 'is man had joked with un down Newlyn.

Now ee knawed why.

Surely they wudn' just goin' t'let un drive off after what ee'd seen? Then again, surely Yak wudn' goin' t'let they just drive off with 'is gear?

Alan M. Kent

Maybe they'd just think ee wuz like the other surfer boys who stayed down here overnight, or some couple who'd just met over a pub in Copperhouse an' come down there fur a bit ov doggin'. But na, 'twudn' lookin' like tha'. They'd prob'ly already spotted there wuz no surfboards on his roof, an' well, the van wudn' 'zactly rockin' t'the movements of erotic love-makin'.

Na, they'd 'ave un.

Yak saw ut comin' in slow motion. The girl an' the boys down there got inta' the Landrover and headed up the beach towards un. Now Yak 'ad promised hisself t'get the starter motor fixed on the van soon as ee'd made the first deal with the coke, an' now, now ov all times, the bugger had decided not t'work. They travelling toward un, seemed to be happening in slo-mo, like none of ut wuz real anymore. The kinda' cunts they were, they surely take un out. No messin'.

The light of the Godrevy beam crossed the ocean again. Ee 'ad about ten seconds t'start the van before the next pass, and before they'd be up to un. Yak turned the key back t'the start position, and with a deft flick of his wrist, tried t'make the right connection. It worked. Ee praised John Wesley and Methodism and Druidism an' anyone else who ee needed t'thank. Spinning sand, ee pulled off the ridge ee wuz on, nearnly 'bout breaking the suspension of the Transit. Nothun' like tha' mattered now. All ee needed t'do now wuz get out ov here. Yak drove madly, crazily, back across the beach, around the old sand quarry, where the Wave Hub plant wuz. Ee looked in the mirror. The fuckers wuz comin' after un still.

Yak pulled out onta' the Hell's Mouth road tha' headed out on the back roads t'Camborne. Perhaps ee cud lose um there: pull off somewhere, or take a diversion down a farm track. Surely they didn' knaw the area as well as ee did? So ee wuz canning it up the bends. Ee 'oped nothun' wuz comin' the other way. For a few minutes, while ee'd skedaddled out ov there, ee'd forgotten about the money ee'd lost, but 'twas back on his mind again now. Yak wudn' goin' t'ave ut naw more. Turn the van around, ee started sayin' t'hisself. So thaas' wha' ee did. Ee reversed inta' turning at the top ov the hill near Higher Pencobben, and turned right.

'Hold yer nerve Yak boy,' ee told hisself.

Voodoo Pilchard

The cocaine thieves had only just got out onta' the main road. Well, they'd quite a load in the back, and the weight wuz slowin' um down. Eventually though, they started t'climb the hill. Yak wudn' takin' naw prisoners in the drivin' department. This wuz one ov his drummin'-style drivin' moments. Steering now chaotically, Yak reached down inta' the side pocket of the door an' pulled out a CD. It wuz some cheap Deep Purple compilation. The first track that comed on wuz 'Highway Star'. Perfect. Paicey began the track with some amazin' fills, and then Glover's bass kicked in. Finally, Blackmore's guitar, Lord's Hammond organ and Gillan's screaming vocals:

NOBODY GONNA TAKE MY CAR
I'M GONNA RACE IT TO THE GROUND
NOBODY GONNA BEAT MY CAR
I'M GONNA BREAK THE SPEED OF SOUND
OOOH IT'S A KILLING MACHINE
IT'S GOT EVERYTHING
LIKE A DRIVING POWER BIG FAT TYRES
AND EVERYTHING

The Landrover wudn' naw match fur the collective power of Yak, Deep Purple an' a Ford Transit. The driver ov the Landrover, steered t'swerve un, an' caught a fuckin' g'eat lump ov' granite gatepost, that prob'ly one time wuz a standing stone on Connor Downs somewhere. The Landrover, didn't flip right away. Instead, ut seemed t'pause fur a minute, before sliding inta' the Cornish hedge opposite and near demonlished tha'. When ut seemed t'lose more grip it turned on its side, the left hand windows and rear windows smashing immediately, and then ut coming t'a halt where the road bent around again t'the right, sliding nicely along the tarmac an' scrapin' ut up t'buggery. Tha' wudn' be makin' ut inta' Troon Motors fur a bit ov bodywork. Na. 'Twas properly trashed: a full insurance write off.

Yak slammed on the breaks ov the transit, comin' t'a slide about a hundred feet away from the remains of the Landrover. From the broken window at the back, one of the packages had fallen onto the road. Yak went back an' picked ut up. Ee didn't really care much about they inside the Landrover. They were clearly comin' around though – and a shotgun barrel wuz pointun' at un over the back seat. 'Twuz prob'ly best t'let sleeping dogs lie. From the crunched surrounds ov the bodywork, ee reckoned ee cud hear ov um groaning. 'Twas time to go before ee got 'is ass blawn off.

When ee got home t'Charlie's plaace, Charlie wudn' there. Ee gave a sigh, an' crashed out on the sofa. In the morning, on Radio Cornwall, they wuz talkin' 'bout a serious road traffic accident down Gwithian. The police were appealing for witnesses. They didn' say nawthun' 'bout naw cocaine. Had someone comed an' collected ut then? Had the police found ut? Ee didn't knaw.

Yak tried callin' his man down Newlyn. It cut inta' 'is answerphone. Ee didn' leave naw message. Then ee remembered; ee'd managed to salvage one bag. Perhaps there'd be a silver lining t'ut all. Ee went out t' the Transit and brought ut inside t'open ut up, away from any pryin' eyes in School Lane. In the kitchen ee found a knife to slit through the packaging. Some best Columbian white wuz what ee wuz 'opin' for.

When the package wuz opened, ee saw what ee'd got: a run ov Tommy's 'Loco' Viagra. Ee read the packet: 'Warning - Use with caution. Do not exceed prescribed dose.'

Star-Gazy Shine – A little goes a long way in adding silky texture.

Instant spray-on shine

• Provides high shine – Contains activated natural blends to help enhance shine

• Silky texture – Excellent for use prior to hair ironing

• Highly concentrated – Lightweight mist pump allows for a fine application – use sparingly

The legend tha' wuz Tommy Curnow wuz in full flow t'the boys on 'is core. 'Twas 5.30am morning shift, an' none ov um wuz much in the mood fur the awkward shrinkage stoping that wuz needed on the 450 fathom level. It required the SIG machines t'be moved along to where management were suspecting tha' the initial finds of gold might be located. They needed to do this, as well as sort out the chutes t'give the boys some room t'work. Right now down there, there wudn' enough room t'swing a cat, tell 'bout a drill bit, or pick an' gad. Tommy though, always 'ad a way of lightening the work with a gag. This wuz today's:

'There's this boy see, an' ee's on holiday in Birmingham. Ee comes across this g'eat church an' ee sees a golden telephone stuck on the wall there, with a sign on ut like, which says '£10,000 per call'. Ee's proper intrigued about this, so ee goes up t'the vicar an' asks un woz up with tha'. Well, ol' vicar says 'tes a direct line t'hebben and that for tha' money you could personally speak t'God. Well, ol' boy didn' have tha' sort ov money on un, so ee went on 'is way...'

The boys could tell this wuz goin' t'be one of Tommy's epic stories, so settled in with their backs t'the stope; one or two havin' a smoak. No work wuz goin' t'get dun 'til Tommy 'ad finished his yarn.

'Anyway... ol' boy is on his way back t'Cornwall, so next ee stops in Bristol Cathedral dunna?. There, ee seen the same golden telephone, with the same sign next to ut. Ee goes up t'the Canon the Cathedral an' asked un what its purpose was. Ee got the same answer back – tha' 'twas a direct line t'hebben, and for tha' kind ov'money you could personally speak t'God. Well, ee didn' have enough money t'make the call, so decided t'head back down the M5. So... ee stops off in Taunton dun't a? Ee goes inta' a church there. Ee finds the same golden telephone and sign. Next ee stops off in Exeter. Ee goes inta' Exeter Cathedral. Ee finds the same golden telephone an' sign. Eventually though, ee makes ut over the border an' crosses the River Tamar. Now ee's back home – so ee d'reckon on goin' in the nearest church an' seeing if there's a golden telephone in there too. So ee goes in dun't a? Finds the same golden telephone. This time, the sign next to ut says 'Fifty pence per call'. Well, ol' boy is pretty 'mazed at this. Ee's proper tickled up ass at the price an' is thinkin' ov makin' a call. The Reverend there comes over to un.

'Reverend,' he goes, 'I've travelled here from Birmingham, an' I've seen the same golden telephone all over the plaace. I've been told 'tes a direct line t'hebben and that the price everywhere else is £10,000 per call if I want to make a personal call t'God. Now, will ee tell me why 'tes s'cheap here?'

Well, the Reverend smiled and said, 'You'm in Cornwall now

boy... This is God's Own Country... and so 'tes a local call.'

Tommy stood back, satisfied that ee'd told the tale well, and given ut 'is best shot. The boys around un groaned, but knew really that Tommy still 'ad the right kind of yip t'keep um entertained. This wuz the sort ov stupid shit tha' kept um goin' underground – when either the damp or the heat made ee feel like jackin' ut all in.

'Well, better make is I s'pause,' Tommy went. 'Shallus see if we'n move the SIG first?'

The boys began to start the process, though not all of um were ready t'move.

'You seen this?' went one of the boys – by the name ov Timmy Pascoe. Tommy'd knawn un a few years now like – worked as one of the ground staff on Saturdays at Treyew Road. Ee wuz pointin' t' the front page of the *West Briton*. There wuz a big story 'bout the graffiti artist who they wuz callin' the Pilchard. Some of the graffiti featured wuz outside of Crofty, but ut seemed the Pilchard had been expandin' his horizons down t'the University at Tremough, an' t'parts of Falmouth. Well, y'd'knaw wha' they'm like down there – all Pimms-drinkin' posh cunts with yachts, cravats an' balconies – and people wudn' very keen on the desecration goin' on. Somethun' 'ad t'be dun about ut, accordin' t'one councillor. 'The young people have got no respect at all these days,' the stupid cunt wuz goin' on.

'Well, ee dun' knaw shit,' went Timmy. 'Everyone in Camborne d'knaw tidn' just youngsters... This Pilchard character, well, ee's a proper artist in my view...'

'People've got used t'ut here now ebm' um?' went Tommy. 'I dunnaw how the bugger gets away with ut t'be honest though. I mean some of the plaaces ent 'zactly isolated are um? The art've got bigger too. You'd think someone wud see un do ut...'

Tommy didn' need t'say anymore. Moast of the boys there thought the same thing. The Pilchard wuz prolific – tha' much wuz true – so why didn't anyone see the cunt at work? 'Twas a mystery an' naw mistake.

'So... are the Tigers goin' t'do ut then?' went Timmy, still 'opin' fur a further distraction before actually startin' any work.

Timmy wuz obviously talkin' about the next few games fur Trura City. All ov of um wuz crunch matches, jostling the top ov the table position with York City an' Kettering Town, which meant that if they won them, they'd be playing in League Division Two. Tommy took a breather from wha' ee'd started.

'You knaw the score Tommy... Wha' ee reckon?'

'Well, if the defence holds... I d'reckon we'm strong enough.... But 'tes goin' t'need some goals too – and looking at ut, I'm not sure the boys is delivering up there right now...'

Tommy wuz speakin' like a seasoned professional – like ee wuz giving an interview t' *Match ov the Day* or somethun'.

But tha' wudn' the real focus of Timmy's interview. Na, wha' ee really wanted t'knaw 'bout, wuz wha' wuz goin' on behind the scenes. Timmy knawed ov Markie Phillips' interests as much as anyone else on the core.

'So is Phillipsy properly in there now then?'

Tommy had been tight-lipped about the wheeling an' dealing goin' on in the background ov the club, but with Timmy ee felt ee could reveal a bit more.

'Well, you'll knaw come Friday evening. There'll be a Press briefing. But yeah – Phillipsy's goin' t'be the major shareholder in the club... Ee's puttin' in a few quid mind...'

'Got tha' sort ov money 'ave a?'

'Well, apparently ee have,' went Tommy. 'Got a lot of fingers in a lot ov pies have tha' boy...'

'Wha'? Butcherin' an' meat packing an' tha'?'

'Well, I think there's more t'his operation these days than tha'...'

Timmy knawed what Tommy meant by tha'. 'Twas the wrong kind of question t'ask what exactly. Like everyone else knawed, 'twas possibly a few illegal activities – but wha' the hell, if Phillipsy wuz man enough t'put up the money, then good on the boy. Half the Premiership wuz prob'ly funded on dodgy money too.

'The name ov his firm goin' on the shirts then?' asked Timmy.

''Es. Fur next season like...'

'Come a long way e 'ave,' went Timmy. ''Mean... years ago like... y'wudn' have thought ut ov un now wud ee?'

'True enough,' said Tommy, who knew a good few of Phillipsy's dealings, but wudn' quite aware ov the specific knowledge his son 'ad about un.

'Beggars cen't be choosers though Timmy... As they d'say, money speaks...'

'Morning,' came a voice down the level, interrupting their conversation about Trura City. It was distinctive enough – the voice of Gerald Matta, chief operating officer of the mine.

'Everything a'right Tommy?' he bellowed in a kindly sort ov way.

'Spot on Mr Matta,' went Tommy. 'We've just started on moving the gear...'

'Splendid... When do you think we can commence drilling?'

'Might be by the middle of the core... either tha', or Af'noon shift can pick ut up...'

'Good. I'm looking forward to what we'll find then...'

Matta looked slightly uncomfortable down there. His type always did. Despite all his experience, management like ee always looked like the least bit ov dirt or grease would scare un. 'Least Matta had a bit ov vision with the mine – an' Tommy admired tha'. Keep ee sweet, an' everything wud be a'right.

'Wha' ee think of that there graffiti up top side then Mr Matta?' yipped up Timmy.

Matta looked a bit puzzled first ov all. Then ee realised what Timmy wuz on about.

'Well, it seems like this Pilchard fellow only targets significant places... so I s'pose we are honoured...'

'That we are,' went Tommy. 'They d'say in the paper there that ee's the Cornish Banksy...'

'Well, in that case... I won't have anyone wipe it quite yet...'

Matta made his way unsteadily back along the level. Tommy an' Timmy ('is pard these days) laughed t'each other. They knew the various bits of graffiti right the way through the mine. Some ov ut prob'ly dated back t' the original Penhellick and Pool Mines of the early nineteenth century, tellin' management and the cap'ns what t'do with themselves. People had been scribbling on the walls down here fur centuries. Why should ut be any different when you comed t'grass?

Crowst came an' went. There wuz always the usual range of jokes at Tommy's expense about Club Rhino and his past collection of lap dancers. This wuz mainly derived from whatever delicate discussion wuz made over the maid displayin' her charms on page three ov the paper. The rest ov the time they yapped about the Wave Hub off the sea down Gwithian. Moast of the boys didn't think ut would work in the long term. If they wanted renewables then why dun't um give geo-thermal another go. Tha' wuz the general opinion. But then these were mining boys, and underground activity wuz wha' they knew best. The ocean? Leave tha' t' the fishermen: the true mentalists.

'Some music boys?' shouted Tommy. Tommy had converted moast of them t'the way of rock while they were underground.

'Not more of tha' fuckin heavy shit Curnow...' shouted back Trudge, who wuz still more inta' his trance an' hip hop nights over Newquay.

'Twas just about the first thing Tommy moved when they transported gear to a new stope – the hanging-looking ghetto-blaster stereo. The thing wuz caked in drill dust, grease and other substances y'didn't want much intimate contact with.

'Yeah,' Tommy went. 'When you'm working with rock, what you need is a good dose of rock...'

From his crowst-bag Tommy took out his latest purchase off Amazon: Ratt's 1984 album *Out of the Cellar*. No other cunt had even heard ov the music Tommy dug out.

'Classic stuff,' went Tommy, an' whacked the CD inta' the player. 'You hear this all the time on the radio in 'Merica...' Like how did Tommy knaw tha' – a cunt who'd got about as far away as Ibiza one week in the 1990s.

ROUND AND ROUND
WITH LOVE WE'LL FIND A WAY JUST GIVE IT TIME
ROUND AND ROUND
WHAT COMES AROUND GOES AROUND
I'LL TELL YOU WHY, DIG

Yeah, dig is prob'ly wha' they did best. Sometimes it seemed like the only way t'deal with the row underground wuz more row. It wuz like y'fought fire with fire. Tha' way the absurdity of wha' they wuz all about (poking drill bits inta' bits ov rock) – seemed t'be a bit less, well, absurd.

LOOKIN' AT YOU, LOOKIN' AT ME
THE WAY YOU MOVE, YOU KNOW IT'S EASY TO SEE

Alan M. Kent

THE NEON LIGHT'S ON ME TONIGHT
I'VE GOT A WAY, WE'RE GONNA PROVE IT TONIGHT
LIKE ROMEO TO JULIET

Trudge comed along and saw Tommy and Timmy prancin' around t'the words, air-guitaring with lengths of drill bits, and pretendin' they wuz onstage at Hammersmith Odeon.

'You two fuckin' look like you just stepped out ov Village People...' ee went.

Ee 'ad a point. They did look a bit fuckin' gay, singin' they sort ov lyrics too. They stopped wha' they were doin'. 'Twudn' really no way fur two hard-rock miners t'carry on. Tommy turned ut down a bit.

'Thanks,' went Trudge, raisin' an eyebrow.

But when a went away gain, Tommy turned ut back up t'full volume. See Tommy, like his son, wudn' quite ready t'give up the rock 'n' roll fantasy – even though ee'd never have said tha'.

When their core finished at one, Tommy stayed on fur a bit in the stope. Somethun' powerful seemed t' be keepun' there. The debris that had comed off the roof of the stope had built up by now, but they hadn't been able to clear all ov ut. 'Twould either be picked up by the next shift, or they'd deal with ut tomorrow. Tommy didn't knaw really whether Matta and the rest of the engineers wuz on some fantasy here. Maybe they'd be better off stickin' t'tin. Tin, y'knawed, an' ut wudn' doin' bad on the stock market at the moment. Why mess with ut?

In the stope, Tommy turned around, and though 'twas well enough lit down there, in the semi-darkness, the torch on his helmet seemed t'catch on somethun'. Ut glimmered in the beam. 'Twudn' tha' unusual really. You usually got ut with a good sturt of tin. This wuz slightly different though. Tommy took his right-hand glove off and reached down inta' the debris. This seemed like a moment straight out ov Indiana Jones. The object that ee wuz reachin' for wudn' no ordinary lump ov rock. Ah naw. Naw ordinary lump t'all.

'Fuuuuuuck!' went Tommy. The word echoed around the stope.

Wha' ee wuz pullin' out wuz a fully-formed nugget ov gold – the kind the geophysics people and the engineers didn't reckon even existed in Crofty. They wuz all about micro-particles

172

and extraction, but this lump wuz around the size ov an egg. Initially, Tommy reckoned on ut being fool's gold (ee'd seen that a time or two down there) but the weight ov ut told un otherwise. From the crouched position ee wuz in, Tommy stood up and brought the lump close to his eye so ee cud closely scan ut. Ee turned ut between his middle finger and thumb, looking at the million-year old object. Then ee moved his hand down to waist level and weighed the dense metal in the palm ov his hand. There wuz buggers who played at gold-mining down west, in the hills above Zennor, but this, this might well be the biggest find ov gold in Cornwall fur decades.

'Why me?' ee mouthed.

Now ee had t'do somethun' about ut. Matta an' the management 'ad naw idea they wuz goin' t'find anything like this. If they did, then there'd be security cameras everywhere, geeking at the workforce t'see what they wuz finding. Tommy reckoned ee 'ad about ten minutes t'make a decision before the cage would be down again with the Af'noon core. Someun' like this would sort un out good an' proper. In 'is mind, ee wuz payin' off a few debts, regardless ov what might happen with tha' tool Yak. Instantly, ee wuz thinkin' about a Mediterranean cruise – or perhaps even one of they luxury American ones outta' Florida with Aerosmith an' Journey as the house bands, an' inevitably movin' Sally and ee over Lanner or Treswithian – away from Trelawny and the worst ov the mephedrone factories. It seemed like Tommy 'ad been waitun' all his life fur this one moment ov luck. This wuz 'is Euro-millions, or the Premium Bonds his feyther never won. Just as ee wuz drifting inta' this kind of fantasy, the reality ov the situation comed back to un again. Perhaps there wuz more down there, still to be found in the debris from the stoping. Tommy put the golden egg in 'is pocket an' put back on his glove again. Ee scrambled around in the broken rock and dust, but there wudn' nothun' more like this; a few tiny seams ov ut maybe – but nothun' you could extract.

This 'ad been what they'd been talkin' about. Ee wuz goin' t'do ut. Ee wuz goin' t'take ut out without tellin' nawbody. Diddlin' the management wuz wha' ee wuz goin' t'do. But so wha'? Anyone in 'is position wud do the same. Somethun' like this they wudn' goin' t'miss anyway. Tommy turned away from

the stope. Ee gave a quick thank you t'the mine knockies fur
revealing ut to un (swearin' ee'd tos um a bit of a pasty corner
tomorra'), and then walked quickly back along the level t'the
cage. The weight of the gold pulled down his pocket on that
side of his overalls. In the shaft ee could hear the new core comin' down.

'Behave like nothun've happened.' Tommy told hisself.

Ee wuz sweating slightly, but then, so what? Tha' wud only
prove t'they comin' down how hard ee'd been workin'.

The doors ov the cage opened an' the Af'noon core comed
out.

'Tommy boy...' they went. 'How's ut hanging?'

'A'right pard...'

'Left ee behind ave um? Eh – Trura City goin' t'do ut ent
um?'

'Hope so,' went Tommy.

'You got t'motivate um Curnow... Sack the manager – Afro
Metters - and get you in there. Thaas' wha' I say... You'd sort
um out... The amount of money the players have now...
They'll be on full-times wages soon wun't um?'

Cards all ov um – they lot.

Tommy wuz glad to be alone in the cage, with the banter
ended. It felt like a long winch up the surface. This wuz like
somethun' out of Mother Goose down Beacon pantomime last
February. Now ee wuz headin' up some magical beanstalk
t'come t'grass. There, nawbody'd knaw shit. An' fur the time
being tha' wuz the best way fur things t'be. Ee took a shower
and cleaned hisself up. Ee placed the gold inta' his crowst bag,
and went t'the car park just as usual. Outside the mine, Tommy
caught sight of the Voodoo Pilchard street art. There was a fair
ol' amount ov ut now on the walls surrounding the mine.
Comin' along Pendarves Street, ee breathed a sigh ov relief.
Whatever voodoo wuz in the air, some good – fur a change -
had seemed to have comed towards un.

Tommy didn' knaw ut then, but there wuz even more magic
'eadin' his way.

Cousin Jack's Cream – Everyday life can be harsh on hair.
Leave-in thickening conditioner
• Moisturizes, strengthens and protects – Moisturizing

Voodoo Pilchard

conditioners and panthenol help strengthen and protect
• Helps protect against sun damage – UV absorbers help
to prevent damage caused by the sun
• Adds body with light hold – This soft, glossy styling
agent enhances body and provides light hold

Earlier tha' day, Yak had tried phonin' his man down Newlyn
again, Somewhere along the line, someone had blabbed hadn'
um? – unless somebody wuz keepin' watch on activities at the
coast. Eventually, after about the twentieth call, a text comed
back to un:

        Not our fault asshole.

Now what wuz a goin' t'do? All his plans were in pieces, an' ee
wuz in pieces too. Ee'd been tryin' t'hide ut from Charlie, but
ee wudn' doin' a very good job ov ut.
    'You're not back on the... y'know...?' asked Charlie.
    'Na – nothun' like tha'.'
    'Y'seem a bit edgy Yak... like y'need somethun'...'
    'Jus' business... That's all...'
    'Business?' asked Charlie, wondering how the fuck his drum-
mer pal (who'd not 'zactly been known fur his Alan Sugar-style
in the cut and thrust of buying-and-selling) could be successful
in tha' kind ov world.
    Charlie didn' like the look ov Yak in this mode. It wuz scar-
ily close t'the way ee'd looked like in the toilets ov *Vic Bars* in
Newquay.
    'What you been doin' anyway?' asked Yak, trying to detract
from his own panic.
    'Song-writing. Done a few demos haven't I? Might want
some drums in there sometime... You up fur tha'?'
    Charlie wuz lying t'hisself really. The song-writing wudn'
goin' as well as ee wanted it too. Ut seemed like every time
some new idea came to un, ee cudn' quite express ut musically.
From time t'time it felt like he wuz facing a musical corner with
no way out ov ut.
    ''Course Charlie... Let me know when...'
    'Later this week maybe... Try an' get Neil over then as well...'
    'Is Bev in then?'

175

That wuz a curve ball. Charlie wudn' expectun' un t'ask tha'...

'Wha' ee mean?'

'Is she... y'knaw... back in the band like?'

Charlie went inta' the kitchen and switched on the kettle. Ee put some spoonfuls of coffee inta' two mugs, slightly regretting this, in the sense tha' Yak wuz edgy enough already without a shot of caffeine racing through is body.

'There ent naw band...' shouted in Charlie.

'But we're recording...' went Yak,

'Yeah – but no band right... Think of ut as just being a session... and tha' you're a session musician...'

'But the four of us... back together... I mean 'tis near as dammit, Balance back again. May as well get Micky in too... an' have a full reformation... The fans out there want ut Charlie...'

By tha' Yak prob'ly meant the hordes that were composed ov Kelvin an' Mel, Boy Bluett (who wuz gearing up fur the army anyway) and perhaps Orange Trescothick (as people wuz callin' un these days after 'is intensive tanning session) and the spirit of Clifford Mellow. No-one else wud give a shit. Clar, the bar steward at Institute wudn' be bookin' em back again after tha' little incident with the urinals.

'Shall I put a statement on-line?! On me website? To confirm... Bev is not in any band... She's playin' again a bit – but I haven't asked her like... Thought you had other plans with EBGBs anyway?' asked Charlie.

'Yeah, well, I did... Well, I still do...'

Charlie brought in a mug of coffee fur Yak, and placed ut on a coaster fur him on his CD rack, near the bands beginning with A, and therefore his 'special edition' AC/DC collection.

'Mind the 'DC there...'

'So the band's not on the radar then...?'

'Na... Best leave sleepin' dogs lie....'

'Micky said Markie Phillips wuz askin' after us the other day outside Headönizm?'

'Woz a now?' asked Charlie.

What, wondered Charlie, wuz Markie asking that fur? Charlie guessed it wuz just a bit of territorial pissing – Markie stampin' his foot on his area. He wuz lettun' um knaw ee wuz watchin'.

Voodoo Pilchard

'Ee's all involved in Trura City now, they d'reckon... With some woman Micky said. Be leavin' we alone I d'reckon... Anyway, you heard from Spyer?'

'Yeah, on e-mail,' went Charlie. 'Apparently ee paid out fur new costumes an tha' fur his new version of Purple Haze, and then at a rehearsal ee told um they wudn' good enough fur the tour – so they jacked ut...'

'So, ee ebm' got nawbody now?'

'Dun't look like ut do ut?'

'All ee got at the moment is a bunch ov costumes... but naw-body t'play...'

This seemd like poetic justice for Spryer both Charlie an' Yak reckoned.

The discussion though, had prompted Charlie t'rethink the future. Wuz ut possible tha' Bev could be recruited again? Right now, ut didn't look very likely – her studies were her priority – not messin' around with music anymore. Charlie looked across at the nervy, smelly, hairy bugger that wuz Yak. Ee realised wha' ee 'ad t'work with. Wuz ut possible again, or no?

Stanking Good Heat Seal – Turn up the heat!
Multi-purpose, humidity resistant styling spray
• Humidity resistant – Helps to ensure longer lasting style
– curly or straight
• Builds body and enhances shine – Clean, flexible styling
ingredients help provide memory and added shine
• Thermal protection – Helps prevent damage caused by
blow dryers and smoothing irons

While Tommy wuz at work an' Charlie was sleepin', Yak had been down Trelawny Gardens t'drop the sole-surviving parcel off fur un. Yak being Yak, ee'd kept a few of the little blue pills fur his own use, but the rest ov the package wuz all fur Tommy. Sally wuz still there tha' time of the day. Yak cudn' really under-stand why Tommy might need a bit of Loco Viagra, when ee had Sally. You cud say wha' y'like but Mrs Curnow, was a hot MILF at the best ov times. Yak gazed at her a bit longer than ee should really. Like Spryer ee 'ad a bit of a thing fur older, more experienced women, and well... currently there wudn' much choice on the streets of Troon.

177

'That it?' went Sally, wondering why Yak had an eye on her cleavage.

This snapped Yak out of the daze ee wuz in, and put un t'mind that ee should go back to School Lane and try an' ring his man again. Ee 'ad t'find out if they'd any idea who'd shafted um. This wuz connected t' this point on Yak's timeline. All the other buggers ee knawed seemed t'be settlin' down around un, an' ee wuz getting' worried ee might be left behind. Maturity wuz a terrible thing – or so ee reckoned - unless ut wuz lookin' at the delights of Mrs Curnow – Cougar *par excellence*.

Sally, meanwhile, put the parcel in the living room, an' didn' think very much more about ut. Her mind at tha' moment in time, wuz more on the next essay she 'ad t'write. The course had moved on a bit, and now she wuz studying some play called *The Rove*r, by Britain's first female playwright Aphra Behn. 'Twudn', in her view, the easiest ov texts t'get her adled brain around. Still, after work, she'd come back an' put in a couple ov hours on ut. She'd left instructions fur Tommy t'cook tea (well, a couple ov microwave-able meals at least) because ee'd be back after morning shift.

Maturity wuz a terrible thing in Tommy Curnow's mind, but ee wudn' s'bothered by ut when ee comed in and found the note from Sally. As well as information about what wuz needed fur tea, she also mentioned tha' Yak had brought over a parcel. Tommy wuz hopin' it might be a few used ten pound notes, but when ee opened ut up, and saw 'twas the promised magical aphrodisiac, he wuz nearnly 'bout just as happy. Tommy checked there wudn' no-one else in the house, fur after all, this wuz somethun' a man didn't want everyone t'knaw about. Ee pulled back the rest of the cellophane around the package, noticing that a few of the boxes had already been taken (Yak, ee reckoned, preparing fur the future, or else fur a glorious night with some maid from over Twilight). Tommy opened one of the packets. This didn' look like quite like the normal packets for Viagra. One of the boys had shown un their type over mine one day. Tommy went through the instructions. Moast of they wuz in Spanish and wha' looked like some weird Chinese writing, but ee cud just about make out the section in English. 'Take one pill half an hour before intercourse' it read. Then Tommy read the packet: 'Warning - Use with caution. Do not exceed prescribed dose.'

'Fuck tha',' Tommy said t'hisself. 'I want the full on Loco Mojo...'

Ee pulled out three ov the tablets and chucked them down his throat.

'Loco lover,' ee went t'hisself.

His intention wuz t'find out wha' kind ov boner ee might get, in advance ov gettin' t'work on Sally.

'Loco... Loco... Loco!'

Christ, ee wuz like Dick Trevithick in an erotic moment.

He wudn' naw fool. Ee knew their sex life needed a bit of a energy. Maybe this wuz the very thing. Tommy wudn' quite sure when the effects of these Loco tabs would kick in. How long did ut take? Did a need any kind of further stimulation? Would ut just happen – or should a spank the monkey a bit? – an' get out a couple ov' old issues ov *Razzle* or *Men Only*. Ee didn knaw an' ut didn' seem t'say anywhere on the packet. Guesswork then, ee reckoned, but ee might knaw a bit more by the time Sally got home. Ee knawed she had an assignment t'write, but then again, perhaps she might be impressed with his reinvigorated desire.

Feelin' good about hisself, Tommy went out inta' the kitchen and emptied out his flask and crowst box. For a moment, this wuz just the same as every other day – only today wuz different wudn' ut? Tommy picked up the weight of his crowst bag, and felt the gold in there. Where cud a put ut? Ee didn't particularly want Sally knawin' about ut yet. Besides, ee'd need t'do some research – find a plaace where it could be valued. Ask Charlie maybe – t'look at some site on the internet perhaps. Some dealer up the line was the best bet. Fur now, he took out the vinyl versions of his Def Leppard albums under the stereo an' hid ut behind them. Ut sat there between 'Pyromania' and 'Hysteria' – perfect rock fur the perfect bit of rock.

Just as ee wuz doin' tha', his mobile rang. Tommy looked at who 'twas. Markie Phillips' mobile.

'Y'a'right Tommy?' came Markie's voice.

'Never better,' went Tommy. 'Wozon?'

'Well – wanted t'check we wuz still on fur Friday... Press launch an' tha'...'

'Yes – still on boy... Naw problem... The Club's got ut all in hand... The lawyers are on ut. Paperwork'll be with ee tomorra' they reckon.'

'And the charity donation's ready...'

Yes. Markie wuz making a donation to the Precious Lives Appeal – fur Life-Limited Children, as well as explaining his financial commitment to the future development of Trura City Football Club.

As they spoke Tommy could feel a sensation in hisself. Ee felt his face getting' redder, his whole body energised and tha' an erection was forming in the new pants Sally had bought fur'n over Pool Market of late.

Fuckin' hell, ee wuz getting' a boner on the phone while talking t'Markie Phillips. What the hell wuz up with tha'? Tommy gave ut a side-on look in the hallway mirror – yes, definite a bit ov horn there ee nawticed in the reflection. 'Look Tommy, I think we need to have a good think about promotion from Conference National...'

'How do ee mean?'

'Well, who've we got comin' up t'play? Newport County away idn' ut? Then after tha', a fortnight later, 'tiz Bath City home...'

'Yeah... thaas' right...'

'Well, what I'm sayin' Tommy, is tha' a few words in the right direction might do ut fur us...'

'What ee mean?'

'Well, you knaw... nothun' different really than the Premiership is ut... the odd game thrown fur mutual benefit...'

The boner in Tommy's pants wuz gaining in size nicely. It wuz takin' a while fur Tommy t'catch on t'Markie's intentions. Then again, ee wuz somewhat distracted.

Suddenly, ee cottoned on t'wha' Markie wuz saying.

'Match fixing Markie? Is tha' wha' you mean?'

'Now, did I say that Tommy? I dun't think I did...'

This wuz how Markie wuz crafty.

'Well, I dun't think we should be movin' in tha' kind ov direction at all...'

There wuz a pause at the other end of the phone. Markie wuz speakin' t'somebody. A woman by the sound ov ut. Foreign-sounding. Lucky bastard. Bet she'd go fur ut widn'.

Voodoo Pilchard

'See Tommy, I got a lot ridin' on this... I have, of late, come into some merchandise – shall we say – that will make me a lot of money... Some of tha' might be put to good use fur the Club.'

Good use. Fuck. Tha' meant Markie's boys talking to some other boys up Newport County and Bath. Deals done. Hands shaken. Lips sealed.

'You do want to see Trura moving into Coca Cola League Division Two dun't ee Tommy?'

'Yes...'

'Well, I think whatever it takes is valid... not just fur us Tommy... but fur the whole ov Cornwall... Imagine the scene in Trura... Open-top bus ride down Lemon Street, inta' Boscawen Street... Fans everywhere.... Just think ov' the excitement in September when we get t'play one of the established teams: Torquay United... Crewe Alexandra... Accrington Stanley... or take on United or Chelsea in the FA Cup...'

Markie had Tommy by the ballsack here.

'We never had this conversation did we?' went Tommy.

'No,' went Markie. 'I dun't think we did...'

'You'll see to ut then?'

'I have people in places who can sort matters...' said Markie.

'Right,' went Tommy. 'That it?'

'Well not quite... Do you see much ov that boy Yak these days?'

Ah fuck, Tommy wuz thinkin'. Wozon now? There were still rumours tha' Yak had been involved in the St Day Post Office job year or two backalong.

'Na... Dun't see un much t'all,' Tommy lied. 'Why?'

'Well, a bit ov business has come to my attention of late... Just thought I might be able to put a few things his way...'

Tommy knew that wuz Markie-speak fur having a double-barrelled sawn-off shotgun against his bollocks sometime soon.

'If you see un...' mouthed Markie.

'Yeah – if I see un...' went Tommy.

'Well, I best be going... Got a lady here who now needs my full attention...'

Tommy could hear her talking in the background, an' wha' sounded like the loud caws ov a seagull or two. Down beach then, givin' 'er one.

181

'A'right. Cheers then Markie...'

Tommy pressed the cancel call button on his mobile.

Ah fuck, the magic goin' his way wuz now takin' a turn fur the worse. Right then, Tommy wuz puttin' it down t'karma and golden eggs. Ee should have declared ut then none of this might have happened. Then again, ee wuz quite enjoying getting is virility back. Yeah, this wuz how ee'd felt with Sally – when they'd first been seeing each other. Ee wuz reckoning on giving her a bit ov a surprise when she comed in later on.

In fact, Tommy wuz really in the mood for a bit ov lovin' when Sally eventually got in the house. He'd been blastin' out every power ballad goin' an' had even gone extra mile. Not only had a put the trimmer on the hairs in 'is nawse, but ee'd also given ut a tidy up down below, so 'twudn' quite s'bushy. The plaace wuz spotless, an' ee'd done a special job on the dining-room table – puttin' out candles, napkins an' the posh cutlery they never normally used, an' tha' Sally said wuz only for special occasions. Well, now ee 'ad 'is Mojo back, that wuz a special occasion in Tommy's mind – aw yes.

Ee did a check outside t'see what sort ov drilgey wuz going' out there. All had gone quiet of late with the Trelawny Chainsaw Crew, and even Mephedrone Towers opposite had gone quiet. Perhaps somethun' else wuz on the street at the moment, fur ee over there certainly wudn' doin' business like ee used t'be. Tommy reckoned there wuz nothun' ee could do right now about Markie – might as well forget about ut fur night, an' wait 'til Friday. 'Least then ee might be able t'influence the cunt. Every now and then, Tommy needed to check the egg of gold wuz still there, and 'adn' moved. This, ee did with increasing vigour as the clock ticked on to when Sally'd be back from Homebase.

Yeah, ee reckoned on tellin' her how much he fancied her in her Homebase uniform. Yeah, she cud go on about Virginia Woolf, Aphra Behn and Sylvia Plath, but in reality all she wanted wuz a bit of good lovin'. This wuz what Tommy wuz thinkin' – and when ee thought about ut, ee knew, deep down how still attractive Sally wuz. Ee knew that from the occasions when ee did take her up Institute, or over Football Club. She still had ut, even at times, if ee didn'. At that particular moment, Tommy looked back an' seen the error ov his ways. Yes – Karen

Mellow would have t'be gived up fur good. Ee 'ad 'is suspicions 'bout 'er ov late anyway.

So, how many should a take? Three seemed t'do the job earlier on. He'd got a boner s'hard an' strong as the Bassett Memorial, but then ee wuz after giving Sally somethun' a bit special. Ee'd read the books – women these days wanted multiple orgasms – not a quick wham, bam an' thank you mam. Ee popped five at first, but then took five more. Then just for luck, ee took two more. Fuckin' hell – with that on board, ee'd be like some kind of Mojo machine – the Ron Jeremy or Peter North of Camborne. How could she resist?

The answer t'tha' seemed quite obvious when Sally got on. She'd 'ad a day ov ut at work – with some couple over Barriper not happy with the worktops they provided, and the new boy off sick from Gardening. An' then the weedkiller delivery manifest wuz all wrong fur the second time this month. At first, she kept goin' on about tha' and then she wuz mullin' over the essay she had to write. Tommy wuz straight in there though, with a glass ov red wine, and the charm and sophistication ov a bloak on extra-strength Viagra. That wuz when she nawticed what ee'd done with the dining-room table. Usually, if Tommy wuz in this kind of mood, ee'd have done somethun' wrong – majorly catastrophic come t'think ov ut (like the developin' ov a pornography empire), but there wudn' much sense ov tha'.

'Thought I might get me hair done this week,' she went. 'I mean, all this time tha' Headönizm's been open – and I've barely 'ad chance t'go in there again since ut started... Jess must be wonderin' whas' on...'

'It looks nice already,' said Tommy, as they ate the Tesco's Finest microwaved Shepherd's Pie they were havin' fur tea.

'Somethun' up with you idn' there?' went Sally, smiling. Ee never paid her compliments like tha'. In her view, her hair needed doin' – but well, if Tommy liked ut – she wudn' complainun'...

Tommy wanted t'tell her about the gold-rush, but not yet, ee told hisself. If ee told her now, tha' might detract from his plans for some hot bedroom action. He pulled out another stop. Ee sat there gazin' inta' Sally's eyes – already startin' t'feel the effects of the Loco Viagra on un.

'You a'right Tommy?' Sally asked. 'You seem miles away...'

'No. I'm fine thanks,' went Tommy. 'Top ov the world, in fact...'

'Did you see that parcel Yak brought around? Funny lad ee is... Comed 'round this morning. I think ee does too many drugs that boy... There's someun' weird about the way ee d'look at me.'

'I did,' went Tommy, ignorin' moast ov wha' she wuz sayin' ov. 'It wuz some old Trura City programmes... from years back. Yak found them down Hayle Car Boot...'

The boner in Tommy's trousers had by now taken on monstrous proportions – or so ee felt. If only ee had been like this when ee wuz running Club Rhino. Well, perhaps not – with some ov the tasty boilers there - ee might have been in even more trouble if tha' were the case.

Sally got up to take the plates over to the sink fur washing up. Tommy cudn' resist ut. Otherwise ee wud have been working against the power ov the Horny Goatweed or whatever else they put in the little blue pills. Ee stood behind her at the sink and put 'is penis against her bottom, rubbing her gently. Sally cudn' quite believe wha' wuz goin' on.

'Mmmm... Someone's feeling sexy,' she said. 'Don't you want any afters?'

'I'd like you fur afters...' said Tommy breathless and husky, sounding like the Obby Stanker equivalent of Barry White.

Sally stood back a little from un, and gived un a double-take. Wuz this the same man who usually just stank of beer and fags and then sprawled out in front ov the telly t'watch football, too tired to do anything else? Physically yes, it wuz him still, but mentally, this wuz somethun' completely different. 'Twas like ee'd 'ad some sort ov personality transplant.

'You a'right Tommy?' she enquired.

Tha' wuz all Tommy needed. His eyes met hers and next thing they knew they wuz snogging like a couple of Trelawny teenagers over park. Their tongues were deep in each other, reaching and clambouring for gold. Sex Voodoo this was. Blood-sugar sex-magick. From the Gods or somethun'. They didn' have much time t'say anything t'each other. Tommy wuz just sayin' somethun' her keepin' her Homebase uniform on – and how much tha' wuz turnin' un on. Sally wuz worried. She moved t'lock the backdoor. Knawin' their luck this would be just the moment when Charlie or Jess might walk in on them.

'Let's go upstairs...' Sally said. 'Give me a minute...'

Tommy wuz left half-dressed in the living room. He elected t'put on Whitesnake's *1987* album. In his mind, ee wuz David Coverdale an' Sally his Tawny Kitaen. Just t'be sure, ee pulled out Yak's box again (that ee'd stashed behind the sofa fur now), and took another five of the blueies. Lovely. 'Twas like ee could feel the testosterone pumping around his body.

If ee wuz right, Sally wud be makin' herself look even more gorgeous. She'd be puttin' on somethun' sexy under tha' Homebase bib ov her's. Tommy decided there wuz no moment like the present so ee stripped off. Ee looked down on his body. A few months ov working below ground 'ad toned ut up a bit – t'the way ut used t'be. 'Es, not bad, ee told hisself.

'You ready?' ee shouted up.

'Almost...'

'What about your assignment?' teased Tommy.

'That'll have t'wait...'

Tommy checked below. Yeah, still hard as rock. This Viagra wuz a wonderful thing. Maybe there wuz a few quid t'be made here somewhere down the line. Not now though. No – now ee wuz goin' t'be a Celtic Love God. Ee ad is golden eggs an' now ee 'ad 'is golden member. Tommy cud feel the blood rushing around his body. Ee cud feel is heart beating faster an' faster. It wuz a nice feeling – like ee wuz young again. Like ee had no cares or worries anymore.

Then ut comed. Sally's voice.

'Ready...' she said, all teasing an' sultry like Carn Brea on a spring morning.

Tommy took a gulp ov air and climbed the staircase. If there wuz one thing ee wuz goin' t'do ee wuz goin' t'show her how much ee loved her. When ee walked inta' the bedroom, Sally's face said ut all. She hadn't seen anything like tha' fur a number ov years. Even her man Ronnie Phillips 'ad nothun' on Tommy.

'Where did ee get tha' from?' she said sexily.

'Thinking 'bout you...'

In seconds, Tommy and Sally were clasped together in a way they hadn't been fur years. Tommy felt rejuvenated, and Sally wuz wonderin' if this wuz all a bit ov a dream. But naw, Tommy wuz touchin' her in all the right places and makin' her feel wonderful. Her nipples went rock hard. Downstairs Coverdale was blasting out 'Is *this* Love?'. Within a few minutes, Tommy wuz on top ov her, finding out if *'twas*, about t'seek another kind of golden moment. Ee wuz pretty panting and puffin' by now, an' t'be honest, Sally wudn' much likin' the sound ov un. Stud, ee might now be, but ee wudn' soundin' right.

'You a'right?' she asked, lookin' up at un.

'Fine,' went Tommy.

The thing wuz ee wudn' fine. Ee cud tell by the way ee wuz breathing, and how 'is body felt. Then ut comed – a stabbing pain all the way through his chest. Tommy grabbed hisself in agony.

'What is ut?' panicked Sally.

'Dunnaw...' went Tommy. 'Me heart I think...'

With tha', Tommy collapsed on top ov her, nearnly 'bout suffocatin' Sally. She had t'push un off onta' the side ov the bed. She didn't much like the look ov 'is eyes. They wuz all glazed over like somethun' wuz seriously wrong.

'Tommy! Tommy!' she shouted, tryin' to get un back. But Tommy wudn' moving much t'all. She checked un below. The hard-on wuz still there – but 'twudn' like ee cud do anything much with ut now.

Shit. She'd warned un. The doctors had warned un. Fags. Booze. Wrong food. The wrong lifestyle. Tommy Curnow – a heart attack waitin' to happen. And now ut 'ad. She moved across the bed to where the phone wuz. This wuz normally the phone she used to moan on to Ursula about the latest bad thing Tommy'd done. Not now. She dialled 999 and asked fur the ambulance service.

'38 Trelawny Gardens, Troon, near Camborne' she said. She listened carefully to the information wanted by the dispatcher. 'I'm Sally Curnow... His wife... Ee've collapsed... Make iss will ee?... Ee idn' lookin' very good t'all...'

Knockie Thickening Glue – Makes shorter styles stand up and get noticed.
Extreme Thickening Glue, direct from Cornish mines
• Extreme thickening – A small amount provides extreme thickness and texture

Voodoo Pilchard

- Extreme hold – Firm, flexible styling agents provide a long-lasting hold
- Quick styling – Fast acting, quick drying

Charlie got the panicked call from his ma shortly afterwards. Ee, in turn, phoned Jess, who'd been workin' late at the salon: some preparatory work fur some Trelawny maid's wedding the next day – third husband. Third time lucky apparently. She wuz old enough, borrowed enough and blue enough t'make this one last a bit longer.

'I's da,' went Charlie. There wuz a seriousness t'Charlie's voice tha' she hadn' heard before. 'Ee've 'ad a bit ov a heart attack...'

This wuz one ov they shitty moments when yer world shifts its axis, and when you ent quite sure ov anything anymore. Even simple stuff becomes weird – like which way is north and wha' colour the sky is. At points like this, nothun' else much matters. Charlie forgot all his ambitions – and Jess closed up the salon as soon as she could. She had t'rush the trial bouffant fur the blushing bride – but who cared? The dream ov Headönizm didn't quite seem wha' ut was – not with her da now in the A&E department ov Treliske hospital over Trura.

Yak an' Micky were boobed up in the main waitun' room, while Charlie, Jess an' his ma were actually close t'one of the treatment bays in which the doctors and nurses were working on Tommy.

Charlie and Jess were still out ov breath from rushing over.

They looked at their ma. Suddenly, she seemed old, like her whole world wuz cavin' in on her. 'Twas as if her own personal mineshaft 'ad collapsed. Both ov um hugged her.

'So, what happened?' went Charlie.

Sally knew this question wuz goin' t'be tricky. She didn' really want t'tell either ov um tha' Tommy an' her were engaged in a moment ov carnal ecstasy before ee keeled over, from well... being on top ov her, and er... in her. Sally wuz feeling guilty because she didn't knaw any better, an' wuz thinkin' that 'twas her fault fur turnin' un on too much. Obviously, 'is heart cudn' take ut anymore. She wudn' be puttin' on that set she'd got from the Ann Summer's party Brenda Penhallurick had down number 30 las' month.

'The ambulance people were brilliant,' said Sally. 'They shocked un back inta' consciouness – and gived un oxygen... I'd seen ut on *Casualty* how they do ut – but 'twas amazin' in real life.'

'Ee knaws whaas' goin' on then?'

'Aw es... Ee wuz conscious an' tha... time they took un out on the stretcher... Aw – you should have seen ut... Everyone wuz out wishin' un well an' tha'... Even Arnie Crago (back from a bit of institutional therapy, an' being looked after by his sister from the up-the-line) comed t'have a gake,'

What Sally hadn't told um wuz tha' she'd got dressed by the time the ambulance had got there, an' the boys from the ambulance crew wuz a bit puzzled why the bloakey they were resuscitating had a massive boner on. Sally'd actually tried t'hide ut, but 'twudn' really helpin' her put un in the recovery position, so she had t'style ut a bit. Thaas' prob'ly the reason now tha' Tommy wuz feelin' his knob wuz somewhat bruised an' battered.

'Ee wuz tellin' me tha' ee loved me... reachin' out fur my arm while ee wuz on the stretcher inside the ambulance... 'Twas lovely. We wuz here in naw time. They dun't half speed along – they new ambulances...'

As his ma wuz sayin' all ov this, Charlie mind went t'all the fuckin' daft things his da had done – even when his own GP 'ad told un t'slaw down a bit.

'That'll be it with Crofty then,' said Jess, but she hardly needed t'say ut. With this kind of condition, 'twudn' likely ee wuz goin' to be back down in the levels very soon.

'What are um doin' now?' asked Charlie.

'Tests – I think... They got un connected t'a drip and they'm monitoring his heart... The doctor said they'd give me an update soon.'

Outside, in the waiting room, Micky and Yak didn' knaw wha' t'do, or say. Micky wuz lookin' at the various Sexually Transmitted Infection posters tha' were pinned up, an' Yak wuz pacin' up an' down – too scared t'look at the posters in case ee 'ad any.

'What's up with you?' went Micky.

'Nothun'.'

Yak knew tha' what 'ad just transpired might be somethun' t'do with the gear ee'd given t'Tommy. Ee wudn' goin' t'say

188

anything though. Nawbody wuz puttin' two an' two together – not yet at least. The other reason ee wuz agitated wuz that this wuz a further blaw t'his dreams of startin' 'is EBGB club. For certain, Tommy Curnow wudn' goin' t'be in naw fit state t'sort anything out, that wuz even if the poor fucker even made ut back home t'Trelawny again. There and then, that 'ad t'be held in mind.

'Tattoo business goin' a'right?' asked Yak.

A daft fuckin' question tha', thought Micky. 'Course 'twas.

'Yeah – more clients all the time...'

'Right...'

There wuz another minute ov silence, before Micky asked, 'Eh Yak – Is Charlie gettin' Balance back t'gether again? I mean...'

Yak looked at un.

'Why?'

'Dunnaw... Just interested.'

Yeah, reckoned Yak. Just interested because ee prob'ly wanted a piece ov ut. But even Yak knawed tha' Charlie didn' really want him back in on keyboards, decks and samples an' shit. If anything wuz goin' t'appen (which clearly it wudn'), 'twas goin' t'be classic rock - no nu-metal, emo or rap-rock fusion shit.

'I've talked to un about ut...' revealed Yak. 'I mean with Bev back on the scene...'

'And?'

'Nothun' doin'...'

'Right.'

'Charlie's not inta' ut at all...'

'I see.'

At this moment, Jess comed out inta' the waiting room. She wuz tearful and upset, knowin' tha' her da wuz in some state in there. Micky moved t'comfort an' hug her tight. She wuz blubberin' big-time, squalin' an' shakin' with worry.

'I's alright... I's alright,' Micky wuz goin' – but 'twudn' t'all.

'I don't want un t'die...' Jess said.

'He's not going to...' went Micky, gently soothing her arms, tryin' to calm her.

Thaas' the way 'tis in these kind ov situations. You can be strong in there, an' then when you get t'think about ut, and wha' might happen, y'lose ut. Wha' wuz ut Charlie said on the road: No. 6 - Keep family ties goin'. Tha' seemed more important than ever now. And what do ee do? Y'put yerself in there dun't ee? Tha' wuz wha' Yak wuz doin' now – thinkin' ov his own ma back home in Troon.

Inside, the doctor wuz askin' t'see Sally.

'Can I talk to you for a bit Mrs Curnow – privately?'

The doctor indicated that what ee wuz about t'say wuz fur her ears only.

'I's alright...' said Sally. 'Ee's me son... Anything you want t'say, you'n say in front ov him...'

'Are you quite sure?'

She nodded. The doctor looked a bit surprised. From his accent, he wuz clearly from South Africa. Over in Cornwall, for a bit of OE - overseas experience. Funny ol' world wudn' ut Charlie reckoned. A hundred years ago – 'twas all the Cornish from Troon, Camborne and Redruth headin' out there to mine for gold an' diamonds, and now, twas they lookin' fur somethun' back here.

'Well... we did some tests... Do you know if your husband was on any kind of medication?'

'Medication? Fur what?'

'Just checking – that's all...'

'Why?'

'I have to be honest with you Mrs Curnow. We found high levels of an unusual chemical in his blood and urine. We've sent it down to the lab for further analysis but we believe it to be a stimulant.'

'What drugs?' went Sally. 'My Tommy wudn' on drugs...'

Her face wuz growin' inta' an Atlantic storm.

'Listen to what ee've got to say ma,' said Charlie.

'Look – your husband's heart is fairly healthy. But this stimulant – it was in extremely large quantities in his body – so much so that his heart-rate would have increased to a dangerous level. That is what caused him to collapse.'

'What kind of stimulant?' asked Charlie.

The doctor looked slightly embarrassed for them.

'I can't be certain, but it looks like your father has had a Viagra overdose.'

Charlie looked at his ma.

'Is tha' right?' ee asked ov er.

'Well, before ut happened, ee wuz unusually... em... sexy...'

Fuck, Charlie thought. Now ut wuz all beginnin' t'make sense.

'I'll leave you to chat,' said the doctor. 'One thing is clear though... we strongly suggest that he gives up alcohol and cigarettes right away – or he may be back in here again very soon. Presently, his liver function is not good and his lungs are also damaged from tobacco inhalation. I'll be honest with you. Both aren't good for his heart. He needs to cut back...'

Charlie's ma looked more embarrassed than concerned about Tommy's alcohol and tobacco intake.

'Charlie, dun't say anything t'Jess... will you? Or anybody else?'

Ah fuck. Here ee wuz – Charlie Curnow – in Treliske with his ma covering up a Viagra overdose just experienced by his fuckwit ov a feyther. Tha' and 'is body wuz screwed up with too much booze an' fags.

NFC see.

Normal fur Camborne.

'Didn' a read the label? You gotta' be careful with tha' kind of stuff...'

'How do you know?'

'Stories ma. Y'hear 'bout ut on the road... Enhancers an' tha'....'

'Enhancers?'

'Yeah – stuff that'll make ee up fur ut all night...'

Charlie knew Spryer ordered out for this kind of shit all the time – especially with some ov the MILFs ee liked t'keep in contact with in Holland.

'I didn' knaw ee even 'ad any in the first plaace...' said his ma.

'Is this the first time ee wuz like tha'?'

'Well...' said Charlie's ma. She 'ad a good think about their sex life. Then she concluded 'What sex life?'.

'Yes.'

'Then the packets must be home there somewhere...'

'What packets?'

'Ee must've got them from somewhere. Has a been t'the doctors lately?'

'Oh Charlie... You know ee dun't trust doctors... Ee wun' have got ut from 'is GP...'

Sally's mind thought back t'events earlier tha' day.

'Aw... Yak brought somethun' round. A package...'

Oh fuck. 'Twas all makin' sense now. They two'd been thick as thieves ov late. Yak 'adn' said anything though. That'all be it though – an' Tommy enough ov a tool t'try anything t'keep his pecker up all night. Ee'd be havin' words. But then, Yak wudn' be doin' ut fur nothun', so wha' wuz ee gettin' back from the deal?

As Charlie wuz processing all ov this, one of the triage nurses comed out. She seem'd t'recognise Charlie. She did a double-take on un.

'Are you tha' Charlie Curnow? Used t'be in the Jimi Hendrix tribute band?'

'Yeah, I am...' went Charlie, embarrassed.

'Aw... I seen ee down Bunters one time... a few years back. They say you been on *X-Factor*... Is tha' right?'

'Shame t'say ut – but yeah, I wuz...' said Charlie.

'Oooh... we dun't get many famous people in here. Tha' your dad is ut?'

'Yeah,' said Charlie.

'Cheeky so-and-so idn' a... Bit ov a scare dun't seem to have hurt un any...'

Charlie cud imagine wha' kind of banter ee'd have been havin' with her. Bet the tool didn' reveal ee'd been on Viagra though.

'He's conscious – you can speak with him if you like, but only fur a few minutes. Right now, he needs rest, and we still need to monitor his heart-rate...'

'Ee'll be stayin' in here then?' asked Charlie's ma.

'Aw yes. Fur a few days... just t'keep an eye on un. Normal procedure that.'

The nurse parted the curtain, and there wuz Tommy Curnow – Troon legend - flat on his back, lookin' a bit rough.

'A'right?' the tool went.

'Oh Tommy... what are ee like?' his ma went, slobbering kisses all over un, an' holding his hand s'tight she might constrict the blood flow t'the rest ov his body.

'Da... glad t'see you'm in the land ov the living...'

'Dunnaw wha' comed over me,' said Tommy, all innocent, like butter – or a Viagra tablet – wudn' melt in 'is mouth.

Charlie and his ma looked at each other.

'Do um knaw? They ent told me much...'

'You gotta' stay in here a few days Tommy. They want t'check everything's back t'normal...'

'Cen't do that. The Tigers've got a Press Launch on Friday night. I gotta' be there...'

'Da. You ent goin' t'be there. You gotta' take ut easy...'

A flicker of annoyance ran through Tommy's eyes. Ee wudn' the type t'take all ov this easy. Ee thought about his golden egg back behind the Def Leppard albums. His mind wuz running t'private nurses an' the kind ov' enhanced mobile care tha' would allow un t'take his position in the directorial box.

'I'll be alright... honest...' said Charlie's da.

'Tommy Curnow,' his ma shouted. You've had a major scare... You'll be signed off work fur a bit...'

Bugger. Tommy's mind raced back to the 450 fathom level an' the gold rush there. Ee wudn' goin' t'let tha' slip away from un. Some other cunt like Timmy Pascoe or Trudge would be in there, finding even bigger nuggets an' smugglin' they up t'grass. Ee cudn' let tha' happen.

'We'll tell the boys on core...' said Sally. 'They'll want t'see you right...'

'Es – let Crofty knaw wun't ee...?'

'Dun't ee worry 'bout a thing...'

'Where's Jess?' Charlie's da mumbled.

'She'll be in in a minute. She's out there with Micky an' Yak...'

'Yak here is a?'

'Yeah,' said Charlie. 'Let's hope ee edn' got any more packages fur ee eh da...?'

'What ee mean?'

'You knaw wha' I'm talkin' about...'

Charlie's da smiled at Sally. It ud taken a couple ov seconds, but ee wuz now realisin' they knew 'bout his erectile 'support'.

'I only wanted t'...'

'I knaw Tommy... I knaw...

'...get ut back to where we once wuz...'

This wuz how the tool could be touchin' at times, and how

you cudn' help but like un. Sally wuz huggin' un good an' proper, like she'd never heard of feminism an' Virginia Woolf. Ut seemed like she'd forgotten about the likes ov Club Rhino and his erotic movie empire as well. Karen Mellow seemed t'have disappeared out ov her memory too.

Charlie tried t'bring un back t'reality a little bit.

'So how many did ee take?'

Tommy blinked as if ee wuz countin' the little blue pills.

'Only a couple...'

'Couple?'

'That dun't sound like wha' the doc is saying... They tested yer blood.'

Tommy 'ad wondered why his arm hurt inside his elbow.

'Might've been a few more... Cen't remember now... Me mind's gone a bit fuzzy see...'

'Tommy,' said Sally. 'The doctor says you'm goin' t'have t'cut back on the booze and fags... or you'll be back in here again...'

'Did a?' went Charlie's da.

Reality hit home. Charlie cud see un calculatin' tha' sippin' orange juice while watchin' some 80s' tribute band up Institute wudn' be his idea of scintillating fun.

'We'll leave ee be fur now...' said his ma. 'I'm just glad you've come round again Tommy...'

'Yeah – Jess an Micky'll wanna' see ee...'

'Send in Yak will ee, as well?' asked Charlie's da.

Charlie nodded. Ee pulled the curtain back, an' waited a while fur Charlie's ma t'kiss un better.

In the waitin' room, Jess wuz still sobbin'. She looked like she'd been pulled through a Cornish hedge-row backwards. Her hair an' make-up wuz all over the place. Still, nawbody from Headönizm or any ov her clients wuz goin' t'see her here wuz um?

From Charlie's expression, Yak knawed 'zactly what 'ad happened.

'A'right is a?'

'Yeah – naw thanks t'you... y'tool.'

'Charlie – I only got wha' he wanted...'

'Didn't ee warn un?'

'No need to. 'Tis all on the packets like. I's not my fault ee went an' took too many...'

Voodoo Pilchard

'Too many? The tool overdosed on um...'

'Really?'

'Yeah – really.'

Jess and Micky were goin' in now.

'Ee want t'see you as well Yak,' went Charlie's ma.

'You'd better go,' said Charlie. 'What I want t'knaw is the deal you two got goin' on though.'

'I's nothun' bad Charlie. Listen, I wanted t'take the lease of Club Rhino off un. Thaas' all. Wanted to start a rock club up see: a Cornish CBGBs. An' well, 'twas all goin' t'plan... sort of... an' yer da asked me about some extras – enhancers like – to see un sorted...'

'I should have bleddy left you in Jimmy Pengelly's shed... locked the door an' thrawn away the key.'

'Na... Charlie... Look, if the band wuz startin' again then...'

'Then...?'

'Well, there'd be no need wud there? This wudn' 'ave happened...' shouted Yak, startin' t'feel the pressure.

Charlie cudn' believe what ee wuz hearing.

'Everyone's askin' Charlie... Even Micky wanted t'know...'

Out of 'is side vision, Charlie caught sight ov 'is ma. She'd been strong so far. But now that the crisis point wuz over, she seemed t'be losin' ut a bit. Charlie didn' have the energy t'yip on t'a tool like'Yak anymore. 'Is ma needed un. Ee let Yak go inta' the treatment area.

'You'm some good t'me...' went 'is ma.

Charlie hugged her.

Just as ee sat down, ee felt 'is phone vibrate with a new message. it wuz Bev askin' how 'twas all goin'. She phoned him about ten times while they'd been in triage. Ee texted her back, sayin' that 'is da wuz doing okay now, an' not t' worry.

Inside, Jess hugged her da so hard she nearnly 'bout knocked over the drip stand.

'Good t'see ee maid,' went Tommy. 'A'right Micky? Think I'd rather have one ov yer tribal tattoos done than have this bleddy stuff in me arm...'

Last t'enter wuz Yak.

'A'right Tommy?' went Yak sheepishly. 'Sorry t'hear 'bout all this...'

'Cen't be helped.' went Tommy, 'cen't be helped... Time-ov-

195

life thing they d'reckon. Dun't ee worry my bewdies, I'll be
back Crofty quicker than duckshit...'

Micky and Jess gave glances to each other. After this kind ov
experience, ut didn't look like tha' wud be happenin' tha' soon.
Fur the next fifteen minutes, there wuz a lot ov nodding' and
sympathetic noises comin' from everyone – with Tommy doin'
his best t' pretend everything wuz normal – except fur the fact
ee wuz in A&E an' 'ad on a hospital gown revealing all the glory
ov his hairy arse.

In the end, Micky an' Jess ad t'go. Their car-park time wuz
up wudn' ut?

'You'd better make 'iss maid. I dun't want ee t'get done.
They'm buggers fur ut up here too so I d'hear... Do ee soon as
look at ee, eh Micky?'

Jess an' Micky hugged un goodbye, and went t'have a word
with the nurse. t'see if there wuz anything else to knaw. As Yak
wuz leaving though, Tommy made a quick grab fur his wrist.

'Aw Yak boy – proper job... I mean, I'll knaw not t'take
s'many next time... Caw d'hell – the boner I got wuz near nuff
the size of Godrevy... Get any more can ee?'

Yeah – this wuz Tommy Curnow. Now as much a fuckin'
loser addict as some of the rest ov um back Trelawny.
Mephedrone. Viagra. Wha' difference wuz there t'all?

''Spect so. Not right away like... but soon.'

'Righton...'

'Look I've been thinkin'... 'bout the Club... I knaw we gotta'
sort ut out. Well, as fortune would have ut, I comed inta' a bit
ov a nest-egg before I ended up in here... an' well, that'll pay
me debts off like... You got the money though – fur me?'

'Na... The deal tha' I 'ad is off.'

'Wha' ebm' ee got any of the song-writing money left?'

'Na.... not anymore...'

Yak 'ad blown ut all on the coke deal.

'Well look,' said Tommy, his faculties quickly returning to
un, 'here's the new deal. I'll keep the lease – but you'n do whatever you want with the Club – just give me a cut ov what you
make.... What ee reckon?'

'Sounds good Tommy.'

They shook on ut, Tommy easing his hand out of the crisp
medicinal sheets.

'One more thing though Yak,' said Tommy conspiratorially. 'These fuckers want t'keep me in fur a week... No can do. I got stuff I gotta' do at Trura City. Can ee see t'getting' me outta' here by Friday? Can ee do ut?'

'Reckon so... ef I bring the van up...'

'Dun't tell Sal, or Charlie, or Jess though... None ov um mind.'

'Dun't worry...'

'Remember,' said Tommy. 'You dun't knaw shit...'

Ee touched his nose, indicating the importance of the secret.

'I dun't knaw shit,' went Yak in response – soundin' like a robot.

Outside A&E, as they all gathered to go home, the triage nurse came up t'Charlie an' handed him a piece ov paper.

'Thaas' me number,' she went, flickering her eyelashes at him, 'if y'fancy doin' somethun' sometime... give me a call...'

Charlie looked down at the number and her name: Jody.

'Y'lucky, lucky bastard Curnow,' went Yak, who fancied Jody quite a bit by the look obm'.

'Me? I'm taken,' went Charlie. 'You'n give her a ring though... I reckon a good woman like she might sort you out.'

No-one said a lot on the way back down t'Trelawny. Ut'd been one ov they sort ov days. Everyone wuz respondin' t'texts or answerphone messages askin' 'bout Tommy.

Tommy meanwhile, wuz in the land of nod, dreamin' about golden eggs an' little blue pills. Tha', an' in twenty years time, how Trura City wud be winning the Premiership.

Peller's Product Spray – Creating a style that lasts all day just got easier.

Finishing Spray

• Rapid drying – A unique blend of magical styling agents reduces the dry time

• Stong hold – Powerful, flexible polymers help provide strong, long-lasting hold

• Clean hold – Spray can be layered onto hair without stiffness of dulling build-up; conditioners and shine enhancers help impart high-gloss and reduce static

So, fur one and all then - the *real* voodoo...

Ironically, or perhaps predictably, 'twas Bev who eventually found out about ut. Her destiny. That wuz a long way off – from triage in Treliske, an' the golden-laced mineral belts ov Crofty, but she wud become the Witchfinder General s't'speak. She wuz the Van Helsing who exposed ut all, found out the truth and combated evil head on. She wuz the one finally brought in as an 'expert'.

So, how come? For happenin' it wuz – even as his da lay in a hospital bed.

Alright then. How the hell did ut happen?

Charlie didn' really knaw. Maybe 'twas the Pilchard's graffiti inspirin' her, or maybe, just maybe, 'twas the other way round: her somehow inspirin' the graffiti. Either way, some shit wuz goin' down tha' Charlie wuz only t'find out about later. In a way, 'twas a serious case of stalking un. Like Twitter on acid. Nothun' like Jody – the nurse over Treliske, or tha' big maid with the boob-tube cleavage up Troon Football Club – but somethun' much more calculating an' disturbing. In another way, 'twas more like the sheer delight ov revenge. Then again, she wuz workin' with real evil; one cosmic force ov destruction happily joinin' with another on the streets of Obby Stanker Country.

Wha' wuz the score then?

Well, ut 'adn' been her just watchin' too many *Twilight* films like half ov the female teen goth-style vampires on Trelawny. Aw naw. See, her family had always had magic run through them hadn't they? Tha' Charlie did know. Accordin' to her mother, thaas' how they'd survived the Nazi occupation, and then after them, the Russians. Thaas' how they'd got through Communism, before Solidarity, Lech Wał sa and the EU opening up borders an' travel. Magic see, in the forests of Quidzin. Snow-fields there, and dark, Northern magic. And then the move to Cornwall – with her father to another place of magic. Old places. Places filled with powerful energies. Ley-lines perhaps. The Celtic dawn. Standing stones. Little people. Faeries. 'Twas only then a short step t'her reading up on Cornish Wicca, to a wider interest in the Craft. Aw yes.

So she had crossed a continent – east to west. Now she would cross an ocean east to west. Go to the home of modern rock music – the blues of New Orleans. Guitars and whiskey. Delta blues an' Dixieland. Boogie-Woogie an' Muddy Waters. John

Voodoo Pilchard

Lee Hooker an' Levees breaking. Elvis an' Mardi Gras. Hendrix an' Howlin' Wolf. Aw yes, all the history ov rock wuz there. See music wuz born there. That wuz the home ov rock 'n' roll but also the home ov magic. And there, more powerful forces could shape destinies, help or hinder life. There, might be found demons, elementals, vampires, goblins... There, could be found Vèvès, Spirals and pentagrams. From all ov this came the triangle of revelation: the three realms ov spirit, energy and body, and from that, the three dolls – the so-called *gris-gris*.

So – with new power from her new relationship – she had dabbled hadn't she? And while ee rose t'new glories, she wuz there beside him – controlling operations – doing whatever needed t'be done. Ee'd even set her up in a lair – a place to practice her dark arts. From her tower, she could watch all life, control it, and manipulate it, just as she wished. Inside it – so they found out later - she shaped her world.

There, she drew symbols. They found them later on the inside walls. Symbols scratched into the paint: ritual drums, Agwe-Taroyo, Ogu-Badagri, symbols for collecting energy, those for the Goddess Erzulie, and finally, those for the God Damballah-Wédo.

There, she might concoct potions. From the ocean would come the desired hallucinogens. She collected them on the beach at night. These were the forces to alter minds, take journeys, and open new doors.

There, could be the ritual creation ov charms and amulets. *Ouanga* would make grant desires, and confound one's enemies and those who had betrayed you. Her new faith had been born of a slave community, and what had she been – what had her people been across European history? Nothing but slaves too: flower-pickers, abattoir-workers, and recyclers fur New Europe's shit. She would no longer be slave – but something else instead.

There, she could create.

So, there were three dolls wudn' there?

Three kinds of pain then: an evil trinity.

The first wuz fur the abasement of the spirit. You sewed a doll out ov black fabric – an' filled ut with organic material. In this case, 'twas heather and gorse from Croft Common close to Charlie's plaace. You cut a slit in the back and sprinkled sharp pepper in ut. Then y'wrote your victim's name on a piece ov paper, and slid that inta' the slit too. You closed the slit with a piece of wire and bent the doll's arms sharply backwards, fastenin' its hands together. In this way, y'made sure yer victim was helpless. No guitar-playin' or song-writing now baby. Finally, you placed the doll in a kneeling position, facing a corner. This way the voodoo works to manoeuvre the victim into a helpless situation and rob them ov their vital energies. Accordin' t'Bev, there were a few dolls similar to these found in the walls of old Cornish cottages years ago. And even these days, during renovations, you might find one or two lurking.

The second wuz fur the destruction ov energy. For this, the *Boker* (thaas' the person making the doll), needed a photograph an' a few hairs of the targeted person. You cut a human figure from thin black paper and attached the photograph with needle and thread to the heart area of the silhouette. The hairs are then glued to the head. Next, the figure if left to decay and as the figure slowly rots away, so the victim loses the will to live and falls more and more prey to insanity. Well, she had heaps ov pictures ov Charlie, and then well, fur hair, there wuz Headönizm wudn' there? Despire some initial resistance, Charlie wuz now getting' his split end dealt with in there – s'long as Kayleigh an' not his sister wuz' doin' the cuttin'. Hair off his head would be no problem. Just watch and wait – thaas' all.

The third wuz the moast powerful, and for the nulling ov the spirit. This wuz needle magic see. Not Micky's tattoos though. Oh no. You make a doll out of soft Cornish clay, bearing all the characteristics of the person you wish to harm. If possible, y'get hair from the victim, or a small piece of his clothing (Even better - she 'ad one of Charlie's still sweat-ridden towels from a Purple Haze gig). You work something of tha' inta' the clay. This enlivens the doll see. All is ready for what needs to be undertaken. Then you shoot the concentrated, negative emotional load into the doll, piercing the image with sharp needles. You'd probably call them pins. Once the whole of the clay doll is pierced in this manner, then it will lead t'the total destruction of the victim. Such a curse wuz best enacted by night in the waning moon, or in the hours governed by the planet Mars. Her lair – even with its disruptive intermittent light – was ideal for watching the sky.

Voodoo Pilchard

And wha' do um say?

Tha' there's a thin line between love an' hate.

'Es.

So, what wuz the doll-maker's name?

You d'knaw her well enough. Like Charlie, y'first seen her walkin' up t'Troon through Beacon like the old man on the cover ov Led Zeppelin *IV* - only with shoppin' bags from Tesco. Thaas' when ee fell fur her. Between Bev the first time 'round and Bev the second time 'round.

In electric pastyland, she wuz Voodoo Chile, Child and Queen, and her name wuz Yeugen Zbarashchenko.

Logan Stone Spray – It's about time for a hairspray that works fast as you need it.

Working Spray

• Rapid drying – A unique blend of styling agents reduces the dry time

• Flexible Hold – Workable and balanced polymers provide a long-lasting hold

• Clean hold – Spray can be layered onto hair without stiffness or dulling build-up; conditioners and shine enhancer help impart high gloss and reduce static

There were several important missions on tha' week in Obby Stanker Country. The first was bein' undertaken by the various incarnations of the 'shadowy' and elusive Pilchard. The original Pilchard, 'ad upped 'is game 'adn' a? 'Twas nearnly 'bout 'zactly wha' Micky had predicted – that the by now 'legendary' artist would develop a few more high-profile pieces. Word wuz spreadin' quickly now. One 'ad gone up within a couple ov days ov Tommy's incident, an' Charlie an' Micky'd gone 'round t'see ut. If South Crofty wudn' high profile enough fur'n, then this new piece wuz a work of plain genius. Ut had gone up on the side of an industrial estate down the bottom end of Camborne, by Treswithian. The plaace had started life as a dairy back in the 1980s, but had long since been abandoned, now tha' all the milk comed from up the line. Ut was made of that kind of knocked-up galvanised steel that characterised that particularly – ahem - innovative period of industrial architecture so to speak – forming the perfect canvas. Not only tha', but

201

ut wuz a heaven spot too – cars pullin' off the A30 onto the roundabout there were bound t'see ut, but ut could also be seen goin' the other way – so any despondent emmets slowly trekking their caravans t'the east cudn' help but nawtice ut as well. The amazin' thing about ut wuz uts enormous size. 'Twas the same style an' everything – but the work took up one of the whole panels on the side of the unit.

'Ee's gettun' better...' went Micky with some degree ov satisfaction tha' ee'd been there from the start, an' had one piece already installed in his Camborne Ink emporium.

Ee wuz right. Not only wuz the piece imitating the Pilchard's original stencil, but the fish had been filled in – with wha' looked like a sort of street take on Celtic knotwork. The black and blue theme remained (this was the hall-mark ov an original), but had been highlighted with other colours. Shit, this wuz the sort of thing you cudn' just throw up. You'd need ladders an' a team t'help. Charlie looked on with a kind ov awe at what 'ad been created. This confirmed that the Pilchard cudn' be a lone worker. Neither wuz a no ordinary fool with a couple ov cans ov spray paint.

'I'm getting' some pictures,' went Micky. 'This is it mate. I'm settin' up a website... Maybe then, ee'll contact me... Yeah – then sort out a book later on.'

'You reckon? Looks to me like ee wants t'remain anonymous.'

'Mark my words Curnow – in a few years time, no bugger'll be heading straight t'St Ives fur the Tate. They'll be stoppin' off here in Camborne... t'see the work ov an urban legend...'

Other Pilchard graffiti wuz continuing t'develop on the streets around the town – but accordin' t'Micky – who wuz now the world's leading expert on his work, they weren't originals. Besides, whoever tha' crew were, didn't have the same boldness as the real Pilchard. Ee wuz creatin' art, whereas they wuz just buggerin' about. That said though, the Pilchard wuz rapidly creatin' a new identity fur young people in the area.

'I forgot t'tell ee... There's some bloakey up Pool Market – on the skate stall there – an' ee's pushin' Voodoo Pilchard hoodies. Shit design an' tha' – but ee d'reckon ee've sold 'bout a hundred in the past fortnight... I told un t'take ut outside Trura City fur the final game ov the season – sell um in the car park like...

Make a mint.'

'You got a tattoo design lined up yet then?' asked Charlie.

''Course mate... No-one's asked fur one yet... but 'tes only a matter ov time...'

Charlie glanced up at the street mural again. Whatever people said about the Pilchard – and ee thought back t'when ee first saw a piece, back at Centenary Chapel – the artist had brought some passion back to the area that wuz sorely lackin' before. Pride maybe, identity or somethun'. Maybe ut 'ad been there before when the likes ov Condurrow and Grenville 'ad been workin'. They'd touched on ut a bit with Balance. This pilchard design though, this piece ov street art wuz allowing people – both young an' old – t'claim somethun' back. Fur one thing, 'twudn' the fuckin' Eden Project fur change, or eco-homes or surf-pods that no fucker cud afford anyway – or the latest shite initiative t'bring prosperity back t'Cornwall. 'Twas a tide tha' no fucker really seemed able t'resist. 'Mean, MK, the Stannary and Trescothick 'ad all had a go, but there just didn' seem the will sometimes. Maybe, 'twas too late – the dam 'ad already been broken – and the annihilation allowed t'spread. Tha' wuz one reason Cornwall was now officially shit. Under Labour, Scotland, Wales an' Northern Ireland 'ad all gained devolved power. Now the Tories were back in, a devolved Cornwall seemed even less likely than under the previous lot.

'Gotta' go,' went Charlie.

Micky gived un a glance, then ee remembered the ledger on the desk. Kayleigh wuz givin' un a trim up Headönizm tha' morning.

'Dunnee trust Jess then?'

'In my experience,' went Charlie. ''Tis best not t'let anyone from yer family do anything like tha' to ee...'

Charlie said ut with conviction.

''Mean, would you let anyone from your family do a tattoo on you?'

'Fair enough,' said Micky. 'I wudn' let um near me. Let's go then...'

This mission wuz unfortunately very much related t'the second mission happenin' tha' day. The one thing Markie Phillips 'ad these days wuz power. Ee cud do whatever the fuck ee wanted. Ef Charlie had knawn, then ee'd have thought of road les-

Alan M. Kent

son No.10 – Know your enemy. But Markie'd come a long way from sawn-offs an' stockings over 'is head. Ef ut meant building a plaace in some 'green field' site where ee shouldn't, then a few notes ov higher denominations in the right direction would put the planning committee on 'is side. Buildin' wuz just another string to 'is crooked bow. A little bit ov arson wuz nicely puttin' rid t'the competition on Obby Stanker too. Ef ut meant keeping his current squeeze sweet, then consider ut done. Thaas, more or less wuz wha' wuz on.

That little find ov high-grade cocaine down Gwithian beach had really set un up nicely ov late. Yeah, ee had a few mules distributin' ut across Cornwall. Good sales too, down Penzance an' over St Ives – as well as the usual in Redruth, Camborne an' Newquay. Fuck Yak. Tha' tool wuz too weak t'do anything 'bout ee now. An' well, ef y'decided t'work in tha' kind ov business, well, y'cudn' go inta' like a fuckin' innocent. Y'had t'be tooled up with the manpower an' weaponry – else you may get stung – 'zactly like wha' happened t'Yak. And who wuz Yak anyway? Just some goon who'd helped un along the way.

The only thing nigglin' ov un, at the back ov his mind wuz ef Yak put two-an'-two together an' decided t'grass un up – an' tell the police 'bout that little job back St Day. Same thing with Curnow see. Only ee seemed t'knaw 'bout Clifford Mellow. Well, come t'think ov ut, then there wuz Trescothick, Ally – an' tha' tosser Davey too. Come t'think ov ut – ee 'ad quite a few enemies out there. Still, the point wuz tha' Markie 'ad enough money t'watch an' monitor all ov those cunts. Yeah – ee cud be their Big Brother. So thaas' wha' a set up didn' a? Ee knew the crack on Tommy Curnow – but also knew ol' man Curnow'd be makin' the press launch.

But then, Markie wuz pullin' down dark forces wudn' a? Yeah – ee'd get whatever she needed. How cud a put ut? Well, like all the Cornish before un, ee 'ad a little bit ov magic on his side didn' a?

So thaas' why his boys 'ad been watchin' Headönizm very fuckin' closely. Ee already knawed Curnow and Micky 'ad gone off somewhere tha' morning – but ee also knew they'd be back. Ut wudn' take much – only fur Curnow just t'pop in there. There wuz a difficulty ee knew. Curnow, being fuckin' Curnow wuz a bit of rocker wudn' a? Gettin' a fuckin' short back an' sides or a Grade One buzz cut wudn' an option fur the cunt. These days ee wuz lookin' a bit like a younger Chris Cornell or Eddie Vedder. But then Markie knew the ego on un too – an' now tha' ee wuz back with tha' posh bit from over Trura, ee knew ee'd want t'be lookin' good. So ee'd told his boys, that ee didn' care how long ut took, just keep watchin' – and when ee went in, pop in yerselves fur a bit of a trim too. Now, when Jess founded Headönizm, she didn't have a clue that the plaace wud be under this kind of micro-scrutiny. And her, well, she wuz normally s'dizzy with the customers an' products an' tha', tha' she didn' even nawtice the salon wuz being 'monitored' on a daily basis.

The two grunts didn' quite get the mission really. They wuz more used t'kickin' in doors, makin' sure unruly customers paid up, or of late, carrying sweeteners up the line t' Newport County an' Bath City, than on this caper.

'Why the fuck d'Markie wun't a piece of Curnow's fuckin' hair?' they wuz goin'. 'Dun't make sense t'me.'

Anyway, in spite ov the fuckin' three weeks ov waitin' they'd 'ad in Troon – parking their several different vehicles in various locations in Fore Street, so as not t'be nawticed, finally the wanker Curnow pulled up in his old Peugeot didn' a? Ee an' Micky got out and walked straight in the salon.

'We dun't even knaw if he's goin' t'get a trim like...'

'Maybe the cunt's goin' in fur a tat or a tan...'

Na. Fulla' ego the cunt might be, but ee wudn' the type fur one ov Micky's tats, and neither ov um cud see un in the tanning booth.

This mission wuz go then.

Both ov um got out of the van, an' crossed over t'the shop. Inside, Curnow wuz already in a chair, bein' dealt with by the maid who they now understood t' be called Kayleigh, Mel an' Jess wuz ut the desk. 'Twas actually a bit unusual fur three bloaks t'come in at the same time, o'course. Jess had been a bit distracted ov late – wha' with her da an' then her idea fur a Cornish hair an' beauty products range – but she managed to raise a smile.

'Morning gentlemen,' she said. 'What can we do fur you?'

'Bit ov a trim,' one of the grunts went.

'Me too,' said the other.

'Well, Mel'll do you – and if you'd like t'follow me...'

Instantly, Mel wuz flirtin' with um. Yeah – they looked a bit rough, but they looked muscley enough. 'Mean, that wuz one of yer jobs wudn' ut? Give out a bit of flirt – and then, well, they might come back. Ut didn' mean like she wuz goin' t'cheat on Kelv or anythin'. One ov the grunts wuz reckoning tha' ee'd knawed her face from somewhere – some film ee'd watched on the internet. She looked like some Porn actress ee reckoned, but ee didn't say anything though.

'Ooo – y'got lovely hair,' she wuz goin' t' Grunt Number One.

They could hear Curnow talkin' t'Kayleigh,

'Yeah – just make sure the ends are lookin' good...'

'How's your dad now?' went Kayleigh.

'A'right. They say his heart-beat's back t'normal – so thaas' a good sign...'

'Jess said ee got t'stay in Treliske fur a bit longer yet...'

'They wunt un to... but y'knaw wha' ee's like...'

The two grunts kept swivelling their eyes over t'where Charlie wuz. They wuz watchin' where his hair fell onta' the floor.

'So... goin' anywhere nice on yer holidays this year?' asked Jess t'Grunt Number Two.

'Na. Dun't think so. Me an' the lad there went up t'South Wales las' Sunday though...'

'Oh – nice there edn' ut?'

Mel realy didn't knaw very much about the ex-Steel working an' coal-mining district of Gwent.

'Didn't see much ov ut t'be honest. 'Twas a bit ov business like...'

'Oh... very nice... Now... do you want me t'take in the sides or not?'

'Yeah – a little bit please...'

Jess twisted his head back t'the position she wanted un in. Fur some reason ee seemed t'still keep lookin' t'the left where Kayleigh wuz workin' with Charlie. Jess reckoned ee fancied Kayleigh a bit. She already 'ad Bluett fancyin' her – an' tha' wuz bad enough.

'You always had ut longish then Charlie?'

'Yeah – since school,' ee wuz saying. 'Gives me power... like

Samson... I need ut at the moment. Tryin' t'write some new songs...'

'Aw... Lovely... wha' kind then? More ov tha' heavy rock...?'

'Sort ov... Love songs mainly at the moment...'

'Nice.'

'I've got a few demoed up but fur sum reason I'm findin' them hard to write right now...'

Yeah, Kayleigh prob'ly didn' knaw tha' Charlie wuz thinkin' ov some phat, downtuned riff tectonics rather than somethun' she might hear on *Now That's What I Call Music Vol.500*. Never mind though. 'Least she wuz interested.

That wuz the truth though. Ee wuz finding the writing harder than ee thought.

Mel, meanwhile, wuz workin' with the other one. Ee wudn' 'zactly a barrel ov laughs t'be honest. She thought she recognised un from somewhere. Ut might have been over Twilight sometime or maybe down the Happy Hour on Saturdays down Rose Cottage.

Both ov um looked over every time Kayleigh an' Curnow shared a joke. Both ov them clenched their fists a bit. They knawed Markie didn' go much on un – an' they'd both have liked t'smack un one. In the corner ov their eye, they also kept a watch on Micky – who was by now, at the bookings desk, checking the internet for pictures of websites devoted to street art and graffiti. There wuz obviously nawbody in fur a tat that day – or even fur a design consultation.

'Much on at the weekend?' Mel tried.

'Na – not a lot. Might go watch Trura City...'

'Oh – yes... some big matches comin' up fur they ent there?'

The stylist named Kayleigh didn' seem t'have taken tha' long with Curnow. She had the mirror at the back of his head showin' what 'twas all lookin' like.

'So, you out on tour again any time soon?' she wuz goin'.

'Na... gived tha' up fur now... Hey – 'tis lookin' good maid... thanks Kayleigh.'

Fuck, Curnow wuz getting' out ov his seat already. Ee wuz walkin' past them – an' on the way out ov the salon. The cunt obviously wudn' be payin' seein' as how ee wuz family. Ee did pause though, t'see wha' Micky wuz lookin' at on the internet. They turned their heads back to where Kayleigh wuz. Curnow's

Alan M. Kent

hair wuz still on the floor right now, but in seconds 'twas goin' t'be swept up an' put in the bin. Markie wudn' go much on ut if their mission failed. Expulsion wud be guaranteed. They wudn' step foot in Cornwall again – not unless they still wanted their bollocks intact.

'Excuse me,' went Grunt Number One, 'Sorry to ask – but can I use yer toilet a sec?'

Mel wuz surprised at the request. No-one normally stopped the cut, just to use the loo. What wuz ut: weak bladder, prostrate or somethun'?

'Yeah... 'course...' said Mel. 'I's back there my lovely – just on the right...'

Tha' wuz Grunt Number One's cue to move. Kayleigh already 'ad the dustpan and brush ready to go. Ee had t'do somethun' here. Ee put his hand in his pocket and yanked out some spare change – pretendin' t' accidentally drop ut.

'Aw shit,' ee went. 'Sorry...'

Kayleigh came to his assistance right away. While she wuz on the left, searchin' fur a couple of twenty pence coins that had rolled under one of the styling units, ee bent down an' grabbed a handful ov Curnow's hair. Job done. Ee placed the hair in his pocket and nodded t'the boy still in the chair. While down there, ee wuz sneaking a quick peek at Kayleigh's shapely ass, fantasizing about ut a bit, before ee got up and she handed him the remaining coins.

'Thanks,' ee went.

Then she bent down and brushed up Curnow's hair. Ut ad been close but the cunt had done ut. Ee carried on the pretend mission and went t'the toilet. In 'is pocket, ee doubled-checked the fistful ov hair wuz still there. Why the fuck Markie wanted this – ov all things – ee didn't rightly knaw but there 'twas – dun an' dusted. He opened his flies and took a satisfying piss. Then afterwards ee nawticed the sign above the toilet: 'Due to work today on the Trelawny Adit, do not flush'. So ee didn't. Ee unlocked the door and came back inta' the salon. By now, Curnow had gone, and the maid called Jess wuz just finishin' up on his mate.

'Do you want some anti-frizz spray on this?'

'Spray? Wha' for?'

'Well, Troon see, This is special Anti-Frizz. We go through a lot ov ut up there. I's the mist an'tha' see. It'll stop ut frizzin' up...'

'Okay then.'

So the Grunt 'ad the Anti-Frizz.

'I didn'... ah... flush... in there...'

'Aw – dun't ee worry... We've had problems ever since we've moved in. They'm still working on the Adit see... an' apparently thaas' all connected with the sewers an' tha'.'

Grunt number one nodded, noticing how stylish 'is mate now looked.

'Shall I finish you off then?' went Mel.

Ee sat down back in the chair an' she carried on.

'Can ee do me ears love?' ee went.

Mel hadn' really gone inta' hairdressin' t'be trimming the unruly ear hair ov portly forty-year bloaks, but still, there 'twas.

When ee looked in the mirror, ee went, 'Lovely job tha'... Best haircut I've had fur years...'

The both paid up and tipped well. When they were outside, both Jess an' Mel commented on wha' nice chaps they were. Unusual t'get the pair ov um in at once. Moast bloaks comed in on there own. Tha' led um to question whether they wuz together-like, but na, they wudn' tha' way inclined – 'specially the way one ov um wuz lookin' at Kayleigh's ass. What they didn' knaw ov course, wuz this wuz how evil operated on the Great Flat Lode.

'Spot on,' went Number One Grunt.

'Caw d'hell... I'd go fur that Kayleigh in there... Let's come back here again...'

'Not fur now... Look Markie's goin' t be like a pig in cherks when he sees this lot...'

They got back in the van again, did a quick three pointer in the middle ov Fore Street an' headed back down through Beacon, zippin' too quickly past a few skaters who flicked um the vs. One of they kids had a Voodoo Pilchard hoodie on. Number Two Grunt in the passenger seat nawticed ut, but didn' think nothun' ov ut. Ee got out his mobile and phoned Markie.

'Mission accomplished,' ee went.

Number One Grunt asked, 'Where does ee want t'meet us?

The usual...'

Number Two Grunt nodded.

'Yeah,' ee went, closin' his phone. 'Down Godrevy.'

The third mission goin' on tha' day wuz at Sally Curnow's house. Obviously since Tommy's incident, she'd been off work. Gerald Matta'd been round t'see her, as well as Timmy Pascoe an' Trudge from over mine. The boys 'ad all 'ad a whip 'round.

'Tell un 'tis fur a golden phone on the wall. He'll knaw wha we mean...' offered Pascoe. 'We'll try t'pop in an' see un later on this week.'

Then, so had just about everyone else from Troon – moast ov um nawsin' around t'be honest, rather than any genuine concern 'bout Tommy. See, Tommy wuz always someone people wuz interested in. They made their mist-filled, gorse-ridden, mine-collapsed days seem a bit more multi-coloured – and well, excitin'. Perhaps Sally cud see tha' now from the number of well-wishers an' cards tha' had been dropped through her letter box. Even tha' bitch Karen Mellow 'ad phoned her up t'see how she wuz doin' and ask how Tommy wuz feelin' – which wuz 'nice' in a way.

When she'd got back that first night, her and Charlie 'ad had a hunt around fur the pile ov Viagra tha' had put Tommy in hospital in the first place. They soon found ut behind the sofa, and didn't quite know wha' t'do with ut. Sally looked at ut as if 'twas some kind of malevolent force operating in her closed domestic world. She wanted t'chuck ut out in in the bins right away – but Charlie knew tha' his da would prob'ly go spare if they did tha' (considerin' the probable cost ov um too!). Instead, he put the box on top ov his da's stereo an' just left ut there. Ee nawticed the case ov Whitesnake's *1987* album there, where his da had left ut. Tha' had prob'ly contributed a bit t'un bein' s'horny as well. The Cov always got un grindin' 'is hips over Institute whenever 'twas on the jukebox there.

'I got an essay t'do,' his ma wuz goin'. 'I'll have t'phone me tutor an' get an extension...'

'I'll do ut ma. Whas' his number?' The tutor was sympathetic. 'Twas a she actually (a right Virginia Woolf by the sound ov her), an' she'd give his ma a fortnight's extension due to extenuating circumstances.

In this way, Charlie helped her.

'He d'need things fur hospital...' she wuz fussin'.

A few things maybe, but not the fuckin' huge holdall she now seemed intent on packin'.

'Ma...' went Charlie. 'Calm down...'

At this rate, 'is ma wuz goin' t'have a heart attack as well.

She looked like she needed someone like old Mrs Williams t'come along and make the tea. Then have a chat 'bout this an' tha'. But they both knawed she wudn' goin' to.

Even Clifford Mellow might do at this point – t'add some hilarity and absurdity to the proceedin's. But ee wudn' there either. Close – across the park and down cemetery – but still not there.

An' fuck, where the hell wuz Ursula? She cudn't get hold ov her over in Spain. She wuz prob'ly outside on the patio, baking her bingo wings an' drinkin' shots of Sangria, laughing at how cold an' wet 'twas back home. .

As they were organising the holdall, the front doorbell went. Charlie went. Ee wuz fully expectun' ut to be fuckin' Anglian Windows wantin' t'offer some new double-glazing or a conservatory. Tha' or the fuckin' Jehovis back again, tryin' t'get Troon on the straight an' narrow. Instead, 'twas fuckin' Ronnie Phillips wudn' ut? What did ee want? The cunt wuz lookin' a bit older, a bit tubbier, but still the same fuckin' Mount Hawke self-styled shag-master, who'd turned his ma's head a while back.

'Long time, no see,' the cunt went. 'How are you Charlie?'

Charlie didn't knaw wha' t'say.

'I's not a good time,' he managed t'say.

'Yer ma in?'

'Like I say,' went Charlie. 'Ut idn'a good time?'

'I knaw...' went the shag-master. 'Look, I dun't want naw trouble. I just comed 'round Charlie – t'offer me support...'

'Who es ut?' shouted his ma from inside the kitchen.

'Nawbody,' Charlie shouted back in.

Ronnie didn' much like tha'. You could tell.

'Look, just tell her I'm there if she d'need anything...'

Ronnie stepped back a bit bit, then walked down the drive and turned inta' the path. Charlie watched un. Ee did a double-take. Yeah – tha' wuz his fuckin' old battered Escort estate wudn' ut? An' who wuz in there beside un? Only Karen Mellow.

Fuck, Charlie cudn' keep up with this lot. Now she wuz shacked up with ee. She gived un a nod t'say hello, and wound down the window.

'A'right Charlie love? Some sorry t'hear 'bout Tommy...'

Yeah, right, thought Charlie.

'Got Ronnie lookin' after me an' the kids now...'

He nodded. Charlie looked in the back ov the car. There seemed like hundreds ov fuckin' tackers 'eaved in there all fix-ated on Nintindo DSs. Whenever Charlie looked at um, ee always worried one ov um might look like his da – from some past condom 'accident' a few years back. The littlest one now – Morwenna – the offspring ov her an' boy Clifford wuz lookin' at un through the Winnie the Pooh window blind. How old wuz she now? Three and a bit prob'ly.

Charlie remembered the time when she wuz born, an' how despite the increasing quicksand beneath Clifford's feet, how happy ee'd been. His expression altered. Karen wuz a good maid. She deserved a bit ov happiness. Ronnie wuz prob'ly old enough t'be her fuckin' feyther – but wha' wuz new there? Stuff like tha' never mattered on Trelawny. Karen had lost her looks a bit now. They'd been goin' when his da had lined her down Club Rhino t'help un select the 'artistes'. But still, before now, Charlie knawed why his da liked her. She 'ad the curves 'is ma didn'. Charlie reckoned the last few years had been hard on her. Eventually, ut d'take ut's toll ee reasoned. But then, just maybe, Ronnie might be able t'save her so t'speak, an' then her kids wudn' end up like moast ov the little fuckers on the estate here – filled with mephedrone, knives an' anything else illegal they could nick.

Ronnie drove off. Charlie reconsidered the cunt. Just maybe, maybe, they'd managed t'escape the voodoo pilchard tha' everyone else seemed t'be goin' through. Ee comed back in.

'Is ma wudn' stupid. She'd heard their voices.

'Tha' Ronnie?'

'Yeah...'

'Wha' a want?'

'Just t'see you wuz a'right...'

'Oh...'

'You knaw who ee's shacked up with?'

His ma nodded; her lower lip quiverin' a bit. She'd heard ut up work, but hadn' said. Fur a second there, there seemed a moment ov regret, but then she picked up Tommy's crowst bag and tidied ut away, and ut went again.

'You ready then?' ee asked.

'Yeah…'

This meant they'd be headin' up t'Treliske once again t'see wha' state Tommy wuz in, an' how much ee wuz moanin' about the food on offer. In her bag, she had a load of Get Well Soon cards tha' people had dropped in fur Tommy, stuff from his core, bits an' pieces she knawed ee liked.

'You had your hair cut?' asked his ma. 'Looks nice…'

'Yeah,' went Charlie. 'Over Headönizm…'

'Mmm. They've done a nice job. Bev'll like ut I spect,' she teased.

After the shock ov Ronnie and Karen, his ma seemed t'be back t'her old self.

They got inta' Charlie's 306 an' drove off. Charlie took the route down through Park an Tansys, where lots ov Voodoo Pilchard graffiti adorned moast ov the urban environment, an' even on some of the long-standin' mattresses an' sofas tha' had been 'eaved out in the gardens there.

'Look at ut all,' went his ma, tutting slightly. She wudn' on about the mattresses or sofas either.

'Yeah, terrible idn' ut?' offered Charlie.

Elsewhere, Yak wuz on a mission too. In his pocket, ee had Jody's number. Well, worth a go wudn' ut? It went straight t'her voice-mail.

'Ah… a'right? This is Charlie Curnow's friend here – Yak. I – ah – wondered if you'd like to go fur a drink some time? I seened you at Treliske the other day like… Give me a ring back when you get this message. Ah – bye. '

Ah fuck. Yak knew ee sounded a proper tool on there – cakey as 'ell. Ee almost dialled again, then thought fuck ut, she wun't even call un back anyway. 'Twas Charlie she'd wanted wudn' ut?

So ee got on with the other mission ov the day. That wuz the prisoner release deal ee'd made with Tommy. Yeah – ee wuz goin' t' break un out ov the Alcatraz Island tha' wuz Treliske Hospital, an' endeavour t'get un over Treyew Road fur the Press night an' instigation ov Markie Phillips as controlling owner ov the Club. 'Twas a breaking out ov Fort Knox Bullion

213

Depository-style operation, requiring a goodly bit ov planning. S'far as he knawed, Tommy didn't have much kit widn', so a quick trip t'Matterland would sort un out with some kaks, socks an' clothes. But then, 'twas a press do they were heading toward, so Yak brought along the only suit that ee had, hopin' 'twould fit Tommy.

Precisely how Yak got Tommy outta' South Crofty Ward wudn' goin' t'be common knowledge fur some time, but it basically involved the serruptitious use ov a laundry bin and Yak gettin' hold ov a cleaner's outfit and ID badge the day before, which ee craftily enhanced with his own image (courtesy of the media production firm and forgers tha wuz called Kelv an' Bluett). T'be honest, once ee'd picked up the bin in the link corridor, ee wuz actually surprised at the ease ov which they'd done ut. Security there didn' seem a t'give a monkeys – well, the plaace wuz almost too big really t'keep a proper eye on. 'Twas s'leisurely, Tommy wuz thinkin' they almost 'ad time t'stop off at the café fur a cup ov tea an' a chococlate brownie.

'Best t'get ee off site,' Yak shouted down inta' the laundry bin.

'A'right then...' said a voice under the sheets.

'You ent goin' t'keel over or anythun' are ee?

'Naw chance...'

'What've the doctors said?'

'Nothun' much... Silly shits... They d'knaw I'm a'right...'

'You knaw Sally an' Charlie's comin' up this af'noon dunnee?'

'Are um?'

'Yeah...'

'Well, I did tell um I wudn' goin' t'miss the Press Conference.'

This wuz Tommy's usual kind of logic – the kind tha' ee'd employed all the way through Club Rhino.

'All we gotta' do is stay outta' their way,' ee went. 'Otherwise, Sal'll have me back in here 'gain...'

So thaas' how Tommy zoomed past reception at Treliske, and then ended up in the car park near t'Yak's battered van. A few minutes later, ee'd got changed in the back, and wuz boobed up in one ov Yak's suits.

'How es ut?' asked.

'Bit tight in the crotch you, an' in the shoulders, but ut'll do...'

'Where shall I go?'

'Anywhere – just not here...'

Yak drove off. Just as they wuz pullin' out, up from the roundabout comed Charlie's 306.

'Duck, y'cunt...' went Yak, pushin' un t'the floor.

Tommy went inta' the well ov the seat. Yak looked away. Hopefully Charlie wudn' catch um. Ee'd be too bothered about getting' his ma up there.

'See us did um?'

'Dun't think so...'

'Look, go down Malpas by the river there – an' park up fur a bit. Then you an' I can sort out the deal on the Club... Let's you an' I talk a bit more 'bout the fixtures and fittin's...'

Just as Yak parked up – so they cud look up at the renovations being dun on the central spire of the cathedral, ee got a text. Bath stone see, Like Mundic block. Waaste o'time in Cornwall – 'gainst the rain an' wet.

Yak looked at ut. It wuz Jody – she wuz interested on goin' on a date widn'.

'Who's tha?' asked Tommy.

'Nawbody,' went Yak. 'She's a nurse...'

'Nurse eh? Very nice Yak... very nice indeed... Kinky like...'

Yak texted her back.

'Eh? Knaw wha' I meant t'tell you... Markie Phillips wanted t'have a word with you. You'n see un later if y'like – over Treyew... I dunnaw wha' ee d'want – d'you?'

Fuck. If the prospect ov goin' on a date with Jody the nurse wudn' enough t'make Yak kack his pants, then a bit ov a chat with Markie wuz sure t'cause ut. There wuz na getting' away from ut: a right hard bastard a used t'be – an' a right hard bastard ee still wuz. Yak gulped and did a little silent scared fart.

At Treliske, Charlie and his ma parked up, and walked across to the main building. Ironically, Tommy wuz in South Crofy Ward wudn a - in wha' wuz known t'anyone in Cornwall, as the Tower Block. This involved walking what seemed t'be the equivalent of a five-mile route march through a link corridor, then takin' the lift up t'the required ward. Charlie held his ma.

He knawed she got nervous in these kind ov situations. Seeing Tommy lying there in the hospital bed wuz likely t'make her squal a bit.

'Crofty at home fur un, an' Crofty in here,' said Sally philo-sophically, as if 'twas Tommy's destiny. Ut 'ad the hubris of voodoo pilchard completely.

'We've come t'see Tommy Curnow...' said Charlie softly t'the nurse at the desk.

She raised her eyes a little. Charlie knawed wha' tha' meant – tha' ee'd already established hisself as a bit ov a joker, vagabond and general tool.

'He's down here on the left... We gave him his own room for a bit more rest...'

Tha' prob'ly meant ee'd been annoying the fuck outta' the other patients, so separating un wuz the best thing they cud do. His ma seemed pleased at tha' though – like ee wuz gettin' spe-cial treatment. The nurse disappeared inta' one ov the rooms on the left, just ahead of them. She came out again shortly.

'I'm so sorry,' she went, 'Ee's gone!'

'What ee mean?!' went Charlie's ma, all shocked an' dis-mayed.

'I checked him earlier – not long before you got here... and he was here then...'

'Can people just leave then?' asked Charlie.

The nurse hurried back to her desk.

'Well, they can discharge themselves if they want – but Mr Curnow didn't indicate to me that he was going to do that...'

'Ah fuck,' went Charlie t'hisself.

'Does ee do this kind ov thing often?' asked the nurse.

'Well, I dun't think so – not normally,' said his ma. 'I mean this is the first time ee've been in hospital fur years...'

'I'll just tell Sister - an' then phone Security.'

Fuck, tha' wuz all they needed now. An APB for all units t'watch out fur a tool in his late forties, in a ass-less hospital gown, prob'ly hopeful ov listening t'some old-school heavy metal, an' stalkin' the corridors of Treliske.

'Ut'll be fur the football,' said Charlie.

His ma had forgotten.

'Aw yes – ee wuz on about tha'...'

Charlie explained to the nurse how committed ee wuz t'the

success ov the Tigers. Promotion, see. League Division Two in the offing. She understood. Apparently, Tommy'd told her tha' Sunday's game against Newport County wuz crucial if they were goin' t' go up.

She moved to the phone on the desk and spoke to Security.

'Yes – a white male. Late forties. Missing from South Crofty Ward... Can you investigate?'

'How wuz a? Was a alright?' asked Charlie's ma.

'Seemed to be... I mean his chart was showing great improvement – since when he was brought into A&E earlier this week... I think the doctors were pleased with his progress. We haven't had one of those kind ov overdoses before...'

She looked up at Sally. Sally ignored her.

'We should go look fur'n,' said Charlie.

'Would you like to pick up the rest ov his things?' the nurse asked.

In the room, were a number of Get Well cards and on the floor, a copy of this week's *West Briton*, turned t'the football pages at the back. Sally took the cards.

'Hope you find him,' said the nurse.

'Yeah, me too,' said Charlie.

Charlie felt the same kind of panic as ee did when they'd been chasing Trescothick up t'the Tamar Bridge backalong. Now ee wuz on a quest t'locate his own feyther. Fuck, ee wuz beginning t'wish ee'd stayed on the road. On the road, y'only 'ad t'think 'bout one o' the eleven lessons at a time usually. Here, y''ad t'think about all ov um at the same time. An American tour with Purple Haze sounded like heaven compared t'all ov this. Maybe Spryer wuz right. Maybe they should have listened to un. Cunt, ee might be, but an' alright cunt at times.

'Shallus go Treyew Road?' asked his ma.

'Na. Thaas' too obvious. Ee'll knaw thaas' the first plaace we'll look...'

'Ee've gotta' be there tonight though...'

'Well, thaas' when we'd best catch up widn'? Otherwise 'tis like lookin' fur a needle in a haystack...'

The odyssey t'locate Tommy then – wud have t'wait 'til the evening. But then, well, then, they'd have a good chance ov locatin' un. Trura City ground wuz goin' t'be like instant GPS.

E'd stick to ut like a magnet does t'steel. The tool just might have made ut easier fur um.

Meanwhile, deep in the west, Trescothick wuz definitely on one – if not 'zactly on a mission. His own brand ov the Black Panthers, or rather the Cornish Tigers, wuz gearin' up (as usual) fur the forthcomin' glorious revolution. Whilst ee cud see wha' wuz happening locally with all the Voodoo Pilchard stuff (ee himself, always a trendsetter so ee imagined, 'ad already invested in a hoodie up Pool Market – so ee cud be 'down with the kidz' on the estate), Trescothick had gained enough subscriptions, donations and investment (by other rampant politically viagra-ised nationalists) in the Cornish Tigers to begin covert operations.

While ee wuz fancyin' the ass off Kayleigh, Boy Bluett, who of course, wuz now gearin' up fur service in the real army, 'ad offered his services as technical support fur the training. Yeah – this wuz the same Boy Bluett who had helped t'mastermind Tommy's porn empire a while ago – now apparently the biggest expert on military procedures since Andy McNab. Bluett was absolutely Bravo Minus Zero. Trescothick himself wuz puttin' the previous military failures ov the Cornish down to their poor levels ov fitness. The twenty-first century had taken them away from their super-fit roots deep in the mines, an' too many of um wuz pied-up on pasties, Roskilly's ice-cream, saffron cake an' the good value Chinese take-aways available down Cross Street in Camborne. Tha' needed t'be offset. The fact tha' Tommy Curnow wuz in hospital with a suspected heart attack hadn' given un much confidence in the wider health and fitness of the Cornish nation – especially if some serious civil disobedience wuz on the cards.

'General' Bluett and 'Field Marshall' Trescothick were therefore havin' a tactical planning day down Trescothick's mother's plaace down Park an Tansys. Trescothick, not havin' naw proper job, an' havin' more time on his hands than sense, had been researchin' the now popular sport ov 'coasteering' as a training methodology. Ee sat there, admirin' his new sleeve tattoo in Cornish, as ee wuz explainin' the phenomenon.

Bluett's response t'all ov tha' wuz brutally incisive: 'Wha' the fuck is tha'?

'Let me explain,' went Trescothick, who wuz still lookin'

tanned t'fuck an' 'ad actually – fur once in his sad fuckin' life - been attractin' lots ov admirin' glances from all the single mums down there (new hairstyle an' all see). 'We are talking about using the opportunity provided by marine geology and the coastline for moving in the 'impact zone' where water, waves, rocks, gullies, and caves come together to provide a high-energy environment'.

Bluett nodded and asked. 'So i's like orienteerin' - but along the coast?'

'Yeah,' went Trescothick. 'Thaas' the top an' bottom ov ut...'

'But ent ut dangerous?' asked Bluett, raising an eyebrow or two.

Trescothick could hardly believe wha' ee wuz hearing. This wuz the boy who in a couple of weeks would be joining up the Rifles and shipped out t' Sangin Province before he knew ut. A body bag an' a flag-lowering cavalcade through Wootton Bassett were real possibilities.

''Course ut's dangerous,' ee went. 'Thaas' the whole idea. If we want t'train the Tigers properly, then ut's got t'have that factor t'ut...'

'But what if somebody dies?'

Trescothick looked up in intense prayer and meditation at the black an' white St Piran's Flag mounted above his ma's fireplace.

'This is war,' ee went. 'People die.'

'Right...' went Bluett, a bit nervous, an' like Yak over Malpas, kackin' his pants slightly.

'The boys ov 1549 wouldn' have asked that now would they?'

Bluett didn' rightly knaw much about 1549 but reckoned prob'ly, na, they wudn' have been kacking themselves in quite the same way as ee wuz now, even if they wuz hung, drawn an' quartered.

'We, my boy, are from the same stock and nothun' scares we...'

'So we'm goin' coast-eer-erin'?'

Bluett could hardly even say the word, let alone actually think about doin' ov ut.

'Yeah...

'So, is this like tha' there wild swimming everybody d'go on about?'

Here, Bluett wuz thinkin' about the middle-classes ov England. who over the last few years seemed t'have given up on chlorine and temperature-controlled public swimming baths, and were plunging inta' any kind ov mountain lakes and water-falls across the country just fur kicks. Believe ut or not, Dozmary Pool wuz the latest trendy location according to BBC Radio Cornwall ('Complete sacrilege,' Trescothick 'ad gone – ut being the imagined last resting place ov King Arthur's sword, Excalibur).

'Wild swimming's fur the English,' went Trescothick. 'What we'm doin' is a bit more like ut...'

Bluett cud see tha' 'Cothick wuz in a lock-an'-load kind ov mood today.

'I wuz doin' wild swimming over the old granite quarries over Praze-an-Beeble,' ee said, 'before the English even invent-ed the term...'

Like as much, prob'ly the ancient Celts wuz doin' ov ut cen-turies ago if Trescothick usual line wuz t'be heard.

'Besides,' ee went, 'The ancient Celts wuz doin' ov ut cen-turies ago.'

'Will we be doin' any tombstonin' sir – because if we are – then count me out...'

Jeez, Trescothick wuz thinkin'. Wozon widn'? Just because there'd been a few high-profile media cases ov underaged an' boozed up twats from up-the-line down over Newquay breakin' their necks doin' a bit of cliff-jumpin', the boy Bluett seemed t'be a bit panicked.

'There'll be none ov tha', went Trescothick. 'Not on my com-mand at least...'

'Good to hear sir,' said Bluett. 'So what do us need?'

'I've made an ordinance list.'

Trescothick went through it.

'3mm full body padded wetsuits. 65N Bouyancy Aids with adjustable shoulder straps, side panel adjusters and chest/waist straps. Suitable impact water helmet. Suitable footwear i.e. training shoes or thick-solded wetsuit boots.'

'Where do us go?'

'Ann's Cottage Surf Shop, Fraddon, an' the Army an' Navy Stores over Redruth. I have the sizes ov all the recruits, but we should obtain some spares too. There will almost certainly be

Voodoo Pilchard

others who wish to join the 'cause'. I am sure.'

Ee said the 'cause' like 'twas the Force.

'Generel Bluett, we shall be operatin' in tha' moast special ov environments... The Cornish foreshore...'

Apparently, tha' happened t'be 'zactly where the 'impact zone' wuz.

Now Bluett didn' really knaw shit. Perhaps tha' wuz the reason ee wuz signin' up t'be canon fodder in Afghanistan. In fact, that wuz one ov the ways in which the British Army throughout the centuries had signed up personnel of the likes of Bluett – people who didn' knaw shit. But wha' ee did knaw wuz that the foreshore wuz one of they plaaces that the Cornish wuz always arguing about. If 'twudn' with the Council, 'twas with Prince Charles and the Duchy. So perhaps 'twas apt tha' whatever operations Trescothick had got planned, was happenin' there.

So tha' wuz the week ov missions on Obby Stanker. An' suddenly wha' wuz looking impossibly difficult at the beginning ov ut, wuz now looking piss easy: public art, covert operations, secret missions, escapology an' decent haircuts. Tha' wuz the really scary thing 'bout all ov ut.

Scarier still though, wuz tha' somewhere out there, on the coast, there wuz the Voodoo Queen, just watchin' and waitin'.

Flighty Chough – Get ready fur rapid curls and save valuable morning minutes.
Liquid Curl Definer
• Cleaner definition – Unique styling properties provide weightless detail to wavy or curl hair
• Long-lasting bendable hold – Helps condition and protect curls while creating durable body and bounce
• Reduces drying time – Specially formulated to help reduce drying time

The fust thing Charlie nawticed about 'is da wuz wha' the fuck kind ov a suit did a have on? Ut looked like the kind ov thing y'wudn' even donate t'yer local Oxfam charity shop, or even take down Hayle Car Boot, let alone put on fur an important press conference ov this kind. Then ee realised where ee'd seen ut before: Yak's ma's plaace, hung up on the side of 'is wardrobe

221

there next t'his old Castle Donington posters. The tool 'ad tha' on fur any kind of posh do (which t'be honest, wudn' very often in Troon: the occasional wedding, funeral or court appearance, an' so on). So 'twas all makin' sense, particularly when ee'd seen Yak's battered van in the car park. Charlie'd decided 'twudn' the best thing t'bring his ma along t'the event at Treyew Road. Fur one thing, she'd awnly sit in the audience glowerin' away at Tommy fur breakin' out ov South Crofty ward, prob'ly puttin' un off the task in hand, and fur another, Charlie wanted t'keep his ma as far away as possible from the likes ov Markie Phillips an' any ov 'is crew. So she wuz home still, frettin' over Tommy and trying t'get t'grips with her Aphra Behn. Naw doubt she'd be on the blawer t'Jess an' Ursula too.

The plaace wuz proper packed you. People wuz crammed in the main bar ov Trura City's social club, an' a few 'ad t'stand out-side. Good job 'twas good weather tha' May evenin' with a bit ov sunshine, else they'd be shafted. All the local newspapers were represented – includin' the *Wessen Morning News* (as 'is da called ut) – and the local radio stations: the BBC, Pirate an' Atlantic FM. 'Twas a big deal you. The Club 'ad laid on a few free drinks an' a bit ov a buffet. Even Timmy Pascoe an' Trudge wuz there from Crofty – helpin' out a bit, organisin' ov the tables and chairs. Fuck me, Charlie 'ad even had a quick yap t'Sam Polglaze. In the time Purple Haze had been away, ee'd progressed up the ladder of journalism an' wuz now Deputy Editor on the *West Briton* wudn' a? Ee didn' seem very surprised at the way Balance or Purple Haze had gone.

'Thaas' the way ov ut, idn' ut? All these bands from Cornwall tha' I seen – I cen't think ov one ov um who actually made ut,' ee went, being the voice ov experience. 'Still, glad t'hear you made a bit on tha' Chakira hit… I danced t'ut a few times over L2… 'Twudn' too bad t'all.'

There. Tha' wuz the high point of Cornish-style media praise: 'Twudn' too bad t'all'. Hardly a glowing five-star review in *Kerrang!* magazine wuz ut?

Now Tommy wudn' chairman ov the Club's managerial committee. Aw naw. That wuz left t'an old boy by the name of Roger 'the Boot' Tremaine who'd seen the club rise up from the South Western League. Ee played fur the Tigers in the '60s and '70s apparently – bit ov a legend an' star player back then, and tha' reputation 'ad catapulted a inta' the role of chairman fur a number ov years. There didn' look much life in the bugger; well, ee 'ad arthritis in both knees now didn' a?. Tha' wuz part ov the problem Charlie suspected. None ov um wuz man enough t'resist the take-over bid assembled by Markie an' his cronies.

A lot ov people wuz goin' up t'Tommy an' shakin' ov 'is hand though, an' askin' un if ee wuz a'right, and tha' they didn' expect un t'be outta' hospital s'soon. Charlie cud see his da makin' light ov ut all – sayin' how 'twas actually a bit ov a heart murmur and not really a heart attack t'all. None ov what the doctors said 'ad seemed t'have made a blind bit ov differ-ence. In the best... er... George Best-style, ee wuz still knockin' the ale, back an' smoakin' like a train every s'often in smoakin' shelter outside, pretendin' nothun' 'ad 'appened. Out there ee wuz smirking with anyone female, an' bein' the normal tool ee wuz back Institute. All around un seemed t'be a bit ov activity, with various reporters placing microphones on stands on the desk at the front ov the room. There wuz even a last minute turn out by the television cameras an' reporters ov BBC *Spotlight*, who must have felt tha' they ought t'cover ut as a bit of a sop to the stupid Cornish. ITV 'course, 'adn't even both-ered. They wuz based up in Bristol now, and didn' give a fuck wha' happened beyond Exeter, let alone over the River Tamar. An' Trura, where wuz tha? There be dragons. Camborne, well, that wuz just beyond the pale as they say, an' Troon wuz where the natives ate their children. They'd never venture tha' far down. There, they didn' even speak English. This wuz Trescothick's point see. The media wuz shaftin' ee all the time.

The really odd thing wuz that Markie Phillips wuz no-where t'be seen. 'Mean, you expected a t'be there schmoozing every-one like the slimey cunt ee wuz. But na, there wuz no clue t'where ee wuz tall. The A and B teams ov Trura City were all in too, as well as the youngsters from all the different squads t'see wha' would be announced. On the video screens they wuz building up for the crunch match between them an' Newport County. An away game – with bus-loads ov fans from Cornwall expected t'make the journey up there inta' South Wales. They wuz doin' good business with the merchandise as well. There wuz black an' white colours everywhere you, an' you cudn' miss the club's badge – the St Piran's cross and Trura Cathedral. The bar wuz busy too. Even if y'didn't necessarily agree t'wha' wuz happening with the Club, y'cud get trolleyed on Skinner's real ales, and be happy with yer life. There wuz a definite buzz in the air though, as if things were goin' t'go mental any minute now. Ut wuz a feeling that Charlie got sometimes before the big gigs they'd done as Purple Haze. Then, 'twas like ut dun't really matter wha' you played, people'll still go nutty fur ut.

Charlie watched his da carefully. You cud see un lookin' carefully at the clock on the wall. 'Twas comin' up fur half-seven, when the press briefin' wuz due t'take place. His da and the various other members of the committee took their places at the front ov the room. The plaace began t'settle down. Just as this wuz happenin', from out the bogs walked in Yak didn' a? The bugger wuz movin' oddly, like as if 'is ass wuz on fire.

'A'right Charlie?' ee went.

'Not really,' said Charlie nonchalantly. 'Had t'be you who busted me da' out ov Treliske wudn' ut? Me mawther wudn' happy t'all – havin' been dragged up here all the way from Troon... t'find ee'd dun a bit ov a Houdini act.'

'I didn't have a choice,' went Yak.

'All fur EBGBs wuz ut then?'

'Yeah...'

Yak wuz fidgetin' on his chair.

'Whas' up?'

'Me guts is playin' up... 'Tis hellish you.'

In reality, Yak had spent the last hour in the toilets with a severe case of the trots. Ee wuz nervous see, about what Markie Phillips wuz goin' t'say to un – or more importantly, wha' ee wuz goin' t'do to un in the way ov fists, kicks an' punches.

The room hushed.

Roger 'the Boot' Tremaine wuz on.

'Ladies and gentlemen, may I extend a warm welcome to you here tonight at Treyew Road, the home of Trura City Football Club. I would like to thank you and members of the media for attending tonight's press briefing. We are, as you know, on the brink of real achievement for football in Cornwall: the entry ov Trura City into Football League Two...'

Ee paused fur a cheer. The crowd gave ut.

'We are fully aware of the importance ov Saturday's away game at Newport County, and of course, in a fortnight's time, the end of season match home here at Treyew against Bath City. Tonight, however, what we shall be doing, is explaining the future direction of football here at Treyew Road, and introducing our newly-gained sponsor and major share-holder in the Club. It is with this kind of financial backing that we hope to take Trura City forward inta' the remainder of the twenty-first century.'

A few whispers went around the room.

'I would now like to hand you over to Tommy Curnow who – as many ov you know – has been a constant voice ov reason and attention t'detail in this year's committee... Tommy...'

'A constant voice ov reason,' Charlie said t'hisself. 'Since when?'

Like the twat paid real attention to detail as t'how many Viagra ee'd shoved down his throat.

Like the others, Yak wuz clappin' as Tommy stood up.

'As some of you know, I nearnly didn' make ut tonight – but thanks to some favours I did with a few nurses up Treliske, I managed to be here...'

A few ov the more beered-up boys in the A and B teams cheered a bit at tha'. This wuz Tommy's typical bullshit gift o'the gab, but they loved un fur ut.

'Tonight is a very important night for the Club. Now, later tonight, our new shareholder will be going through the committee's vision for the Club and its hopeful future within League Division Two. As you know, the FA have a number ov criteria which have to be in plaace for the club to be ready for promotion. Many people have been working throughout the year, to have all of this ready...'

Tommy paused so tha' the crowd could clap.

'Thank you kindly,' ee wuz goin', like ee wuz some sorta' cocky stand-up comedian. 'My job tonight, however, is to introduce to you our new controlling shareholder and sponsor. The person I want to introduce I have known for a number of years, and may I just say tha' ee is quite a remarkable individual. Not only has 'ee built up – from virtually nothing – a substantial business empire in West Cornwall – but he has also a constant charitable presence in the community (more of which in a moment). The committee and I feel confident that this individual and his various business interests will catapult the Tigers into the next phase of our development. I feel sure that he will be with us not *if* we enter the Premiership, but *when*... Ladies and gentlemen, may I introduce to you Mr Markie Phillips...'

Charlie's da made a little side movement with his hand which wuz the cue fur someone behind the bar, t'press play on the CD player there. Smooth see – honed from years ov experience up Institute. Like always though, 'twas a bit ov a cock-up and the track comed on a bit later than ut should really. Still, from one ov the side rooms, out walked Markie Phillips with two ov his gorillas – all three ov um in sharp suits. None ov yer Matterland rubbish this lot. Charlie recognised um instantly. These wuz the two grunts who'd been sat next to un in Headönizm the other day. So at tha', Charlie cudn' help but wonder wha' they wuz doing in the salon? Bloaks like they never just got their hair cut in a place. There must be somethun' more behind ut. Ee'd make sure Micky and Jess knawed as soon as ee seened um. The music that comed on wuz Survivor's 'Eye of the Tiger'. Fuck me, 'ere ee wuz – Markie Phillips, thinkin' he wuz Rocky Balboa – 'bout t'save Trura City single-handedly.

RISIN' UP, BACK ON THE STREET
DID MY TIME, TOOK MY CHANCES
WENT THE DISTANCE, NOW I'M BACK ON MY FEET
JUST A MAN AND HIS WILL TO SURVIVE

That wuz true enough certainly. Ee'd dun 'is time in Exeter prison, an' ee wuz always takin' chances. Ee'd be joggin' 'round Redruth next, an' askin' after Adrian.

SO MANY TIMES, IT HAPPENS TOO FAST
YOU CHANGE YOUR PASSION FOR GLORY
DON'T LOOSE YOUR GRIP ON THE DREAMS OF THE PAST
YOU MUST FIGHT JUST TO KEEP THEM ALIVE.

Yeah, reckoned Charlie. Bet Clifford thought tha' too.

After the first rousing chorus, Charlie's da hurriedly make a cut-the-music sign with his hand, and the 1982 AOR classic faded out. 'Ad time stood still? This wuz wha' they used t'put up with over Grouter Park when they wuz still kids. Wha' wuz ut like!? They'd 'ave fuckin' Tina Turner's 'Simply the Best' on next, followed by Queen's 'We are the Champions'.

Markie took the centre seat on the front desk, next t'the rest of the committee, while his two grunts sat on the side, pretendin' t' look like intelligent financial gurus instead of hired muscle. As ee stood up, the crowd gived un a big clap. Fuck me, Charlie wuz goin', cudn' they see through anything? Here wuz Satan standin' before um, and they wuz praisin' un like he wuz Jesus Christ arriving in Cornwall with Joseph ov Arimathea.

Markie knew how t'work the audience. Tha' wuz wha' wuz so scary. Ee didn't say a thing, but just gently undid his jacket, took it off, and rolled up his sleeve, showin' a brand new tattoo on his thick bicep ov Trura City Football club's logo. Ee pointed at ut with 'is forefinger with a bit ov attitude. By the look ov ut, Charlie knew in an instant 'twas one ov Micky's pieces.

'Tha' ladies and gentlemen,' said Markie. 'is my faith an' commitment to this club.'

He paused fur effect, like a great orator. The crowed cheered wildly.

Wuz tha' wha' the gorillas were in Headönizm for then? Maybe t'suss the plaace out fur a bit ov bespoke inking. Maybe, Charlie concluded.

'I am here this evening to announce my successful buy-out of a 51% stake in the club, and my commitment to offer financial support here for the next five years. My business interests have given me the opportunity to do this, and I feel confident that we can have a harmonious relationship...'

The committee an' Tommy were clapping at what ee said. Tha' wuz Phillipsy up there goin' on like ee wuz John F. Kennedy about t'lead everyone who supported the Tinmen t'the promised land ov milk an' honey.

'On each ov your seats, you will find a folder containing a prospectus and business plan of all the projected incomes and investments concerned with the club, as well as our vision ov where myself and the committee see as an appropriate direction. You will notice that over the next few years, I am proposing the development ov a new stadium for the club, which will allow its continued expansion and centrality as a leisure facili-

Alan M. Kent

ty in mid-Cornwall. Not only will it be the home ov the Tinmen, but also a concert venue for major international recording artists.'

Fuck, this wuz now dangerously close t'Charlie's world ov rock 'n' roll and far away from the smell ov Deep Heat muscle rub an' sweaty shin pads. Stud spanners an' early baths this wudn'.

Down the front, the reporters were busily noting down everything he wuz sayin', seemingly rapt in his words, an' tha' in this economic climate, ee wuz offerin' to transform the club an' offer a well-needed economic boast to Cornwall. Charlie felt like ee wuz hallucinatin'. This wuz wha' ut had come to wuz ut? Him, listenin' t' a villain ov the first order, convincin' half ov Cornwall tha' ee wuz a sound an' reliable bloak.

Fur the next ten minutes, Markie – an' his financial advisors (tha' wuz the grunts beside ov un) took the audience through the future. Ee'd even had architectural drawings ov the new stadium dun up hadn' a? Well, 'twas all lookin' like somethun' y'might be able t'sell t'the International Olympic committee or FIFA, tell 'bout Cornwall Council or the local press. They wuz lovin' un fur ut. All their dreams an' ambitions were encompassed in 'is every word. So this, this wuz what all the cash-point robberies 'ad been about wuz ut? All the deals? All the art-gallery robberies? All the kickings-in ov innocents? Yeah, this wuz wha' 'twas all about. At the end of his presentation, the architects had comed up with a projected video sequence of the ground, from both a player's point of view, and then from a fan's perspective. Well, the audience wuz in raptures wudn' um? You nearnly 'bout saw grown men crying. Jaws dropped. Saliva dripped. 'Twas orgasmic. Fuck all the rugby now. With this, well, Cornwall could take on anyone. Yak seemed t'also be astonished by the images, an' even Charlie himself felt drawn inta' the wonder ov wha' wuz bein' offered. Ee 'ad t'snap hisself out ov ut sharpish, an' plant 'is feet back on the ground again.

'Now – ladies an' gentlemen, I won't bore you anymore for now. But members of the press, at this point in the evening's proceedings, I doan't mind takin' a few brief questions...'

Markie sipped some water.

'Will you be sponsoring the new kit?' – this, from the bloak from Pirate FM.

'I will,' said Markie. 'To my left, is an example of the home and away strips that we are proposing.'

The two grunts held up two new shirt designs. On them wuz Phillips' name in bold lettering. The new material an' style looked amazin' – like they'd just been flown in from the World Cup. Ut made the old kit look like 'twas from the 1930s.

'Do you propose to be hands on with the team and training?' – tha', from the maid from BBC Radio Cornwall.

'No. The team is the concern of the manager alone. I'll be leavin' all ov tha' to Dave there...'

At this point, City's long-standin' manager Dave Metters, who'd got them this far, breathed a bit ov a sigh ov relief. Ee put back on his City cap onta' 'is greying Kevin Keegan-style afro. Ee cud sleep well tonight back his plaace over Trispen.

'Will you be buying in any new players fur the new season?' Tha' wuz from Sam Polglaze. You cud tell – there wuz still the same attitude on un as when ee'd interviewed Balance over Troon Methodist Chapel all tha' time ago.

'I suspect tha' we will, though at this stage, the present team seem to be doing a very good job already...'

The team nodded their affimation – and tha' this Phillips bloak didn' seem a bad ol'boy all towld.

Charlie waited fur a moment of silence in the discussion. In fur a penny, in fur a pound ee reckoned. Ee just chipped ut in there, like a perfect David Beckham-style free kick. The shot at goal wuz perfectly timed an' almost caught the 'keeper' off balance.

'There are concerns tha' your business interests are not always legitimate... How do you answer those claims?'

Charlie watched his da crumple. Ah fuck. Tha' wud be ut.

Little discussions rumbled around the room. A few others 'ad heard the same thing. A bit ov a wild card wuz this Phillips boy, the old timers reckoned.

Ee watched Markie. Just fur a micro-second, there wuz a look in his eye tha' went 'I've been rumbled' but the cunt wuz stone cold cool, there wuz naw takin' tha' away from un. But ee'd knawn who'd asked ut. Markie didn' falter one bit though. Curnow ee'd have later when the time wuz right.

'Those accusations are grossly unfounded. I welcome public scrutiny in all my operations and business interests, and say to everyone here, speak to my accountants, my employees and my customers...'

'I think... ah... that ut is time to draw a close to questions at this point,' went Tommy sensitively. 'And may I suggest that we move to the second part of tonight's evening... the presentation....'

Tha' shut down any kind of dissent in the room. The radio and tv stations had perked up a bit at tha' last question though. A bit ov controversy wuz wha' they media fuckers wuz always after. Anythun' plain-sailing didn' interest they t'all.

'Yes... Now – as you know Trura City's long-term charity has been the Precious Lives appeal for life-limited children.... And to add to the total already collected this year: five thousand pounds on the gate an' at club events, Mr Phillips would like to make an initial donation of some ten thousand pounds.'

More clapping.

Some young, vibrant an' nubile presenter from BBC Radio Cornwall wuz up there collectin' one of them big cheques that had been made out t'the appeal. Tha' wuz ut then – Markie, Roger 'the Boot' Tremaine, his da and she wuz in there posin' fur photographs. Markie gived her a kiss on the cheek, followed by his da – who aimed fur her lips an' ended up somewhere near her ear. 'Twas lookin' like the overdose hadn't fully worn off then. The cheque 'ad exactly the right appeal to the doubters. Completely orchestrated see. Cen't be all bad then, Charlie cud sense um saying, if ee'n afford t'lay out tha' kind ov money fur charity.

Suddenly, Yak went mental.

'I cent' stand ut anymore...' ee said.

WTF? Charlie went.

'I gotta' find out wha' ee want with me. I ent goin' t'have me bollocks blasted off... no way.'

Yak wuz up stroathin' across the room, towards where Markie wuz. Everywhere wuz chaos now. People wuz stretchin' their legs, getting' more beers from the bar, or takin' a piss break. Tables were scattered an' the chairs out ov their rows. Still, Yak wudn' lettin' any ov tha' stand in his way. Charlie cud only watch on at a distance.

They'd just finished all the photo opportunities when Yak got to um. Tommy nawticed un first ov all.

'Yak boy? What ee want?'

'T 'ave a word with Markie...'

'This idn' quite the time nor the plaace fur ut...'

'Yeah – well, my poor fuckin' arse cen't take ut anymore... I'm scared Tommy. I wanna' knaw wha' ee wants...'

Markie wudn' thick. He sensed what Yak wanted an' stepped in. His gorillas watched closely. Markie had one eye on Charlie as ee wuz speakin' t'Yak.

'Mr Phillips,' went Yak nervously, 'I heard you wanted t'talk t'me...'

'Thaas' right Yak...' went Markie.

'Ut seems my people found somethun' important ov yours on the beach down Gwithian the other day...'

'Really?'

'Yeah... Your cocaine wudn' ut?;

Markie put a kindly hand over Yak's shoulder an' forced un inta' a corner near the club's kitchen hatch.

'Well... Yeah...'

'Look, Yak. I dun't want naw trouble. But you did end up wrecking one of my Land-rovers down there. A full write-off. Coppers involved too. We had t'act very quickly not to have the 'consignment' taken from us. Hear about tha' did you?'

Aw fuck, Yak had forgotten about all tha' with the Land-rover.

'But we do go back a goodly way dun't us Yak?'

Yak remembered the St Day Post Office job. Europe's 'The Final Countdown' wuz blastin' out. Tha' wuz clear in 'is memory.

'See, you helped set me on the road I'm on today Yak...'

Both Tommy and Markie's gorillas wuz lookin' on carefully, making sure they made a move if anything kicked off. One move, an' they'd bundle the cunt right out onta' the pitch, an' give un a bit of a pastin' in the goal-mouth: the hands or fists of God if y'like.

'So look Yak. I want you t'forget about tha' – and maybe I can forget about the damage to my vehicle... How does tha' sound?'

'Ver... very good,' went Yak.

'Boys,' called Markie. 'Can you escort Mr... Yak... t'the car park? In my car, you'll find an envelope... A bit of compensation fur ee. Well, y'set up a good deal down Godrevy... I cen't let tha' go un-nawticed so t'speak.'

Yak looked puzzled and worried.

'Let's just say we'm quits yeah?'

Markie launched Yak towards his gorillas. Yak didn' like t'think about wha' wuz about t'happen next. They proceeded through the main bar doors an' out inta' the packed car park. Charlie wuz reckonin' ee wud need t'advertise fur a new drummer fur any projected session work. 'Twudn' likely ee'd be goin' on any date with Jody very soon unless 'twas straight through the swing doors ov A&E with a face like a welder's bench.

Tommy meanwhile, 'eaded over to where Charlie wuz. Ee wudn' happy thaas' fur sure,

'You fuckin' idiot,' went his da, tryin' t'whisper an' failing. 'What did ee mean by askin' tha'? You almost blew everything Charlie...'

'Ut had t'be asked da,' went Charlie.

'Fuck off home if you'n goin' t'be like tha'...'

'Right,' said Charlie. 'I will... but remember I'm yer lift at the moment. I dun't think Yak's goin' t'be in a fit state t'drive...'

Charlie's da didn't 'zactly fancy hitch-hiking along by Chacewater, so ee eased off a bit. Ee bit 'is tongue.

'Da. All I'm sayin' is tha' ee's trouble... Just be careful thaas' all.'

Tommy knawed ut really. He knawed Charlie wuz right. The away game on Sunday at Newport County wuz already won – thanks t' the sweetener tha' had been paid. Ee wudn' be tellin' anybody 'bout tha'. If anyone found out, well, tha' wud be ut. Trura City wud be expelled from any promotion, prob'ly the Conference National too, an' payin' off the fines fur years t'come.

'You'n see ut though Charlie?' 'is da went. 'See wha' he's doin' fur Trura, fur Cornwall? See how proud people are here. The likes of Trescothick cudn'd do this... I knaw Markie's naw angel, but then, who is?'

Charlie looked around un. Fur once, the people ov Trura and wider Cornwall seemed t'be happy. None ov um wuz angels – but fur a change, they did have smiles on their faces.

'I knaw.' went Charlie. 'I do knaw...'

'Let ut go then,' said his da.

'I cen't,' went Charlie. 'Thaas' the problem...'

'Go back t'yer music then,' said his da, which wuz somethun' ee'd never normally even think ov sayin'. 'Thaas' where you'm best off...'

'Perhaps I will,' went Charlie. An' ee thought ov Balance, Bev, an' the Pilchard all at once. A holy trinity shone forth.

At this point, Yak walked back inta' the club. Surprisingly, ee still 'ad all his teeth left, and didn't look scat up any. In fact, ee wuz smilin'.

'Tommy,' ee went to un, handin' over the envelope in his hand. 'There's the money fur the fixtures an' fittun's yeah? I cudn' go forward with ut, unless you wuz sorted. We'm square now – so I reckon EBGBs a go-er. I'n start bookin' some bands now.'

Charlie's da looked in the envelope.

'How much?'

'Five grand,' went Yak. 'From Markie... fur a bit ov business ee owed me for...'

'Proper,' went Tommy. 'Want a pint do ee?'

'Na... I'm a'right fur one now. I'm meetun' tha' Jody ent I? – fur a drink in town... She just text me. See you two later.'

So tha' wuz Yak outta' ut. Knawin' ee, Charlie might find Jody in 'is spare roomn, time ee comed back.

Charlie's world collapsed a bit at tha' point. That old mine-workings-sinking feeling. Now even Yak wuz in cahoots widn'. Resistance wuz futile, so ut seemed. Ee cudn' go anywhere. Ee wud have t'wait fur 'is da. Ee'd have t'spend the rest ov the evening avoidin' Markie. Still, ee wuz big enough now, fur everyone inside t'want a piece obm'. Yeah – Markie Phillips 'ad a rock star aura to un these days. The fuckers inside the Club wuz even queuing up for 'is autograph alongside the rest ov the current A team squad.

Charlie went out on the chewing-gum splattered terraces an' looked across at the sacred turf of Treyew Road. Ee knew the club wuz goin' up inta' Football League Two. 'Twas in the air – a given. But somethun' wudn' right about ut. This wuz Cornwall, where nothun' went right, and when ut did, well, you didn' believe ut wuz true. Inside, right on cue, wuz Tina Turner's legs struttin' away t' 'Simply the Best' with every drunken tool singin' along to ut like they'd already gained promotion.

In the chill of the evening, Charlie didn' care about promotions. Instead, ee wuz havin' premonitions. Ee wuz being held by Bev, an' she wuz back in the band again. Ee wuz in her bed next to her, on a tour bus, ploughing all the autobahns of central Europe somewhere, knawing all ov this lot wuz just a bad dream. Shame wuz, ut wudn'.

The mutterin' grounds-keeper (who wuz pissed off because ee 'ad t'work later than usual coz of the press conference) wuz turning off the flood-lights. Areas of the pitch were consumed with blackness, just like Charlie's heart. Unstoppable now, voodoo pilchard, voodoo pilchard, voodoo pilchard, voodoo pilchard tumbled around the four chambers ov ut like there wuz naw tomorra'.

> Smuggler's Super Strong Liquid Treatment – 60% stronger hair.
> Helps repair and rebuild
> • Strengthens and protects – Our exclusive complex joins forces with UV protection to help replace lost minerals and proteins
> • Repairs from the inside out – Marine extracts and vegetable proteins replenish every strand while special silicones protect the surface, leaving the cuticle smooth and healthy
> • Seals split ends – The complex, marine extracts, silicone and proteins create the ultimate power team to seal split ends

There wuz a tomorra' though.

Trescothick gived Charlie a call didn' a? Did Charlie fancy goin' out an' doing a bit ov coasteering with un?

'Y'never knaw' said the modern An Gov ov Park an Tansys, 'ut might inspire some new songs...'

Like fuck. Charlie wuz stugglin' t'write anything new at the moment anyway.

'Whaas' ut all about?' asked Charlie.

Trescothick explained in tha' cakey way ov 'is.

'Who wuz goin'?'

Trescothick said there wuz a few ov um, including Boy Bluett. Ee'd roped in Mel an' Kelv as well. In fact, tha' pair wuz supposed t'be quite good at ut – havin' experienced somethun' similar on holiday in France.

'Would a need anything?'

Trescothick 'ad all the gear necessary. Might need some shorts an' a towel, bit ov crowst an' a drink maybe.

'Could a bring Neil an' Anthony?'

"Course you can boy,' went Trescothick.

Now, like moast ov the adult population ov Cornwall, Charlie did 'is utmost normally t'avoid any contact with the sea. The general idea tha' moast ov the Cornish spent their time in the ocean – well, wuz flawed really. See the real Cornish (not all the surfer twats up Perranporth or Newquay, who wuz main-ly neo-Cornish emmets anyway) knawed the power ov the sea all too well. Y'only 'ad t'listen the radio over a typical summer (when they wudn' talkin' about Trura City's glorious new stadi-um) t'hear how many tourists had died around the coast (rip currents, climbing cliffs, old adits, an' dinghys were the top offenders) t'make ee understand its danger.

The awnly real exception wuz the fishermen – and thaas' because they wuz mental. Yeah – mentalists fur a living tha' lot. The yacht brigade – well, they wuz just playin' at ut wudn' um? – the boat equivalent of wild swimming instead of full-on coas-teering. But this time, Charlie succumbed. Well, knawin' wha' ee did now, about the state of Trura City's backer, ee didn't rightly care fur 'is own safety, seemingly let alone anyone else's. This coasteering thing looked a bit ov an adrenaline rush. Besides, anything usually involving Trescothick or Bluett wuz bound t'be a bit ov a laugh. Ut'd be good to hang with the old Balance crowd – an' catch up a bit with Mel and Kelv.

'Do I have t'wear a beret?'

At this, Trescothick paused fur a bit.

'Ut would help if you wanted t'look like the rest ov the Tigers?'

'The Tigers?'

Trescothick explained about his new an' improved para-mil-itary outfit (a new branch of the KLF – the Kernow Liberation Front), an' tha' this wuz all part ov their on-going training pro-gramme for when ut all kicked off. That wuz apparently the day the Cornish wud be housed in townships, with a curtailment ov their basic human rights an' their need ov saffron cake. A lot ov ut Charlie had already garnered from Micky. Ee knew well Trescothick's political ambitions. T'be honest, moast ov ut Charlie agreed with. Ee knawed the score. Had done, ever since ee wuz a kid. Everyone did on Trelawny. 'Twas just Trescothick's methods really tha' they disagreed.

'But by peaceful means,' Charlie wud go.

'Na,' went Trescothick. 'We'm beyond the point ov turnin' back...'

See, if Charlie wuz more the human rights ov Pearl Jam, then Trescothick wuz the agit-prop anger ov Rage Against The Machine wudn' a?

'Ut dun't involve any surface-t'-air missiles then?'

'Not this time around...'

Charlie found out the where an' when, and wha' time ut wuz expected t'go on to. Well, there wuz Bev t'think about. Like his ma, she 'ad an assignment t'be written, so Sunday sounded a good day fur ut. Ee'd see Bev in the evening.

'One thing Charlie,' went Trescothick. 'All ov this is strictly top secret... Do not reveal the names ov any ov the partici-pants, take any photographs... or ask too many questions...'

'But they'll know who I am...'

'Yeah – but you dun't count,' went Trescothick haughtily.

'Oh. Cheers...' went Charlie.

'I'm not being funny Charlie, but you are not yet a fully signed up member ov the Tigers... Besides, you've been on *X-Factor*. Everyone knaws you already. You ent... covert enough...'

Not covert enough. Fuckin' 'ell. Tha' wuz Charlie's life over, right there an' then.

'Is Bluett then?'

'Yeah – ee's second-in-command...'

'Is ee "covert" enough then?'

'Yeah. 'Course.'

'I see. But i's alright fur Neil an' Anthony though? Y'knaw his problems an' tha'...'

Trescothick knew.

'Aspergers an' ADHD idn' ut? Might do un some good...' ee went.

Ee 'ad a point. Fur a tool, sometimes Trescothick wuz a'right.

Charlie phoned Neil an' told un about the activity. Yeah,

Voodoo Pilchard

Neil reckoned 'twud be a good break from the routine at Tesco, and somethun' tha' would serve Anthony well. Apparently, the last time the school took un on an outward bound centre, ee'd had a great time, an' wudn' naw trouble t'the instructors t'all. Yeah, but this wuz Trescothick and Bluett. Boath of um wuz still tools ov the first order. Even though Charlie 'ad agreed t'ut, ee wuz perhaps expectin' an emergency call to the coastguard at some point in the afternoon, an' then a helicopter being dispatched from down Culdrose. Even another trip inta' Treliske A&E might be on the cards with a new incident ov NFC: Normal fuckin' coasteering.

Downstairs in Charlie's house, Nurse Jody wuz makin' herself some breakfast, wearing one ov' Yak's shirts tha' wuz shawin' just about everything., especially when she bent over t'take the milk outta' the fridge.

'A'right Charlie?' she went. 'Fancy meetin' you here...'

'Whaaaa?' went Charlie, tryin' t' avoid seein' wha' ee shudn'.

'Nice plaace you got here. Proper job-like, fur you an' Yakky...'

Who d'fuck wuz Yakky?

Her eyes looked upwards t'Yak's squat upstairs.

Yakky now wuz ut? 'Twudn' be naw use askin' tha' tool ef ee wanted t'go coasteering. Na, ee'd be full-on steerin' his way through Jody's cleavage – an' hopin' fur more games ov doctors and nurses tha' afternoon. 'Twas lookin' like EBGBs wuz on the back-burner fur a bit while Yakky got 'is somewhat EB and slightly GB end away. An' there Charlie wuz thinkin' tha' might be the perfect debut venue to try out some ov 'is new songs – in a kind ov unplugged, acoustic set.

Today, o'course, the game wuz on wudn' ut? Half ov Cornwall'd be travelling up the M5 an' headin' over the Severn Bridge t'Newport. Saturday'd given um time enough t'recover from Friday night's celebratory hangover. How many times did um sing 'Simply the Best'? His da 'ad gone o'course – with some of the boys from over South Crofty. Not a lot ov gold wuz bein' dug tha' weekend y'cud tell. No doubt Markie Phillips wud've gone too, in order t'show his newly-found allegiance – prob'ly chauffeur-driven these days up the A30 by his goons. The radio wuz all full ov ut – one of they 'Will the last one over the Tamar Bridge' turn the lights out?' moments. Apparently, Newport

County wuz named The Ironsides after their steel-making industrial past – so here 'twas, the Ironsides versus the Tinmen – a real grudge game ov heavy-metal football. The Tinmen really needed a win. A draw wudn' be enough t'give um the right amount ov points. But Newport County, well, they wuz fighting relegation see, an' the points would mean as much t'they as t' Trura City.

Charlie left 'Yakky' and 'Nursey' alone in his house. His *room-ov-'is-own* plan 'ad gone properly tits up ov late, an' so ee got inta' his Peugeot t'pick up Neil an' Anthony down Portreath. Apparently, Jess wuz goin' t'meet Ally an' lil' Megan in town t'do a bit ov high-street damage on their debit cards. Then Ally wuz goin' t'help make some of these new Cornish products beauty range wudn' she? – an' then test um out. Well, considerin' Ally's business experience with Pasty-Pronto, she knawed a little bit ov how t'get ut out there. Charlie wuz still in a bit ov a daze t'be honest, but then 'is eyes suddenly opened much wider when he checked out the street furniture ov Troon. The whole fuckin' plaace had been bombed with orange an' red Voodoo Pilchard stencilling. You cudn' move fur ut on the Co-op an' the Lloyds Pharmacy on New Street. Even the pub an' chip-house had been done over. Curiously, the Pilchard appeared t'have left Headönism alone.

'Fuck me,' Charlie went.

Jimmy Pengelly wudn' be happy either. By the look ov ut, they'd dun over 'is shed too. 'Spect Arnie Crago's and Georgie Angov'd be havin' some of ut too. They'd prob'ly done the remainder of Arnie's roses an' 'is shed too. True enough, the artist 'ad had a go at Trelawny too. Moast of the diggers an' plant equipment had got a tag on um. *Cormac* had got used t'working down Trelawny. They knawed tha' each night 'twas best t'cover up the cab windows an' tha' (to stop windows being broken, an' drive offs by the tackers) – but they'd been seen to as well.

Micky texted un, as ee drove along Newton Road:

Seen ut all. Not the real Pilchard though!

Things wuz getting' a bit outta' hand now Charlie realised – but then, wha' cud ee do about ut?

Everyone got there didn' um? – down at the National Trust car park at Godrevy, just off Gwithian Bridge. Mel and Kelv wuz already kitted out in their body-padded wetsuits, an' were testing the weight an' feel of their buoyancy aids.

'Are you in the Tigers then?' asked Neil. 'I mean full-on members...'

'Na... not really,' went Kelv. 'I mean, the bank didn't like ut much when I moved inta' the world ov porn, so I don't think they'd approve any terrorist activities do you?'

'We are not terrorists,' went Trescothick – slightly on one. 'I prefer the term freedom fighters...'

This wuz comin' from a boy who wuz strugglin' t'put on his wet-suit and stragglin' around the shore like a huge, beached whale. Twudn' helped by bad-mouthin' the National Trust as imperial fascists who support the English state.

'Some ass on un,' went Mel. 'Orange too...'

'Make sure you've adjusted the straps properly on your buoyancy aids. They should be tight, but not constrictive.'

This wuz comin' from Boy Bluett, who apparently would be commanding the operation from the cliff-top. You 'ad real confidence then in the whole operation, knawin' tha' ee'd done the risk assessment too.

Charlie, Neil an' Anthony wuz gettin' kitted up. You cudn' help but laugh at the state ov ut. Both Neil and Charlie wudn' very comfortable in wet suits t'be honest. The only one who seemed t'knaw wha' ee wuz doin' was Anthony, who wuz already dressed for the water, an' ready to go. How comed all the surfin' emmet cunts looked s'cool in their Gul wetsuits, when everyone else looked like the biggest knobber going'?

'Which direction are we going in?' Anthony wuz askin' ov Boy Bluett.

'Due north,' went Bluett.

'I think you'll find it's actually slightly North-northwest...' corrected Anthony.

'Yes – thaas' what I meant,' said a flustered Bluett.

Y'had t'hand ut to un. Anthony looked like ee knawed more about map-reading, tidal conditions and the natural world ov the rock pools than just anyone else there. Ee wuz already identifyin all the plants, types of rock, seaweed an' shells.

As they were toolin' up, another van pulled up, with the

Cornish Tigers in ut. Fuck, they wuz really lookin' like a bunch ov IRA terrorists from another era.

'They got balaclavas on,' nawticed Neil.

'Yeah... Thaas' coz they're on real ops training... went Trescothick. 'This is a real simulation see...'

'I see,' went Charlie.

'Charlie Curnow,' ee went t' the masked raiders – introducin' ov un to the masked raiders.

They all nodded t'each other like 'twas a familiar name.

Tha' wuz a bit scary Charlie reckoned – that the para-militaries knawed who ee wuz.

'This is Neil, his son Anthony, an' thaas; Mel and Kelv...'

'A'right?' everyone went, like y'do if you'm cakey in Cornwall.

'A'right?' everyone went back, which they wuz..

'Y'might want some ov this,' said Trescothick, openin' up a cool box, which contained about a dozen chilled cans ov Red Bull.

Trescothick wuz already on his second can.

'I'll have one,' said Anthony.

'Na. I doan't think thaas' a good idea do you?'

Anthony looked at his father in a sort of Dr Bruce Banner turning inta' the Incredible Hulk-kind-ov-way – a look tha' Charlie knew intimately by now.

'You'm hyper enough Anth,' went Neil. 'You d'knaw tha'...'

Anthony looked at the ground, obviously a bit pissed off tha' everyone else cud have one.

Charlie bent down to un.

'You got Jedi powers Anth...' went Charlie. 'You have a high midicholorian count already...'

Anth smiled a bit more now.

'You got the way with un there,' said Neil. 'You wud be great with kids Charlie...'

Charlie gived un a look that wuz t'be read as fuck off, not on yer life, never, ever.

By now, there wuz quite a crew ov um down there, and the uniform look ov the collective, not t'mention the balaclavas ov one or two ov um, wuz attracting some interest from the general public, who generally comed down here t'walk their dogs an' get a bit of air, then pop over Hayle for a bit ov shoppin' at the new M&S store there. Ov late though, this wuz the centre of all the work on the Wave Hub project, so there wuz a bit ov interest in observin' all o'tha' operation too.

Ah fuck. You ebm' seen nothun' like this 'ere coasteering fur a fuckin' laugh. Charlie hadn' had s'good a giggle since well, prob'ly the last time ee'd seen Clifford dancin' up Institute a few years back. At that time, well, the tide wuz almost in around Magow Rocks which is where they wuz goin' t' start, and the idea wuz tha' they wuz goin' t'make ut up past the Cleaders an' around Godrevy Point, then on to Mutton Cove – on ta' Castle Giver an' up t' the Knavocks t'pick up the road down t'Gwithian Churchtown. The core thing about ut wuz y' 'ad t'have a crew up on the cliffs watchin' out fur ee. 'Twas ideal if they had phone or mobile communication with they below makin' their way round the inter-tidal 'impact' zone.

The basic objective wuz t'move as quickly as y'cud through the landscape. Havin' said tha' as moast ov um wudn' tha' fit, and Trescothick the least fit ov all ov um. There were plenty ov stops, mainly t'look at usually inaccessible rock pools an' ledges. A few ov the more organised members of the Cornish Tigers had brought snorkel masks, and they wuz dippin' under every so often, t'see what wuz beneath the surface. The first big waves started t'hit as they proceded over the Cleaders rocks. From here, the three islands of Godrevy were in good view, so you got a reasonable view ov the lighthouse. Charlie wuz explainin' the tale about Virginia Woolf and her novel t'Mel.

'Thaas' interestin'... I heard tha' someone have bought ut. They wuz sayin' tha' in the *West Briton*... Apparently, they'm goin' t' start trips out there again from Hayle...'

'Not in weather like this though surely?' asked Neil.

The foam wuz bein' cast up a bit, and the swell quite fierce already, even on a fairly reasonable day in May.

Trescothick wuz makin' up fur lost time. Perhaps the Red Bull wuz kickin' in a bit. Ee looked like some sad version of Jackie Chan at one point, flicking between the ledges ov the Cleaders, an' then then doin' a bit ov a belly-flop in the ocean. Up on the cliffs, Bluett an' a couple ov the other Cornish Tigers brigade were watchin' out fur them, seeking obstacles and dangers tha' might confront the party in the 'impact' zone.

Alan M. Kent

Anthony seemed t'be lappin' ut up.

'Daddy, look down here...' ee wuz going.

Neil ad a look an' saw a couple of largish dogfish cruising around the shallows.

Neil held Anthony's hand as the negotiated a particularly gnarly piece of barnacle-edged rock.

'Hey Mel,' said Charlie, jumping down. 'Do you remember they two bloaks who comed in Headönizm the other day – while Kayleigh wuz cuttin' my hair?'

Mel thought fur a bit. Kelv listened on.

'Yeah – think so... Comed in together didn' um?'

'Know um do ee?'

'No – but I've seen um around Troon before... an' over Twilight...'

'Do you know they'm workin' fur Markie Phillips? I seen um Friday – over Trura City football club... They wuz with un.'

The news slightly disturbed Mel an' Kelvin.

'Dun't want their sort in there,' said Kelvin.

'Na. Thaas' right,' said Charlie, grunting, as ee mounted a massive piece ov granite. 'Did they ask any questions or any-thing?'

'Na... Not really,' went Mel. 'Should I tell Jess?'

'Dun't say anything fur now... Just wondered thaas' all...'

As Mel, Kelv, Anthony, Neil an' Charlie were progressin' ahead, the Cornish Tigers seemed t'be takin' an unusual inter-est in the status of Godrevy Lighthouse as they were passing ut. Charlie nawticed tha' Trescothick, in particular, wuz keenly tak-ing notes. Up on the cliff, Bluett wuz scanning ut with 'is binoculars, making mobile phone calls to Trescothick below.

'Y'interested in the lighthouse then?' asked Charlie.

'Not really,' lied Trescothick. 'Just the bird life over there, thaas' all. Apparently, somebody've seen some cormorants out there lately... I read about ut on the RSPB Cornwall website...'

'I like them,' went Anthony. 'Their wings are weird – like dragons...'

'How far across then - from the shore here – to the island then?' asked Neil.

Trescothick listened in on this bit ov yap.

'Not too far... but further than y'think. Three quarters ov a mile perhaps...' offered Charlie.

'Easy rowing or no?' asked Mel.

'Take ee moast ov the day,' chipped in Kelv. 'The swell stops ee I d'reckon. Every three strokes forward, you'd go one back...'

Still 'twas where some of the old lining boats used to come out years ago – lookin' fur mackerel and pilchards..

Trescothick stepped away from the main group bit, and dialled the number fur Bluett. Charlie climbed out of the pool ee'd found hisself in t'earwig on the conversation.

'We'll need fast motor boats – rigid inflatables...' Trescothick wuz sayin'. 'An' we'll need t'look carefully at the tides... Landin' will be the issue. Over...'

A garbled message came back tha' Charlie cudn' hear.

So whatever Trescothick wuz plannin', ut involved Godrevy in some capacity. Charlie looked over the bay t' where St Ives wuz. Prob'ly on a day like today the plaace wud be filled with Wallis, Nicolson, Lanyon and Hepworth acolytes. Wuz tha' the tool's plan now? A potential launch at St Ives from the top of the lighthouse. Na. Surely ee'd learnt his lesson there? More likely with this crew, they'd paint a St Piran's flag on the bugger an' reclaim ut fur the People's Republic ov Cornwall. Either way, 'twas a bit of Woolf's *T'the Lighthouse* tha' wuz in the offing. Trescothick caught Charlie overhearin' un. Ee pressed the red button an' cut the call.

Charlie nawticed a change in Anthony's usual hyperactive behaviour. Fur once, ee wuz actually standin' stock still.

'Over there,' ee went. 'Look. There's a woman.'

The little cunt had some keen eye-sight. Nothun' seemed t'go past un, tha' much wuz true. Ee made a little dive down inta' one ov the smaller trenches filled with billowing seaweed.

Everyone stopped coasteerin' t'look across. The woman had long, dark hair, an' looked dream-like, as ef she wuz a ghostly presence, rather than a real person. Even more incredible, she wuz standin' up on the balcony, next to the glass ov the shipping light itself. A few seagulls circled the top of the lighthouse as she stood there. From here, they had the appearance of circling crows.

'Hello, hello out there,' Anthony wuz goin', waving to her. Ee had both hands in the air. She didn't respond though.

'She's mean,' Anthony mumbled to hisself. 'She's a witch...'

Neil overheard un but didn't think much ov ut. What

Anthony 'ad said wuz like somethun' out ov a *Famous Five* story. Ee'd come out with tha' kind of stuff lately – but then, ee'd been consuming adventure stories at home all the time. The problem wuz they just cudn' get un t'read anythin' at school.

The woman seemed to realise they were watchin' her, an' so she stepped down inside ov the structure again. When she wuz gone, ut wuz as if she 'adn' been there t'all.

'I thought nawbody wuz out there these days. Automated idn' ut?' asked Kelv.

'Yeah, they are,' went Mel, 'but like I said, I d'reckon someone's bought ut... Could be they... Cen't see naw boat moored up though.'

Charlie listened intently and watched Trescothick's reaction. The other Tigers with un seemed t'be lookin' fur his response. Ee gave none.

Fuckin' 'ell, they 'adn' made ut that far around the coast. Everyone wuz already knacked.

'I'm sweatun like a poultice...' observed Orange Trescothick, sniffin' both of 'is armpits.

'Time fur a bit ov crowst then eh?' went Kelv.

Everyone sat down. Partially, their food an' drinks had been carried by Bluett this far, and he managed to scramble down to them. A hot drink went down well.

'Anyone know how Trura is getting' on?' asked Kelv.

'Nil nil apparently,' went Bluett. 'A bloak up on the cliff told me, who'd been listenin' to the match live on BBC Radio Cornwall.'

Well, at least they 'adn' conceded anything wuz the collective thought ov all the coasteerers.

'I'm like Obi Wan an' Jar Jar when they go in the Bongo,' went Anthony, ducking beneath the surface of a large-sized tidal pool..

Only Charlie knawed what ee wuz on about – a sequence during *Star Wars Episode I: The Phantom Menace*, in the waters ov the planet Naboo, when, with Qui-Gon Jinn, they had left the Gungans.

'See un now,' went Neil, reflectively. 'You wudn' knaw there wuz anything wrong with un... Just playin' away there like any normal six-year old...'

Charlie wuz listenin', but still carefully watchin' Trescothick for clues. Ee appeared t'be discussing elements ov the Ten Point plan with other members of the Tigers.

'Charlie?'

'Charlie?' Neil 'ad t'say again. 'I do want t'lay down the guitar parts – fur the new stuff you're recordin'... honest... but Ally an' I... I'm not sure we'm goin' t'make ut... Things are hard at home right now. We'm arguing all the time.'

That stopped Charlie from focusing on Orange Trescothick fur a bit. Neil wuz shakin' his head a bit an' Charlie cud see tears formin' in the corners ov his eyes.

'The stress ov ut all?'

'Yes-shh,' Neil went, squalin' slightly.

Charlie moved around t'shield Neil from the other para-militaries on operations.

'I'm always here mate,' ee said.

'I know, I know...' said Neil. 'but when y'have kids. y'dun't expect this do ee? Y'want everything t'be perfect dun't ee? An' well, I dun't think ut ever will be... not any more...'

Charlie looked over at Anthony. Like any other six-year old, now ee wuz throwing pebbles an' rocks inta' the water, each one getting progressively larger. Each time ut made a splosh ee shivered with the sea's power and the sheer delight in wha' ee wuz doin' ov.

Charlie grabbed Neil.

'Look at un...' said Charlie. 'Now... look... If not fur you, then look fur me.'

Trescothick wuz now givin' un bits ov custard cream to feed t' a friendly seagull.

'I cen't look,' went Neil. 'Every time I see un, I wun't t' nearnly 'bout break down... Tha' wuz ut Charlie... Ut wuz tha' tha' wuz getting' t'me at tha' Hard Rock Hell event in Prestatyn...'

'Look at un fur me,' went Charlie. 'Honestly Neil, I knaw ee got 'is problems an' tha' – but never mind, y'knaw – thaas' yer prosperity, yer beauty, yer love, yer health... Anthony... well, Anthony's everything I'm tryin' t'write about Neil.'

Neil stopped squalin' fur a second an' listened.

'An you an' Ally... you'm made fur each other. Never forget tha'... Stay strong... boath ov ee. You've been through too much t'let ut go.'

Alan M. Kent

Charlie knawed Ally cud sometimes be a pain in the ass, and sometimes she didn' think much of ee, but that wudn' the point – not now, at least. The point now wuz helpin' Neil through all ov this. All the other crap: Trura City, 'is da, the Pilchard, well tha' wuz just nothun' in comparison.

'Yer a good mate Charlie,' Neil said.

As Neil wuz recoverin', Charlie saw Trescothick on a mission with the balaclava crew. Ee cudn' quite work ut out, but ee cud swear tha' the Orange one 'ad a crafty set of blueprints of the lighthouse in his hand, and wuz checkin' the detail ov ut with the real thing opposite. So this wuz clearly a reconnaissance mission. There wuz time enough fur un t'put ut away, in 'is waterproof rucksack before Charlie an' Neil reached um.

'Ready fur the off then?' asked Trescothick.

'Yeah – ready fur some more,' went Charlie.

Trescothick signalled t'Bluett tha' they'd be startin' again.

Charlie hung back a bit t'see if Trescothick wuz goin' t'look again at the lighthouse. Ee didn' though, an' instead went stankin', swimmin' an; climbin' on ahead ov them – heading up to the Point. Above them wuz an old tumulus Charlie knawed ov (ee'd climbed to ut often as a kid). Es, a plaace where the old Celts had come t'bury their dead, an' look out on t he ocean – a tomb with a view if y'liked. Yeah – when 'is day comed, thaas' the kind of thing ee wudn' mind. All the time 'twas givin' un a few song-writing ideas.

Just here, the scramblin' got more intense. You left the water behind fur a bit an' pushed up the cliff-face a little more.

'Look at me,' shouted Anthony.

Ee wuz up t'the top ledge before anyone else.

'Go careful,' advised Neil.

'Daddy hurry up. Dun't be soooo slow...'

Neil wuz startin' t' realise tha' a few months workin' at Tesco wudn' quite leavin' un s'fit as playin' a gig every night, where you'd sweat buckets an' keep moving. Charlie didn' dare laugh, because ee wuz feelin' ut too. Ee hoped Bev wudn' be too much in the mood fur ut this evening, because ee knew ee wuz goin' t'ache t'buggery later on.

'Go easy,' ee cud hear hisself saying.

Once 'round the point, things got a bit easier, even though the cliffs were higher, and Bluett an' the support crew seemingly a long way away. 'Bout here at Mutton Cove wuz where all the seals gathered. T'be honest, they didn't seem that bothered by the presence of Trescothick's coasteerin' crew.

'Don't go too near their calves,' wuz the general advice tha' seemed t'be given.

'Daddy, look at them!' said Anthony with a sense ov amazement an' wonder. A few of the female seal cows slid inta' the Atlantic. 'They look like mermaids!'

No-one else wud have made the connection, but Anthony did.

'Ee's got an amazing imagination,' said Trescothick. 'The next generation ov creative spirit of the Cornish see...

At tha' moment, Trescothick's phone rang. He took the call. 'Twas obviously about the footy.

Ee put the phone back in his pocket.

'One nil,' ee went. 'T'Trura... Five minutes t'go 'til full-time. Stoppage time yet mind'

Well, tha' news just about boosted everyone on, t'make ut around the next section of the impact zone. This wuz the section they called Kynance. This wudn' the one down on the Lizard but another section of rock heading north until you got t'Nathaga Rocks. Nathaga wuz where ut might get a bit more difficult. Bluett 'ad forewarned um t'be fair, an' calculated a bit of rope might be useful, t'help pull people up – especially the less experienced ones – like well, Neil an' Charlie. The view from there wuz pretty spectacular though. You cud see up t'St Agnes, an' then on this particular day, further up the coast, almost 'til Newquay. At moments like this you cud understand why every tool in the country wanted t'drive down here an' have a piece ov ut. If you wuz Cornish, then at times like this, you actually realised who you wuz, an' what the plaace meant to ee. This wuz wha' Charlie meant by seeking solace in the Celtic West. This wuz ut. This, ee supposed, wuz what Trescothick, an' 'is asshole ov a feyther were fightin' for. On different fronts sure – but the same battle fur Cornwall – wha' wuz the joke his da towld un? – God's Own Country.

'I's beautiful innut?' went Anthony, who fur a moment there, wuz soundin' like nawbody gived up any dialect fur standard English. Six year olds in 1825 'ad prob'ly sounded the same.

''Es,' went Charlie.

From Nathaga, the party 'eaded inland. All towld, they'd been on the go now fur about three hours, an' fur a high-intensity sport such as this, tha' wuz enough. Towards the south, you cud see Camborne lurking in the distance, Carn Brea – a g'eat brown, sleeping monster on the horizon – an' beyond tha', Obby Stanker. They wuz stankin' now back down the road tha' lead down inta' Gwithian again. Nawbody there knawed ov ut o'course, but all ov um went past the point where Markie's gimps had crashed the Land-rover fulla' Yakky's stolen cocaine. If you looked close enough you cud prob'ly still find traces ov ut on the road. A few Chelsea diamonds on the road surface wuz all anybody nawticed. Up Higher Pencobben a few bullocks looked down upon them, and out to sea, the seal cows blew air out of their nostrils as they surfaced from catching pilchards an' other fish tha' comed in on tha' tide.

All the world seemed at peace, and the Tinmen had apparently won against the Ironsides, but from the way Trescothick wuz carryin' hisself an' his smug orange face, Charlie knawed tha' some serious Shock an' Awe wuz bein' planned. For wha' purpose though, ee'd yet to determine.

'Thank you Mr Trescothick,' went Anthony, as they got back to their cars. 'I had an awesome day... Next time though, can *I* wear a balaclava please?'

Tamar Super Strong Daily Shampoo – Strong hair starts from within.
Strengthens and Protects
• Strengthens – Super strong compound penetrates deep into the hair to help re-build internal structure
• Gently cleanses – Mild River Tamar extract suitable for coloured-treated hair, gently cleanses and helps prevent further damage to hair
• Enhances shine – Conditioning ingredients help improve the feel and intensify surface shine

Ee wuz on his way back home when ut happened. Ee'd just been in t'see how 'is da wuz doin'. Thaas' when they had un. The fuckers 'eaved un in the back ov the van in one go. There wuz a lot of cunts in there. Ee cud tell. As they hauled un up one ov they put a canvas hood over un, and tied ut around his throat. Thaas' when the dislocation started. Fuckin' 'ell - all Charlie ever wanted wuz an easy life. Why did everything have t'be s'difficult? All ov the road lessons ee 'ad learnt, merged into one big fuckin' problem now. Ee was shaking with fear. Feelin' around the inside of the van he felt the wooden floor and sides ov ut. It 'ad been boarded out – the kind of van bands used to gig in. Somewhere in 'is mind, ee recognised ut, but cudn' plaace ut fur the moment. There was a smell of tobacco and maybe some cannabis too. None ov the fuckers seem to speak but ee cud hear ov um breathing deeply. Ee wobbled about at first, then, just as he found his balance, an' orientated hisself, they roughly put his wrists together and positioned cable ties around them. They cut into his skin and hurt t'fuck. This wudn' the way 'twas meant t'be. Ee was meant t'be at 'is home in School Lane, listenin' t'music an' tryin' t'write new songs. The van was moving quickly, takin' the corners way too fast. Ee felt the rear wheels hit the corners of pavements. clunking at the metal of the wheel rims. As they hit one particularly tight bend, Charlie couldn' stop hisself from falling over onto the floor. One ov the cunts laughed at un. This wudn' good. This wudn' good t'all. Charlie'd 'ad moments where ee'd been shit-scared before, but nothun' like this. This wuz up a notch, and naw mistake.

They were well-disciplined you, this crowd. No conversation. Nothing that might give them away. There wuz nothin' that gave Charlie a notion of who they were. Fuckin' 'ell – Charlie'd come 'ome t'escape riding around in the back of a van. 'Ere ee wuz again – bumpin' around in a bugger.

Ee felt the road surface change slightly. It became bumpy – obviously pot holes, and the driver slowed down to negotiate them. Where were they? They hadn't come too far. Wasteland prob'ly, around Pool or Crofty – already ear-marked fur development. Tha', or United Downs somewhere. Eventually, the van came to a halt. There wuz movement. The fuckers in the back opened the door and got out. They shut the rear doors on un. Ee was left alone. Outside, ee cud hear muffled voices. This wuz ut Charlie reckoned. A few slaps around with a baseball bat – or somethun' more pleasant like a good knee-cappin'. 'Least ee'd seen a bit ov the world. 'Least, ee'd tried.

What 'appened next wudn' no real surprise. Ut 'ad t'happen really didn' ut? 'Twas unfinished business. One of the rear doors opened an' two people got in. Charlie sensed they were carryin' something.

'Curnow y'cunt,' comed a voice, slow, hard and bruised. It was unmistakable. Markie Phillips. His voice wuz older somehow, wiser, nastier, an' filled with hatred and self-loathing..

'What ee want?' replied Charlie, his voice nervous and uncertain.

'A bit ov payback,' went Markie.

'Payback?'

''Es. Well, we got unfinished business ebm' us?'

'What business?'

'Aw y'knaw – that little difficulty I 'ad with yer mate Mellow... I mean 'twas all nearly sorted an' then well, you fucked off didn' ee? See, I been meanin' t'catch up with ee... fur a bit...'

'It's over,' went Charlie. 'Long time ago...'

'Is ut be fuck? What about Treyew Road and the other night then? Your bewdie ov a cuntin' question...'

'Goin' t' slap me around with a heavy object are ee?' asked Charlie. 'Just like with Clifford...'

There wuz a pause. Markie laughed.

'Na... we got somethun' better planned fur you boy...'

We?

Who the fuck else wuz with un?

We?

'I have been waiting fur this moment,' came another voice. This wuz soundin' like somethun' from a fuckin' Bond movie. This voice wuz female, and familiar. Charlie put ut all together within a nano-second. That wuz Yeugen. Where the fuck 'ad she popped up from? Aw fuck, here 'twas. This was her little bit ov revenge on un – fur betrayin' er – fur goin' an snoggin' Bev. An' yeah, 'course, all that time down Club Rhino, she always 'ad the hots fur Markie. Ee knawed ut. Perhaps tha' wuz wha' wuz wrong with they together in the fust plaace. When every other cunt thought ee wuz the wust tool in the world, she still defended un. Fuckin' 'ell. Now both ov um workin' together on un. Where wuz Trescothick when y'needed the cunt?

Now ee knawed how Clifford 'ad felt. So, her an' Markie.

Voodoo Pilchard

What – partners in crime? Charlie'd never seen ut comin' – but ee wuz quickly puttin' ut all together. How cud a have been s'fuckin' thick? Obviously, she was a woman scorned. Hadn' a fuckin' learnt anything? A road lesson fur ee there Curnow. Behave like a tool an' ut'll come back an' bite ee in the ass when you'm least expectin' ov ut.

'I loved you Charlie Curnow,' she went, and then laughed like a witch. Charlie didn't knaw ut then, but she wuz the Voodoo Queen – 'is worst nightmare.

Ee didn' knaw wha' the fuck t'say.

'You hurt me...'

Charlie wuz beginnin' t'wish ee 'adn' set his eyes on her that time. How cud someone so lovely become s'evil s'quickly? Well, perhaps tha' wuz the way ov the world. People becomes bitter when stuff dun't work out. An' now, wha' wuz the fuckin' attraction t'Markie Phillips? If there was one knobber ee wished fur er not t'be seein', then ut wuz him. Givin' her one then, that or as ee later found out, ee'd set her up in a nice little spot on the coast. Good sea views an' tha'. Ut would've made Virginia Woolf jealous at least. So now, they wuz goin' t'hurt him. Ee cud feel ut comin' a mile off.

Ee wuz workin' ov ut out. Money – tha' wuz the attraction. Markie 'ad money t'burn – and she'd be happy t'ignite the lot fur'n.

Ee thought ut over. Last thing ee'd 'eard 'bout Yeugen was tha' she'd fucked off back to Poland. The economy 'ad got better there. She'd earned enough in Cornwall t'fund er place at university, and tha' wuz tha' – one ov they chalk ut up t'experience moments in life. Obviously, the People's Republic ov Cornwall 'ad a greater attraction to her than Charlie first realised. Right there, right now, ee wuz feelin' properly shafted. Ee'd thought better ov her. But then she wuz the perfect partner fur Markie wudn' she? Tha' wuz Markie's skill, see. Ee cud turn an' twist the knife like no other. Es – Curnow's old girlfriend: fuckin' proper job.

Pins in the doll eh – and worse? Many dolls perhaps. A little trio. And worse.

'Thought we'd have a bit ov fun with ee,' went Markie.

Charlie knew Markie's idea ov fun. It was right up there with the shotgun placed on Neil's ball bag, an' raidin' art galleries.

Charlie knew the rumours too – about the cash-point robberies. Had t'be Markie – ee wuz the only fucker in west Cornwall who'd chance his arm at jobs like tha'.

'Feyther a'right is a?' went Markie, throwing tha' in there at Charlie, jus' fur fun. 'Pity tha' Club ov 'is went tits up... 'twas a'right there... Still, ee an' I seem t'be doin' a'right over Trura Football Club now. Ee've recovered well from tha' heart scare ee had. Support the Tinmen a bit dun't ee? Seen ee there at match-es with the kid – Anthony idn' ut? Shame you'm such a knob-ber though...'

Charlie thought back t'Yeugen dancin' at Club Rhino a while back. Ee 'adn't liked ut. In this moment, Charlie wuz wonder-in' if there wuz any way she could be turned back from the dark side. Cud ee talk to er about pickin' ut up again? Na - truth towld – 'twas prob'ly too late.

'Jimi Hendrix idn' ut?' went Markie.

'What ee mean?'

'Who you've been impersonatin' fur the past few years...'

''Twas a tribute band...'

'Took drugs though didn' a?

'A few...'

'Liked t'pop a bit ov speed an' LSD from what I've read...'

''Es...'

'We've been thinkin'.... well, we d'reckon you should try a few...'

Ah fuck, went Charlie t'hisself. Ee might have knawn wha' wuz comin'. Clever these pair. They wudn' goin' t'mess un up physically – that wuz too easy. Na – they 'ad somethun' alto-gether more interestin' planned. Yeah – harm un mentally – thaas' the ticket.

So, 'ere it comed.

Markie undid the hood Charlie wuz wearin', and yanked ut off his head. The two ov them had balaclavas on but Charlie knew their eyes. S'pause it might have been useful to have tha' kind ov gear on first ov all, but ut didn' matter much now. Ee knawed both of them now. Still, the first thing ee did wuz to look up at Yeugen. The same eyes ee 'ad once loved, now as cold as the forests outside Quidzin. She tapped her knuckles on the side of the van, and the other crew who had been waiting outside, came into the van. They bundled in, and held Charlie down harshly. Charlie knawed um – two ov um wuz the boys who'd been watchin' un in Headönizm and then over Treyew Road. The other gorilla wuz Markie's usual muscle – the one with the neck tattoo. Ee knew what wuz comin'.

'Knaw wha' this is? went Markie.

He held up a wrap of paper with something inside ov ut.

Charlie knew ut wuz a drug ov some kind, but not precisely what was contained in the wrap.

'A bit ov meaow meaow – with a few grams of speed, coke and ecstasy thrown in... Trelawny-style bit ov bucket... Should sort ee out nicely...'

Charlie wuz shakin' with fear by now.

'Give ee a proper Jimi Hendrix experience eh?'

Markie forced open his mouth. Charlie tried to clamp his teeth down on his hand, but some other fucker had a pair of forceps stuck in 'is mouth just to make sure ut stayed open.

'Eat ut you fucker!' went Markie. Charlie gagged an' tried not to swallow the wrap. 'Oh – I know, ut ent very nice idn' ut? Good medicine though... especially fur lyin', scheming fuckers like you.'

Charlie watched Yeugen above him. Ee cudn' make out her mouth, but ee cud see the terror in 'is eyes, reflected in her's. She kept starin' at him though.

'Give him a drink!' shouted Markie.

Another tool forced some bottled water inta' Charlie's mouth. The wrap started to choke him. Ee tried spitting ut out, but Markie's hand wuz there to prevent ut. Eventually, after much coughing and force, the wrap went down his oesophagus and inta' Charlie's stomach.

'Another,' went Markie.

Charlie struggled again. This time, they sat on 'is body and legs to stop him from moving. Yeugen turned away. She felt for him ee cud tell – even though, even though...

'Argh...' went one of Markie's gorillas. 'The cunt just bit me finger...'

The gorilla gave Charlie a painful kick in his ribs. Ee'd wanted t'do tha' since watchin' un in Headönizm.

'Let me go you fuckers!' screamed Charlie, but ut wudn' naw good. Na – the next wrap went down easier than the first. Mephedrone, speed, coke and ecstasy gurgling around in his stomach. Nice little cocktail in there ready t'take un t'hell.

'One fur luck,' said Markie, laughing. This time, the cunt sat on Charlie's stomach putting both knees into his armpits.

'I can see you like ut,' ee said.

'Cunt!' mouthed Charlie, trying to turn his head.

Eventually another gorilla held Charlie's head so Markie could drop the bomb into his mouth. Ee gagged and sicked up some phlegm, but Markie wuz ready with a cloth in his mouth. He cud either swallow ut or be suffocated. The bastard knew wha' ee wuz doin' ov.

So, three wraps ov the stuff in his guts. Charlie knew wha' would happen. The trip he wuz about t'ave wuz somethun' ee'd 'eard Yak talk about a few times. Yak knew the effects ov moast drugs. Stuff like this though – fuckin' combo-bombs of mephedrone, speed, coke an' ecstasy were the kind ov thing ee generally avoided.

Charlie cud 'ear ov un: 'Bad news those fuckers... Dun't touch the stuff... I dun ut once, an' the trip wuz real gnarly, nasty-like...'

Charlie knew what ee 'ad t'do. Ee 'ad t'try an' make hisself sick. That way maybe not s'much ov ut would be absorbed. There wudn' long. Perhaps fifteen minutes tops. After that the effects would start to kick in, and Christ knaws what tha' would bring. 'Twudn' 'zactly goin' t'be a light stroll down Tehidy Woods on a Sunday afternoon, feeding the squirrels and ducks. First ov all, ee tried to do it by retching his body and throat, but to no effect. Ee needed his fingers t'stick down is throat, and well, just at this moment in time, they wuz bound behind his back. He knew the effects would come on soon: increased alertness, euphoria, excitement, openness, and a full on psychedelic look at the world of electric pastyland – not, in all honesty, somethun' ee was really looking forward to.

Yeugen looked shocked still. It was the force-feeding of the drug that had given her the discomfiture. But there wudn' much she could do now? She was in Markie's little retinue – an' she 'ad to accept tha' now.

'Any hallucinations yet? went Markie. 'They tell me this stuff is quite good... the best you'n get in Cornwall right now... You'n thank yer mate Yak fur the cocaine. Tha' wuz his little deal.'

Voodoo Pilchard

Charlie was wishin' ee'd actually had the balls to take some of the gear ee'd been offered in the past. That way, 'least ee might know how t'deal with ut. There an' then, ee wuz clueless. Ee clenched his left hand, feeling the calloused tips of his fret-playing fingers.

'You tried any ov this stuff?' went one of Markie's gorillas to him. Charlie reckoned ut wuz the neck tattoo one.

'Na. First rule of business boy. Never try any of this shit. I jus' sell ut, thaas' all...'

'You said just one bomb,' went Yeugen, breaking up their conversation. 'One bomb for him. This is too many... He may die.'

'Ee' idn' goin' t'die. Dun't ee worry. You stick t'yer spells an' voodoo – an' I'll do the rest a'right...?'

Wha' did ee just say? Holy shit.

'The damage – maybe it is long lasting...'

'The fucker's Charlie Curnow – ee's already mentally damaged... This idn' goin' t'make that much difference...'

'We take him somewhere safe then... so the effects may wear off... A room. I will pay for it. A hotel. Or back at the lighthouse...'

'No maid. That idn' the idea t'all...'

Charlie tried to retch to naw effect. 'Least they wudn' pinning un down no more. Lighthouse. Where the fuck did um mean?

'What will you do with him?'

'Let un loose eh boys?'

The gorillas and grunts grunted.

'As 'twas agreed, I d'reckon,' went the tattoo.

'You do wrong here Markie... I do not like this,' said Yeugen. Her sense of justice seemed t' kick in a bit.

'Whether you like this or naw maid, this is what we'm goin' t'do... an' you'd better shut up now... You'm in this as deep as the rest ov us 'ere... Do some ov yer Vèvès an' ut'll be sorted, yeah? '

Markie's words shut up Yeugen. Charlie kept lookin' at her – hoping she might be sympathetic an' help him out of the situation ee found hisself in. 'Twudn' easy fur her though – not now she'd thrown her lot in with ee.

'As we agreed then?' Markie confirmed to his boys.

Alan M. Kent

They placed the hood back over Charlie and all climbed in the back with him. Charlie was writhing around now. The effects were already starting. Ee needed to breathe more deeply. If ee made him sick now, the tightness of the hood would force the vomit back down his windpipe. He'd choke t'death – go the way of all his heroes. Inside the darkness of the hood, Charlie could feel the rate of his heartbeat increase. Now ee knew how 'is da felt on the the Loco Viagra. Ee was truly fucked. Over and over ee thought to hisself – shouldn' ever have got involved – 'zactly wha' Markie wanted un t'feel. So this wuz ut, not a punishment beatun'; more a punishment trip. Nothun' could 'ave prepared un fur what wuz goin' t'appen though.

In the van, ee cud hear Yeugen gently sobbing about what 'ad just happened. It wuz pitiful t'hear, but there wudn' a lot Charlie cud do about ut. Ee wuz tryin' t'keep 'is thoughts focused. Ee thought about his ma an' da (now just about recovered from the scare) and wondered what they were doin'. Ee thought ov is ma back home, tryin' t'write her first assignment fur her course, and then his da, back down Crofty, and then his sister Jess an' her new business – her Cornish hair and beauty products range now comin' t'fruition as well. Fuckin' hell – all tha' world wuz about t'completely disappear. Ee'd just been forced down a rabbit hole an' some cunt had forced a bottle of 'Drink me!' down his neck. Yeah – tha' wuz ut now – *Alice in Fuckin' Pastyland*. White Rabbits. Mad Hatters. Dodos. Cheshire Cats. Caterpillars smoking hookahs. Ee'd be seeing pixies, knockies an' spriggans next. Then mermaids, giants an' fairies back Bolenowe.

This wuz so far from Charlie's normality that 'twas about t'get very bad. Cornwall an' drugs – yeah – it ud always been there… What – old Robert Stephen Hawker, author ov 'Trelawny' (Neil'd done a Hendrix take on ut) wrote half ov his stuff high on fuckin' opium – and then, the 1960s down St Ives. Half the artist cunts down there were high on stuff. Had t'be, t'make such mad pictures. They never said anything 'bout tha' down the Tate. Mentally, ee wuz tryin' t'prepare hisself fur what wuz about t'kick in. Ee knew ee must minimise harm, and reduce the risk as much as ee cud. All tha' fuckin' stuff the teachers told you at school tha' you never thought you'd have t'deal with.

The van wuz moving again – the same sharp turns around the pot-holed streets of Pool and Camborne. Ee was jerked about by the movement – no one gived a shit about un. They just let un slide about so the bomb inside is stomach would fizz and burble better than ever. Bastards, bastards, bastards, ee kept mouthing t'hisself. Nothun' you cud do though. 'Twas in there, goin' round an' round like the headgear at Crofty. Yeah – being absorbed inta' is bloodstream. Enterin' the very soul obm'. Changin' everything. Makin' un look at the world in new ways. Wozon? Well, a fuckin' stomach-full ov drugs is wha' woz on. How bad can ut get?

Aw, worse. Much worse.

Voodoo pilchard see.

Voodoo pilchard, every time.

The bumpy journey worked. Charlie knew the drug was impacting on his perception. New doors opened. Ee was in complete head-fuck mood. Reality shifted. Time stood still and then speeded up again to be super fast. Ee could hear himself, chitterin' on, like there wuz no problem at all. At one point ee reckoned he said how ee loved Markie so much, an' tha' made everyone in the back of the van laugh. Then ee started callin' Simon Cowell a cunt. Past memories collided and rubbed against the present. This was the kind of shit that happened when you were pissed up – only worse.

'Please untie his hands,' Yeugen went.

'Na... be more fun like this...'

'Please Markie...'

Markie, the fuckin' softie – obviously tempted now by the promise ov an evening's shag with this Polish bit - resisted didn' a? When the van comed to a halt, the grunts cut off the cable ties, freeing his wrists.

'Ee'll ave some fun in there with the ghosts an' tha'...'

Charlie heard the van load laughing.

They dumped un in the middle of Troon cemetery, right next to one of the bins where visitors dumped old flowers. Tired and rotting chrysanthemums looked out onto Charlie's face. Ee smelt their decay. The gorillas walked back along the gravel to the gate, and then jumped back into the van. Ee heard ut leave. Everything was silent – scarily silent. Death and drugs. Not a good combination. Charlie was fearing seeing the undead; zombies climbing out of crypts – the sort ov thing half the ASBO-ite tackers liked to test on their Playstations an' X-Boxes ov a Saturday morning.

Ee just about knew where ee was. In the moonlight, formal Victorian headstones and modern Celtic crosses were silhouetted. The names of the dead that Charlie had come to know well over the years, merged and faded in the light. The crosses and headstones seem to move, swaying in the wind, like sheets. Fuck. Ee knawed 'zactly what wuz happening. If there wuz a plaace to haunt an' disturb him, then this wuz ut. Markie Phillips knawed what ee wuz doin' fur certain.

In the distance, ee thought ee could make out the lights ov Trelawny, an' then across the way, the stacks of Condurrow an' Grenville. The drug bomb wuz kickin' in nicely now. Every move ee made wuz enhanced, amplified, and made unreal. The granite of the grave kerbs twinkled brightly at him as if they held diamonds in them. Although night-time, everything was psychedelic. Rainbows descended from off Carn Brea, and sprang across the night sky, all the way down Tolcarne. It 'ad all gone very fuckin' Pink Floyd. This was tales of topographic Troon – Roger Dean's art ov floating islands an' fantastic worlds wuz merging with Mineral Tramways and the horizon's stacks pointing skyward.

'Fuck. Thaas' beautiful,' Charlie heard hisself say.

Ee was up walking now, through the rows of headstones, feeling each one. There was music in his head. Ee cudn' make it out – what it wuz. Bits of Balance. Bits of John Harris. Bits of Hendrix. Bits of everything ee 'ad ever heard in his life – all at once, and then not at all. Other images and sounds were merging and becoming deeper somehow, like what ee'd seen and heard before was something slight and temporal. This was the real music now: the music of the earth. Aw 'es. Now the dead were playing for him, singing for him, making him appreciate all those names and dates carved into the headstones. Enys. Chenoweth. Julian. Chegwin. Fidock. Pascoe. Es – that wuz ut. Ee wuz doin' a bit of Chenoweth. Takin' Fidock. Experimentin' with a bit ov Pascoe. Names ov drugs wudn' they? Not boys who'd worked the adits and levels below.

Ee knew ee wuz on one. Ee cudn' help ut though. Charlie knew ut wudn' 'is fault. Ee wanted to get home – ee knew that would be best – yes, find 'is way to Trelawny Gardens – 'is ma and da's house – and then ee could sleep. Get over ut. Be in a safe place. But ee cudn' find 'is way there. Walls and bushes stopped un, so the whole cemetery became a maze. Like they bleddy carvings up Rocky Valley in North Cornwall ee'd once visited. Each step was difficult, wobbly, unsure as if the world was somehow tipping on its axis. There was nausea too, but not enough for him to be sick. What wuz the use of tha' now anyway? The mephedrone had been absorbed, and the speed, coke an' ecstasy were keepin' un nicely awake. Ee could hear noises comin' from un – songs, words, images, but none ov ut wuz makin' much sense you. Ee wuz prop'ly fucked. Any minute now the piskies wud have un and swap un as a Changeling.

The ground wuz wet – a slight dew already resting on the well-kept grass. Charlie pulled hisself along it. Ee could feel the moisture, but it was cooling, addictive, and made the heat of his body disappear. Ee pooled some of the dew into 'is hand and licked it with his tongue. It felt glorious and wonderful and tasted of the earth. Momentarily, ee wuz back in the back ov the van again, and they were pushing the wraps down his throat. Ee felt like ee would feel that forever – people holding him down, restricting him, constricting every move. Charlie cudn' think straight. For what seemed like an hour, ee kept seeing the face of Yeugen in the way the lichen ran up the rear of one white marble headstone. Then ut disappeared again. This was fuckin' scary, real scary. Charlie knew the hallucinations would get worse before they got better. The best thing ee cud do was prob'ly just hang on as tight as ee could. Stay on the floor, boy. Less far to fall. Harm reduction see. Like all the dead Cornish before him – knowing there was safety in the earth.

If only ee cud get home t'his ma and da's plaace. It wuz a stone's throw really. Not far t'all. Ee called out – opin' some fucker wuz out this late, walkin' their dog. Unlikely though. This wuz the tackers' time ov night, when they controlled the streets and did wha' the fuck they wanted – despite the best efforts ov Operation Goodnight. You wudn' fuckin' dare to go out even if you wanted to. So ee wuz there fur the duration. Whatever visions came to un, ee'd 'ave t'cope with them alone. Ee tried thinkin' ov Yak – wishin' ee wuz there – needin' 'is experience ov the world ov substance abuse. Charlie felt Yak laughin' at un from somewhere distant.

'Take on more orange juice,' ee kept on sayin' to hisself. 'Kiwi fruit – es, they'm good fur ee... Vitamin C offsets the ecstasy yeah...'

Ee knew how incoherent ee wuz getting. Ee began to shiver. Tha' wuz a bad sign. Get cold, an' you were shafted. Death wudn' that far away then. Ee tried to think hisself warm, by flying over Cornwall. Es – thaas' what ee would do – think himself out of his body. Be above hisself, and see hisself down there in Obby Stanker Country. Charlie, you'll be alright, honest. So ee wuz flying in from the Isles of Scilly, over Land's End, and up over St Ives, and Godrevy, and Carn Brea, and Trura an' Newquay. Yes – ee wuz surfing all over the sky with a guitar round 'is neck. Fuckin' 'ell, now ee cud see why half 'is heroes 'ad gone off the boil, when they'd experimented with drugs. How half the fuckers had come out the other side ee didn't rightly knaw? So this wuz the kind of thing Hawkwind got up to regularly in the mid-1970s. How wudn' the fuckers even more wrecked than they were? Ee imagined more surfing then, up across Bodmin Moor, then onto the Tamar Bridge; barrel rolls and carves around the Royal Albert railway bridge and then on up inta' England. There were some on Trelawny who regularly paid fur this sort ov thing. They fuckers ud be jealous ov un, if they cud feel just some of the hallucinations ee wuz havin' right now.

Ee tried taking deep breaths, getting more oxygen in. Prob'ly all that would do, would be to take the drug more quickly around his body. Ee was scared. This would stop eventually – but would there be lasting damage. Look at Druid Dave, all the synapses in his brain seemed to have slowed down. Charlie didn' want to end up the same. What wuz a goin' t'be? Another statistic. Another NFC over Treliske. Jody there, watchin' un come in – just like 'is da. At least, no pixies yet. Maybe ee'd survive ut an' come out the other side.

It wuz just at tha' point – where ee wuz feelin' a little more positive an' in control, tha' things took a slightly more surreal turn. Perhaps ut was the third little wrap that just took the edge ov things and pushed what Charlie could see, that little bit further. Ee'd got up by now, and walked to the corner ov the cemetery where Clifford Mellow 'ad been buried. Somethun' wuz drawin' un there; some energy, or force. A ley-line maybe. But there wuz also something ritualistic 'bout ut – like as if Charlie wuz meant to be there; like ee wuz meant t'see ut. The mound of earth that 'ad once been there wuz now flattened down, an' around the headstone wuz pictures of Clifford's step kids and his own daughter Morwenna as a baby. This was when the reality of Clifford's passing kicked in.

For comfort, Charlie touched the piece of Hendrix's string around his neck. Ee felt the thinness of the Fender light gauge (0.10). Aw es – the spirit of Jimi wuz very much with un, ee reckoned. 'Twas a piece ov light in this dark experience. Charlie wuz thinkin' tha' when ut all 'appened.

Somebody wuz tappin' un on the shoulder. Charlie jumped an' turned around. There, brighter than a tin ingot, was Clifford Mellow, not a day older than when Charlie had last seen un. Time an' decay 'adn't altered un one bit – still the same curly, fuzzy, unstyled hair – and still the muttonchop sideburns. A trip over Headönizm might have sorted un out – but somehow, 'twas too late now.

'Clifford boy, you scared me good an' proper?'

'Wozon Charlie?' went Clifford.

'Been dumped here,' went Charlie. 'Markie's filled me with drugs...'

'Everyone else a'right though, are um?' went Clifford.

''Course,' said Charlie. ''Course... How are you?'

'I'm a'right,' went Clifford. 'Tidn' tha' nice being deaded an' tha', but I'm doin' a'right really...'

'Wha' about Karen an' the kids?'

'Well, I'm watchin' over um Charlie. 'Twas me who sent Ronnie Phillips their way. A good man Ronnie. Ee'll see she right.'

'What you doin' here now though?' asked Charlie. 'Up from yer grave an' tha...'

'I be seeking Papa Piran,' went Clifford.

'Papa Piran?'

All Charlie'd heard ov was Saint Piran.

'Saint Piran you mean?'

'Es... Papa Piran... you can call un tha' now too... You gotta' help me Charlie... Ee's the boy t'save we... If we call un, and ee let's us through, you and I get t'meet someone else...'

'Who?'

'You'll see. Charlie Curnow, you'll see. You just gotta' believe thaas' all...'

Charlie looked at Clifford. Charlie knawed Clifford wuz always the cakiest bugger this side of the Tamar, but this, well, this, was somethun' else altogether. Suddenly, ut wuz feelin' like Charlie wudn' on anything anymore.

With the energy as if ee wuz still doin' a kinky strip up Miners and Mechanics Institute, Clifford began to sing:

'Papa Piran, Papa Piran, open the door,

I'm callin' you, come to me!

Papa Piran, Papa Piran, open the door...'

Charlie repeated Clifford's words.

'What ee doin' ov?' asked Charlie. Wha' the fuck wuz a on?

'Be patient, young one,' said Clifford.

Then again, Clifford called:

'Papa Piran, open the gate for me, oh oh,

Open the gate for me...

The gate for me Papa, so I may enter...

On my way back, I will thank you fur this favour oh oh.'

Charlie repeated the chant. Ee felt a right tool doin' ov ut.

'Thaas' ut,' went Clifford. 'You can see her now. Papa Piran's let you in.'

'Who d'fuck is Papa Piran?' went Charlie. 'An' who's her?'

'Gotta' go,' went Clifford. 'Nice t'see ee gain Charlie... See ee fur a beer sometime up Institute yeah? Mine's a pint of 'Betty Stoggs' a'right?'

'Papa Piran? Her?'

'Work ut out eh? Trescothick d'knaw. 'Ask ee will ee? Aw - say hello to her fur me wun't ee?'

'Who?'

'The old maid... the Oracle there...'

Clifford 'ad gone. Poor fucker, Charlie thought t'hisself. Both of them were victims of Markie's terror.

Charlie looked back across the cemetery. There was a small, frail figure walking toward un. Charlie recognised her instantly.

'A'right Mrs Williams? What you doing out here this time o'night? You ought t'be 'ome right now – what with the tackers out an' that... They'll 'ave ee...'

Then ee realised. Mrs Williams – chapel stalwart and flower changer – was dead. She'd gone on three years ago now. They'd found er body down Stithians Reservoir.

'Charlie Curnow... I ent Mrs Williams no more... aw naw... Now I be the Oracle. That there Clifford Mellow called upon Papa Piran to let you through...'

'Through to where?'

'Here... Dun't ee knaw? The spirit world...'

'But I'm on drugs Mrs Williams – Mrs Oracle... I ent quite right in the head right now...'

'That may be so, but it dun't matter. Not really. Not with what I've got t'tell you...'

'How do ee mean?'

'Well, see, I've gived up all that Methodism... 'Twudn' really me t'be honest. Sebenty-odd years ov ut es enough fur anyone truth be knawn. This world's much more exciting see... Lookee' here at this bewdie...'

From behind her back, Mrs Williams (now the Oracle) produced a snake, a right ol' big bugger of a pissed-off adder.

'Ee d'look some taissy Mrs Williams,' noted Charlie.

'Aw – ee's a'right once you get t'knaw un...'

The snake who was now straddled between Mrs Williams' outstretched arms didn't look too keen on the ritual. She raised her hands above her head.

'Got a name 'ave a?' asked Charlie.

'Aw 'es. Cute idn' a? I d'call un Li Grand Zombi... the serpent spirit... an' ee be the healing knowledge and the connection between heaven and earth...'

Fuck me, Charlie wuz thinkun'. She wuz soundin' 'zactly like one of they there neo-pagans from down Penwith. Charlie cudn' keep 'is eye off the snake. The movements the creature was makin' were intoxicating, addictive.

'See Charlie... I am the Oracle... the Prophet... the Diviner... I know all. I read the thoughts of Rada and Petro Loa, Legba and Elegba, Shango and Chango, Osham and Oxum, Oya and Yansa.'

Who d'fuck were all tha' lot? Charlie wuz thinkin'.

'Right on,' went Charlie, 'but whaas' ut all mean? I mean, you an' the snake there...'

'This is ritual for prosperity, beauty, love and health...'

'For me?'

263

'For you Charlie Curnow... Li Grand Zombi opens the body soul and awakens the *Kundalini*, the snake power'

'*Kundalini*?' asked Charlie nervously. 'That some kind ov Cornish language es ut?'

'No Charlie... it is voodoo...'

'Voodoo? Like black magic...'

'No. White magic... Good magic... It is in you... It has always been in you... The snake senses ut...'

Mrs Williams came closer to him, passing the snake across and over him. Charlie reckoned ol' snake might have been happier sunning himself over some of the concrete buddles still over Condurrow than being danced around him in the middle of Troon cemetery, but there 'twas. Charlie's da wuz always on t'un as a kid 'bout how careful y'needed t'be out there on the moors. There wuz some big buggerin' snakes out there – tha' would 'ave ee soon as look at ee.

'It is only now Charlie, that you have the power to see all of this...' announced Mrs Williams.

'I think ut's the drugs,' went Charlie.

'No matter. It is the person – the individual – the special individual who sees beyond reality... That is you, Charlie...'

'You said you were the Oracle? If you are the Oracle and can see into the future, then what do you see for me?'

'I have told you: prosperity, beauty, love and health...'

'But will I ever be successful in rock 'n' roll? Will I have to sell my soul? Will we ever have a number one album?'

Mrs Williams lowered the snake from above her head, and placed it on the ground, letting the creature go. It slid purposefully over Charlie's feet. pausing there just slightly, and then disappeared into the undergrowth.

'Li Grand Zombi has spoken... I have no answers to those questions. Only you have them... inside of you...'

She laughed a deep laugh..

'I see...'

'Be grateful Charlie for what you have... Most aren't. You can be... In that, lies the truth, the vision that you seek. Now, I must go. I got crowst to make fur tomorrow.'

'You an' Clifford? Will I ever see you again?'

'Depends...'

'Depends on what?'

'The mixture of drugs you take... of course...'

Mrs Williams started to walk away.

'Tell mother I asked after her...'

Charlie tried following but when ut comed to findin' her 'round the corner ov one of the memorials, she wudn' there no more.

Although the Oracle wuz gone, other things started t'stabilise a bit. Maybe ee wuz over the wurst of ut. Leastways the earth didn' quite feel like the swell ov the Atlantic anymore. Ee wuz feelin' sick though, but when ee urged nothun' comed up. He hoped t'fuck ee wuz on a downer now and tha' gradually whatever shit wuz inside ov un, would soon dissipate.

What the hell happened though? Within the last hour ee'd encountered the spirit of Clifford Mellow, heard about Papa Piran, then met the Oracle an' Li Grand Zombi. 'Twudn' right. 'Twudn' right t'all – but what could a do? Lie down an' sleep – thaas' wha'. An' tha' ee did – a long, deep sleep close to the grave ov Clifford Mellow.

In the mornin' some party wuz in changin' the flewers on one of the graves. Charlie sat up straight, having heard all the drilgey. Ee 'oped ee wuz back t'normal. Ee got up and walked along the path out of the cemetery, still smarting from the paranormal, drug-induced voodoo of the night.

'Disgustin' idn' ut?' ee heard one of the party say, 'Drunk's handcart in the graveyard. The Police ought t'do somethun' 'bout ut... I'll tell Combellack.'

Charlie looked back fur Papa Piran – but ee wudn' there. Nor wuz Clifford or Mrs Williams.

Hallucinations – all three ov um, wudn' um?

Yeah. Must've been.

Bolerium Super Strong Treatment – Get your hair in tip top condition with this power-packed weekly treatment. Rebuild and strengthens

•Strengthens – Super strong compound penetrates straight into the cortex to help rebuild the internal structure of damaged hair

• Rebuilds – Rich natural conditioners help enhance the flexibility and increase elasticity to help guard against further damage

- Restores – Wheat proteins and other essential ingredients help restore strength and elasticity

Feeling high wudn' really Charlie's idea ov fun t'all. Even though ee wuz both conscious and cognizant, ee still felt ee wuz hallucinating a bit. However, ee 'ad enough 'bout un, t'be able t'make ut out of the cemetery an' 'ead back inta' Troon. 'Bout the best ee cud manage wuz t'wonder inta' the Trelawny estate. Ee'd never make ut back up t'his place. The ground wuz feelin' like the Atlantic's swell, and every step like ee wuz hangin' off a surfboard on an in-coming wave down Gwithian. The fuckin' tackers everywhere 'ad grawed up these days, but they wuz the same little tools, who'd do anything t'ee fur a laugh. This morning, a few ov um wuz down park shootin' up a new sign about health and safety on the play area tha the council 'ad put up. T'they, some bugger comin' in ov a morning lookin' like they wuz on drugs wudn' nothun' new t'be honest. 'Twas just like any other morning on the estate. Charlie looked at um. This time though, they didn' say much.

'Thaas' Curnow idn' ut?' one ov um went.

They didn' like the look ov his eyes. Ee looked weird somehow.

'Fuckin' out there ee is. Look at un...'

Charlie gaked over t'where they stood. Ee knawed ut hisself. Ee looked a right state. The front of un wuz covered in earth and grass stains, and all 'is clothes were wet from the morning's dew. Ee cud still feel 'is stomach gurgling with all the shit inside ov ut. Maybe if ee got t'his ma and da's place, ee cud be sick and try an' get some ov ut out ov 'is system.

As ee walked, ee wuz contemplatin' what ee'd seen and wha' 'ad been said t'un. 'Twudn' fuckin' real wuz ut? The problem wuz ut felt real. Ut felt like Clifford and Mrs Williams 'ad been right next to un, like they'd never been gone. The reality ov ut wuz what wuz disturbin' ov un. This voodoo shit cudn' carry on, ee told hisself. Ut had t'stop. The other thing wuz, if Markie an' his boys cud do this to un, then there were surely other people receiving the same, or similar fates, on Obby Stanker. Tha' wuz wha' wuz really troublin' un. His mind ran t'Bev. What ef ee got hold ov her? Ee wanted t'protect her, hold her, be with her. Right now, the most logical thing in the world wud be t'ask her t'marry him, t'show how much ee loved her. Shit. Maybe the drugs 'ad adled his mind tha' much, tha' ee wuz now thinkin' along these lines. 'Twudn' normally a line ov thought ee'd have been contemplatin'. But now, well, maybe 'twas different now. Maturity an' mephedrone changed ee a bit.

Then ee thought ov Yeugen back in the frame and hitched up with ee. Now 'twas all makin' sense – wha' Micky 'ad said 'bout un being with someone. And well, 'twas only natural really, she'd want t'be with un. Ee'd treated the Polish well 'adn't a? Charlie weighed ut up. Ee knew Yeugen wuz wrong fur'n in the long term. Bev wuz the one fur ee. But Yeugen, or at least the Yeugen ee knawed when ee wuz with her, was a good person. She didn' have an evil bone in her body. Wha' 'ad happened t'turn ut around? Ee thought back t'wha' she'd said. 'Twas all becoming a blur. Wuz a high then? Ee cudn' remember.

Charlie stanked up the alley t' number 38. Ee pushed the back door open and walked in like a zombie.

'Rough night?' 'is da went, not really lookin' at un.

'Y'cud say tha',' said Charlie.

'I d'reckon they dun't keep the beer right up Institute at the moment y'knaw. I 'ad the same thing the other day... well, before my little heart murmur at least...'

Heart murmur now wuz ut? Tha' must've made ut less threatening in 'is mind.

Charlie went back inta' the kitchen and pulled himself a couple of pint glasses filled from the tap. The coolness of the water refreshed his whole being.

'I need a shower,' ee said t'his da.

'Hang on... hang on...' went his da. 'Why ent you at your own plaace? This idn' a hotel y'knaw...'

'I's a long story. You wudn' believe me if I told ee...'

'Try me,' went 'is da.

Charlie did think 'bout tellun' un fur a minute. But then ee reconsidered. What wud be the point? 'Is tool ov a da wudn' believe un anyway. Ee wuz too much a central strand ov Markie's web these days.

'You d'look like you'm on drugs boy...' his da went, not that Tommy'd ever believe Charlie wud do such a thing..

'Is da had the telly on, but wuz sat in his chair, still in his kaks an' with a cheap Matterland t-shirt on. At the same time, ee wuz engrossed in what looked like a novel. That wuz weird enough in utself.

'What you reading?' asked Charlie.

'Ah... one ov your mother's books? That there Virginia Woolf...'

Ee shawed Charlie the cover. It wuz *To the Lighthouse*.

Fuck, thought Charlie. Ee felt ee must be still on drugs if his feyther wuz reading tha'. With more vigour, still a bit shaky on 'is feet, Charlie climbed the stairs t'the bathroom. Only in the shower did a become a little more human again. The hot jets from the shower head jolted 'is body back to some kind of normality. Ee wuz fully prepared though, fur the effects t'last fur maybe the next forty-eight hours. This wuz a judgment based on wha' ee'd seen ov Yak's little indulgences over the years. Apprently, ut came an' went in this kind ov situation.

When ee comed back down, ut felt like the three wraps were still affectun' un. Is' da wuz down by his record collection, reaching between the Ds somewhere. At this point, 'is da wuz all ass. 'Twudn' a pretty sight watching yer feyther's crack while delving inta' 'is old Def Leppard albums.

'Wha' ee lookin' fur?' Charlie managed t'say. Ee 'ad on his da's dressing- gown on, and went inta' the kitchen t'put 'is own clothes in the washing machine. When ee bent down to shut the door ov the machine, Charlie cud still feel the drugs fuckin' weth un. 'Is head was bangin' and when ee switched the machine on, 'is stomach felt like the washing bouncing around inside ov ut. Feeling ee might be sick, ee went back inta' the living room an' sat down on the sofa.

'What ee think ov this then?'

Ee knew ee hadn' comed down yet, not when his da wuz standun' in the middle ov the room, smiling an' holding wha' looked like a nugget ov gold in his hand.

Fur 'bout a minute, Charlie checked his eyes an' brain wudn' playin' tricks on un. Charlie's da moved ut closer so his son could see ut.

'Tha' fur real?' asked Charlie. Ee wuz thinking ee might still be asking for Papa Piran and observin' ov the Oracle. On the state ov this, maybe wha' the Oracle wuz sayin' wuz about t'come true sooner than ee'd ever thought. Wha' wuz ut she'd said about prosperity? The first thing on her list wudn' ut? Well, here 'twas, starin' un full-on in the face.

'Yeah, fur real,' went his da. 'Gold'.

'Gold?'

'Found ut... down Crofty...' his da went.

'Mean, Charlie'd seen all the media stuff about gold down Crofty. Ee'd reckoned on ut bein' a bit ov spin, t'keep the RDA off their backs – an' tha' the mine had more ov a run ahead ov ut. Ee knew all the papers an' that were full ov shit about a gold-rush in Cornwall, but this, this thing in his da's hadn' looked fur real. Y'cud tell by the way 'twas gleaming.

'D'they knaw? Crofty-like?

'Na. Ent tellin' they buggers. This is mine.'

The cunt wuz suddenly soundin' like Gollum. 'Twas another ov his plans tha' wud see un either a) lose his job, b) be 'ad up fur ut or c) be more ov a legend than ee already wuz.

'I 'oped you thanked the knockies fur ut... with a bit ov crowst,' went Charlie, casually remembering Clifford's pasty business.

Fuck, Charlie's da realised tha' ee 'adn'. Ee'd meant to, but ee 'adn't.

Now, 'twas all becomin' understandable. Tha' was when ee'd taken the Loco Viagra wudn' ut? Ee adn' been down there the next mornin' ad a? – t'toss um a piece of crowst in thanks. Tha' kind'a shit you didn' mess with – not underground. Folklore ut may be, but when you'm working mine, y'always have yer eye on ut. 'Mean, look at they poor fuckers in Chile who wuz stuck down a mine over there. Bet they didn' toss the mine spirits naw bit ov pasty – even with a bit of chilli in ut. In an instant, recovering from a heart attack or naw, ee wud need t'get down there an' deal with ut, or else bad luck wud be forever comin' his way. With the up an' comin' Trura City versus Bath City match, tha' cudn' be allowed t'happen. Ef ee didn' placate the little buggers, then any 'opes ov promotion wuz goin' t'go tits up, Markie Phillips squarin' a deal or naw Markie Phillips squar-in' a deal.

Charlie nawticed his father's face 'ad become pained at wha' ee'd said. Ee'd said ut as a joke. His da 'ad always been on 'bout the knockies ever since ee wuz a kid.

'You a'right?' ee asked his da.

'Yeah. Just gotta' do somethun' thaas' all.'

'Can I hold ut?' ashed Charlie.

That way, Charlie reckoned, ee might realise tha' ee wudn' still trippin'. If the object could be felt, and weighed his hand, then the effect of the drug bombs might have worn off. His da passed ut to un. Charlie felt the gold nugget. Ut fitted in 'is hand nicely, and 'ad an egg shape to ut. Ah fuck, this wuz like a fairy tale wudn' ut? Tha' worried Charlie. Had a side-stepped reality again? Had a staggered inta' the world of Mother Goose or somethun'? Ee needed confirmation tha' ee wuz back from the otherworld of Papa Piran and the Oracle.

'Am I right then? You've sayin you found this golden egg somewhere down Crofty – and that it's now back here in Trelawny?'

'Correct,' went his da, like ee wuz some tv game-show host.

'Anyone else knaw?'

'Na. Not even yer mother... I wanted t'surprise her.'

'This is amazin' da... I mean, really amazin'...'

'Not a bad ol' find us ut?'

Charlie knew the typical Cornish capacity fur understatement.

'Proves I ent the awnly Curnow t'make a mint dun't ut?'

Charlie wuz reckonin' is da wuz talkin' 'bout him then – the money ee'd made off the Chakiri deal.

'I invested mine,' went Charlie, 'in the house...'

'Yeah – but I ent just talkin' 'bout you...'

'Wha' ee mean then?'

'Ebm' you heard? Well, y'knaw Jess... She've been workin' ebm she... on this Cornish products range. Getting they there Gillyflower apples an' Burcombe cherries from down Jimmy Pengellys' plaace... an' all tha' other shit she've been gathering an' developin'. Well, she've cracked u ent she? She got a distributor now. An' 'tis all goin' t'be bottled up an' sold fur hairdressers an' tha...'

Charlie knawed she'd been workin' on ut ov late. But ee didn' knaw she wuz quite s'far forward with ut.

'Tha' right?' asked Charlie. Ee still wudn' certain ef ee wuz out there – still on one from Markie and Yeugen's plan fur un.

'Yeah... Whaas' up with ee this morning Charlie?' 'Tes like you ent weth ut somethun'?'

Voodoo Pilchard

'Rough night,' Charlie mumbled. 'Over-did ut a bit...'

'Well, look, I've been waitun' fur you t'come 'round. See this little golden egg 'ere, well, tes yer mawther and me's future idn' ut? An I dun't want anybody else knawin' ov ut, so look, wha' do ee reckon's the best way t'sell ut? I mean how do I get money fur ut?'

Charlie wuz dumbstruck. Ee didn' knaw wha' t'say. 'Twudn' really the kind of sale y'cud pitch up down Hayle Car Boot, or take in the dodgy pawnbrokers over Redruth. You cudn' put ut in an envelope either an' send ut off t'Cash4Gold either. The postman might do hisself an' injury. Perhaps years ago, in Cornwall, there were maybe dealers who dealt with metals ov this type, an' could give ee a fair price fur ut. Maybe still out there across the world – in places like California and New Zealand – the Cornish might be tradin' a few nuggets, but where did ee go now? Charlie suddenly felt worried. This golden egg wuz somethun' ee didn' want t'cock up fur 'is da, and right now, 'is brain still felt mazed an' adled, like ee wuz in an electric dreamland.

'So wha' ee reckon?' 'is da went, shovelling 'is Def Leppard albums back inta' their place, like ee wuz loadin' a wagon over mine. In the kitchen, the washing machine droned, a drone tha' entered Charlie's mind and sent him spinning back all the time t'last night in the cemetery.

'I... I... dunnaw...' said Charlie.

'But you always got a plan boy?' went his da.

'Yeah... but gold... like this... well... i's unheard ov idn' ut?'

'Wha' 'bout e-Bay?' went his da.

Charlie looked at un, like tha' wuz the stupidest idea on the planet, which in a way, ut wuz.

'Tell ee wha'. Bet Markie'll knaw...' went his da.

Charlie didn' want ee involved in this at all. 'Is involvement would only lead t'a Brinks Mat bullion-style robbery on 38 Trelawny Gardens.

'I reckon the scrapies over United Downs might knaw,' suggested Charlie. 'Mean, they'm always dealing with metal aren't um? Someone must've asked um 'bout gold once or twice.'

'Good idea,' went his da. 'Es. They might knaw somebody in the knaw like...'

This wus ut, wudn' ut, on electric pastyland? If you wuz in

doubt, somebody over United Downs wud knaw wha' t'do. 'Twas a kind ov superhero country, wrecked, shafted, dumped an' shat on by the rest ov Cornwall, but ut always 'ad answers. Maybe Papa Piran and the Oracle wuz pointin' un in tha' kind of direction.

'Cun you go out an' see then?' asked his da. 'I gotta' go over Crofty. There's somethun' important I gotta' do...'

Charlie explained t'his da, how ee wudn' feeling tha' good still. Charlie's da's advice wuz t'put on some old-school metal. That ud sort his brain out a bit.

'Plenty ov new re-mastered stuff fur ee t'choose from,' 'is da went, heading t'the fridge an' pullin' out an uneaten half ov a pasty, Charlie's ma had made earlier in the week.

Charlie explained how 'is clothes were still bein' washed. Charlie's da's advice wuz t' 'eave ut in the tumble dryer, and ee'd be sorted in naw time t'all.

Tommy went out the door, heading off t'Crofty. Charlie wudn' sure whether ee wuz sane again or naw. Ut felt like the whole ov electric pastyland wuz on drugs. 'Is 'ead wuz spinnin' madly, an' his da had gone off underground t'meet with some little people. Pink elephants next then.

Fairy Ointment Relaxing Balm – Enjoy silky smooth results, rain or shine.
Smoothes and Controls
• Smooths and conditions – Proteins and conditioning ingredients help moisturize hair from within, protecting locks while leaving them soft and silky smooth
• Resists humidity – A unique, humidity resistant ingredient provides incredible memory that lasts in any weather, creating an ideal foundation for heat styling
• Saves time - Skinnier strands make heat styling a cinch, the exclusive Headönizm complex displaces water and constricts every strand for reduced drying time and speedy styling

'Found it,' went Micky.

'Wha'?'

''Is gallery...'

The way ee said 'gallery' made ut sound like ee wuz just

releasin' the US government's new military plan fur success in Afghanistan.

'Wha'?'

'Are you a'right Charlie mate? You seem a bit out there like...'

'No. I'm alright honest. Just a bit ov a big one last night...'

Charlie wuz standin' in the middle ov Fore Street in Troon, outside Headönizm. Ee cud smell the fresh lavender fabric conditioner in his clothes tha' ee'd just washed over his ma an' da's. 'Is head still hurt, like a fuckin' massive Crofty rock drill wuz gainin' entry inta' his cranium. An old-school work out ov Saxon, Iron Maiden an' UFO 'adn' worked either.

'Eh, good news about Jess and the products range... Spot on...'

'Yeah, great edn' ut? But listen... you gotta' see the Pilchard's gallery Charlie. You won't believe ut...'

Wha' wuz Micky like? 'Is girlfriend had just netted the best business deal ever, an' Micky didn' seem t'give a fuck. Ee wuz much more interested in the Pilchard's activities.

'I's over Condurrow... Come on – you gotta' see ut.'

'But I gotta' go over United Downs...'

'Don't worry about that... Come on. This'll blow your mind...'

Given the toss up between a stank around a scrapies over United Downs, seeking how t'sell his da's golden egg, or havin' his mind blawn, ee'd take the scrapies right now. In fact, ee didn' rightly knaw how 'is mind might be blawn any further – given the hallucinations ov last night. Still, Micky 'ad tha' way about un this morning, which meant Charlie didn' have much ov a choice.

'Course, Condurrow had been dun up a bit since they wuz kids. All tha' big launch a few years ago about ut being a World Heritage Site had faded in moast people's memories in Troon. The reality ov ut meant tha' just a few more tourists occasionally cycled or walked through the place, thinking they'd accidentally stumbled inta' Baghdad or somethun'. Besides all the stone chippings, explanation signs an' a bit ov tartin' up ov the masonry, not a lot had changed really. 'Mean, in posh places like Trura, y'cud pick up leaflets all about ut, an' tha' and how ut might change yer perspective on the Cornish contribution to world peace, but in reality, 'twas still the same place Obby Stankers dumped their chainsawed Leylandii trees an' old mattresses, an' where a lot of the Trelawny teenagers had their first shag.

'In here,' went Micky. 'Look...'

Micky wuz introducin' the Pilchard's gallery like 'twas the fuckin' Tate St Ives or the Louvre in Paris.

They'd gone around the main engine house, an' come to a set ov old out- buildings and storage sheds, once used to house equipment fur the miners. The roof had gone, and the despite the clean-up fur World Heritage Site status wuz now being reclaimed by gorse and wild buddleia trees.

Here though, wuz where the Pilchard clearly practised and developed 'is pieces.

'See the development,' went Micky. 'From the early designs down here... to these...'

The later designs showed a new complexity to the Voodoo Pilchard product. The same street energy wuz there though, like whoever'd dun ut, 'ad a lightning rod inta' the fear and joy ov the youth ov Cornwall. There were enhancements everywhere, little lines of detail, colours, backgrounds and sheer brilliance which made these stand apart from the other red-and-orange designs being completed by someone else. They kind ov bites wudn' nothun' on these. The site here had been bombed with originals.

'Amazing... idn' it?'

Charlie gasped. When ee stood there, an' saw the vast nature of the canvas, ee gulped in disbelief.

Tha' wudn' all ov ut though.

'Come on... See this lot round here...'

Charlie nervously went forward through the gorse and bracken. The sunlight of the late morning was transporting him back to the blinding light that had accompanied La Grand Zombi. Ee wuz checking the undergrowth fur adders. The fuckers were everywhere this time ov year. Every so often the synapses of his nerves seems to jig him back to the trip as if ee were still there. Micky wuz stankin' on ahead, like the energy of the Pilchard's work itself was now strangely addictive.

They'd come to an old concrete base of a once large building, which seemed t'stretch on fur about quarter ov a mile.

Several ov the tin buddies 'ad been removed from ut, but you could still see the circular bases where they had been mounted. A hundred years ago this place 'ad been buzzing with energy. Now ut wuz strangely still. Charlie looked at the walls. There wuz nothun' to be seen. Instead, the Pilchard had done a work on the floor. On it went, for a few hundred feet, a vast circular implosion of street art, depicting images from the locality, combined with the Pilchard's usual flair. T'say ut wuz impressive, wuz an understatement.

'Fuck me,' went Charlie. 'Ee must've gone through a few cans with this lot... That's a wicked piece of bombing.'

'I know. When I found it, I couldn't believe it,' said Micky.

They both scrambled up on an old tailing to have a better view.

'Local then, is a?' asked Charlie.

'Must be. I mean, he knows this area really well, obviously.'

'I don't know anybody,' said Charlie, 'with that skill though. I mean, when I look back at school, there was nobody that good at art.'

'Might have come from somewhere else,' said Micky. 'You never know.'

There wuz a pause while they looked. Charlie turned t'Micky.

'Not you is ut?' ee asked.

'Wha'?'

'I mean, you're a bit tasty with the tattoos an' tha'. I thought maybe you might have expanded your canvas like.'

'Dun't be stupid,' said Micky. 'I'n work with ink, but not aerosols... This stuff's outta' my league t'be honest...'

'Just wondered,' went Charlie.

'Anyway, what wuz you on last night?' asked Micky. 'You'm lookin' wrecked...'

'If I told you, I'd have t'kill you,' said Charlie.

'Like tha' us ut?'

'Yeah. Ut us.'

As they walked back from the gallery, Micky felt a bit worried about Charlie. 'Mean, these days ee wuz a health nut wudn' a? A bit ov a straight-edger t'be honest. Now ut looked like ee'd been out on the razz, an' got totally shafted.

If ee'd known, Charlie would've appreciated the concern

about his well-being. 'Is head wuz pounding. Ee wuz worried 'bout tha' but t'be perfectly 'onest, ee wuz even more worried about serpents an' their arcane powers.

Pasty ESP – Spike, twist, crimp, bend or define with this versatile paste.
Elastic Shaping Paste
• Elastic – Infused with beeswax for style and bendable texture
• Shaping – Mesh-like fibres create multiple styles – define or separate
• Paste – Highly concentrated, a little goes a long way

Clearly, Micky cudn' go up United Downs with Charlie. 'Is mission there wuz top secret wudn' ut? Charlie left un at Headönizm t'help Jess carry on with her now expanding empire ov beauty products. Well, there wuz names fur ut all – trendy an' corny bits of Cornwall printed on the labels, containers and tins. Micky knew tha' in some ways, the success ov tha' wuz (at the moment, at least) beginning t'overtake his tattoo business. Because they were close now, Micky cud sense Charlie wuz up t'somethun', but ee didn' ask un too many questions. When ee'd asked Yak about the band over Treliske, ee'd nearly bitten his hand off. Like everything else on Obby Stanker, 'twud come out in time.

Charlie felt a bit nervous about driving. Was Papa Piran goin' t' jump out in front ov un down Bolenowe? Was a goin' t' have to put his foot down for the Oracle chasin' ov un once more, an' offering un some more words ov wisdom? Somehow, ut wuz scary. Charlie didn' like t'knaw 'is future in tha' way. 'Is future could come dreckly as far as ee wuz concerned. Fuck, if only ee'd stayed on the road – away from all ov this. A quiet life wuz all ee wanted.

As ee drove, a text comed in from Bev. Ee glanced a look at ut. She wanted to meet up later on. Charlie wudn' sure though, Ee wudn' sure his mind wuz in the right place, an' shit, contemplatin' marryin' her needed t'really be thought through carefully – not with a buzz of meaow meaow, speed, coke and ecstasy in there.

Love?

Tha' wuz somethin' else the Oracle 'ad said. 'Twas all comin' back to un now. So only health and prosperity t'go then? Ee pulled over and texted her back, sayin' ee wudn' feeling too good. Well, 'twudn' a lie wuz ut? Moast people wudn' emerge fur a week after the stuff ee'd 'ad shoved down inta' a his stomach. Ee reckoned ee wuz doin' quite well, considerin'.

Of all the fuckin' scrapies, ee pulled inta' out United Downs (an' there were a good few out there), ee'd chosen this one hadn' a? – a place by the name of 'Crofthandy Recycling'. Fate. Destiny. Hubris. Voodoo Pilchard at work see. The place wuz greasy an' gnarly as fuck. Despite the good weather, huge, brown and oily puddles dominated the entrance t'the scrapyard; this wuz where the big tonnage trucks pulled in an' out. Their loads were regularly checked at the weigh bridge. Next to tha', wuz the scummy little office. Inside a young girl sat examining her nails, bored t'fuck, an' angry tha' she had t'work there instead ov' being a model. Charlie knawed her. She comed from over Beacon.

'A'right?' went Charlie. 'Can I speak t'somebody about pricing some metal?'

'Yeah,' she went, disinterestedly. 'Go over an' see Dave in the shed opposite.'

The floor ov the office was covered in muddy boot prints, like no cunt had bothered anymore. Well, 'twas prob'ly not worth ut. Once 'twas clean, somebody else wud walk in an' mess ut up again. Come t'think ov ut, tha' was a bit like moast ov Cornwall really.

'Okay,' went Charlie. 'Thanks.'

The shed opposite wuz where all the small-scale scrap was checked in. Y'had t' register yer licence plate in case any ov ut proved t'be knocked off – or you'd just done a job on some church roofing lead down Perranwell or Mylor. There were skips filled with gear everywhere: one with aluminium in, another with lead, another with steel. This wuz heavy metal.

'Er... hello... I'm lookin' fur Dave...' went Charlie, shouting inta' the expanse.

A grizzled bloakey turned around from delving inta' one ov the skips, re-lighting a rolly encased in his lips. Charlie recognised un right away. 'Twas Druid Dave – Hendrix's one time roadie. Ee 'ad a faded Donington '85 t-shirt on, when ZZ Top, Marillion an' Bon Jovi were headlining. Classic.

'Fuck me,' went Charlie. 'Whas' a Liskeard boy like you doing down here?'

'Charlie – how's ut going?'

'Good. Good,' went Charlie, when 'twasn't really.

'You've moved then?'

'Well, I wuz workin' fur this scrappy up Menheniot you, but with the recession on an' tha', well ee packed in… and then this comed up down here…'

'You commuting then?'

'Na. Got a new maid down this end…'

'Got ee,' went Charlie.

Charlie cud see Druid Dave lookin' at his neck. Despite his scrappy gloves an' grease, ee still should be standin' on top ov Carn Brea in white, holdin' a golden sickle with a bit ov mistletoe on un fur good luck.

'Still got the string I see…'

'Yeah – 'twas good fur the tour,' went Charlie. 'Honest. Brought us a lotta' luck.'

'Still goin' then – the Hendrix thing?' ee asked enthusiastically.

Charlie hated givin' un the truth.

'Na… We split… Tryin' t'do my own stuff again now…'

'Well, hold on t'tha' string mind. Only pass ut on, when you think somebody else really needs ut. 'Tis a good talisman tha'… I tell ee tha' fur nothun'…Protection see. Anytime you want t'come 'round an' talk some more Hendrix – you give me a shout a'right? I got these new bootlegs off the 'net see.'

'Yeah, cool,' went Charlie, but right now, Jimi Hendrix was the last thing on his mind.

Druid Dave moved over t'the scales expectin' Charlie t'be handing over some scrap metal.

'What've ee got then?' ee asked.

'Nothun''

'Nothun'?'

'Not t'day at least,' said Charlie quietly. 'Listen… I need a bit ov advice like… I happen t'have come by a bit of metal like… an' I want t'knaw where t'sell ut.'

'What kind of metal?'

Dave comed in closer.

'Gold.' Charlie whispered.

'Gold. Hell, we dun't get much ov tha' in...'

'Yeah, I know... '

'How much?'

'Well a palm-sized nugget... 'bout the size ov an egg...'

'Big then. Knaw the quality do ee?'

Quality? Neither Charlie nor his da 'adn't really thought 'bout tha' much. 'Course, there wuz different carats wudn' there?

'This is from the ground,' Charlie said. 'Raw. Just mined like...'

'Not processed then? Not alloy?'

'No. Cash4Gold idn' goin' t'do ut.'

'Well, price ov metals these days,' said Druid Dave, 'size of ut... as you mentioned... tha' should bring in a pretty penny...'

'What we talking?' asked Charlie.

'Dependin' on the quality, but a good few thousand...'

'Really?'

'You been doin' a bit ov mining lately thun?' asked Dave, knawin' ov the Camborne gold-rush.

'Na,' said Charlie, smiling. 'Still inta' me heavy metals though...'

'Look, I knaw the very company who'll give ee a fair price fur ut. Up the line mind. You'll have t'take ut up to um to value... In London I think... I got their card an' number somewhere here.'

Dave went over t'his desk an' scrambled around fur a bit, pullin' out a couple of drawers filled with spanners an' wrenches.

''Ere 'tis look. Liquid Gold: Gold Exchange Services. We dun't get much in here – but the odd bit occasionally like. Thaas' who we d'call. They'll sort ee out Charlie...'

'Cheers. Like the shirt Dave... There then... wuz ee?'

'Yes – been t'everyone since 1980. Even the new ones... Download an' tha'...'

Fuck, tha' wuz thirty years ov metal, not countin' his days as Hendrix's roadie. Druid Dave wuz a legend, now workin' as a scrappy out United Downs. Such wuz the way ov the world. His life had been devoted t'metal in all its guises. Respect then.

'So when you headlining Donington then?' asked Dave.

'Ah – might have had dreams a few years ago, not now though... Be happy with a spot down Tyack's Hotel ov a Friday night...'

'Charlie – you still got ut boy. You never knaw...'

'Eh, you knaw Yak's got a new club opening dun't ee? EBGBs. Down the old Club Rhino...'

Druid Dave ad never been down Club Rhino, but ee knew it by reputation.

'Rock an' metal,' said Charlie.

'Very much needed,' Dave went, 'in these days of *X-Factor*...'

Charlie reckoned ee wud keep 'is audition fur tha' quiet fur now.

'Cheers Dave.'

'Let me knaw how you get on.'

'I'll see ee right fur ut mind...'

Charlie headed back to his car, driving off. Ee felt the spirt of Hendrix run through un once again. Ee left Dave t' the next customer who'd brought in a load ov old copper wiring. Well, there wuz good money in ut these days wudn' there?

Time Charlie got back, 'is da wuz already nestled in his chair, looking at the glimmering egg, as if ut 'ad been left on earth from an alien visitation.

'How did ee get on?' ee asked.

'Liquid Gold, here look...'

Charlie passed him the card.

'They'll pay you for ut...'

'Who gived ee tha'?'

'A bloak I knaw up United Downs...'

'Legit is ut?'

Charlie thought about Dave. A more legit bloak didn't exist. The fucker had worked with Hendrix.

''Course...'

'What do I need to do?'

'Phone um. Make an appointment. They'm up the line – in London. You'll have t'go up... They'm proper gold dealers da.'

'Right-on.'

'Anyways, how did you get on over mine?'

'Alright I d'reckon. I went down to the 450th level... an' made me peace with um... 'Twill be a'right again now.'

Charlie checked 'is head. His da wuz havin' conversations with pixies down mines. How mental wuz tha'?

'They'd forgived me,' ee went, like ee'd just been t'some subterranean confession.

Some Voodoo Pilchard this wuz.

'I put in a good word fur Trura City too...'

Like the knockies wuz controlling the fate ov everything now wuz um? 'Course, Charlie's da didn' say nothun' 'bout Markie's deal with Bath City. Charlie didn' say nothun either 'bout 'is own fears ov someone or somethun' controllin' him.

'Eh – they've found more gold down there?' his da went.

'What, like the egg there?'

'Na – just traces ov ut... Worth mining though... The boys've been on ut. while I bin 'ome 'ere. Timmy an' Trudge wuz tellin' me all 'bout ut.'

'No nuggets though...?'

'Not so they wuz saying...'

Right there and then, both ov um knew that the likelihood wuz they'd have done just the same as Charlie's da. 'Homers,' thaas' wha' they called ut over mine, an' had done so fur a thousand years. A few homers once in a while, well, ut greased the wheels of the winding cables didn' ut? A few more feet along the shaft an' well, Crofty'd do well enough anyway.

'So you goin' t'ring um?'

'Right away,' said his da.

'Ring who?' came a voice entering the back door, and now standing in the kitchen.

It wuz Charlie's ma, home from shoppin' over Trura.

'Nawbody... A surprise,' went Tommy. 'Wait an' see...'

Charlie had a quick yap with his ma, and then went 'ome. Ut had been a long ol' forty-eight hours. Least now, his da wuz set up for a few quid. Ef ee played ut right, ee'd be sorted fur life. Meanwhile, Charlie knew tha' the Pilchard 'ad stepped things up a gear. Life wuz goin' too quick fur'n, but like the Trelawny Bucket ee'd had, ut was somehow strangely addictive. Recent trips (both the real and the hallucinogenic ones) 'ad given un new insights, and maybe even new belief. Waitin' an' seein' wuz the only thing ee cud do now.

Alan M. Kent

Lyonesse Hair Lotion – You're an original – create the style that's exclusively yours!
Versatile Styling Liquid
• Medium hold – Styling ingredients from the isles of Lyonesse create long-lasting memory and texture
• Reactivates with heat or water – Water-based formula allows for easy restyling
• Helps eliminate static – Wheat-derived conditioners help smooth the surface and reduce static

The row tha' Markie Phillips an' Yeugen had after the little trip t'the dark side they'd given Charlie wuz, accordin' to those who heard part ov ut, a conflict of epic proportions. While Markie thought gettin' 'is end away with Charlie's ex-girlfriend would be the kind ov revenge on Curnow ee'd always been seekin', the top an' bottom ov ut, was, that Yeugen didn' go much on ut. What Markie Phillips 'ad not been reckonin' on, was that although she had been scorned by Charlie in favour of his previous girlfriend, the Polish were an honourable and dignified people. She wuz thinkin' she'd made a mistake by even linking up with Markie in the first plaace. Still. she cudn' do much about ut now. 'is boys 'ad given her Curnow's hair fur her magic. Thaas' wha' she'd wanted she'd told un. With tha', wud come power t'um both. The three dolls wud sort ut. *Gris-gris* wud control fate in Obby Stanker.

Markie though 'ad been doin' a bit ov diggin' ov late. Gettin' 'is own back on Charlie wudn' goin' t'be nothun' compared t'what ee wanted t'inflict on Ally an' Neil. Why them? Well, Neil'd been the goon who'd taken Ally away from un in the first place, all them years ago. In Markie's mind, that needed t'be paid for. Secondly, Ally not only left un for Neil, but she'd also been associating with Clifford Mellow. She knawed enough – just like Charlie did – to put un inside fur a very long time indeed. It just wudn' do in Markie's mind. Ee wanted control ov the situation because tha' wuz the sort of bloak ee wuz. As fur business, or well, the usual amount of thieving, gambling, arson and extortion ee normally wielded out on Cornwall, that wuz actually goin' quite well – well enough t'fund Trura City. Well enough, so that ee could keep ut fairly arm's length. The wuz a recession on – enough tools out there t'do is dirty work fur'n – however and whenever ee wanted ut. But that wudn' be good enough here. Aw naw. This time, 'twas personal.

Hopefully, ee'd have fried Charlie's brain fur a bit. Now ee'd set is mind on Ally an' Neil. You'd have thought tha' Markie might have made 'is move a while ago – maybe when Neil wuz away tourin', but na, that would have been too easy, too predictable. Having Neil 'ome, would mean that ee could really turn the screws. There wuz a bit of a rumour goin' round about Charlie Curnow an' that heap of shite – Balance. Apparently, one of their songs had netted them a good bit of money. Well, in Markie's view, ee'd be havin' some of that perhaps. The plan wuz easy. Ee reckoned the best way to get at Neil and Ally was t'kidnap one ov their kids. A little bit of kidnapping an' extortion might be fairly easy. S'thaas how ut comed about.

See Markie 'ad the connections now. Ee could do what ee wanted. Money talks. Speak t'the right people and grease the wheels. an' anything is possible. Fuck, this bugger had ambitions. Some people were sayin' ee even had political ambitions: maybe running for councillor on the local elections. Charlie knew ee could front it out: well, you could change people from voting black t'white if you had the money and the persuasion. On top of tha', ut wuz common knowledge that Markie wuz lookin' fur investments 'zactly like the one at Treyew Road. All tha' fuckin' crooked money needed t'go somewhere an' make un a bit more. There wuz a lot ov talk goin' 'round. Some was sayin' ee wuz now up fur buyin' out the Cornish Pirates. Others reckoned ee next 'ad Redruth Rugby Club on his mind. 'Twas a buyer's market – an' all, an' nawbody knew tha' better than Markie hisself. Fuck 'is police record. If you had cash, you cud do wha' you wanted.

Splashing the cash wudn' 'zactly the only thing Markie wuz planning though. Oh yes, ee'd been down Gwithian, an' eyed up Godrevy lighthouse. Since Trinity House had pulled out a few years back, an' got rid of a keeper over there, they installed an automatic system. Well, since then, the plaace had become pretty much derelict. Markie been speakun' t'some of 'is 'advisors' and they reckoned there wuz a pretty penny t'be made on ut. Years ago, day-trippers used to head out there each day in the summer, fur picnics and cream teas. Tha' seemed to have stopped towards the end of the twentieth century, but Markie pitched new trips out there from Hayle harbour. Well, since Harveys 'ad gone on, over a hundred years ago, there was bugger all else to come out of Hayle. 'Twas the sort ov development idea that you could suggest t'anybody with a suit on these days, an' see um go fur ut. All the fuckin' trendy Virginia Woolf fans would be queuing up they reckoned. Do Eden, then the Tate, an' then pop out to the most famous lighthouse in the world. It wuz a sure-fire winner. Throw in a bit ov crap about modernism and the Ramsay family an' the middle-class literary types who read *The Guardian* would be eatin' out of their hands. It had the right ticks: classy, green, right next to the new Wave Hub in St Ives Bay. Markie Phillips see, wudn' naw ordinary fool. Since wrapping up the affairs ov Pasty Pronto, and negotiating (on behalf ov Karen and the Mellow estate) the sale t'Ginsters, Markie knew the big boys – the buggers with addresses in Exeter an' Bristol who seemed t'control everything goin' on in Cornwall. 'Es – with Markie the pies were getting' bigger an' his fingers deeper in um.

Fur now though, ut wuz as useful as a criminal base as any ee 'ad. The good thing about ut wuz its separation from the mainland. An island state. Its own rules see. Devolved. Nawbody even knew you wuz there. So, ee'd set up Yeugen there. It would be her witch's tower in the west. So, there wuz magic next to un now.

But the rest ov the time ee was still the old bastard who'd shafted everyone on Trelawny fur years. That wuz long behind un, but the bugger had a long memory. See, ee might be knockin' round with Yeugen, but Ally wuz still the apple ov his eye. Shame wuz that eye had become twisted an' s'bitter. The job wuz well-organised though. Charlie'd give un tha'. When did um strike? Well, the opportune moment came down Portreath Primary School. There'd been talk still ov un movin' schools, but like everything in education, things moved rather more slowly on the ground than the education department of Cornwall Council thought. As usual, Anthony had been put in isolation, just before dinner time. The class teacher had put up with un all mornin' but when ut came to ut, she wudn' goin' t'allow un – fur a laugh - t'eat the goldfish in the tank in the Key Stage 1 room. It had taken her and a couple of teaching assistants to get un where ee needed t'be. They wuz goin' t'have t'call the parents in again – and prob'ly get un inta' a special school tha' week. Some days the bugger wudn' say a word. Next day, ee'd fuckin' trashed the classroom, all because someone had taken away one of his colouring pencils. Markie done his research mind – 'ad one of his grunts watch un fur a few weeks (just the same as weth Charlie): time ee went to school, time ee went home, what part of the playground (if any) ee spent 'is breaktimes in. Aw yes, 'twudn' no amateur operation this.

The thing is tha' when a kiddie goes missin', there's not much the parents can do. All they can do is blame each other, an' any fucker who d'get in the way. So thaas' wha' Neil an' Ally did. How did ut happen? Well, luckily fur Markie's gorillas, Anthony decided that ee wuz pissed off with being in isolation that day, so ee climbed out the window. There were bars on the fucker, but being a bit bendable like, ee'd gone straight through them and comed out of the office where they put un to calm down. Anthony didn' give much ov a fuck 'bout authority on any level, so once ee wuz outside, well, then the fucker made a run fur ut. Where wuz a heading? Prob'ly down beach, if truth be knawn. A bit ov' coaseteering wuz 'is actual plan. This wuz just the right moment fur Markie an' 'is boys t'strike. Proper old paedo-stuff it looked like. As ee ran down the road, they lured un in with some Star Wars toys.

'There's more in the back,' went one ov Markie's boys. 'Have a gake if y'd'like… We got a whole Venator-class Republic attack cruiser in there…'

Well, even Anthony wudn' immune t'the power ov some Star Wars toys. An' the Venator, well, tha' wuz one ov the best kits going. A prestigious model – about a thousand pieces. How cud the poor little fucker resist? Like a little pilchard caught off Nathaga Rocks, ee fell fur ut hook, line an' sinker.

Prussia Cove Slick Style – Smuggle a shine, with polish and control.
Texture and shine
• Sleek texture and definition – Lightweight, glossy ingredients from Prussia Cove enhance texture and creates definition
• High Shine – Activated natural ingredients help to enhance shine

• Finishing polish – The fine textured base and emollient conditioners create a lightweight formula, perfect for finishing

There wuz hell up you.

There's nothun' worse than when a kid goes missing. The build up t'ut all wuz quite slaw really, t' begin with. At the school 'twas afternoon registration tha' made all the staff worried. Ee wudn' there. Nawbody had seen un dinner time either. They just checked the room they'd put un in fur time out. The little sod wudn' there. Gradually, they comed t'realise tha' ee must've gone out the window. So the search widened didn't ut – t'the playground, an' when a wudn' there, well, 'twas time t'call the police. Mrs Evans, the head-teacher reckoned this kid wud be the death ov 'er. She sat in her office, knawin' tha' safeguardin' wuz the big issue at the moment, and tha' the school had probably failed in its duty ov care. Tha' wuz it she reckoned. Her job would be on the line now. There'd be governors' meetings an' what not. There wuz a bottle ov gin she kept in the bottom drawer ov her filing cabinet just for special occasions like this. While the rest ov the staff were out looking fur Anthony, she poured herself a large glass an' took a couple ov paracetamols. Like the mephedrone kids ov Trelawny, right there an' then, she didn' give fuck.

As with all these kind of things, first, 'twas quite low key really. Y'think ee've just gone off somewhere, t'prove a point, t'wind people up. The police kept ut quite calm. They'd do a sweep ov the school again, t'check nothun' had been missed, an' then expand the search t'the village. Already ov course, they wuz thinkin' about the coast, and shit, the sea down Portreath wuz fairly fuckin' rough at the best ov times, an' even on a summer's day like this, wuz lookin' powerful. The beach wuz pretty full too, with a lot ov emmets down there, tryin' to get tans an' pretend they wuz actually in Tenerife. There wuz a lot ov kids running about – Anthony could be anywhere down there by the sound an' look ov ut.

So 'is parents would have t'be told wudn' um? They wuz difficult enough already what with all the behavioural issues goin' on. Ally opened the door holdin' Megan in her arms. She'd been puttin' out the washin' hadn' she? Neil wuz at work, checkin' off the fruit an' vegetable delivery tha' had just comed in. The police informed her ov the situation. A family liaison officer wuz in there straight away, trying to alleviate her fears and makin' sure she knew they were doing their level best to find her son. Ally phoned Neil t'let un knaw. Ee didn' pick up right away – but phoned her back about fifteen minutes later. Ee'd be home, naw problem. As y'do in these kind of circumstances, you want t'knaw the ins and outs of wha' happened. So the police explained t'Ally what had happened earlier tha' morning. Ut wuz also becoming clear t'they, tha' Anthony wudn' no ordinary little kid either.

The police in Camborne 'adn' quite 'ad a case like this t'deal with fur a while. 'Mean, there wuz the occasional kid who went missing, then the usual custody battle disappearances, where a father had grabbed a kid outside McDonalds or somethun', and there wuz a right ol' row/discussion/slanging match goin' on. but this, this seemed a little more serious. They were makin' house-t'-house enquires along the road by the school, but nawbody had seen nothun'. Normally, by tha' stage you've got a few leads, a few ideas as t'where ee might've gone, but here, well, 'twas like ee'd been abducted by aliens and clean disappeared off the face ov the earth. The other parents wuz askin' questions ov the school now, so some officials wuz brought in from the education department. In fact, ut wuz Geoff Hawkins wudn' ut – who wuz now boobed up at the school gates, takin' a bit ov the flak. Inside, Mrs Evens wuz hittin' more ov the gin, while her staff didn' really knaw wha' t'do.

'Course, some local tool had phoned the media 'adn' um? So they wuz startin' t'turn up by the end ov the day. 'Nawsin' about wuz their only objective wudn' ut? A few other tools gived um a bit ov background on Anthony didn' um? Yeah, basically ee wuz a violent little fucker who the school cudn' control, and yeah, my daughter wuz put in hospital by un earlier this year. Tha' wuz really helpful like. All ov this wuz startun' t' come out s'fast, tha' Geoff Hawkins wuz havin' difficulty controlling wha' information went out, an' wha' didn't. Ee may as well ov got a huge fuckin' loudspeaker, an' stood on the cliffs up Western Hill an' broadcast ut t' the world an' his brother.

By the evening, a full search of the Portreath area wuz being conducted. Tha' wuz the next step really. Culdrose had sent up a rescue helicopter an' ut wuz spending its time initially scanning Illogan and Nance Woods, then moving out s'far as Penpraze an' Tehidy. Meantime, the coastguards had been trekking both west an' east along the coastal footpath. One team had headed as far east as the Gullyn Rock; the other had gone west in the direction of Porth-cadjack Cove. They found nothun'. 'Course, if the western team had carried on a bit further down the coast, they may have actually comed close t'where Anthony wuz. But then, nawbody knawed tha' then? How cud um?

Word had gone round the village tha' Anthony Davey had gone missing. Now, moast people there knawed tha' Anthony wudn' quite right in the head, an' wuz a bit well... special... like, but they liked Ally an' Neil a lot. They wuz good people, wudn' um? So a few villagers wuz out there too, with sticks an' a bit ov tough Cornish attitude, searching around the plaace. The biggest worry wuz some ov the old mining shafts you. Moast ov um had been sealed up, but a few remained uncapped. If ee'd gone down one ov they, well, they didn't hold out much hope ov findin' un. On these sort ov events, the first twenty-four hours are crucial in tryin' t'locate the missing person. After tha', ut all becomes more difficult. Trails go cold an' information becomes more difficult to obtain. The world moves on, an' people forget. With this case though, any kind ov leads weren't just cold, they wuz in sub-zero temperatures. 'Twas later tha' evening tha' the police were havin' t'contemplate tha' Anthony 'ad not just gone missing, but tha' ee'd been abducted.

Ally wuz holdin' out better than Neil t'be honest. The thing with Neil, wuz tha' since tha' time down on the coast with Charlie, ee'd be re-thinking Anthony, an' realising just how special ee wuz. Ee'd come t'realise tha' ee didn' want un any different. Yeah, ee wuz a weird little fucker, but ee wuz Neil's weird little fucker. Thaas' wha' wuz bringin' on the sobs upstairs an' tha' ee didn't knaw wha' t'do or say. Guitarists see – always emotional, moody cunts. Ally wuz more realistic about ut all. She knew she had t'keep her shit together just t'get through. She wudn' 'zactly religious t'all but she found herself prayin' t'God t' keep un safe and not let un come t'any harm.

News ov ut all had started t'filter across Obby Stanker

Country by now. Charlie an' Bev contemplated goin' down t'Portreath t'Ally an' Neil's plaace – but there wuz nothun' they cud really do. Besides, their little plaace probably cudn' take many more people inside ut. All Charlie cud do wuz text um and offer 'is support if they needed ut. Mel, Kelvin, Jess an' Charlie's ma and da did the same thing. Nawbody really knew wha' t'say though. Despite them being down on the coast, Trelawny Gardens wuz quiet tha' night. Parents had probably asked their own tackers t'make sure they wuz inside. The tackers sensed their parents meant ut too – like as if there wuz evil in the air. So, instead of shootin' stuff with the BB guns, they wuz inside on their Wii's shootin' stuff in fantasy worlds, where animated characters were rescued from being locked up in tall towers.

The kids down Portreath meanwhile, were pretty shook up about Anthony's disappearance. The ones in his class, perhaps fur the fust time, wuz learnin' tha' bad things happen; that the world wuz a fuckin' scary plaace at times. Anthony wuz weird, they all knew tha', but ee wuz always funny in the classroom – they way ee wound up the teachers an' dinner ladies an' tha'. Ee'd be just havin' a laugh somewhere they told themselves as they snuggled down in their Toy Story-duvet covers. Overhead, the search-and-rescue helicopter continued looking relentlessly.

'Is kidnappers meanwhile, had kept un in the van fur moast ov the day. The kid seemed t'be happy enough in there, constructing the Lego kit. They bought un a happy meal over Pool McDonalds as well, so fur him initially, 'twas just like a bit ov an adventure. Ee wuz startin' t'ask a few awkward questions though – like when wuz his ma pickun' ut up, and when ee might be goin' home fur his tea an' that. 'Course, at some point, one ov Markie's boys had t'tell un tha' wudn' likely t'happen in the near future. T'give Anthony credit, ee didn' squal or anything at that, an' seemed t'accept 'is fate a little more. The problem ee comed back with though wuz about his medication. Tha' wuz the one factor Markie 'adn' seemed to have taken inta' account. They tried t'establish wha' the medication wuz and wha' might happen if ee didn't take ut.

'I go a bit weird,' wuz Anthony's response to their questions.
'Wha' kind ov weird?'

Alan M. Kent

'Mummy says I get violent. Sometimes I break things... I throw around my Lego.'

Ah shit. So they might need t'hold un in somewhere like a padded cell, t'save un from hisself. 'Is medication wudn' somethun' tha' wuz goin' t'be easy to obtain. Ee wuz goin' t'have to go without.

At the moment, ee wuz still in his Portreath School uniform. Markie wudn' stupid though. Ee knawed tha' ee'd need a bit ov kit fur'n t'manage un. So tha' wuz all organised on the island. The transfer across would come later tha' day under cover ov darkness. Well, this wuz when all the day visitors down Godrevy Point 'ad gone home, and when Markie's gorillas cud launch a small motor boat across. T'ensure Anthony wudn' knaw where the hell ee wuz, they put a hood on un. From the top ov the tower y'had a good view of the Bay. And ov course, this wuz where Yeugen had nawticed Yak's little shipment, an' 'ad intervened in its distribution around Cornwall.

'We're goin' t'play a game,' the boy with the neck tattoo went.

'What kind ov game?'

Well, i's a bit ov an adventure. You have t'try to guess where we'm goin'...'

Anthony quite liked the sound ov tha', but ee didn't like ut s'much when they bundled un a bit and put the hood on un. Ee seemed t'go all quiet an' shivering when tha' happened – like ee 'adn' expected the violence of ut.

Markie's gimps wudn' likun' ut much either.

'I dunnaw about all ov this,' one ov them wuz goin'. Ee 'ad kids hisself, an' the prospect ov one ov they in the same situation didn' go down well with un.

'Tell Markie tha'. Do you wunt t'keep your bollocks or no?' said the tattooed one. 'You're being paid well enough pard...'

Anthony wuz still, lying on the back of the van. In his hand he'd manage t'hang on t'a Lego clone-trooper figure. Tha' wuz about the only thing tha' wuz keepin' un going at this point.

They moved un out ov the van down on the Sands, and carried him over into the motor boat. Shortly, ee wuz on board, feeling the rocking sensation of the boat heading over the water to the island. The tide and winds were in their favour tha' night so it didn' take too long to make the crossing. They brought the boat in at the western landing place an' then marched un up the path. To their right, wuz the old abandoned crane, down by the shore, and nearer the lighthouse itself, the old oil store. Anthony wuz goin' t'be held in on the second level, in a locked and screened section of the room that Markie's boys 'ad set up. The boys wudn' allowed t'go up any further – the top three storeys were Yeugen's domain, and were kept secret.

She comed down t'meet them though.

'How is he?'

'Quiet.'

'Has he been t' the toilet?'

'Not yet.'

'Take him... Make sure he's okay. There are spare clothes an' things for him to do in his room.'

Markie'd set up a kind of a play area fur Anthony. Ee knew that the kid might be with um for some time. This wuz composed ov a few more Lego kits as well as some games for un t'play on a newly-installed Wii system. Anthony wuz being monitored very carefully. Ee didn't seem t'want t'get changed out of his school uniform though – but then again, ee did take his shoes off. By the way ob'un, ut seemed like ee wuz thinkin' ee'd be back in school pretty soon.

The whole hood thing had failed though. Anthony wudn' thick. Within a few seconds ee'd realised where he wuz when they took it off his head. He nawticed the round walls of the tower.

'Is this a lighthouse?'

Nawbody answered un.

Ee looked out one of the windows an' saw Godrevy Point.

'Caw... Is this Godrevy?'

Ah shit. The kid had already worked ut out.

'It is,' went Yeugen.

Anthony did a bit ov a double-take on her. He recognised her from the other day when he'd been coasteering with his da, Charlie an' Trescothick's army. Ut wuz the witch. Now even Anthony wuz old enough an' sensible enough t'knaw tha' askin' her if she wuz a witch wudn' be the best move ee'd ever made. Her presence did scare him though. Maybe ee even sensed she wuz the Voodoo Queen in all ov this.

'Are these fur me?' ee managed to say.

On the floor of the second level were a range of Star Wars Lego kits fur him to occupy himself. One of Markie's boys also passed un' over the Venator box with the near-complete model inside of ut. This, ee got excited about again, an' seemed to forget the anxiety of the previous few minutes.

Outside cud be heard the buzz of the engine of a helicopter comin' in from the east. Yeugen an' the gorillas already there didn' need t'say anything. They knew 'twas Markie arrivin' bang on time. Yeah. Markie wudn' the sort t'cross t'the island in a motor boat. Well, these days 'twud mess up one of his flash suits wudn' ut? Na, there wuz enough money on tap t' fly in these days. In fact, given the hold-ups all the time on the A30, Markie wuz findin' ov ut very convenient. Ee'd even gone up t' the match in Newport in the helicopter. The old landing pad on the island, ov course, had been used to ferry occasional equipment across, an' 'ad needed a bit ov work, but of late, wuz proving very useful. Yeah, there wuz the base down at Stithians abattoir, but this, out here, wuz a bit more like ut, completely away from prying eyes.

What did Markie want t' come out ov Anthony's abduction? That wudn' 'zactly clear really to his inner circle. All they'd knawed wuz that somehow this kid's parents had done un wrong in the past. Markie wudn' too forward about the fact tha' ee still fancied the ass off Ally t' Yeugen. All ee wuz sayin' t'her wuz tha' Ally an' Neil needed sortun', an' tha the best way ov hurtin' they, wuz t'take their kid away. In the end, ee didn' want money from um. 'Mean, they didn' really have much in the first plaace so what would be the point of askin' fur that? The song-writing money wuz just peanuts really. Na, wha' ee wanted wuz a bit more ov a guarantee tha' Ally wudn' goin' t'say anything – an' tha' maybe, ee'd just spend a bit ov time with her, t'have another go an' see ef she'd give un a second chance – an' leave tha' loser Davey. 'Twas flawed logic, but well, power corrupts dun't ut? Ut makes ee act in ways you normally wudn'. There wuz a further reason fur ut all though. What ee wuz aimin' fur wuz t'create a climate ov fear around electric pastyland tha' would make un look even more ov a hero. With the right manipulation ov all ov ut, ee cud end up looking like a hero – bringin' Anthony back t'his parents.

Somethun like tha' wud only enchance his 'Precious Lives' reputation.

The helipad could be found just inside the outer wall of the the lighthouse complex. The helicopter itself could head back across t'the mainland now. Markie grabbed his case and ducked below the rotating blades. Ee made is way over to the tower. 'Twas a pleasant evening ee nawticed. The lights ov St Ives and Hayle twinkled in the distance. A warmish breeze came in off the Atlantic. A perfect summer's evening all towld. Ee gived a glance up the coast t'Portreath, where ee knawed things were probably not goin' so well. Inside the lighthouse tower, 'is boys were on the bottom layer, awaiting further instructions.

'You got un thun?' went Markie.

'Yeah. Ut all went t'plan...'

'Easy wuz ut – with the Lego?'

'Aw yeah... Ee fell fur ut...'

'Good... I towld ee so.'

'Wha' next then?'

'We just have t'wait.'

'She up there?' asked Markie.

'Yeah, she's there.'

'Where's the kid?'

'In the storehouse fur the moment, havin' somethun' t'eat...'

'Keep un there. I need to speak to her... Oh, keep a close watch outside. Monitor the island for me. Make sure you keep an eye on what's coming across from the mainland...'

'Righton Markie...'

The grunts went out and left Markie to climb the radial staircase to where ee'd find Yeugen. Markie wudn' quite sure about wha' ee wuz involved with, with her. Mean, the bitch wuz sexy as fuck at times – ee cud see why ee'd been tempted. Then other times, ut seemed like she wuz still in love with Curnow – an' tha' nothun' else seemed t'matter much. 'Is contract with her wuz important though. She wuz sealin' the deals on much ov the Eastern European end ov things. Ee knew ee needed her kept sweet. But in 'is mind, ee wuz still imagining Ally. Ee cudn' help ut. Thaas' who ee'd wanted, the one who ee'd always wanted. In another world, tha' kid below wud be 50% 'is.

In the top room of the tower, Yeugen wuz at work, sat cross-legged on the floor. Magical arts were in process. Markie almost didn' like t'disturb her. Ee stood there fur a while watchin' her, nawticing the drawings on the walls: the magical symbols, numbers and calculations of her Vèvès. Above both ov them the tower lantern gave its flash every ten seconds, white in sectors 22-101 and 145-272 degrees, and red over the Stones in the other 101-145 degrees. Magical numbers those, for a long period of time now: preventing loss ov life and others not coming to harm out there in the Bay.

Ee coughed t'let her know ee wuz there. She turned around.

'That ut?' ee said.

Yeugen opened her hands. In them, a small clay doll, with pins stuck in it.

'That's him,' she said. 'Przyniesie to mu zaszkodzi ...'

Her Polish made her activities seem all the more convincing, and all the more magical.

He nodded fur her to translate.

'It will bring him harm,' she said.

'Proper job,' went Markie.

Ee realised that actually, ee did love her, an' kissed her passionately. Amongst the Vèvès an' numbers, they made an evil kind ov love.

Eden Project Re-Works – Freedom of movement means unlimited possibilities.
Versatile texture cream
• Re-workable – Bendable pliable plant formula for easy restyling
• Clean texture – Light cream base with tropical biome-derived conditioners to help provide moveable texture
• Multiple styles – Apply to damp hair for a soft finish or to dry hair for separation and added texture

Nawbody had found un overnight. The police held a meetun' in Portreath Church hall t'discuss the collective strategy with the community. In other words, they wuz feelin' a bit clueless, an' thought they'd best see wha' everyone else thought. Well, people didn' knaw wha' t'say did um? Ee'd clean disappeared. Abduction wuz lookin' more an' more likely. Every known an' registered paedophile in the area wuz receiving a visit from the police. Up Exeter, the Child Protection unit were monitoring the kiddie-fiddler websites t'see if anything wuz being discussed or disclosed. There wuz nawthin' though. No new leads.

Back in Neil an' Ally's house, a couple of things wuz happenin'. Like in all these kind ov cases, the coppers wuz havin' t'investigate Ally an' Neil's movements yesterday as well. Like, as if y'd kidnap your own kid fur some reason. Well, ut had happened hadn' ut? – so they had t'rule ut out. They wanted the ins and outs of cat's arsehole on tha'. They even wanted t'knaw where Neil'd been working in the previous six months.

'I wuz on tour.' ee went.

'Who with?'

'Our band – Purple Haze...' ee said snivelling.

'Where?'

'I dunno... Everywhere. Lots ov gigs across the country...'

'I see.'

'Can we verify that?'

'Ask Spryer – our manager... Thaas' his number there...'

An so ut went on.

Outside, the search had widened. Redruth an' Camborne were now under scrutiny. They'd gived up on the coastpath t'be honest, though there wuz the feeling amongst the coastguard tha' they ought t'keep any eye out for a body being washed in by the tide. Nawbody wuz tellin' Neil an' Ally tha' though. The day 'ad brought in another raft ov media interest too. Ut being summer, and the fuckers on the papers an' on tv havin' fuck all else t'write about, ad made ut one of their lead stories, hadn' um?

Charlie cudn' stand ut any longer. Ee went down there t'try an' see um, but their house wuz inaccessible. If you wudn' family you wudn' goin' in.

'I'm 'is best mate though,' Charlie wuz sayin' to one of the coppers.

'No access mate,' the copper went. 'Sorry...'

Up on Trelawny 'bout the only useful thing they cud do, wuz organise a set of flyers an' posters with Anthony's face on um, t'see if ut would stir up any knowledge in the general public ov West Cornwall. Even the tackers up there got involved, goin' around t'any telegraph post, an' stapling on an A4 'Help find Anthony' poster. Within the day, they'd just about covered

Alan M. Kent

Redruth, Pool an' Camborne with as many posters as there wuz bit ov voodoo pilchard graffiti. In fact, in some cases, the posters 'ad been pinned or taped straight on top of the Pilchard's work. Well, when a kiddie wuz missin', ut didn't seem t'matter much any more? The same thing had gone on down Portreath and Porthtowan, an' someone 'ad gone t'Hayle an' Gwithian as well.

The police knawed they wuz losing ut. In a couple ov days, the public an' the MPs would be askin' questions ov um. Why hadn' they found this dear little boy yet? How cud um be s'fuckin' useless? Wha' wuz um doin' ov you? They began a new round ov discussions with Ally an' Neil, in an effort t'solve where ee'd gone. Any relatives? Any problems like? Wuz ut absolutely and categorically their kid? Then there wuz questions about anyone who might do they harm. At tha', there wuz a slight pause on Ally's behalf, but she dismissed ut as soon as she even thought ov ut. Well, tha' wuz all a long time ago, an' so she'd heard, ee wuz with someone else now, and doin' very well. So she said nawthin'. Plus, she didn' knaw if she wanted ut all t'come out – what she knew 'bout un. She wuz pretty thinkin' 'bout Charlie though – an' wished she might have a private chat widn' but fur now, considering the quantity of support there in her home, tha' wudn' goin' t'be possible. Neil 'ad a think too – ee didn' knaw ov anybody – not since they wuz kids at least. The police then, wuz shafted. They had nawthin' t'go on, so you knaw how 'tis, there wuz lots of press conferences and briefings, tha' were basically bullshittin' the public.

Charlie wuz tryin' to work out where ee might have gone. Ee wuz reckonin' on they two havin' a bit of special relationship really, bondin' over Naboo and Obi Wan Kenobi. From tha', cud a work out where ee'd gone? 'Twas causin' un a lot ov mental anguish. Ee wondered how ee might cope if ee wuz in Neil's situation? Fur wha' seemed like days, there wuz no solace. Ee even tried to write ut out – t'exorcise the demons ov ut by puttin' it inta' a song, but ut wudn' happening. 'Twas driving un insane really.

'Don't try t'force ut too much…' Bev wuz going. 'Just let it come naturally…'

But the thing wuz. This wudn' natural. Thaas' what ee wuz feeling.

Voodoo Pilchard

Charlie wuz beginning to wonder ef comin' back here wuz the right thing t'do at all. Despite Neil's worries, maybe if they'd still have been in the collective protection of Hendrix, none ov this wud have happened. Ee touched Jimi's string t'try an' gain some guidance. Nothun' seemed t'come however.

Yak wuz all too philosophical about ut.

'Yeah, thousands of kids go missun' every year... They never find um. They just act like ut hasn't happened. Me and Jody wuz talkin' 'bout ut. '

Ee wuz tryin' t'be logical about ut all. But when your emotions are involved, how can y'be? At this point in time, Charlie wuz feeling tha' ee wuz needin' not just the road lessons ee had, but a whole new set. Now you wuz beginning t'understand pain an' anguish on a whole new scale. 'Twas like some cunt wuz out there ill-wishin' the lot ov um.

Three days had passed now, an' there wudn' naw progress (not least, tha' anyone in electric pastyland cud see). Ut had made the national news now. Yeah – Cornwall, tha' wuz an easy place t' lose kids wudn' ut? Charlie saw people bein' interviewed down Portreath. The shock ov ut all wuz becomin' very clear t'see. 'Twas when you heard people speakin' dialect on national telly, well, thaas' when ut's always hammered home. The awnly thing they cud do wuz t'just step up the campaign t'find Anthony. Over the Eden Project, at the usual indie music sessions, they'd had a minute's prayer fur un, an' some of the proceeds ov tha' wuz being put inta' a Find Anthony Fund.

Jimmy Pengelly had even hastily organised a benefit concert down Centenary Chapel. Ee'd even asked Charlie t'sing with um – a version of Hendrix's 'The Wind Cries Mary' which ee did. A couple ov hours rehearsal with the Holman-Climax male voice choir, an' ut sounded brilliant. In another world, ut would have been some kind of charity single. Just about all ov Portreath and Obby Stanker Country wuz in. Ut made his ma and is da squal a bit – 'twas so emotional over there you.

'Y'knaw you've always got a plaace here with us,' said Jimmy Pengelly.

Fuck, how the world had changed on the flip ov a coin. Fur a second, at the emotion ov ut, ee wuz contemplatin' ut – if ut wud only bring Anthony home.

The one-eyed minister, the boy who'd Charlie'd first seen

trying to scrub off the voodoo pilchard graffiti, well, ee wuz leading a collective service t'pray fur Anthony's well-being and tha' ee soon be bought home safely. Yeah – like all the congregation there, Charlie wuz hopin' tha' in God's Own Country ee just might be located somehow.

> Penwith Moors Wild Wax – A new way to wax baby!
> 3-dimensional texture and flexible hold
> • Waxed satin finish – Non-oily cosmetic wave combined with heather and gorse from the Penwith Moors to produce a waxed satin finish
> • Pliable texture – Fine and flexible all the time
> • Light mist aerosol – Easy to apply to all lengths and hair types

Nawbody back Centenary knawed ut, but ee 'ad been located. The bugger who'd dun ut wuz Trescothick.

See, Tresothick 'ad been monitorin' very closely the activities takin' plaace on Godrevy. Charlie had picked tha' up. Ee knawn ov the Orange one's interest in the island when they wuz coasteerin'. Trescothick see, didn' go very much on Markie Phillips, an' all his pretend support fur Cornwall with Trura City football club. Ee also 'ad a gut feeling about Clifford Mellow's murderer. Fur ee, Phillipsy wuz a kind of rottenness at the core of contemporary Cornwall, one worse than the development and tourist agencies put together. Ee wuz tha' worst kind ov Cornish, who shat on their own doorstep, and wud do anything s'long as ut guaranteed them a bit ov money. So fur the past few nights ee'd pulled up his little Bedford Rascal van on the road t'Godrevy Point an' just watched wha' wuz goin' on. Y'had t'hand ut to un. Shit terrorist an' tha' re wuz, ee wudn bad actually at a goodly bit ov military reconnaissance. Ee'd seen all the comin' and goings on the island fur the past few days like, an' nawticed a white Transit pullin' up – not t'mention the motor boat goin' out there. Why the fuck in the darkness ee 'ad asked? There'd been the helicopter landings too. Yeah, ee'd nawticed tha' a few times. Didn' really knaw who 'twas but 'course, ee 'ad 'is suspicions.

See, ee 'ad his high-powered binoculars trained on the lighthouse tower didn' a? Straight t'the lighthouse every night see.

An' well, as ut goes, ee'd been watchin' each of the windows t'see what wuz goin' on. An' yeah, ee'd seen that woman a few times out there – the one they'd seen while out coasteering. She wuz weirder than assholes she wuz – out there all on her own like. But then, Trescothick 'ad a bit ov an epiphany didn' a? The showing forth tha' comed wuz after earlier tha' day ee'd been listenin' t'the latest about the disappearance ov Neil's boy. Trescothick 'ad a fondness fur'n especially after ee'd asked un fur a balaclava next time they went coasteering. Now Trescothick wudn' a man too keen on the media institution tha' wuz Radio Cornwall – ut, in his considered view, bein' infiltrated from top t'bottom with English imperialism. However, the news tha' Anthony had been abducted coincided with un seeing, just briefly, wha' ee thought wuz a little boy's head silhouetted in one of the windows ov the second level of the lighthouse. Initially, ee didn' want t'make the connection, ee really didn', but then, when ee sawed un again – just briefly, ee knaw somehow 'twas Anthony. Yeah – definitely ee. Tha' geeky fuckin' look 'bout un.

Now any sane person might, at tha' point, have called the police an' gived um the kind of lead tha' wud result in Anthony being swiftly reunited with his family after a tactical raid on the hostage's environment. Trescothick though, saw this as just the right opportunity t'start implementin' a number ov the objectives ov the Cornish Tiger's ten point plan. Ee took out his mobile an' made the first call. The chain tha' ee wuz about t'start wuz the culmination ov months of planning. A continuum ov phone calls would be made across God's Own Country uniting the freedom fighters of Cornwall. Wha' 'ad up until tha' moment, been just a proposed offensive, wuz about t'become reality on the ground.

'Lock an' load,' went Trescothick.

His unit knew instantly. Mission Godrevy wuz go.

Mackerel Works – Go hi-def. Spike it up and fish for compliments!
Extreme texture and shine
• Creates texture and definition – Flexible resins and fish-based conditioners provide texture and definition
• Excellent control – Thick, softening formula is perfect

for hard to control hair types
• Intensifies shine – Activated maritime blend to enhance shine

Another day had gone past, and still, there wuz no news. Neil an' Ally wuz in pieces wudn' um? 'Twas becomin' clear tha' mentally an' physically, they cudn' take much more ov ut. Geoff Hawkins wuz doin' his best t'help, an' losin' ut big time - an' recalling his days as a bit of a hippy at Elephant Fayre – ee'd suggested a bit ov meditation, t', in his words, 'Will Anthony back to us'. Well, Neil an' Ally wud try anything but it didn' seem t'do a lotta' good. The police's attention 'ad turned to the school itself and the safeguarding procedures they obviously didn't have in place. Before you knawed ut, Mrs Evans wuz off work wudn' she – due t'stress apparently – an' little knawn to moast of the community, 'ad gone on a bit ov a gin bender down her place in Carbis Bay. The school wuz vaguely carryin' on, but 'twudn' looking like anybody wuz tha' bothered really about National Curriculum test results or what levels the kids were achieving. The remaining staff had set up an 'Anthony' board where the kids could post their thoughts about Anthony, an' place drawings ov un.

Charlie had now managed t' meet up with Neil an' Ally – they'd asked fur a bit ov space from the police, which they'd willingly granted. 'Twas as if Charlie didn' knaw um anymore though. Neil'd gone right inta' hisself, an' wuz upstairs playin' odd snatches ov Hendrix over an' over again. Ally wuz devotin' her energies t'Megan and doin' her best – still ironing Anthony's shirts for school.

'I gotta' believe he's goin' t'come back Charlie…'

'Yeah… I understand…'

Ally looked like she wanted t'talk. At one point, she looked like she wuz goin' t'ask Charlie's view on somethun', but then Neil came back downstairs an' put her off.

'I'm there fur you both… Bev an' me… you knaw tha' dun't you?' went Charlie.

'Yeah, cheers Charlie. We really appreciate tha' dun't we Ally?'

If they'd knawn ov wha' wuz on further t'west, they might have 'ad a bit more hope. Trescothick's unit had met 'round his

mother's earlier tha' day t'discuss tactics. The exact detail ov
the 'rescue' mission nature ov the squad's objective wuz quite a
closely-guarded secret, but all ov them there cud tell tha' ut
wudn' just a bit of a day-trip out the island. Trescothick
explained the sensitivity ov ut to them. It wuz definitely on a
need-to-knaw basis. All they needed t'knaw wuz tha' their previous plans for an attack on the island remained the same

Come the evening, thaas' when they deployed. They knew
wha' time Markie's helicopter would come in, so waited until
after then. Tha' wuz usually about ten o'clock, an' even then,
this time ov year, the sky over the Atlantic still held onta' the
last of the light. The real darkness awnly hit at eleven, so thaas'
when the first rigid-hulled launches hit the water. Where did a
land-lubber Trescothick get they from? Well, like Yak, ee 'ad a
few contacts down Newlyn too. The trawlermen wuz always up
fur the 'cause', or so ee said. The Tigers' faces were all blacked
up, and they 'ad on the standard KLF-issue black fatigues. In
this way, they could move easily by the cover ov darkness.

Last to deploy wuz Boy Bluett. Ee'd be takin' a squad around
the eastern side of the central island, t'give um a bit ov a surprise attack tha' end. Now seein' as how ee wuz second-in-command at this point in the Tigers' history, ee 'ad a bit ov a notion
ov the sensitivity of their mission. 'Obi Wan' wuz the code
name they wuz givin' to Anthony an' ov course, ee wuz their
prime objective. A second objective however, wuz t'deal with
Markie's boys, and bring Phillipsy back here t'the mainland. A
plan had been drawn up t' incapacitate un, an' start interroga-
tion procedures – prob'ly over United Downs somewhere. At
the very least, Trescothick wuz aiming fur a confession about
Clifford Mellow, but also anything else about his illegal activities. Less wuz knawn about the witch of the island. Tha' wuz
perhaps the one thing tha' wuz making Trescothick nervous. Ee
didn't knaw wha' kind of powers she had. Pagans, ee didn'
mind. There wuz a few on um in the Movement, but this one,
she wuz out there.

Everyone had synchronised their watches. The attack wud
begin at two minutes t' midnight. Tha' wuz Trescothick's standard starting time fur any covert operation – him being a bit ov
an Iron Maiden fan see. See, now they were heading out on the
dark waves of the Atlantic, ready t'do battle. Ut wuz a proud

moment fur all ov um. This wuz wha' the Tigers wuz all about
– direct action, makin' good the wrongs suffered by the Cornish
people. The bows ov their launches hit hard against the waves.
A salty spray caught their faces. Closer t' the island, they had to
manipulate a course which took them out of the beam of the
lighthouse itself. It was also necessary t' cut engines then, an'
row the last expanse of water. The aim wuz t'be both silent an'
deadly. One unexpected difficulty they had to face wuz the various vessels out in the bay laying the cable for the Wave Hub.
At tha' point all of the Tigers held up rods t'make ut look like
they wuz jus' goin' out for a bit of a night-fishin'. The boys on
board the cable vessels even waved um on, not knawing anything ov the magnitude of what wuz going to happen.

Now, as for weaponry, with a unit of this type, tha' wuz kind
of improvised t'be honest. Trescothick had his contacts mind –
mean, ee wuz probably the awnly tool in Britain who'd taken
private delivery of a Starstreak missile – an' ee'd been 'opin' fur
some decent automatic weapons, but 'twudn' forthcoming; certainly not fur this mission at least. Moast of the Tigers there, 'ad
improvised sawn-off shot-guns, air-rifles and BB guns. This wuz
typical Obby-Stanker ordinance. Whether ut wuz powerful
enough fur Markie's gorillas wuz yet t'be seen.

While they were waiting, Bluett wuz on one, 'Fuck me. Have
anyone else tried tha' Cash4Gold thing yet?'

Nawbody else had.

'I did. Sent off me dead gran's old earrings. Didn' get much
back. Two pound bleddy fifty...' ee went. 'Well I towld um they
could keep their two pound fifty... fur tha' money – so they
sent um back...'

Ut sounded like twudn' the sort ov thing tha' wudn' goin'
t'provide the kind ov on-going funding the KLF wuz goin'
t'need fur their future development.

At precisely 11.58pm the mission began. The two groups
stepped ashore. Lights were still shining in the windows of the
tower as they made their way stealthily up the paths on both
sides of the island. All ov um were crouching, turning every so
often to monitor activity. Trescothick's group were takin' ut
steady, spreading out to mount the attack from all sides, including the north, where the raincatch area wuz. By about five minutes past midnight, they'd made ut as far as the oil store.

Now, Bluett's group wuz goin' a bit more steadily on the eastern side ov the island, with the boys with ee askin' un more about Cash4Gold an' tha' and whether 'twud be worth their while or naw. Things seemed t'be goin' well, Bluett noted over his radio t'Trescothick. In fact, ut seemed t'be goin' a bit too well. There wuz one potential difficulty with the whole operation though. One hint tha' anything wuz on, amongst Markie's boys, and their refuge wuz easy wudn' ut. All they had t'do wuz get in the tower an' shut the door. That'ud be ut then.

Trescothick knawed ut. ''Twould then be like one ov they there Irish Round Towers... We'd never penetrate ut...'

They'd go up the inside, and come out on the balcony. From there, ut could be a complete pin-down situation, with the growing dawn exposing their positions even further. Na, securing the door 'ad t' be the prime objective above all else.

As before though, whenever Trescothick planned an attempt at revolution, ut didn' go quite the way ee'd conceived ov ut. See, Markie an' his boys wudn' stupid. They knew someone might be watchin'. After all, the amount ov firms ee'd put out ov business, well, you could expect someone tryin' t'get even. They'd littered the plaace with trip wires see, and well Trescothick happened t'accidentally stumble inta' one. Despire being a bit more focused on Cash4Gold than he should've been, Bluett wudn' have done nothun' like that see. Well, heading off t'Afghanistan, ee had such IEDs on 'is mind all the time didn' a? The effect of this wire though was to sound an alarm and set off some bright arc-lighting in the central compound. Fur Markie's grunts, this wuz the signal that they 'ad a security breach. So they wuz out there within an instant, nawticing that the island wuz over-run with invaders.

T'call any ov what happened in the next ten minutes a thing of beauty an' wonder would quite wrong. Nawbody had a fuckin' clue. 'Twas really, the blind fighting the blind. The Tigers blawed off every kind of weaponry they had, moast of ut missing their targets completely and t'be honest makin' a bit ov a mess ov the historically preserved walls of the lighthouse complex. Likewise, Markie's boys, though used t' a bit ov fisticuffs, wudn' that much handier with the pistols ee'd issued them. In fact, they had just about more hope ov hitting' one of the seals over Mutton Cove than hitting one of the Tigers. Weaponry therefore proved a bit incompetent. Hand-t'-hand wuz the way to go. Trescothick had trained his boys in the art ov wrasslin' fur this very kind of scenario, so they wudn' doing a bad job at confronting the tactics of Markie's forces.

Bluett's team arrived a bit later than anyone else, an' so made keeping the lighthouse door open their priority. At all the row, Markie had comed down, followed by Yeugen, an' ee wuz doin' his level best t'stop Bluett's team. Near the door, ee'd a store ov automatic weapons, an' while blocking an' battling Bluett, was dolling out the AR-15 machine guns. In an instant, Trescothick saw that they wuz outmanoeuvred and outgunned on all levels.

'Abort the mission. Obi Wan is over. Repeat. Obi Wan is over,' ee shouted. 'Retreat!'

Bluett didn have much hope ov holding out against Markie, and let go on the door and went flyin' off down the slope to the helipad. Moast of 'is squad 'ad aleady followed Trescothick's orders and were heading back down to the eastern landing point.

'Next time, you come back, bring a proper army!' roared Markie.

'We are,' teased Trescothick, like a true commander, lettin' the rest ov his squad get the hell out.

'Have they come for Anthony?' asked Yeugen.

'Doan't knaw... Someone've told um somethun'...'

Markie's mind wuz fulla' dark mistrust an' fear.

Curly Piskey Sculpting Foam – Make waves with smooth, silky, static-free style.
Conditioning style foam
• Medium hold – Styling and bodifying ingredients with panthenol to help provide long-lasting memory and texture
• Defines cut and controls fuzz – Conditions to help smooth the surface to control static and enhance curls.
• Helps prevent moisture loss – Our activated Piskey Blend with moorland heather helps balance moisture and prevent dryness

In trying to allow the others time to leave the island in retreat,

Voodoo Pilchard

Trescothick wuz the one who couldn't quite get to the rigid-hulled motor boats in time. The pasty intake had gone up ov late (in direct response to the stress ov plannin' all the coasteerin' an' the Godrevy operation), and tha' had made un a little more sluggish than the others. While the rest ov the Cornish Tigers went on training weekends up on Bodmin Moor, doin' route marches ov Ten Tors-type proportions, Trescothick mainly stayed at home, designing the website an' pushing out the propaganda. In truth, ee wuz an orange-coloured fat fucker too slaw t'catch duckshit, so thaas' why Markie's boys easily took un out with a tackle worthy of the props ov the Cornish Pirates pack. Fuck, ee wuz always bein' took out, naw matter wha' ee did fur the revolution. Lass' time around 'twas some little fucker from Trelawny, an' now 'twas Markie's muscle. There wuz no messin' with um. Off comed the balaclava and beret first ov all. They chucked ut over the cliffside inta' the Atlantic swell.

'I's tha' twat Trescothick,' said one ov the boys, instantly identifying un.

'Do what y'like,' said Trescothick. 'I shan't speak... You'll get nothun' from me. I shall have a name perpetual and a fame permanent and immortal. Me am beth hanow heb dewath ha bry bisgwethack rag nevra...'

'Y'reckon,' went Markie Phillips. 'Well, well, well, if we haven't been and caught the leader of the revolution here in Cornwall... Well done boys... This is the ace in the pack... Dun't worry about the rest... Not when we've caught Public Enemy Number One...'

'They'll be back fur me,' went Trescothick, like the Last Cornish Action Hero standing.

'Na, they wun't,' said Phillipsy. 'They think you'm a cunt... an' you are a cunt... so don't bank on any SAS-style rescue mission.'

'Where do ee want un boss?' went one of Markie's boys.

'Inside... In the 'lab'...'

'Righton...'

Lab? That sounded fuckin' sick. What was a now? Not only Cornwall's biggest gobshite, but now fuckin' Frankenstein in 'is secret lab. About ten ov Markie's boys bundled un along, giving un a good few punches an' digs as went. Trescothick wuz takin' ut all. Ee knawed there wuz naw gain fur Cornwall, without a

305

Alan M. Kent

bit ov pain. In his mind, ee wuz trying to psychologically prepare fur what wuz to come. Ee knawed ut wudn' goin' t'be
pleasant. The Cornish Ten Point plan came to the forefront ov
'is mind. If ee kept thinking of tha', then all would be well.
Trescothick wuz thinking ee wuz just the latest in a long line of
Cornish heroes who'd suffered for their land. Before ee entered
the 'lab' the gimps blindfolded un.

Inside the lab, which wuz on the bottom floor of the lighthouse tower, they stripped un down, to his fuckin' stupid lookin' grape smugglers, tossing away 'is clothing to the wind outside. However Trescothick wuz goin' t' be getting' out ov there,
ee wuz goin' to be doin' ut in 'is pants alone. Maybe ee could
draw on legend – tha' a mermaid or a seal wud rescue un. Na.
Shit like tha' didn' really happen, unless you wuz on drugs or
mephedrone or somethun'.

'Fuck me, you'm some orange,' went Markie. 'What happened?'

'Got tanned didn' I? - over Jess Curnow's new salon...' pleaded Trescothick.

'Canned?'

'No – tanned...'

Unable to see, Trescothick felt them push him down onto an
inclined table. They bound his hand and his feet, so the latter
were at the uppermost end. In another world, 'twud be nice an'
kinky – especially with someone fanciable like Jess Curnow or
tha' Kayleigh maid - but this, this wuz fuckin' bad news. They
strapped down 'is head too – right down at the lower end.

'In my line ov work,' Markie wuz goin', 'occasionally, you
have to deal with shite and clean ut up... Now, our little bit ov
fun here, is me dealing with you – my next lump ov shit...'

Trescothick sensed wha' they were going to do. They wuz
goin' t'waterboard un. Torture across the world would be one of
'is specialised subjects if ee ever got on Mastermind. Ee tried to
struggle but cudn' move an inch. Ee wuz goin' t'have to be very
strong here. Ee called down the spirits of Michael Joseph an'
Thomas Flamank an' fuckers from 1549 - like Humphry
Arundell an' Henry Bray, an' anyone else who wuz watchin'.
They took a double-folded towel and pushed ut down hard on
his mouth. Then, one of the gimps picked up a salt-water-filled
water can, and started to pour it very slowly onto the towel.

Trescothick could feel the towel becoming wetter and wetter. Any moment soon, the torrent would fall down his throat and gag him; then give him the sensation that ee wuz drowning. Ee cud already taste the salty water on his tongue. For a bit, the pouring seemed to stop. Trescothick could feel 'is heart beat increasing, pumping vigorously against his chest. Ee wuz trying to breathe, but was finding ut more and more difficult. Hold yer nerve ee wuz telling hisself.

'What do you know about me?' asked Markie. 'Come on – I want some answers…'

'Nothun', Trescothick shouted. They moved the towel away from 'is face, so ee could breathe and speak more easily.

'If you go to the law, to the coppers, an' tell them what you know, do you know what's going to happen to you?'

'No.'

'More of this…'

Markie nodded, an' the towel wuz back on his face again. Because 'is feet were elevated, the effect of the waterboarding wuz worse. Trescothick wuz counting. There'd be around 20 to 40 seconds of the cloth over his mouth and nose. Then the water would be poured. There it wuz. He could feel the presence of the stream – about twelve inches above his mouth. Entering. Then the first gag reflex. The sensation ov drowning. They left the cloth on just long enough fur it take effect. Fuck. Ee cud feel himself blacking out. Then the towel was off again.

'I don't want to drown you Trescothick, not really,' Markie wuz going, slowly, almost caring for him. 'See, I want you to go safely back to Camborne… not ever darken my door again… Do you get that? Well, have a think about ut.'

The towel was back on again. It felt heavier this time, like it was saturated. Breathing wuz more difficult. There wuz no time to prepare, to swallow air. Bastards. Trescothick wuz beginning t'wish ee'd exercised a bit more now, an' tha' he'd made ut back to the boats. Fuck this, 'twas only goin' t'get worse. Outside of the dulled world ee wuz in, ee cud hear the cunts counting up to twenty. Ee counted with them. Ee got to 14 before the water started to enter his mouth. The convulsions were worse this time, hurting his neck bones, 'is lungs craving to spit out the water. The salt made it even worse. Ee wuz floating downward now in the deep, with the crabs, the shells, the seaweed and the pilchards. Momentarily, ee thought of the pain of the tattoo ov Michael Joseph's words on his arm. Then there wuz light again. Markie wuz directly over him, gazing down on 'is eyes. Ee spewed up the water from 'is lungs, coughed and gagged in front ov un.

'Glad you'm likin' ut... Know where I learnt this?' asked Markie.

'Iraq?' asked Trescothick, like a twat. As if.

'Aw naw... Exeter prison... That time I got put in fur that job over Tuckingmill... yeah... Any cunt who done wrong on the inside, this is wha' we used to do... Never any problem again once they experience this... But you, Trescothick... we dun't seem t'be breaking you yet... For moast people, ut seems t'be enough just thinkun' 'bout ut... but you... well, you'm harder than I thought... Must be the berets boys, eh?'

Trescothick heard all the cunts around un laugh. Ee'd have they back one ov these days, dun't ee worry.

'Once more...' commanded Markie.

Phased and simulated asphyxiation wuz wha' ut wuz. Trescothick knew ee'd be traumatized by ut years later. Ee knew ee'd be waking up in sweats. Ee knawed they cudn' carry ut on too long though. Any more than about twenty minutes ov ut, an' ee'd be a goner. Maybe thaas' wha' they wanted. Then again, there were too many boys watchin' this time. Markie wudn' like tha' ee didn' think. When ut comed t'death, ee liked ut secret an' hidden – not public executions. If ee cud survive this one, then ee might have made ut through.

The towel wuz on again. It wudn' sea-water this time though. Naw, this wuz beer. Hang on, 'twas St Austell Brewery HSD. Trescothick cud recognised the taste anywhere. There were worse ways t'go Trescothick reckoned. Ee cud feel hisself starting to gag but tried to divert as much of ut as possible inta' his stomach. Even then, ee only reached fifteen seconds before ee blacked out. When they felt 'is body relax at the point of death, the towel comed off, and ee wuz able to breathe again.

'Your favourite, eh Trescothick...?'

Markie had a pint of HSD in his hand.

'Okay,' ee went. 'Tha' wuz the warm-up game... Pre-Season so t'speak...'

Trescothick tried to speak, but Phillipsy put his hand over his mouth.

'Ah... someone d'wun't t'confess to me... Well, too late fur tha' now... A little bird told me you've been sayin' all kind ov shit 'bout me over Obby Stanker...'

Trescothick knew there wuz wurst t'come but kept his nerve. If Michael Joseph could stand it, then ee could. Markie wuz tryin' t' wind un up.

'Your're tougher than I thought 'Cothick boy,' went Markie. 'Boys, show un what we've got...'

Trescothick watched as much as ee could from 'is immobilised position on the inclined table. Two of Markie's boys opened a box near the door of the room, and took out a serious ghetto-blaster stereo, then beside ut, opened a case full ov what looked like about a hundred CDs.

'See I been watchin' you Trescothick – fur a long time... Mess with me and I'll mess with you...'

'What ee goin' t'do now?' asked a by-now, very scared Trescothick. Ee wuz sensing the evil of wha' wuz comin'.

Markie walked slowly around the table ignoring Trescothick's gaze at un.

'You an' your fuckin' pretend army think they can take the likes ov me out do you?'

Trescothick didn' answer.

'Well, do you?' Markie shouted.

'No,' said Trescothick, even though ee thought yes.

'See in Cornwall now, I own everything. I own all the meat production fur the pasties, I own the drugs, I own Trura City Football Club, an' anything I don't own, I can influence the way I want ut. Devolved power in Cornwall. Well, thaas' me, tha' is. Do you get that Trescothick?'

Markie made a move to grab Trescothick by the neck but then realised ee was naked apart from a pair of sad lookin' Speedo-style underpants. Ee wudn' about to grab they – not yet at least.

'Yes,' coughed Trescothick.

'I own your ass as well Trescothick. Say it...'

'You own my ass,' said Trescothick. Under his breath, Trescothick wuz cursin' Markie in Cornish. Where wuz a bit of Curnow's voodoo when y'needed ut?

'Say it again…'

'You own my ass…'

'Good. Now, you being a para-military Trescothick, you should know all about psychological warfare don't you?'

Trescothick tried to lift his neck up.

'Not really.'

'Well, I do,' said Markie. 'In fact, me an' the boys here have been studying it in some amount of detail. Oh yes.'

Bastard, Trescothick wuz thinkin'.

'I know you've heard of the Black Panthers, but have you heard of the United States 361st Psychological Operations Company?'

'No Markie,' went Trescothick, 'I haven't.'

'Well, you'm goin' to get a bit friendly like with their methods… See out here, on Godrevy, naw-one can hear you scream.'

Fuck. This wuz soundin' like the first Alien film. 'Cothick ud seen ut a few times.

'What you going t'do to me?'

'Boys, just give un a little blast… a taster of what's to come…'

One of Markie's gimps took a CD out of its cream and pink-coloured case and put it into the player. Trescothick's eyes darted from side to side, his anxiousness reaching new extremes. The sweat started to pour off him.

'This should culturally offend you nicely…'

From the stereo came music. Ut was the kind ov music that Trescothick instantly recognised as English-style folk music, played by some 70s' sounding band. As the song built, the discomfort increased fur Trescothick. All of the cells in his body seemed to be responding to it; and the music was cajoling them into spasms of terror he had never experienced before.

'Stop it,' Trescothick begged.

Markie shook his head. The gimp didn't move to the pause button. The nod meant play it a bit longer.

On it went:

AND WHEN THE MEETING IT WAS DONE, SHE CAST
   HER EYES BOUT
AND THERE SHE SAW LITTLE MATTY GROVES, WALKED
   IN THE CROWD
COME HOME WITH ME, LITTLE MATTY GROVES, COME

HOME WITH ME TONIGHT
COME HOME WITH ME, LITTLE MATTY GROVES, AND
SLEEP WITH ME 'TILL LIGHT.

Everyone watched Trescothick's eyes. They glazed over. His fists started to tighten again. This was worse than the waterboarding. Ee wondered if Michael Joseph 'ad had to stand anything as awful.

'That'll do,' went Markie. He moved his hand for the gimp to stop the music.

The room became silent again, aside from Trescothick's deep breathing.

Eventually, Trescothick breathlessly managed to ask, 'Who... Who wuz tha'?'

'The very best in English folk music...' went Markie.

Trescothick screamed.

'Only 'Matty Groves' off *Liege and Lief* by Fairport Convention.' said Markie.

Fuck, Trescothick, was going. The high point of English electric folk in the modern era. Ee didn't think ee cud stand ut any more.

'Got anything you want t'say to me?' asked Markie in a whisper.

'No.'

'You sure? Maybe you want to go home to mother's plaace in Park an Tansys an' never come out again... Maybe you want to stop speaking to Curnow or Ally eh? Maybe you ent goin' t'do anything like tonight's raid again?'

Trescothick wuz moving his head from side to side, struggling in the straps.

'Maybe you'll never show up at Gwennap Pit with a fuckin' bazooka an' try an' take me an' my boys out – eh, you cunt?'

'No... I wun't,' went Trescothick. He wuz breaking. He knew ut. Ee didn't want to, but 'twas unstoppable. English folk music, in Trescothick's view, wuz a kind ov juggernaut ov evil that polluted the wondrous heritage west of the Tamar. He knew ee cudn't last much longer. Waterboarding, the experience of drowing, well, that wuz survivable. This, this hurt hard.

Markie asked him again, 'So you goin' to stop now Trescothick? You an' your fuckin' little poncy army?'

Alan M. Kent

'Yeah...' he said, almost sick with anxiety.

'I dun't believe you,' shouted Markie. 'Do you believe him boys?'

'No,' grunted the gimps.

'No-one believes you Trescothick – not yet, at least. Now, do you knaw wha'? I'm goin' to leave you now... I got other fish to fry see....'

'Dun't leave me,' pleaded Trescothick. Ee'd cracked. Ee'd tell all if Markie wanted.

'Well, I will, but the boys here'll keep ee company fur a bit... Aw... an' I believe we got some more music t'bombard ee with...'

Trescothick wuz wishing for anything that ee 'ad his iPod an' earphones there with a good bit of the Holman Climax on ut, the Fisherman's Friends, Dalla, Big Al Hodge or even some Balance wud do.

'What us ut?' asked Trescothick.

'Turn ut up boys – volume 10...'

In his daze, Trescothick was calling out for Alan Stivell an' Brenda Wootton.

Markie drank the remainder of his pint ov HSD, then picked the exact artists ee wunted to use on Trescothick. Ee handed the ten CDs to one ov his gimps: more Fairport Convention (*Live at Cropedy* this time), Steeleye Span, Lindisfarne, Pentangle, The Albion Band, John Martyn, Richard Thompson, Dave Swarbrick, and then *101 Best Morris Dance Songs in the World... Ever*.

Last of all, the killer - Seth Lakeman.

'When ee's broken, come an' get me.'

The first song of ee comed on, and Trescothick shook and cried like a baby fur the next twenty-four hours. Evil beyond evil had reached new heights in electric pastyland.

Mermaid Fast-drying sculpting spray – Great-looking hair is no accident.
Medium hold finishing spray
• Body, control and shine. Medium, flexible styling ingredients and our activated blend of rock pool botanicals help enhance shine and body with memory
• Excellent working spray – Easy to brush through, reactivates with heat or water

312

Voodoo Pilchard

• Added protection – Helps protect against sun damage

'Twas Anthony who eventually freed Trescothick from the psychological hell tha' wuz the music of the English electric-folk tradition. While Markie wuz upstairs, getting ut on some more with Yeugen, they'd neglected t'think that the tacker posed any danger. Wrong. If Anthony could get out of the window down Portreath Primary school, then a locked door wudn' goin' to pose un any trouble t'all. Ee dismantled the Venator takin' one or two sections of Lego he reckoned might be handy. A bit of tidy work with they on the lock ov the door soon 'ad ut released.

Ee crept down stairs. Ee wuz still slightly scared, because there'd been a lot of gunfire earlier on, but now, tha' 'ad all seemed to have died down. All ee could hear wuz the dulcet voice ov Seth Lakeman:

OUT OF THE MOONLIGHT IN THE MONTH OF MAY
THIS SHIP WOULD TAKE HER LAST BREATH.
HER FULL MAST IT WAS DRAPING,
LIKE A MERMAID SHE WAS DRESSED.

HER LONELY HEART IS SETTING FREE,
ALL HER CARES THEY WENT SAILING OUT TO SEA.

Actually, Anthony wuz quite liking wha' ee wuz hearing. Well, 'twas makin' a change from all tha' heavy rock stuff 'is da played all the time. But Trescothick wudn' looking very good t'all. Besides all the groaning ee wuz makin', 'is body 'ad also gone a weird orange colour to match his face.

Mr Trescothick, Mr Trescothick,' went Anthony. 'Why are you on that table? Why are you s'orange?'

Trescothick opened his eyes. There wudn' much life left behind them. You cud tell ee 'ad gone past breaking point. Anthony cudn' work out why Trescothick wuz in this position.

'Is ut a game?' went Anthony.

'Naw. 'Tis naw game boy... They been torturing me. Taking me t' the limits ov endurance.'

So, ee wuz right. Anthony wuz bein' held here. Mission 'Obi Wan' might be back on again.

Trescothick looked down on his tattoo for guidance an' inspiration.

'Can ee undo the straps fur me? But first of all, turn tha' row off will ee?'

Anthony moved to the stereo and pressed the stop button. Trescothick's mind regained some ov its sanity. Once with him again, Anthony undid the straps that 'ad kept Trescothick there for what 'ad seemed like an age.

'The witch is upstairs,' went Anthony.

'Markie?'

Anthony didn' really knaw who tha' wuz.

'There is a man with her I think. I cud hear them on the floorboards...'

'Where's 'is men?'

'In the store-room outside. They're eating.'

'Come with me...'

Now Trescothick wuz up on 'is feet in a pair of Speedo grape smugglers not really best kitted out fur combat.

'I need clothes though...'

Near the old oil-fuelled boiler of the tower, wuz a set of dusty overalls.

'What about these?' went Anthony.

'Bewdie.'

Now Trescothick still didn' have any shoes, but at least a wudn' lookin' quite s'orange.

'Have we got any weapons?'

There didn' seem t'be much there. Anthony dug inta' his pockets an' pulled out a load of Lego.

'Thaas' no good. Guns, knives or somethun...'

Anthony shrugged his shoulders.

'Alright, we'll have t' deal with the muscle first ov all, then Markie okay?'

Although Trescothick wuz feelin' like givin' the grunts a bit ov R & R time ov ut on the waterboarding table, ee knew this wudn' the time for ut. Escape with Anthony wuz really the main objective. Getting off the island right then prob'ly cudn' be done though. Ee'd have t'signal t'his units out there, an' that could only be done if the muscle wuz dealt with. There wuz only one thing fur ut. They'd have t'seal the guards in there as best they could. Trescothick didn't knaw if the storeroom that they were in would have a lock on it, but the tower 'ad a padlock tha' wuz open. He took ut and ran over to the storeroom. Carefully, he eased the door shut, and then whacked on the lock. The clasp shut an' they were sealed in there.

'Fuckin' ell!' ee heard them say. 'Wozon here? I's the Orange fucker – ee've escaped.'

Trescothick looked at the state of the lock. Ut wudn' hold forever. If they battered the door, the metal of the hasp would fracture, an' they'd be out. Ut did give ee an' Anthony some time though. At the banging on the door from his grunts, Markie broke away from Yeugen's arms. Ee got dressed an' came running down the stairs. The first thing ee nawticed wuz tha' the lock on the door t'Anthony's room 'ad been picked.

'Aw fuck. Ee's out...'

At that point in time, ut wudn' really the fact that Anthony had escaped that bothered him; ut wus more the fear ov un actually hurtin' hisself out here, falling off the island, or playin' with one of his weapons that scared un. Despite ut all, Markie cud be sentimental at times. Tha' wuz one of the things that drew women, an' perhaps even Yeugen, to him.

Another run of stairs told him that Trescothick wuz free too. That wuz really worrying. A terrorist and an Aspergers and ADHD-kid workin' against un.

'No, no. no...'

Suddenly the rules weren't fair any more.

Down the bottom room, Markie cudn' undertand why the door there wuz open. Ee eased ut back inta more ov a half-way point. Just as ee did tha' Trescothick rammed the door shut, so that his hand got caught between the door and the frame.

'Shit!' he went, in some considerable pain.

Outside, ee knew tha' his boys were locked in the storehouse. While ee wuz crumpled in agony, Trescothick gave Phillipsy a swift an' hard kick in the bollocks. Ee felt them with his toes – so the aim must have been been good. Phillipsy forgot about 'is hand, and shifted both of them to his groin.

'I've seen you before,' said Anthony peerin' down at un from above.

At this Anthony took a few bits of Lego, an' used them as weapons of mass destruction on Markie's body. Yeah, this wuz a bit of voodoo needle magic back at un. A particularly pointy bit of technical Lego comed down on Markie's nose, then a very knobbly bit wuz used on his nipple. Ut wuz a move Anthony had practised a few times in the playground. Then ee forced another bit between 'is toes and twisted ut. This made Markie writhe in pain.

'Good work private,' went Trescothick. 'Search his pockets...'

There were keys in the left trouser pocket.

'I wonder wha' that opens...'

'There look...'

Towards the window wuz a steel cabinet – obviously used to house weapons.

'Open it up.'

Anthony tossed the keys over to Trescothick.

'You little bastard,' snarled Markie at Anthony. This wuz 50% spermatozoa from Davey. Ee should have blasted um off when ee had the chance. Ee wudn' be here then.

'Keep un there...' said Trescothick.

Anthony lifted up Markie's shirt an' made a move t'jam a particularly nasty looking cone-shaped piece of Lego inta' his belly button.

'Na... Please,' went Markie. 'Not there... Not there...'

The tacker held ut just long enough fur Trescothick to remove and unlock one of the AR-15 rifles that wuz part of the island's arsenal.

Hearing all the drilgey, down the stairs comed Yeugen.

'What are you doing?'

'What ee think we'm doin'? Escapin' my 'andsome,' went Trescothick.

'You won't get off the island, not this time of night... No-one can. It's too dangerous.'

'I d'knaw you a little bit more than you think,' said the Orange one. 'I remember you when you used t'shake ut around a bit down Club Rhino. Now look at ee... like you'm lady ov the manor out here... set up by 'is money...'

'Stop him!' moaned Markie. But Yeugen wuz naw match fur a highly-trained operative like Trescothick and a tacker like Anthony.

The pair ov um headed up the spiralling stairs of the building heading fur the top.

'This is prob'ly not a good move,' Anthony wuz mouthing.

'Where do we go when we get to the top?'

As ee wuz running, Trescothick got the point ee wuz makin', but 'twas too late now. Markie was up and after them, taking two steps at a time.

'Watch!' went Anthony.

He threw out as many Lego wheels and circular bricks as he could. The bricks bounced nearly down the stairs, bowling out Markie's feet in one clean motion. The cunt went flying' right back down the second level, busting his knee.

They were further up the tower now, inta' Yeugen's quarters. Glancing in, Trescothick noticed the Polish food she'd got it, and then on the next level, the spooky magical items. They kept going to the fifth floor. Despite 'is injury, Markie wuz catching up with them again.

'Take that...' went Anthony.

As they manoeuvred inta' a position to climb onta' the exterior balcony, Anthony began grabbing any Lego he could out of his pockets and thrawed ut at un. The cunt had t'duck an' dive good an proper, as some ov the constructions were a bit meaty t'be honest.

'This is what I'm like when I can't have my medicine.'

Clearly, the lack ov ut 'ad energized 'is combat skills.

'See,' went Trescothick. 'The boy here can deal with you. And so can I Phillipsy. You think you'm the big I am – but you ent. In fact, you'm nothun'... All that back there. Think I'd break did you? Well, I haven't! We're still here, coming t'get you.'

'Yeah,' went Anthony sounding like Robin t'Trescothick's Batman.

'Yeah,' went Trescothick.

When they reached the door to the balcony outside, there wuz only one thing t'do, get out there, and slam the door shut.

'No lock again,' went a disappointed Trescothick. Whatever they might do to close an' secure it, surely at the end of the day, with a good bit ov brute force, Markie and his boys wud break through.

Perhaps comin' up here wudn' such a good idea, Trescothick now realised. About the best form of defence they could find, were some rusty steel poles that had been left up there from some repair work on the roof. They wudn' hold long though.

Alan M. Kent

Anthony and Trescothick caught their breath back, and eased around the lantern at the top of the lighthouse. The plaace wuz amazing. Not only wuz there the view up and down the coast, but also the pulse of the red and white light. The spot wuz prob'ly one of the moast beautiful plaaces you cud be in Cornwall.

Markie wuz back banging on the door again, and then, after a while, ut stopped.

The both breathed a little more easily and looked behind them at the huge lens of the lantern. 'A' frames ov metal struts encased the glass.

'Shoot out the light,' went Anthony.

'What?'

'Take ut out...'

Trescothick cud see what ee meant.

'It's the only option idn' ut?'

'Yeah.'

If the light went, ut wud be nawticed all the way down the coast. The coastguard wud be informed right away, and they'd have t'get a team from Trinity House out there to repair the light.

Now in reality, Trescothick 'ad never actually fired an automatic weapon in 'is life. Even though ee made a big noise about 'is tactical expertise, when ut combed down to ut, ee didn' really have fuckin' clue. Still, ee nervously squeezed the trigger ov the AR-15, an' bits ov glass shattered and went everywhere. Anthony made a dive fur ut under the metal base of the lantern, while Trescothick vibrated backwards at the recoil of the weapon. Ee stopped squeezin' the trigger when ee nearnly 'bout toppled over the edge of the balcony. Fuck, 'twas s'close tha' ut wuz awnly Anthony's hand tha' saved un from fallin'.

The lantern wuz in a right fuckin' state – and looked very sorry fur itself. Trescothick felt a bit pitiful fur ut, seein' as how ee'd 'ad t'shoot up a bit of genuine Cornish history. The light didn't go right away. Ut seemed t'hold out hope ov shining a bit longer than ut wuz meant to, but then whatever bullets had gone inta' its bulbs and reflectors seem t'take effect, and then the light died. Everything went quiet. The damage to the lantern caused the whole island's electrical supply to fuse. The darkness ov the balcony wuz eerie and disconcerting. People on the mainland wud have t'have takem nawtice. Somethun' must be majorly wrong over Godrevy ef the light 'ad gone out.

'I can't be here any more,' went Trescothick.

'What ee mean?'

'We're a covert operation,' ee went t'Anthony. 'People cen't find out tha' 'tis we who saved you like…'

'Why not?'

Trescothick looked at un.

'You wudn' understand. We got this ten-point plan see… an' well, I've only done about one and a half ov ut tonight… If I'm found here, the other seven and a half ov ut won't get done,'

Ee started t'leave. They cud boath hear a chopper comin' in, t'whisk Markie an' Yeugen away. From the balcony, they observed the two ov them running down t'the helipad.

'In a minute, when they've gone, go inside Anthony… Don't worry. Ut won't take um long fur somebody t'find you. Then you'll be back home with mum and dad…'

'And you?'

'The Tigers – they'll be waitun' fur me out there off-shore. I'll take the boat back t'Obby Stanker…'

So Anthony stayed on the island, while Trescothick went from the lighthouse. Fur now, ee'd let Markie go. There'd be time enough some other day t'deal with ee. In fact, ee reckoned ee'd knawed the very crew t'sort un out.

Rocky Valley Sculpting Gel – Like rock!
Maximum hold and control
• Stong hold and texture – Firm hold styling ingredients help provide a textured look
• Excellent for wet-looks – Shine enhancing conditioning ingredients from Rocky Valley, make this the perfect choice for wet looks
• Intensifies shine – Activated Headönizm Blend of algae, aloe, and rosemary helps enhance shine

Frustrated tha' ee cudn' access Trescothick an' Anthony on the balcony, and mightily pissed off that a tool such as the leader ov the Cornish Tigers, and an Aspergers- and ADHD-affected kid had nearnly 'bout wiped out his grunting and gorilla-like protectors, ee an' Yeugen had fled from the tower down to the helipad. A call t' his man would guarantee the chopper be here shortly. Ee 'ad un on emergency stand-by fur this very kind of scenario, and tha' would be worth every penny right now. This wuz one plaace where ee didn' want t'be found.

Fuck his gorillas now locked away in the storehouse. Unless Trescothick set um free, they'd have t' look after themselves. The lock there wudn' keep um tha' long. If they made 'iss, they cud get down to their motor launches an' make their way back t' the mainland. Right now though, ee had t' look after number one – well, an' 'is number two ov sorts: Yeugen. She'd been shocked at all ov the night's events. In her mind, her tower had been an impenetrable fortress, a plaace where she might practice her dark arts, an' now ut had been over-run, degraded and violated.

'You need t' make yer voodoo work harder,' said an angry Markie. 'Or what am I payin' you for? All tha' effort fur the hair hadn' really paid off have ut?'

'How do you know? Have you spoken to Charlie lately?'

Ee didn' care t' be honest. Separating himself from a child-abduction scandal wuz now 'is major objective. A bit of calmness an' an alibi at another one ov 'is operations would be all that it should take. A shocked press release about events on Godrevy Island would put things right – and how saddened ee wuz to find that the abducted Anthony had been found on 'is property. What evil there wuz in the world these days? Wuz a a'right? Did a need anything?

As Markie's rescue chopper came in, ee looked down at the state of his leg. There, the maiming ov his knee had been caused by the malicious use of some Lego, not to mention the other needle-like stabs at his body. Ee never knawed ut had such power. Was tha' revenge fur him an' the shotgun aimed once at Neil's package all them years back?

'I have had enough of this place,' went Yeugen. 'Now what we do scares me a little...'

'I's too late t' be scared now m'andsome,' said Markie.

'No. I know the truth. You have not wanted me as your lover. You have just wanted me as your power: a stick to beat others with. '

Markie knawed she wuz right. Ee didn't knaw wha' t' say t' her.

Voodoo Pilchard

'I go home now... Back to Poland, yes?'

She edged away and turned her back to him.

As his private chopper rose into the air, in the darkness ov St Ives Bay, Markie tried to look below for Trescothick, a boy ee now knew had too much on un.

'Look there,' went Yeugen.

The helicopter lights picked out a small, innocent form. On the lighthouse balcony, stood Anthony watching them, and waving.

Below, although they couldn't be seen from above, Markie's boys managed to break out of the storehouse and saw the helicopter rise into the night. In an instant, they saw tha' the lighthouse lantern wuz broken. The beam had stopped.

'Ee dun't give a fuck 'bout we look,' went one of the two grunts whose hair Mel had cut up Headönizm.

'We'd best skiddaddle then...'

High in the tower, Anthony surveyed the items in Yeugen's room – not knowing what they were all for. Ee did find a few pictures though, ov his da's friend Charlie Curnow on one ov the tables. That, ee thought, wuz a bit weird. Downstairs in the lab's torture chamber ee found the water-boarding table an' the stereo. In the CD player there wuz still a Seth Lakeman album. Ee listened to ut until he fell soundly asleep. 'Is da didn't have any ov tha' kind ov music, and ut soothed un.

The Trinity House emergency technical crew got across there in the morning. They'd comed up from Falmouth docks. The plaace wuz in some state you. A technical report would have to be sent back to their planning centre at Harwich in Essex. Ut turned out t'be a helleva' job t'repair all the glass an' the lantern. Yeah, fuckin' hell, whoever had done ut, used automatic weapons t'scat ut up.

In the base ov the tower, they comed across a small boy sleeping. When ee told them 'is name ut soon becomed clear that ee wuz the missing kid half ov Cornwall wuz currently searching for.

'I'm Anthony Davey', ee went. 'Pleased to meet you...'

'And you...' went the foreman of the Trinity House team.

'Are you here to rescue me?'

'I s'pause so!'

'Can you wait a minute? I need to gather up all my Lego...'

From the look ov ut, all his construction kits were as smashed up as the lantern, While they inspected the rest of the lighthouse, Anthony gathered up all the blocks that had been strewn around.

Fisherman's Friend Super Clean Spray – Create strong looks with this lightweight spray.
Medium hold finishing spray
• Adds body and shine – Medium hold, flexible conditioning ingredients from the deep sea provide fullness and shine
• Quick drying – Fast drying fine mist spray provides a dry application
• Adds protection – Helps protect against sun damage

'They've found tha' little boy.'
    'Ave um by gar... That's good... I wuz some worried fur'n.'
    'It must be true. I heard ut down Aldi's this mornun'.'
    'Where did um find un?'
    'Well, from wha' they'm sayin', 'twas down Godrevy island, in the lighthouse there...'
    ''Ad a been abducted then?'
    'Well, so they say...'
    'At least ee been found. And thaas' the main thing...'
    'Have the police got anybody fur ut then?'
    'Naw... not s'far as I knaw... Apparently they'd gone from the island, an' jus' left un there t'fend fur hisself...'
    'Poor little mite...'
This wuz the conversation Charlie overhead in the Co-Op up Troon later tha' day. Charlie knew already. Ee'd got a text from Neil. 'Twas all very puzzlin' though - how the hell ee'd got out there, and then, ov course, Charlie already knew tha' Trescothick wuz sizin' the plaace up. At the moment, the puzzle ov ut wuz still confoundin' un. Bits ov ut were seemingly solved, but then, the full story wudn' come out until a few months later. Ee wuz goin' t'have t'be patient – a bit like the rest ov Cornwall. The bottom-line wuz tha' Charlie wuz just relieved fur Neil an' Ally. Perhaps, ee wuz hopin', they might just realise wha' they'd got. Neil o'course, had been on the brink ov understanding tha' before Anthony'd been snatched.

Now maybe, Ally wuz too. That understanding would hopefully pull um back together again.

'I see the cashpoint's been repaired, look...' went one of the women.

Charlie had nawticed ut too. Now they'd installed fuckin great concrete bollards outside of ut t'prevent anything like tha happenin' again. Ut looked like something you'd only find in the middle of Washington D.C. let alone in the middle of electric pastyland.

Back Portreath, the plaace wuz jubilant. There wuz t'be a special party at the school, to celebrate Anthony's return an' just about the whole village wuz out there to welcome un back as ee climbed out ov the back ov a police car.

'Thank you driver. Tha' wuz amazun'' ee'd gone t'the police driver, havin' (unlike moast of the tacker population in Trelawny) never been in a police car before.

'Dun't forget yer Lego,' the cop driver had gone.

Ee passed Anthony the bag of bricks an' instruction leaflets.

'Ma – whaas' the fuss about?'

'You,' went Ally. 'You'm back safe an' sound...'

Well, when ee wuz ready fur ut, the police wanted a few words. Now, Anthony being' a bit sensitive – an' a bit ov a Jedi - 'ad already worked out wha' might be opportune t'tell the coppers an' what not to. Bein' a bit selective with the information wuz perhaps a skill (honed from years ov touring) ee'd learnt straight off 'is feyther. Clearly ee'd been abducted, but there'd been naw ransom fee asked for, so 'twas hardly a kidnapping job.

'Did you get sight ov any of the people who took you?' the family liaison officer was gently askin' him.

'No. They were all wearing masks...'

'Did they say anything to you about why they wanted you?'

'No. They just gived me some Lego outside school.'

'Did they hurt you or touch you in any way?'

'No.'

Moast of Anthony's answer began with No. The police wudn' getting' very far t'all widn'.

'Can I go out now?' ee pleaded. 'I want t'play Obi Wan versus Darth Maul...'

The police let un go.

'Twas very puzzling, very fucking puzzling indeed. Almost as puzzlin' as all tha' voodoo pilchard taggin' over west Cornwall, which the police were also tryin' t'crack down on. If awnly they cud catch a litte bugger in the act.

Life started t'get back t'normal though for Neil, Ally, Anthony an' Megan. Just as ut wuz, Ally felt her phone buzz with a text.

'Twas a number she didn' knaw, but in an instant she knawed who 'twas. She read ut.

I am sorry.

'Who's tha'?' asked Neil.
'Oh... nawbody,' responded Ally. 'Just Headönism askin' if I want t'cancel my appointment today...'
Ally didn't like lying. But ut had t'be done.
Later tha' day, when the house wuz a bit more peaceful, she texted the number back.

Trust me. I wont grass u up.

An' tha' wuz the last piece ov communication she wuz ever t'have with Markie Phillips. You'll see why.

Charlie'd been curious too, an' 'ad headed down Park an Tansys t'see if Trescothick wuz home.

'Naw, ee idn' here me dear,' went Tre-terrorist's cakey ol' mawther. 'Comed in late, then ee wuz up early t'go down B&Q – on 'bout the need t'buy a new chainsaw...'

'Oh... Thanks,' went Charlie.

Tha' seemed a reasonable purchase 'til ee thought 'bout ut. Then ee remembered wha' Micky had said about the Trelawny Chainsaw Crew. Now the KLF (the Cornish Tigers) were joinin' up with the TCC (Ut wuz hard t'keep up sometimes with the nationalists and the pensioners). The other interesting thing wuz tha' yeah, Trescothick had been out all night. Bluett wuz next on his calls t'find out wha' 'ad been goin' on. When ee rang the doorbell ov 'is plaace, there wudn' naw response. Nawthin' new there. Ee wuz probably sleepin' in, after some early morning epic viewin' ov repeats of *Star Trek: The Next Generation*, a few cans ov cider, and an epic wank thinkin' 'bout

Kayleigh. Ee did, however, nawtice a set of black military fatigues, a BB gun an' a balaclava 'eaved down on the kitchen table. Certainly there'd been KLF activity of late then.

Right now though, the answers – like the new songs – just wudn' comin'.

Cornish Gloss Drops – Get your shine on!
Frizz-free Defining Polish
• Creates a silky, smooth finish – Lightweight ingredients help smooth the surface and leave hair soft and silky
• Long-lasting shine – Our exclusive Headonizm blend of chamomile, jojoba and heather help provide shine and reflection
• Helps resist humidity – Frizz-free, smooth shine in all climates

Cornwall 'adn' really seen anythun' like ut.

'Mean, there'd been the rugby before up Twickenham, but nothun' this close t'home. Trura wuz packed you. You cudn' move. Ef you were sensible, then you'd got there early in the mornin'. Anytime later than tha', an' you wudn' goin' t'get in t'all. All the normal shite tha' accompanies any sporting event in Cornwall wuz expanded upon ten times wudn' ut? Y'had people out with giant pasties an' surf-boards; other cunts dressed up as red-legged choughs and then even more people had the black and white of St Piran's cross daubed on their faces. These were the national colours yeah, but they happened t'be the colours of Trura City too. The club's potential place in Football League Two 'ad caught the imagination ov just about everybody. Shops 'ad ut plastered all over the plaace, while the various media were running interviews with players, coaching staff, the club's directors, and fans – in fact, anyone who 'ad a big enough gob on um to say somethun'. An' certainly sayin' somethun' wuz Tommy Curnow who'd turned overnight inta' a bit ov a media personality. The tool wuz doin' 'is best t'be on every panel, in every newspaper an' speak t'anyone who even 'ad the remotest interest in the final match ov the season. Ut made un feel s'good, ee might not even need the Loco Viagra any more. 'Is pecker wuz up sure 'nough. Tha', Sally 'ad nawticed.

Alan M. Kent

Because ov the expected traffic chaos, buses an' coaches were just about the only thing being allowed inta' Trura. They'd organised ut so tha' people'd park outside and then catch them t'the ground. 'Course Treyew Road wudn' tha' big a venue wuz ut, so extra stands an' seatin' had been constructed outta' scaffoldin' in advance ov the game. See, there wuz the Bath City crew t'take inta' account too. They'd come down in a good few numbers too – in spite ov the fact tha' they wuz just mid-table. Well, last game ov the season wudn' ut? – and you could guarantee 'twould be a mad day out down there in Cornwall. Never mind the result. They 'ad good beer didn't they? The Cornish had comedic value too. Worth goin' for.

Tickets fur the game 'ad sold out well in advance, and wuz goin' fur stupid prices on e-Bay. Some cunts, ov course, wuz makin' a killun', havin' no real interest in football, but a big interest in increasin' the thickness ov their wallets. So there were touts aplenty outside, an' on all the routes comin' inta' the ground. Everyone wuz tryin' t'make a bit on the game. Y'had a load of burger an' curry vans out in the car park, and then, from Pool Market wuz the bloakey selling the knocked-up Voodoo Pilchard t-shirts. They'd become almost an unofficial team shirt by now, especially amongst the younger elements ov the supporters. What wuz amazin' wuz the sense ov pride goin' on – tha' a club s'lowly as Trura-fuckin'-City 'ad made ut t'this point in their career. Even ef the buggers didn' do ut, then they'd still have dun an amazin' job t'get this far.

But then, moast people wudn' even contemplatin' tha'. They 'ad t'go up didn' um? 'Twas almost feeling like 'twas part ov some revolution: that somehow, ef they'd got this far, well, Cornwall might be a proper territory again – an' not just some county boobed on the ass end of England. All the fuckin' stuff done in the past t'make the rest ov the world nawtice the Cornish wudn' matter any more. Gettin' the team in there might encourage a few more fuckers t'vote Mebyon Kernow next time round. Trescothick knew tha'. Ee an' Bluett wuz one ov the first lot there. They wudn' goin' t'miss this fur nawthun'. Events ov late, an' now this, wuz progressing part of their Ten Point Plan nicely – even if Bluett didn' really knaw wha' 'twas all 'bout. Shit, this wuz is last big adventure before goin' off t'join the army – well, the British army this time – not the KLF.

Voodoo Pilchard

Charlie 'ad t'hand ut to 'is da and the rest ov the club's management. A fair bit ov organisation 'ad been put inta' the match. Down in the 'Piazza' in Trura, any bugger who hadn't got a ticket, could go down there an' watch a g'eat live video screen. The match wuz goin' t'be broadcast by the BBC as well, an' live commentaries were being lined up fur local radio. Interest in the match wudn' only comin' from home. Some of the Britain-wide papers 'ad picked up on the fact tha' fur the first time in history. a Cornish team might get inta' Football League Two.

Everybody on Trelawny 'ad gone up. Troon itself wuz nearnly deserted. Charlie 'ad even managed t'encourage Bev t'go, an' Yak 'ad brought along Jody, who wuz now as inseparable from him as 'is drum kit an' a few medicinal substances normally were. 'Course, Bev wuz there with her da too – who wuz a bit of a Trura City nut. Leastways ov late, ee didn' seem t'mind hangin' out with the Trelawny crew now tha' well, Charlie, wuz a home-owner, and tha' Tommy wuz on the committee. Glancin' around the crowd in the west stand, you could sense the anticipation, an' tha' near 'nough every bugger there prob'ly had some lucky charm on um (or 'ad already prayed t'the knockies), 'opin' that the boys would pull through. Neil, Ally, Anthony an' Megan wuz there too – recovered a bit from their ordeal. Neil seemed fairly relaxed, but Ally wuz still a bit on edge. She wuz watchin' Anthony like a hawk, fearful ov anything else happenin' to un. On Charlie's advice, she'd been givin' un a lot more Omega 3, which seemed t'be helpin' a bit with 'is multiple conditions. The little fucker 'ad clearly learnt a lot durin' 'is kidnappin' ordeal about self-resilience and survival, not t'mention inflicting damage with piece ov Lego. As they stood waitin' Charlie 'ad a bit ov a yap widn'.

'You a'right?' he asked.

'Yes thank you,' went Anthony. Ee wuz always polite like tha'.

'Who's goin' t' win t'day then?'

Charlie wuz expectun' un t'say Trura City, but tha' wud've been too simple. Ov late, the Aspergers had been more prominent, an' ee'd become obsessed with football data.

'I am not certain,' said Anthony. 'I examined the form ov both clubs on the internet, and found that they are more or less

327

evenly matched. I think you will find that Bath City have had a good run lately, so the odds are not stacked in Truro City's favour...'

Holy shit. Charlie nearnly fell over. Ee 'adn't expected Professor Stephen Hawking to answer him. Six year olds now, talking about a statistical analysis of football.

'Ee's been on ut all week,' went Neil. 'The school's now sayin' he might be talented and gifted at mathematics... They gotta' keep challengin' un.'

'Said much else 'ave a? About the kidnappin' I mean,' asked Charlie.

'No. Nothun' much...'

Charlie wuz goin' t'ask ut now, whatever.

'Markie Phillips wudn' ut?'

Neil didn' much want t'hear 'is name let alone discuss ut like this. Ee nodded.

'Thought so. Bastard.'

'I's over now Charlie. Thaas' the main thing...'

Charlie sensed the pain ov ut all. Ee 'oped tha' Ally an' ee would be able t'move on from ut. Perhaps sometimes y'cudn' though, Perhaps sometimes, events in the past keep hittin' the present, an' keep givin' ee a smack in the mouth. Perhaps Ally an' ee wudn' ever quite come t'terms with wha' Markie Phillips 'ad done, and neither wud ee ever come t'terms with they two bein' together. Thaas' jus' the way 'twas you. Destiny. Fate. Hubris. Voodoo Pilchard.

Earlier tha' afternoon, while ee an' Bev ad been waitin' fur Micky an' Jess t' arrive, Charlie had gone up t'the bloakey sellin' the Voodoo Pilchard shirts in the car park. Ee'd wanted a nawse at wha' wuz on offer.

'A'right?' ee'd gone t'Charlie.

Ee knawed un. Ee'd seen Charlie up market a few times.

'Nice shirts,' went Charlie. 'D'the Pilchard knaw you'm sellin' um?'

'Yeah – the Pilchard's a mate ov mine...'

'Really?'

'You seen his gallery then?'

'What gallery?!'

'Well, you cen't be too much ov a mate if you ebm' seen 'is gallery...' joked Charlie.

'Where us ut?'

'Back Condurrow. Go have a stank 'round there an' you'll see ut...'

'Oh,' went the bloakey – not feelin' quite as confident anymore. 'I must see un about tha'...'

'How much then?' asked Charlie.

'A tenner each.'

Charlie scanned the run ov shirts on the tarpaulin. Ee had t'hand ut to un. The boy 'ad not done a bad job. The print wuz clear an' yeah, ee'd managed t'capture the street energy of the Pilchard's early stencil work.

'That one please,' went Charlie.

Ee bought a black t-shirt with a white print on ut. A good souvenir ee reckoned. One day, ut might be iconic, important, an' inspirational even.

Charlie had ut clutched to un now as they stood on the terraces.

'Look out,' went Charlie, leanin' in t'Micky an' Jess. 'There ee is...'

Across the field, they cud all see Tommy Curnow full ov ut, meetin' and greetin' the officials, and everyone else who ee felt merited a handshake. Wuz this the same tool who sat at home in 'is kaks reading Virginia Woolf an' listening t'Def Leppard? Yeah – ut wuz. Ut wuz also the same tool who'd cashed in 'is golden egg. Ee'd ad a little trip away up t'London 'adn' a – on the advice ov Charlie an' Druid Dave? Charlie had tried t'get the final figure out ov un – as t'how much Liquid Gold wuz offerin' un. 'Twas quite some sum apparently, ee'd understood in the conversations ee'd had with 'is da: more than moast ov Trelawny wuz getting' from Cash4Gold that wuz certain. Charlie wuz reckoning on the dense quality ov the find. A figure of some twenty grand had been talked about. No wonder 'is da wuz lookin' s'happy over the other side ov the field. Christ, t'day ee'd even managed t'drag their ma up for the event. She wuz stood next t'un – all glammed up; her hair newly-done over Headönizm – an' attractin' the attention currently ov the referee (who wuz from up Barnstaple way), an' ad decided she wuz a bit tasty. These days, though, Tommy wuz a bit sharper, an' escorted Sally away from un to meet the elderly Mayor ov Trura, who was there with 'is missus permed t'the nines, all boobed up in 'is chains and regalia.

Treyew wuz gettin' packed out now. In the distance. you cud look west, back over Nansavallan Woods t'electric pastyland. The sunshine wuz streamin' in. Jess wuz happy. She'd advised the girls t'use some ov her new UV protection products, an' every so often, she wuz giving out free literature about Headönizm an' her planned beauty products, shampoos, sprays an' conditioners. Well, everything wuz a business opportunity wudn' ut? Micky meanwhile, wuz demonstratin' some pictures ee'd taken ov the Pilchard's gallery. 'Is next plan wuz t'secretly camp out there on the old Condurrow site, an' see if ee cud find out the artist's identity. So far, ee'd told naw-one, not even Charlie. Besides Micky 'ad 'is own suspicions.

Charlie meantime, wuz scannin' fur Phillipsy. The cunt had t'be there. The Club had some sort ov VIP tent erected in the car park, so prob'ly, ee'd still be in there at the moment, poncin' around with the other members of the committee and various dignitaries who'd been invited. Charlie wudn' the only one interested in ee right now. Trescothick 'ad 'is eye on un too. Fur the orange one, gettin' rid ov Phillipsy wuz now as much a priority as anything else in 'is Cornish Tigers ten-point plan – and as the days ov summer wore on, ee reckoned ee wuz comin' close t'executing a plan that wudn' fail. Right now though, the fucker wuz tuckin' inta' a hot dog sausage t'sustain un fur the duration ov the game. Final whistle on Markie wuz comin' soon though. Ee liked tha' feelin' almost as much as the fried onions an' tomato ketchup.

Three o'clock wuz approachin'. Thaas' when ee caught a glimpse of Markie. The fucker wuz limpin' down the steps towards a position behind the dug-outs. Ee wuz chattin' to the team manager Dave 'Afro' Metters. Charlie wuz tryin' to read the conversation. The way tha' Markie wuz chattin' to him seemed all too calm, like ee knew City wuz going' t'win. You could see the fear on Metters' face as ee assumed 'is place in the dug out. A win wuz the only route fur'n today. Lose an' ee'd be out on 'is ear – a pariah forever. Ee'd never make ut out ov Trispen again without some cunt offerin' advice on how ee should have run a 4-4-2 or 4-3-3 instead ov 'is planned 4-3-2-1. Win – an' ee'd be a national hero: a kind of Alf Ramsey fur Cornwall. The same could be said ov the team, who were receiving a standing ovation as they comed on the pitch. Lose an' well, they may as well pack up an' live east of the Tamar forever.

Bath City had been given a good welcome too, but you knawed how football worked. The crowd, who wuz basically 95% Trura City, needed t'intimidate the away side as much as possible. Puttin' um off the ball or any move wuz basically the crowd's tactic. Given this, the Bath City players didn' much like the look ov the somewhat ferocious Cornish crowd. There wuz a look about um tha' reminded some ov the players of an as yet un-named tribe's ritual night in Papua New Guinea. T' they, 'twas seeming less like a footy match, an' more like some gladiatorial conflict. Should um just fuck off home now an' be done with ut? Maybe.

Boy Pritchard – Trura City's star striker wuz limberin' up out there on the pitch stretchin' out 'is calf muscles. There'd been a lot of discussion in the local media tha' ee wudn' 100% fit fur the game. Apparently ee'd been suffering from some ankle injury – but ee wudn' goin' t'miss this, not fur anything. This wuz where ee wuz hopin' t'join the legends like Roger 'the Boot' Tremaine, in Trura City's hall of fame. The referee 'ad moved out t'the centre circle now – havin' 'ad a last look at Sally Curnow's legs – an' hopin' t'show her ee was a fit bugger, even though ee wuz in his late forties. The crowd had gone quiet. They'd hushed t'hear the whistle.

A sustained peep came from the centre ov the pitch, an' the game wuz on. Go t'any football ground in Cornwall, and you'n expect t'hear a lot ov 'poetic' language bein' shouted at both the home an' away team alike, as well as the presiding refereee. Charlie wuz opin' Bev wudn' be too shocked. Jess, Mel and Ally – well, they were prob'ly a bit more used to ut, havin' grawn up on Trelawny. But as the game started, 'twas comin' thick an' fast. Charlie wuz always somewhat amazed at the fruitiness of the comments ov some ov the pensioners there, who normally wudn' even contemplate usin' such four-letter words, but who on the terraces just let rip. At times, ut seemed only the right thing to do t'join in with the old-age delinquents.

'Come on you fuckers!' wuz one ov the more polite addresses to members of the Trura City squad tha' afternoon; this from a boy who must've been near shakin' up eighty.

Alan M. Kent

The game wudn' naw Troon AFC-style meander against another local club from West Cornwall though. Boath teams knawed wha' ut meant. The crunches were coming thick an' fast, an' the play end t'end stuff. Two minutes in, an' Bath City were in Trura's half. There wuz an outswingin' corner taken by Bath City, from the right by-line. Tha' wuz nicely cleared by Adam Vigus, City's keeper. The attack kept on comin' though. An in-swingin' corner next, taken by Andrew Davies – Bath's winger. Nigel Caddy – one ov Trura's backs made the clearance though. The next run comed from Trura, up from the full-backs t'the front-line. The ball's delivered t' Craig Williams, and then there comed the first headed effort from Boy Pritchard. Unfortunately ut missed, to the left ov the goal. 'Twas a bit messy fur the next few minutes. Caddy's bleddy well done fur handball, and concedes a free kick t'Bath City. The direct free kick is taken by their No.9. Tries a shot at goal dun't a? – aimin' t'be a bit ov a hero. Vigus is on ut though. Cheers go all around the ground. 'Twas a beauty stop you. Trura broke fur a bit then, but the offside rule is laid at Pritchard idn't ut? The official who raises the flag get a good booing from the home crowd.

'Y'need a fuckin' poker up yer ass, linesman,' shouted one ol' boy on the terrace.

Basically, ee did. 'Twudn' no offside s'far as the Trelawny crowd could see. There's a foul then on Pritchard idn't there? Ee looks t'be writhing around in agony like – an' thaas' a problem fur Trura. Ef ee's out, then we be fucked, moast people wuz thinkun'. After a bit ov magic sponge though, ee's up an' at ut again. Metters is runnin' up an' down the line idn' a? – shoutin' out instructions tha' the players seem t'be ignornin' from their Afro-haired leader. Still, thaas' wha' managers have t'do dun't um? Stu Curgenven is up fur the free kick. Ee tries a shot at goal, but ut idn' happening. Bath City are comin' back at um now. Good clearance again by Caddy. At the moment, ee's the one savin' Trura City. Y'have t'say though, tha' the midfield ov Bath City ent up t'much. 'Twas like their legs 'ave been tied together. Still you ent goin' t'moan are ee? Trura City just need t'keep up the pressure though. There's a header from Curgenven, but ut d'go straight over the crossbar. Fuck. Tha' wuz close.

Voodoo Pilchard

We'm on the twenty-fourth minute by now, an' things are startin' t'go Trura's way. Then on a run, there's an unfair challenge ent there, on boy Sean Clemo? Ee be one of the players who City poached off Troon actually. Got a lotta' potential this lad, because ov 'is speed. Quite right. The Bath City boy is booked fur ut.

'Glad you ent completely bleddy blind ref,' comed a shout from down front.

Tha' sorted ut a bit. The Bath City players wudn' very happy about the decision and wuz still moanin' about ut to each other. Thaas' when Trura made their move. The first goal comed from a perfect square formed by Curgenven, to Clemo, and then back t'Curgenven again. Straight in there you – from just inside the penalty area to the bottom right corner ov the net. There 'tis. Trura City 1. Bath City 0. The plaace erupted. Charlie watched Markie. Ee wuz up on 'is feet, noddin'. An fuck, there, Yeugen next to un, clappin' gleefully.

The crowd wuz singin' a bit now. 'Twas mainly creative and abusive (towards the other teams at least) adaptations of stuff like 'Lamorna', 'South Australia', 'The White Rose' and 'Trelawny' (the kind of thing the Holman Climax boys'd sing). Charlie liked what they'd done with ut: 'And have they fixed the where an' when? And shall Trura City die? Here's twenty thousand Cornish men, will know the reason why.' The Falmouth Marine Band wuz in there too. They tools wudn' a real Royal Marine band – just a few boys with upturned oil drums who liked t'make a lot ov row. Still, all ov tha' wuz nicely puttin' off the Bath City players – moast ov whom 'ad never seened anything like ut before. Well, they wuz fuckin' Cornish wudn' um? Mad fuckers.

In the thirty-seventh minute, Pritchard 'ad another shot on target but 'twas blocked good an' proper by Bath City's goalie. Shit, 'twas a good strike too. Tha' really needed t'have gone in. There wuz still time yet though. There wuz another effort on goal by Clemo, but ut missed, just to the right of the posts. Their keeper didn't even move – ee wuz so confident ut wuz wide. Clemo gave a little gob ov spit down to the grass at the disappointment. Trura seemed t'be getting a little edgy, but Charlie wuz thinkin' tha' they wuz still one up. Tha' wud be enough. A win wuz all ut needed. A second goal comed though

Alan M. Kent

– just before the referee wuz to blaw fur half time. Ut wuz a repeat of the move Curgenven an' Clemo 'ad made earlier on. This time though, Pritchard wuz there on the end ov ut. The ball comed from just outside the penalty box inta' the bottom left corner ov goal. Their keeper didn't have a chance. Bewdie. Now Trura wuz two nil up at half-time: a very comfortable place fur um t'be. All they had t'do now wuz hang onta' ut, an' not cock ut up in the second half (as ut so often 'ad been in the past, down in the lower leagues ov the south-west).

Moast ov the crowd on the terraces dispersed fur a bit, heading for a pie an' coffee, or relieving themselves in the bogs from the first pints ov the day. Jess went marketin' to anyone who would receive a leaflet, while Neil took Megan an' Anthony off t'get some low-*everything* food. Bev 'ad gone too, so Charlie wuz left standin' with Ally. Ee an' her – always awkward. Had been fur years you.

'You knawed who took un then?' asked Charlie.

Ally didn' answer.

'Why are you coverin' up for un? Do you still love Markie or somethun'?'

'No. I's not like tha'…'

'Is nemesis 'ad some hold on her.

'Then wha'?'

'Ee's not all bad…'

'Since when?'

'Well, ee knows I know too much Charlie. I just want to let go ov ut all now…'

'There want be any more?'

'No. I'm sure…'

Charlie didn' get Ally sometimes. She wuz one of the reasons the band wudn' be gettin' back together. Ee knawed ee cudn' do anything about ut. Ee wudn' aware though until later on, quite wha' fully happened at half-time. Bev 'ad left um to use the toilets 'adn't she? They were t'be found over the eastern side ov the field. As you can imagine, the facilities were near at breakin' point today, with almost ten times the normal attendance in. Well, football grounds dun't normally pay too much attention t'the facilities fur women, so there wuz a huge queue snakin' around the clubhouse. Bev 'ad naw choice though. She 'ad t'go. Ut wuz the coffee tha' Charlie 'ad bought her earlier

334

on. An' well, other things too.

As she queued, she nawticed a slender figure who'd already managed to get to the ladies. She wuz walking back to the ground again. Bev wudn' naw ordinary fool. Well, she wudn' be, doin' wha' she wuz doin' at university. The moment she caught sight ov the figure, she knawed who 'twas. She stepped out, so the figure would have to stop.

'It's Yeugen isn't ut?' asked Bev.

'Yes... And?'

'I know you. You used to go out with Charlie Curnow...'

Yeugen put this girl's narrative together. She wuz Charlie's old girlfriend, the one ee'd betrayed her for. She wuz the one ee'd returned to. She fully knew they were seeing each again. She wuz spending a lot of time at Charlie's house – so much time, Yeugen thought she might have even moved in with him. Markie's gorillas had kept her informed.

'I don't want to speak to you,' said Yeugen.

'But I want to speak to you,' said Bev, hopeful ov a peace settlement tha' only women seem t'be able t'negotiate.

Yeugen tried to move, but Bev blocked her.

'Please...'

Yeugen would hardly look inta' Bev's eyes.

'Look, I just wanted to say I'm sorry... about you an' Charlie. We – I, didn't mean to hurt you... It's nothing personal... really...'

The Polish girl's face wuz hard and unbending – a kind ov granite expression tha' you didn' want t'mess with.

'You're with Markie now aren't you?'

'Maybe,' came the response.

'He seems to be doing well,' went Bev, 'with the Club here an' that...'

'Yes... That is true.'

Yeugen raised her eyes to Bev. Now she could see wha' Charlie found attractive in her. There wuz a dark temptation there, an otherworldly aura, that initially, would tempt any man.

'Is he alright?'

'Who?'

'Charlie..'

'I mean, after the...'

Yeugen stopped herself. She wuz goin' to say drugs, but she knew ut wasn't a good move.

'After what?'

'I've said too much... Ask him yourself. Does he not tell you the truth then? Just like Charlie I think.'

This worried Bev, What did she mean? She'd be havin' this out with Charlie. Had a betrayed her now? She didn' think so, but ut put her on edge. Yeugen still seemed to care about him, despite everything.

Thaas' when she nawticed Yeugen's bag. Ut ad been slung over her shoulder during their conversation. Inside wuz a pro-gramme from today's match, but also wha' t' Bev looked like *gris gris* bags – little bags ov voodoo magic. She cud tell. She'd studied this stuff fur long enough now. In there, would be Charlie's hair and other tokens she had collected from him, zappin' all ov her boyfriend's energy an' spirit.

'*Gris Gris*,' she mouthed. 'Charms... *Ju Ju*... I's you isn't ut?'

Ju Ju wuz the other West African name fur them.

Bev made the connection. Any ill-wishin' comin' Charlie's way ov late 'ad been down to her.

'No. Not *gris gris* at all...' Yeugen mouthed. The very fact tha' Yeugen knew wha' she wuz talkin' about only served t'demon-strate her guilt.

Bev needed to grab the *gris gris* an' destroy them. She alone, knawed their power. She made a move for Yeugen's bag. It was only casually placed on her shoulder. One tug should do it. Around the two ov them, other women could see that things were getting a bit heated. A Bath City an' a Trura City fan argu-ing perhaps, over the ref's first-half decisions.

Bev made her move, but Yeugen held onta' the bag. A scuf-fle began. Interest in getting to the toilets before the second half began, shifted onta' these two young women.

'Give it to me now,' requested Bev.

'It's my magic,' went Yeugen. 'No concern of you I think...'

A few male Bath City supporters went past.

'Whoah boys... Look – a bitch fight... Get on! This is better than the footy.'

Tha' turned things up a notch. Yeugen hadn' been com-mandin' a drugs empire from Godrevy fur nothun', She'd learnt a few moves off Markie an' 'is gorillas over the last few months. She soon managed t'knock Bev t'the floor an' keep her there. Her hard, stiletto boot was on Bev's stomach. Yeugen wuz watching her intently.

'Not there, no, please...'

For a moment, Yeugen didn't really know why this girl Beverly wuz panicking so much about her stomach. Surely there were more painful places fur her t'be pined down? Then she realised. Not there. Not there, because she wuz pregnant. So, Curnow's child eh?

'A baby yes?'

Bev had no course other than to nod.

'His?'

'Yes...'

Yeugen released her foot away from Bev's womb. She laughed as she walked away.

'Look at you... I hope you and he will be happy now. I won't be here any more to upset you. Soon, I return to Poland yes, takin' what I've earned with me.'

Bev wuz able to sit up now tha' Yeugen had gone.

'You a'right my lover,' asked an old lady, obviously a long-standin' Trura City supporter – all kitted out in her black an' white woollens.

'Yeah, sort of...'

'She wuz a nasty piece ov work. Emmet wudn' she? – judgin' by her accent.'

'Yeah,' nodded Bev.

Bev recovered an' waited longer in the queue so she could use the toilet. Then she returned to Charlie on the terraces. By the look ov her, Charlie cud tell tha' somethun' 'ad 'appened, but in the crowd, right now, 'twudn' the time to talk to her. Besides, the second half wuz starting. Instead, Bev snuggled inta' Charlie an' held 'is hand very tightly. She watched the second half, but her mind wudn' really on ut. Instead, she had lots of questions running about her brain, trying to shoot for goals.

The two teams had, ov course, swapped ends fur the second half. Trura City comed back on to jubilant applause. They were that close now you. All they had t'do wuz hold their nerve. Sadly, that wudn' t'be. Within the first eight minutes ov the second half, Bath had scored two goals. The first wuz a bewdie shot from one ov their mid-fielders – a David Beckham-like free kick inta' the back ov the net. Vigus looked gutted. Ee wuz shoutin' shit at 'is defence t'get um inta' some sort ov shape. Tha' advice completely failed though, when a boy called James Davies – one ov Bath's front pairing, put one straight in. So there 'twas – two two. The home crowd went a bit fuckin' quiet at tha' last shot. They knew they needed the points here. Ut had t'be a win, to put um in the top two. Only two clubs went up you. The three points would move um up from third place t'first in the league.

Trura were gatherin' their strength again. There wuz another good run by Clemo, who produced a right-footed shot from just outside the area tha' went wide ov the goal. 'Twudn' t'be though. Frustration wuz creepin' in now. Charlie cud feel ut in the players. They were gettin' too aggressive and not thinkin' enough ov skill and tactics. Curgenven wuz in the box again – a nice delivery inta' the top ov the goal, but the keeper wuz on ut. Trura kept at ut though. Then the right piece comed together – a free kick awarded to Pritchard, an' the shot t'be taken by Clemo. In ut fuckin' went. Trura wuz singin' all over again. Charlie saw ut. Nawbody else in the ground around him seemed t' nawtice ut, but ut wuz the slight delay in the way the Bath City keeper moved. Like 'twas an objective ee'd been trainin' for. From the goal, ee glanced back over t'Markie. Ee looked like ee nawticed ut too, but instead ov enquirin' like Charlie, seemed t'fully accept the decision. Charlie's eye went back t'the keeper. Ee wuz keepin' 'is head down in case ee gave anything away. Prob'ly the two goals tha' had comed earlier on were real ones, unexpected in the order ov things. That one though, wudn' quite right. Charlie looked across the crowd again, Nawbody seemed t'mind. They were too busy realisin' that the club wuz now definitely heading for Football League Two. Did ut matter tha' the match had been thrown? Probably not, in the bigger scheme of things. Tha' wuz sport all over these days. 'Twas all about the money – nothun' else. Maybe Bath City had made a good few quid on ut – their own golden egg so t'speak. Next session, maybe with a few more expensive players on board, they might get t'the position Trura wuz in. This wuz the real game bein' played.

What wuz Bath goin' t'do next? Have a few more pretend shots on goal, but not really bother? Tha' seemed the order ov the day from about the fiftieth minute onwards. 'Twas like there wuz naw energy in um any more. This cud now be a bit ov a walkover fur Trura. If Markie'd fixed ut, then a 3-2 victory wudn' be enough. Ee'd 'ave wanted a drubbin' t' formally announced 'is place in the order ov things. Charlie reckoned there'd be another goal sharpish. Trura kept passin' the ball upfront t'good effect. T'give Bath some credit, their defence had some crunch tackles against Trura, an' looked like they meant business. The fix then, had obviously been with the keeper. Tha' wuz when boy Clemo got scat over didn' a? One ov the Bath defence caught un a beauty. 'Twas a late tackle mind, and the tool deserved t'be sent off. Tha' left Trura one man down too – boy Clemo had t'be helped off. So Metters called for a substitution didn' a? The player who was brought on, wuz one of the old gang – before the Club's recent run ov success. Charlie knawed ov un – a hard fucker by the name of Paul Norrish, who played a lot ov Rugby for Redruth a few years back. Norrish wuz nearnly 'bout forty now, but ee 'ad the experience fur a match ov this magnitude. Over the other side ov the pitch, Charlie saw Markie standing around Clemo, opin' t'look sympathetic t' the boy's injury. By the look ov ut, a bad hamstring injury.

Norrish didn' take any prisoners. Ee wuz prob'ly the kind ov player Markie wud like. Tha' said, ee wuz a bit ov a crowd favourite too. The cunt liked leapin' over the corner flags an' doin' a kind ov jig if ee scored. You'd often meet un out clubbin' over L2 an' Twilight. The tool wuz too old fur ut, but reckoned ee cud still pull; the reason ee'd 'ad a couple ov divorces behind un. At Norrish's presence, Bath City made a substitution too. Some young kid comed on t'replace one of their midfielders, who t'be perfectly 'onest, 'ad been a bit lacklustre throughout. So 'twas heads down then, for the final fifteen minutes ov the match. The earlier end t'end stuff had disappeared now, because moast of the players were dog-tired. Only Norrish seemed t'have the pace. Markie wuz up on 'is feet all the time now. Yeugen wuz next to him. They didn' look very close though. Not like Bev, who wuz still clutching 'is hand, and cuddling him.

'Go on Norrish. Make 'iss boy!' shouted Tommy, s'loud you cud hear ut over the other side of the ground, where all ov

Trelawny stood.

Norrish seemed t'take tha' as 'is cue, and picked up the ball off the new kid from Bath City. A run saw un go around a couple of defenders – somethun' tha' ee'd learnt from 'is rugby days, an' then a little chip saw the ball spin inta' the goal mouth. The keeper, who Charlie wuz watchin' intensely, seemed t'react in good time, stretching fur ut as ut sailed towards un. On any training session in Bath, ee'd have got ut, but not today. Fur Charlie, ee wudn' reachin' high enough. Matter did ut? Na. The fuckin' ball pushed against the back ov the net. About fifty photographers moved t'capture the shot, an' Norrish runned over t'his team-mates fur a celebration. Then the cunt broke from they, an' headed t' the corner flag. Ee did 'is usual jig with the crowd copyin' un. Tommy wuz over the other side ov the pitch jigging around too – like some Loco Viagra 'ad just hit un again. Next thing ee wuz there kissin' Charlie's ma in jubilation.

Yeah – ut 'ad been a complete fix: an 'enhanced' game Charlie reckoned, but nawbody seemed to mind. There wuz just ten minutes to go, with prob'ly about three minutes of stoppage time. All they had t'do wuz hold out. A bit ov needless passing wud do ut. Just keep Bath off the ball. There were the usual last minute breaks on their behalf: a few cack-handed shots at goal tha' resulted in Vigus havin' t'move a few feet. Other than tha', Bath didn' give um any further trouble. A 4-2 win then. The crowd booed the referee fur the long stoppage time, but then the final whistle came. Fur a few seconds, 'twas like the crowd 'ad t'realise wha' 'ad just occurred. Tha' really hadn' happened 'ad ut? The players on the pitch were the same. The Trura boys looked stunned. The Bath players just sat down. Charlie viewed ut the same way ee 'ad while under the drug cocktail. It felt hallucinatory, unreal – outlandish even.

What followed wuz chaos. The crowed leapt over the barriers an' invaded the pitch. Fur a while, ut looked like one ov they mad moments in other countries, where people might just fire off a few shots from sub-machine guns in joyous celebration. The Trelawny crew leant on one of resting posts, an' watched the enormity of ut all.

'They have been successful,' said Anthony. 'I am so pleased.'

'Me too,' went Charlie. 'Good inut?'

Voodoo Pilchard

Even though ee wudn' convinced ov the 'honesty' ov the performance, Charlie cud still see the wonder tha' ut had become fur other people. Hell, the fuckers ov electric pastyland and Obby Stanker, 'ad needed somethun' like this. Charlie wuz reminded ov wha' Ally 'ad said earlier about Markie Phillips: 'Ee's not all bad'. Maybe then, there wuz hope.

Charlie realised tha' sometimes deviance had its place. Judgin' by the look on people's faces, ee cudn' say a lot t'all. When you get tha' level ov emotional understandin', thaas' when you need t'write. Charlie cud feel the need t'do so as soon as ee got home. Whatever 'ad been stoppin' un before wuz comin' to an end.

The jubilation tha' followed wuz unimaginable. Across the whole ov Cornwall, people basically went apeshit. They now 'ad a club in Football League Two. A few years ago, tha' had been unimaginable. Now, 'twas a reality. Ut felt like the earth 'ad shifted its orbit, an' tha' now you cud justify your plaace in a footballing world. Wetherspoons' pubs (now all with shite Cornish names like *Try Dowr* or *Rann Wartha*) changed barrels again as thousands reached new heights of alcoholic inebriation. Businesses prepared for nawbody t'turn up on Monday, their employees phonin' in sick, but actually nursin' massive celebratory hangovers. The Council went inta' an emergency planning scenario such wuz the scale of devastation expected in town centres after the celebrations. Riot squads were dispatched t'Trura, Newquay an' Camborne.

The Trelawny crew had followed some of the celebrations in Trura City Centre. There 'ad been alcohol, karaoke, dancin', an' the singing of old Cornish songs that would have made Jimmy Pengelly proud. Tommy wuz arseholed. Fur once, even 'is ma had sunk a good few Bacardi and cokes, and everyone else wuz slammin' inta' the Skinners and HSD like their wudn' naw tomorra'. The only one not quite partyin' as much wuz Bev. Accordin' t'her, nothun' wuz wrong though. Her da had been there too with um, knockin' back a few shorts an' extolling the merits ov bein' a long-term support ov Trura City.

'Whaas' wrong?' asked Charlie.

'Yeugen. I saw her.'

This wuz one ov they 'aw fuck' moments. Charlie knew she wuz back in Obby Stanker Country.

'Tell me the truth Charlie. She mentioned something that worried me. She asked after you – if you were alright ... 'after the' something... What was that something?'

'I haven't been seeing her or anything,' Charlie said, pleadin' 'is innocence.

Then ee had to tell her about the enforced trip ee'd been on. Bev wuz shocked.'You cud've died...'

Charlie 'ad not said about meetin' Clifford or Mrs Williams, an' prayin' to Papa Piran and meeting the Oracle. Tha' ee reckoned wud, be a step too far, even fur Bev. In hindsight, maybe if ee'd told her, ut might've explained a lot.

Bev almost told Charlie wha' she'd found out about Yeugen, but she reckoned tha' this wudn' the right moment. So she kept ut secret. More worrying, wuz the notion tha' Yeugen could now be ill-wishin' the baby inside her tha' as yet, Charlie knawed nothun' about.

On Sunday morning, there wuz goin' t'be an open-top bus parade in Trura, with City holding the Cup fur winning the Conference National league, guaranteeing their promotion. Tommy wuz lined up t'be on the bus with the team, alongside Roger 'the Boot' Tremaine, an' Markie Phillips. Ut happened, an' 'twas amazing t'be honest. The bus began by comin' down Lemon Street, an' then ut pulled inta' Boscawen Street. The place wuz heavin'. There wuz balloons, ticker-tape, bands, speeches an' joy never seen before in Trura.

Tommy never made ut though.

See, when their coach pulled back inta' Troon the site tha' greeted them wudn' the kind of alcoholic devastation expected by Cornwall Council over in Trura, Newquay or Camborne. Ah naw, 'twas a very different kind of devastation altogether. As they pulled over the hill from Beacon, near t'where Troon Cemetery wuz, ut was pretty clear tha' somethun' major 'ad 'appened on the estate. There wuz blues an' twos everywhere, an' the spinning orange lights ov Cormac contractors could be seen. Their vehicles were moving too, already seemingly shoring up a broken landscape – odd fur a Saturday night.

On the bus, everyone went silent, an' just gaked out the window. After the match there'd been a major downpour – one of they extreme weather events y'd'seem t'get every now an' then – like wha' 'appened up Boscastle a few years back. 'Twas over by the time everybody 'ad got down inta' the town centre, but back Trelawny the downpour it seemed, 'ad had dire consequences.

Charlie's ma wuz the first t'nawtice ut. She wuz up front on the coach.

'Oh-my-god,' she went. 'Look at numbers 34 and 36...'

Everyone looked. You cudn' actually look at numbers 34 and 36 because the houses wudn' there anymore. Fuckin' hell. Ut looked like a 10-on-the-Richter-Scale earthquake 'ad hit the estate. Shock an' terror went through the coach. You cud feel ut.

The coach driver pulled inta' the estate, but a road block had been set up by the police. Combellack wuz there. Ee got on the coach. 'Ere we fuckin' go. Wozon then?

'Good evening, ladies and gentlemen. I am sorry to tell you that there has been a major incident here this afternoon. Following the rainstorm we had, it appears that the remainder ov the old Trelawny Adit wuz overwhelmed with water, leading to its collapse. This collapse has resulted in several properties on the estate falling into the remains of the adit...'

Shittin' hell.

'Anybody hurted,' asked Tommy, 'or deaded?

'No. As far as we know, the properties affected were empty at the time...'

A collective sigh ov relief went through the coach. People were soberin' up sharpish.

Nearnly 'bout everyone on the coach 'ad questions fur Combellack which ee cudn' possibly answer. 'Twas clear though, tha' the work Cormac 'ad been doin' ov late 'ad been as a direct response t'concerns about the structural safety ov the man-made adit. Naw wonder Headönizm 'ad had such problems with its sewage an' water supply over the preceding months. Now the bugger had collapsed, an' taken a couple of properties with ut. This kind ov thing wudn' that uncommon in Obby Stanker Country t'be honest. 'Mean, moast ov the homes there were built over some kind of mining tunnels an' galleries. You did yer purchaser's mining survey an' took yer chances. There wuz the occasional collapse at times. One wuz down Pengegon the other day, when some bit ov a boy's back-garden disappeared. But two houses? Tha' wuz somethun' else.

Alan M. Kent

It wuz voodoo pilchard turned up another notch.

'Can us get in there?' asked Charlie's ma.

''Fraid not,' went Combellack. 'It's too dangerous fur now... The engineers are in there right now, seeing wha' needs to be done...'

Tha' wuz ut then. Nawbody on the estate wuz goin' home. Fur Charlie, tha' meant 'is home wudn' be a room ov 'is own fur some time.

In the morning, while the rest of Cornwall wuz jubilant, Trelawny wuz takin' a long, cold hard look at utself. When they went over t'have a gake, 'twas clear that the hole that had emerged had spared a few things, but taken others. Part of the playground an' garages 'ad gone in, and the remains of 34 and 36 could just about be seen. You didn't like t'look too far inta' the hole though. 'Twas very fuckin' black an' scary.

Tommy should've been sobbin' fur joy 'bout Trura City. Ee wudn' though. Ee wuz sobbing in sadness and worry instead. See, the collapsed adit 'ad left their house in tact, but ut had taken Tommy's mundic block shed. Somewhere in the abyss, were all 'is Trura City programmes, 'is rock memorabilia, an' 'is collection of rare 80s' porn mags. Tha' represented disaster on a new an' unexpected scale.

Amidst the horror, there wuz one ray of hope. Tommy suddenly remembered the money ee'd got fur the golden egg.

'We'll be a'right,' ee said to Sally. 'Dun't ee worry...'

Amongst the morning's news stories, events at Trelawny Gardens had now gone t'top ov the pile. Trura City's success was somewhat negated by the catastrophe tha' had occurred.

Along Polgine Lane, a black BMW pulled over. The rear tinted window buzzed down, an' a face looked out upon the devastation. Ee rubbed 'is knee a little, where the pain from 'is Lego-wielding attacker still grated.

'Shame,' ee went. 'They may as well knock the whole estate down an' start again...'

Ee ad a point t'be honest. Whatever wuz goin' t'happen, Trelawny Gardens wudn' goin' t'be the same ever again.

After Trura City's promotion, this wuz now the icing on the cake. Although Yeugen had been with un earlier tha' day, ee knew their arrangement wudn' goin' t'last tha' much longer. Although ee wuz pretty pleased with the weekend's event, ee

344

wudn' goin' t'be s'pleased when ee looked at the state ov 'is bank account on Monday morning. Yeah – the fuckin' bitch 'ad cleaned un out hadn' she? – only learning 'is PIN numbers and then pissin' off home t'Poland. She wuz the cash-point thief now. She'd been in 'is various other banks too – an' 'ad the money transferred t'her own private account. Trura City wudn' quite be gettin' as much as they thought from un. Any plans fur new Stadium fur Cornwall were swept clean off the table.

Trura City themselves might need t'think again sharpish 'bout who their sponsor wuz fur next season in League Two. Markie didn' knaw ut then, but there wuz a brave price on 'is head. The bounty hunters ov Obby Stanker 'ad agreed ut the day before the adit fell in. Arnie see, had replanted 'is prize-winning roses, an' wuz up fur ut.

Crowz-an-Wra Volumizing Spray – Spritz on maximum volume.
Root lifter on the move
• Maximum life – a blend of naturally derived heat ingredients help provide extra volume to blow-dried style. Ideal for the festival season
• Adds fullness – Panthenol helps to think hair and add body
• Highly concentrated – Lightweight mist pump spray allows for an even application – use sparingly

Yak had been fartin' around with his newly-acquired club, the very beautifully-named EBGBs 'adn' a? The tool seemed t' be on ut 24/7 more or less, thaas' when ee wudn' seein' Jody. 'Mean, Jody wuz rapidly becoming part ov the fixtures an' fittun's of Charlie's place ov late as much as Yak already wuz . So much fur Charlie's room ov one's one. Amongst all the bad news 'bout the abduction ov Anthony, an' the collapse ov the Trelawny Adit, a few good things had comed his way. Trura City wuz goin' up, but more importantly, his ma had passed her *Voices an' Texts* unit 'adn' she? A grade 2 pass apparently. which wuz good enough fur her t'be moving onta' the next stage of the course. In the future she wuz goin' t'be tackling the immensity ov the nineteenth-century novel. Tha' wud be meanin' Tommy'd be contendin' with a bit ov Jane Austen, Charlotte

Alan M. Kent

Brontë, Elizabeth Gaskell an' George Elliot now. She wuz readin' Charlie the opening lines ov *Pride and Prejudice* before goin' up Homebase one morning.

'It is a truth universally acknowledged, that a single man in possession of a good fortune, must be in want of a wife.'

'That true us ut?' asked Charlie.

Well, his da now 'ad a good fortune, but ee suppawsed ee already 'ad a wife.

'Dunnaw,' went 'is ma. 'I's one of the moast famous lines in the whole of English Literature though...'

T'Charlie a bit ov Jane Austen, Charlotte Brontë, Elizabeth Gaskell, an' George Eliot sounded like ut wud have the kind ov language in ut that would be even more distant from his ma's usual experiences of the drecklys, m'andsomes and proper jobs ov Obby Stanker. Still, ef she liked ut, then, tha', well, tha' wuz vitty enough fur ee.

'Ut d'sound like ut's a bit sarcastic t'me,' went Charlie.

'Do ee think so?' went his ma.

'So they wuz the forerunners then, ov Virginia Woolf really then, wudn' um?'

'Yeah, I suppawse so, when you put ut like tha'... Tha' George Elliot 'ad t'assume a male name just t'get on y'knaw...'

Charlie thought ov 'is own personal lighthouse ov the last few weeks. Woolf had had a fascination with ut, and now, so did Charlie. Wha' the fuck 'ad gone on down there out Godrevy? Everyone's lips were sealed. Nawbody wuz opening their gob – which on Trelawny – wuz unheard of. Usually, somebody 'ad a bit ov a tale t'tell. And well, somehow ut went against the natural proclivities ov his people didn' ut? 'Mean, the Cornish cud yip up fur England cudn' um? Ee'd better not say tha' t' Trescothick though. Perhaps the Cornish cud yip up enough fur themselves.

Havin' dropped the stories about Anthony an' Trura City's promotion (though boath 'ad made stonkin' on-going items), the papers. telly an' radio wuz fulla' ut about how the Tory and Liberal Democrat Coalition government wuz now quite sympathetic t'devolution in Cornwall. Their MPs wuz now talkin' about a *Senedh Kernow* – a devolved Cornish Assembly wudn' um? Well, sometimes in history some times things are meant t'be. an' some times things just happen by chance. Charlie wuz t'find tha' out sooner than ee thought. The chance tha' had happened ov late wuz that the Prime Minister ad been on holiday in Cornwall (prob'ly up somewhere posh like Rock, Daymar Bay or Padsta') an' his missus 'ad 'appened t'give birth t'the baby daughter down here – the sprog popped out over Treliske apparently. They wuz goin' t'be callin' her Endellion, after the female saint up North Cornwall way. Apparently, tha' made No.10 a bit more, well, sympathetic t'the Cornish situation didn' ut? 'Awnly thing wuz, the Cornish might have t'vote Tory forever, an' amongst the Liberal-Methodist tradition tha' existed all the way across Obby Stanker an' beyond, tha' wudn' likely t'last long. Prob'ly fur Trescothick an' the rest of the Cornish Tigers 'twudn' be good enough, but 'twas a start, eh? A bit more ov the Ten Point Plan nailed.

'Assembly'?! Fuck an 'Assembly'. Wha' we need is a full parliament,' Charlie cud hear um sayin'.

'Least maybe there wudn' be the need ov munitions, Starstreak missiles, or balaclavas any more: the Kernewek Jihad might even be over.

Trelawny wuz in even more ov a state than 'twas normally in – an' usually 'twas in some state. All sorts ov work wuz goin' on underground t'help seal the land-surface and prevent any further damage. The saving ov number 38 Trelawny Gardens 'ad been a close run thing though. Cormac 'ad got in there fust ov all, an' strengthened the land immediately around um. Tha' meant tha' fur a while at least, they cud move back in. The other two houses were unrecoverable, an' 'twas unlikely tha' the land there wud ever be built on in the future. The playground cud be made good again, but then you wuz talkin' prob'ly sixth months t' a year, just to make ut safe fur kiddies t'walk on. Because ov tha', the fuckin' tackers wuz back on the prowl again every evening. Operation Goodnight well, had t'be said Goodnight to.

There'd been a lot ov legal to-ing an' fro-ing too, about who exactly wuz responsible fur the adit. In the end, ut 'ad comed down t'the Council, an' they wuz in a pretty good mood t'pay up a generous bit ov compensation. Put tha' with Tommy's golden egg, and well, the Curnows 'ad a tidy bit put by. Fur now though, they wuz carryin' on as normal, as if there wudn' a massive hole outside their back gate inta' which the rest ov the row 'ad fallen. The adit's collapse continued to form a major source ov conversation over the next few years. Hell, 'twas almost as good as Tommy Curnow's porn empire a few years back.

Charlie'd found 'is creative powers had miraculously somehow returned to un again. Ee'd started to really worry about his ability to write decent songs anymore. The thing wuz with the whole process waz that you cud create the kind of kick-arse rock that wud staple your ears back with wonder on an acoustic guitar. If the melody wuz right, ut didn't matter if ut wuz composed on an acoustic or electric guitar, 'twud have the same power. An' when Charlie thought about ut, all the bad-ass tunes ever thrown out inta' the world of Metal, well, they all relied on the melody didn' um? Once tha' wuz nailed, you had people in the palm ov your hand. If Iron Maiden an' Metallica did ut tha' way when they wuz composin', then so would ee. Perhaps, 'is full return to the solace of the Celtic West wuz the right thing to have done. After the madness of the past three years, ut had been good to get back to 'is roots and recharge the batteries.

'Is first gig fur a long while wuz on. Ee'd been posterin' around Camborne an' Redruth – not the stupid mad-cap fly-posterin' ee used t'do with Balance, but a more targeted campaign, in the right trendy shops and 'appenin' locations. 'Charlie Curnow: Acoustic set' ut read, with a mean an' moody lookin' image ov Charlie tha' had been taken up Croft Common by Bev. The gig wuz t'be at EBGBs wudn' ut – an' Charlie's set wudn' goin' t' zactly be the grand rockin' opening that maybe Yak wuz dreamin' ov. Then again, 'is name might pull a few punters in.

'Hardly kicking supreme amounts of butt though us ut?' Charlie had said t' Yak. ''Tis unplugged y'knaw... Eric Clapton-an' Nirvana-style...'

'Ut dun't matter Charlie... You'm a legend boy... Besides, if people wunt t'boogie we'll be holdin' the traditional EBGB alternative an' rock disco afterwards...'

'We?'

'Yeah – well, me an' Micky...'

Tha' sounded like a recipe fur disaster. They two cunts wuz always arguing the toss in Balance.

Voodoo Pilchard

'Headönizm's sponsorin' ut see...'

Ah. Now 'twas becoming clearer. 'Twas the old story: money talked, or ut least stylin' products did.

Bluett 'ad gone 'adn' a? Charlie'd seen un go off on the train at Camborne. Nawbody else seemed t'give much ov a fuck. Well, there wuz Kayleigh, who havin' resisted 'is charms fur a month or two, finally recognised tha' ee wudn' a bad ol' boy all told – an' tha' she'd write to un on e-mail. That gived un a bit ov hope at least.

Charlie mentioned the gig and the necessary publicity machine.

'Postering?' ee asked. 'Ah fuck Charlie, I d'love doin' all ov tha'... sneakin' around in the middle ov the night an' tha'...'

'Ut idn' like tha' anymore though boy...'

'Ah – things is just startin' off again – an' now I'm goin' away like...'

'You nervous?' asked Charlie.

'Wha' – about wha' might happen?'

'Afghanistan?'

'Well, not really,' ee went, 'not after me an' the Tigers freed tha' little kid...'

As usual, Bluett had said too much, an' ee realised ut.

Charlie'd worked ut out anyway.

Bluett's train wuz pullin' inta' the up platform. Charlie watched un give a quick look around at Camborne – home of boy Trevithick, home of Charlie Curnow, rock god, and home ov Obby Stanker Country. The next time ee'd be here, the fucker wud been walking up the hill ov Trevu Road on the way t'Beacon and Troon. His army boots would make a good imitation of the noisy stank the hobnailed boys used t'make years ago.

'Take this with you,' said Charlie.

Ee passed Bluett the necklace on which wuz attached Hendrix's 0.10 gauge guitar string. The synapse-damaged Yoda tha' wuz Druid Dave 'ad passed ut on t'Charlie an' now Charlie wuz passin' ut on again – just as its original owner 'ad wanted.

'I cen't take tha',' went Bluett.

'Yeah you can,' said Charlie. 'When you come back safe an' sound, you can *personally* give ut back to me.'

'Fuck, Charlie. I dunnaw wha' t'say.'

Hendrix 'ad protected an' given hope t' thousands in Vietnam an' now 'twud do' the same fur Bluett in Helmand Province. As 'is train headed up the line, Charlie cud hear 'All Along the Watchtower' playing. As ee got inta' his car, ee softly sang the song for Bluett in the hope ee wud eventually come back where ee belonged t'be. Ee prayed tha' on 'is particular watch ee wudn' be trippin' naw IEDs.

Yak 'ad been workin' hard t'transform the former lap-dancing an' porn empire inta' a reputable institution. Ee'd even 'ad responsible discussions with the police about parking an' late-night noise, an' Constable Combellack (still recoverin' somewhat form the shock ov the adit: ee'd been first on the scene see) 'ad been down there t'give the plaace a once over. Fuck, Yak 'ad even managed t'secure an alcohol license. T'Charlie tha' sounded a bit mental on behalf ov the authorities t'be honest; givin' the moast unstable 'medicinal' user ov Obby Stanker free reign ov the optics. Ah well. Never mind.

Who gived a fuck?

'Mean, after all, your house could fall down an adit at any time cudn't ut?

A bit ov a buzz had gone around about the plaace – well, from Hayle t'Trura at least – an' ee wuz hopin' that anyone who remotely 'ad any decent musical taste wud turn up. Things seemed t'be goin' well with this maid Jody. Well, ut turned out when she wuz not wearin' her nurse's outfit at Treliske or in Yak's bedroom, or bending over Charlie's fridge, she wuz a bit ov a goth. So well, Yak had been blastin' out the Sisters of Mercy, some old-school The Mission, an' a bit ov retro Southern Death Cult. Micky'd been in there too, tartin' up the sleazy purple design of Club Rhino with a few tribal Celtic pieces, and then, the masterstroke: ee'd managed t'secure part ov the large voodoo pilchard graffiti piece down the dairy at Treswithian. They wuz goin' t'scat up the plaace there fur the development of some new eco-homes, so Micky asked if ee cud have ut. 'Twas now boobed up in the middle of the club, near to where the lap- and pole-dancers had once got changed, or rather got undressed. The thing wuz 'full-on'.

'Ideal,' went Micky, 'fur the realm of the pilchard...'

'Ut looks amazing. Micky,' went Charlie. 'Now, I knaw wha' I wuz goin' t'ask you...'

'Wha'?'

'Tha' tattoo... the Trura City one...'

'Wha' fur Markie Phillips...?'

'You did ut then?'

'Yeah. 'Course. Tell cud ee?'

'Did a pay fur ut or...?'

'...or wha', I did ut as a favour while ee set up a little protection racket?'

'Kind ov?'

'I's Jess... I worry tha'...'

'Well, the fucker paid fur ut. Can't say fairer than tha'. In fact, I inked over some of the old stuff he had there... Y'knaw crappy stuff he'd had done years ago... in Exeter prison I think... Ee paid me well fur ut too.'

'Just wondered,' went Charlie.

'Ee said ee wuz goin' t'get some more done. In fact, ee wuz talkin' about tha' voodoo pilchard design I 'ad ready t'go...'

Charlie wudn' too happy to hear tha'.

'What?'

'Yeah, the pilchard design...'

Charlie had t'be careful wha' ee wuz sayin' now.

'But tha' belongs t'the people of Obby Stanker,' ee went. 'Not ee...'

'Well, I ebm' seen un lately anyway... s' don't you worry. I'll let y' knaw if ee comes in.'

'Thanks,' went Charlie – but 'twas still disappointin' news t'even knaw ee wuz contemplatin' ov ut.

A few wuz in later tha' evening, t'see 'is set. All basically 'twas wuz Charlie, sat on a stool on stage with a microphone before un. This wuz the very stage where the maids, a few years ago, 'ad shook their bits before a droolin' male audience ov Cormac employees, migrant workers from Latvia and Poland, an' a few pervy locals.

'Don't worry,' Charlie said before ee began, 'I won't be doin' naw pole-dancin' fur ee...'

Tha' set the mood – tight but loose, so t'speak.

'My first song tonight is a nod t'the past... I'd like t'dedicate this t'Boy Bluett, who, as some of you knaw, ent here tonight. We wish un' well, we really do. Go safe, boy. This is 'All Along the Watchtower'.'

Alan M. Kent

T'begin with, Charlie's vocal wuz a bit raw, but ut soon settled down. The power an' simplicity ov his strumming seemed t'silence People. Even Neil realised how good a guitarist Charlie'd become.

'This is a new song... Yeah, you can get your beers now... I's called 'Lighthouse'.'

Fuck, 'twas a compelling bit ov music. Probab'ly 'twas closer t'Seth Lakeman than Iron Maiden, to be 'onest, but havin' said tha', given a metal make-over by some bad-ass producer like Kevin Shirley or Ross Robinson, 'twud be the sort v thing tha' wud have people's lighters in the air in the big arenas. You cud feel the brooding nature ov ut.

'Stonking song.' Yak wuz goin', trying to work out the drum beats an' patterns that might go down on ut one day. Neil too, wuz wonderin' where the lead might come in, an' where ee might be adding some solos.

'I'd like t'thank Chakira fur this next one... fur puttin' ut in the Top 40 for us...'

'What are you on?' wuz then played in a stripped-down, unfunked, un-rapped over piece, which brought a few good memories back. Anyone who'd not been there in the days of Balance realised wha' a good song ut really wuz, not knowin' that the bugger up on stage wuz the author of the chart-topper.

'As you may know, I wuz once on *X-Factor*...' Charlie wuz going. 'Yeah, well, they only let me sing about three or four bars... I didn't have enough soul apparently. Hopefully, this one's got some soul. I's called 'Coming back.'

'Twas quite a piece tha'. You cud imagine ut with a full-blown orchestra at the Royal Albert Hall, maybe ut ud be double-tracked on the album with the Holman-Climax choir addin' an ethereal feel.

Charlie did a few more new songs of the same quality, and then trawled the back catalogue of some classic rock: Free, AC/DC. a bit ov Led Zep. Tha' got the place up fur the steamer ov a disco tha' followed. Anyone who 'adn' seen Charlie sing before wuz mightily impressed; anyone who 'ad dun, realised tha' all tha' time away on the road with Purple Haze had honed un inta' a gifted showman an' singer. Obviously, an awareness of the skills of Hendrix an' other blues-rock artists before un,

352

'ad helped his song-writing no end. This wuz Ivor Novello award-winning stuff and naw mistake.

After the shaw, Charlie rested his back against the old undressing rooms ov Club Rhino. Ee felt happy tha' ee'd given ut his best shot tha' night. Inside, Micky wuz firin' up the dance floor with a bit of Rob Zombie.

'Charlie, tha' wuz brilliant. They loved ut? Listen, can I talk to you a minute... It's important... really important.'

Ov late, Bev had been a bit withdrawn with un. Charlie'd put ut down t'a lot of things really. She'd been involved in organising a big academic conference down Tremough on folklore an' superstition, an' there'd been all the stuff with Neil an' Ally. Then there wuz tha' little encounter with Yeugen over Treyew Road. Now she wuz needun' t'talk to un. When maids generally have tha' kind ov tone in their voices, ut usually meant somethun' serious wuz up. You'd learnt you'd dun somethun' wrong, or they wuz about t'drop ee like a g'eat heavy stone in Stithians Reservoir. Everything with they pair 'ad been goin' along s'nicely as well. Well, s'well in fact, Charlie 'ad been contemplatin' a more serious future fur um. Ee 'adn't towld her yet, but well, ee wuz thinkin' strongly tha' she should move in with un. She'd be ready then fur the new academic year down uni, an' the plus factor ov this, o'course wuz tha' ut would encourage Yak an' Jody t'move out an' maybe get their own pad together. Ee'd have a room ov one's own – awnly sharin' ut with her. Bewdie like.

As they wuz speakin', Charlie's phone went. Like a tool, when ee should have left ut go to voicemail, ee answered ut didn' a? Bev turned away from him. Ee reached fur her hand, which she gave him hesitantly. She wuz makin' ut clear though, tha' this phone call wudn' much appreciated at this particular moment. Inside the club, the reception wudn' tha' good.

'Hang on a minute,' ee wuz sayin' to the caller. 'I got a bad signal in here...'

Ee stepped outside. In the distance, on the horizon, ee cud see South Crofty's head-frame towards the west. There wudn' naw flicker of Godrevy though. The news had reported how the lantern down there needed considerable repair.

Bev 'ad followed un outside an' she stood in front ov un, a silhouette with Carn Brea behind her.

'Ah Pete, how are you?' went Charlie.

'Pete who?' whispered Bev.

'Pete Thomas – you know, the producer – the record company bloak,' Charlie said, away from the phone.

Bev wondered wha' ee wanted. Ut 'ad been a while. Why had a phoned up Charlie outta' the blue? Besides, whatever ee wanted, ut wudn' be as important as wha' she needed t'tell Charlie.

On the phone, Charlie wudn' sayin' a lot. Ee wuz mainly doing the listening. Inside the club, Micky wuz progressin' to a bit ov Linkin Park, an' getting' the crowd going. Every so often, ov course, ee wuz throwin' in the name ov their sponsor Headönizm an' how later on, they be givin' out some free hair an' beauty products. Well, yer average rock fan these days, wudn' yer greasy grebo of yore Ah naw, now they wuz coiffured an' street savy. Think less Status Quo c.1974, an more current Welsh noisesters, the Lost Prophets.

Bev wuz pickin' out a bit ov the conversation.

'So you thought ov us then?' Charlie wuz goin', an' then a little later. 'Yeah – got lots ov new songs... Been playin' them here tonight in fact...'

When Charlie ended the call, Bev cud see him lookin' t'the west in a moment of rapture. Charlie knawed ut too. 'Twas like the moment when the architect's drawings of the new Trura City stadium fur Cornwall had been revealed.

She left him to is thoughts fur a moment, and then asked, 'So?'

Ee turned to her. She saw the animation and wonder in his eyes – something she knew an' loved about Charlie, but 'adn' seen fur a while.

'Tha' wuz Pete Thomas...'

'Yeah – and...?'

'Ee wants t'work with us again.'

'Us?'

'Balance...'

'Well, the remains ov ut...'

'Go on?'

Charlie wuz speakun' fast.

'Ee wants t'form a new band. Shape ut from the beginning. Rod Smallwood-style. Build slowly, steadily an' grow a new rock band over the next ten years...'

'You, Yak an' Neil?'

'Yeah – an' you?'

'See – ee's been given an executive position on a new off-shoot of EMI records. They've asked un to find the right band... Well, ee 'ad faith in us, didn't ee, a few years back? – only we cocked ut up didn't us? When ee found out about the Chakira hit tha' prompted un t'get in touch again.... Ee wants a mee-tun' with us.'

Suddenly, all the grind, all the toilets, all the wraps ov Trelawny bucket ee'd 'ad to endure and all the hard, road les-sons ee'd learnt, looked they wuz about t'pay off.

'I can't do it,' said Bev nervously. 'Don't put me in there.'

'What ee mean?'

'You, Yak an' Neil – but not me...'

Charlie reckoned ee knawed why. She'd given up rock 'n' roll fur academia now. Bev didn' see her future there, swingin' around her bass like Steve Harris, the way she used to, the way the crowd loved. Ee understood. Ee really did, but they, well, they were a winnin' team. Given a bit ov' time, ee'd convince her.

'I understand – I mean, I know you got other fish t'fry at uni now... but you won't need no back-up plan. Pete's serious this time. I knaw ut.'

'Ut idn' tha' t'all...' went Bev. 'I's more serious than tha'...'

'What's more serious?'

Could anything be more serious than wha' wuz currently on the table? Charlie wuz beginning t'worry now. Ut looked like she wuz goin' t'squal. Wuz she goin' t'ruin this moment fur'n, this moment ov triumph?

'Come on Bev, talk to me...'

Voodoo pilchard, voodoo pilchard, voodoo pilchard, voodoo pilchard. Like drums ut wuz, tumbling around the chambers of his heart.

'... Tell me whaas' wrong...'

Bev wudn' look at un. Ee moved to hold her, holdin' her s'tight as ee'd ever had, as tight as 'is tool of a feyther, holdin' tha' golden egg.

'I can't be in the band – not any more. I'm pregnant.'

Did she say tha'?

Alan M. Kent

'Mean, did she really fuckin' say tha'?

'It changes things Charlie... It was bad enough before contemplating telling you. Now, there's all this stuff with Pete Thomas. You won't be wanting it – the baby I mean – not now you'm s'close.'

Certainly this wuz about as voodoo and as pilchard as 'twas goin' t'get. Magic an' stinkun' fish eh?

'I's definite? I mean, naw mistake like...'

'No. I was late. So I bought a test. Then the doctor confirmed it.'

Charlie thought of all the tackers ee'd ever known. Tha' little fucker with the BB gun who'd helped un save the day, then Anthony – who despite everything – could be an amazin', incredible kid. Now, one wuz headin' right his way – a visceral thunderball ov love an' energy.

'Na...' went Charlie. 'Na... I mean thaas' brilliant!'

'What do you mean?'

'Tha' I'm goin' t'be a da... My ma's goin' t' go mental...'

'You're happy about ut?'

'Yeah, really, really happy...'

'But we weren't planning on ut or anything. I mean, I think tha' condom the other day... the one you wuz worried about...'

Shit, Charlie 'ad been plannin' stuff ever since ee cud remember: plannin' the next gig, the next song, the next album, how the tour would be, what the album cover would look like, what merchandise they'd have, what the band wud be doin' ov in five years time. Fur once in his life, ut wuz good t'have somethun' tha' wudn' planned.

'I's fine,' went Charlie. 'I'm happy with ut.'

'But the band, the new band I mean?'

'Look, there's no reason why you can't have the baby an' be in the band. Lots ov rockers have their kids tour with them now. I mean, i's part ov life idn' ut? 'Mean, ef ut works out with Pete Thomas, there'll be Anthony an' Megan t'think about too.'

Ee 'ad a point.

'So you reckon I can be a yummy mummy, an' rock?' she said jokingly.

''Course...' said Charlie Curnow.

'You buggers comin' back in or no? asked Yak, standin' there lookin' pleased as punch with his new club. 'So, what ee think

356

Voodoo Pilchard

ov EBGBs then, eh?'

'Nice one Yakky,' went Charlie. 'I's rockin'...'

'This is the future fur me,' Yak wuz goin' t' Jody. '*I'm* sorted. *We're* sorted.'

They went back inside t' join everybody else – Jess, Kelvin, Mel, Ally, Trescothick (who didn' look quite so out ov plaace due t'his new Emo haircut an' the fact that the darkness of the club wuz hidin' 'is all-out orangeness) an' Druid Dave, wearing an original Saxon 'Wheels of Steel' tour shirt. Out on the dance floor wuz Charlie's da, already a bit hammered, gettin' down t'some serious air-guitar t' the (retro an' corny, for EBGBs at least) sounds ov Bon Jovi's 'You Give Love a Bad Name' – which on reflection, ee wudn' any more.

'Sheer class,' ee wuz goin'. 'Eh Micky, 'eave on 'Livin' on a Prayer' next will ee boy?'

'I wun't tell Yak yet,' went Charlie. 'Dun't wunt t' ruin his evening.'

''Course,' went Bev, feeling her womb, and realising that they were now becoming a power trio. Better than 'The Experience' or 'Purple Haze' though.

Charlie smiled at her. Ee raised his glass an' toasted somewhere distant, in the afterlife, Papa Piran, Clifford Mellow, and finally, Mrs Williams. On drugs ee might have been, but the Oracle had been right all along. Coming his way finally, seemed t'be prosperity, beauty, love and health. Proper job.

Nansavallan Woods Super Clean Extra – Strong hold doesn't need to be heavy-handed.
Firm Hold Finishing Spray
• Maximum body and shine – Firm hold, flexible conditioning ingredients from Cornish woodland help provide fullness and shine
• Quick drying – Fast drying fine mist spray provides a dry application
• Added protection – Helps protect again sun damage

They found Markie Phillips' 'devolved' body a couple ov months on. T'be 'onest, there wudn' a lot left ov the poor bugger. The new owners ov Chycarn Farm up Croft Common wuz sortin' out their yard, when they decided t'move an ancient, an' unusually strong-smellin' dung heap. On Monday mornin', one of the workers up there (a cakey boy by the name ov' Owen Richards, who in the evening used t'regularly drink twenty pints over Grenville Arms, and then wuz up at four o'clock in the morning t'milk cows), wuz using a pitchfork t'stram in a last bit of rotten hay, and 'appened t'nawtice a left hand stickin' out the top ov the steaming mass.

First off, ee reckoned ee wuz still pissed from the night before. But tha' wudn' the case. So secondly, ee'd reckoned someone 'ad fallen in there, accidental-like, but when a made a grab fur'n, well, the whole bleddy hand comed out didn't ut? Ee nawticed quick enough tha' 'twas neatly severed at the wrist. Thaas' when a screamed, dropped the hand, and thought ee'd better phone the coppers sharpish. See, nothun' decomposes s'good as when 'tes put in a dung-heap. Worms, flies an' dung d'do a proper good job you. After the police 'ad constructed a white investigation tent over the heap, so the story went, the skull 'ad already been picked clean – s'white as Gwithian sand.

The police finally identified un through 'is tattoos an' dental records. They'd been down an' 'ad a word with Micky. Yeah, the Trura City logo was one of Headönizm's pieces, thaas' fur cert. Micky'd checked 'is records an' the client 'ad been a Mr Phillips (Best keep ut formal, Micky reckoned). Well, the coppers didn' knaw how t'puzzle tha' one out, sure 'nough. They knew Markie well enough though. Moast of the coppers on the case 'ad knawed ov un fur years – an' 'ad wished some bugger might have done this job, wha' five or ten years ago. Certainly the rate ov serious crime and drug dealing would have been cut markedly. Half the bleddy population of west Cornwall 'ad reason 'nough t'take un out. Nawbody wuz sayin' nothun, but when ut all comed out in the newspapers, Boy Trescothick 'ad a wry smile on is face. So did the Trelawny Chainsaw Crew, who proudly displayed their own tattoos, fur weeks afterwards. 'Twas lookin' like Papa Piran 'ad helped everyone get some old-fashioned revenge on the taking of Clifford Mellow.

NFC see.

Normal fur Camborne.

An' when Markie's affairs were wound up, an anonymous letter (post-marked from some place called Quidzin in Poland) comed inta' the cop-shop at Camborne, an' ut told ov um where they might find a few interestin' bits an' pieces. 'Es – a look around down the abattoir down Stithians gived um lots t'do. Down there, in one of the killing sheds, they found a numberplate-less JCB mechanical shovel, with – accordin' t'the forensic boys - dust on ut that matched up t'the location ov nearnly a dozen cash-points all over Cornwall. Stoved in behind that bugger was a number ov works ov art, that eventually got returned t'collectors and gallery owners from all over Cornwall. Plans too, fur a huge raid on the Tate St Ives.

In the safe, wuz some even weirder shit: a frying pan with a dent in ut, which they eventually connected with the murder of Clifford Mellow. Then, over in one of the rooms over Godrevy Lighthouse, three dolls, Vèvès scrawled all over the walls an' other 'classified' items. Accordin' t'the papers, they wuz fur Black Magic – Voodoo-style. The police asked an expert fur help in understandin' ut all – a maid called Bev Bennets who'd happened t'be doing a Ph.D on witchcraft down the university at Tremough. She cud identify an' classify ut all. The photo, the hair, the name on the piece ov paper all told her who 'twas. The shocker wuz ut turned out t'be her fella' who 'appened t'be the fixation ov the so-called Voodoo Queen.

When tha' happened, well, ut all comed a bit full circle, like the life-cycle ov the common or garden *Sardina pilchardus*.

The police though, wuz dealin' with another incident around the same time as all this wuz goin' on. 'Twas awnly a stone's throw away really from Chycarn Farm. Yeah, Constable Combellack 'ad been patrolling the estate one night on the latest and newly-re-invigorated phase ov Operation Goodnight. Ee'd been scanning' the adit works earlier on but then pulled around the corner ov Polgine Lane, where there were a few recycling bins. A figure wuz at work on um, with a set of stencils, working 'is way along the side of the paper and card container. In an instant, Combellack knawed what the little shit wuz up to. Ee called fur back up, suspecting tha' ee'd found one of Camborne's now notorious graffiti artists at work. The kid wuz intensely involved with wha' ee wuz doin' – Combellack observing the orange an' red designs emerging. Ee stopped the car, and got out surreptitiously, walking over to un with a set of handcuffs at the ready. When the kid stood back to admire his work, well, thaas' when Constable Combellack made his move.

Alan M. Kent

Now Combellack wudn' the speediest fuckin' copper on the block (t'be honest ee wuz slower than the fat orange Tre-terror- ist), but this arrest, wud go down in history wudn' ut? Ee, Combellack, had caught the Pilchard at work. Proper job you.

Ee cuffed the kid's wrist first, and then moved his knee inta' his back. Tha' helped force un t'the floor. The second wrist wuz then very easy.

'Get off me y'wanker,' the kid went. 'I ent dun nothun'.'

In the process, the kid's hoodie fell back onta' his back, so Combellack cud see his face.

'So, you're the Pilchard are you?'

The kid didn' say a thing. Ee wudn' admittin' nothun'. Combellack searched un' an' read un his rights. Ee'd seen un before, Combellack reckoned, an' ee 'ad prob'ly gived un a warnin' in the past.

On the pavement still, wuz the kid's rucksack. When the other units turned up, Combellack wuz able t'search ut.

'You wun't stop the graffiti – not ever!' went the kid as he wuz bundled inta' the back ov a transit. Defiant little tool ee wuz.

'A'right boy... but we've stopped you, haven't we?' said Combellack. 'Would you like to tell me your name?'

'Fuck you.'

Nice.

Inside the rucksack, as well as various other stencils, orange an' red spray aerosol cans, the police found a tin of cannabis, a bong improvised out ov a coke bottle and a loaded BB gun with plenty more pellets in the side pockets.

'Tooled up then?' inquired one ov the other officer at the scene of the incident.

They took un straight down the cells down Camborne Police Station t'see if ee'd cool off a bit. Ee wuz prob'ly high on mephedrone or blaw anyway. 'Course, wha' the police cudn' possibly knaw wuz that this wuz the now-grown up tacker who'd once helped Charlie an' Yak defeat the misguided inten- tions of the Kernow Liberation Front and their missile attack on the Tamar Bridge. Tha' wuz unlikely t'be taken inta' considera- tion when ee'd be up before the juvenile court in a couple ov months time.

In the cell though, the kid wuz unremorseful. Ee wuz sittin'

360

on the plastic mattress, carving a little Voodoo Pilchard symbol inta' the all-too-soft plaster ov the walls there.

> St Piran Freeze and Shine Super-saint Spray – Give your hair the 'super-saint' hold with memory.
> Firm hold finishing spray
> • Provides powerful, long-lasting hold – Firm hold styling ingredients from the dunes of Perranporth provide long-lasting finish and memory
> • Intensifies shine – Activated Botanical blend of algae, grass, and rosemary helps to enhance shine
> • Added protection – Helps protect against sun damage

Tommy comed home from mine that night pretty chipper with hisself. All day long ee'd been hearing ov the crack 'bout Markie Phillips an' tha'. Ov late, Markie seemed t' be pullin' back from investing in Trura City, an' Tommy wudn't too happy about tha'. Then suddenly, the fucker seemed t'disappear over night. Ee wudn' responded t' any calls to his mobile or is home or business numbers. 'Twas real weird. Trura City needed t'look fur alternatives now. Perhaps Crofty might step in.

'Whas up with you?' went Sally, intrigued.

'Twudn' Markie Phillips tha' wuz on 'is mind though.

'Life's good Sal...' ee went. Tha' wuz a new one fur Tommy. Ee never said stuff like tha' normally. No-one did in Cornwall. Only tourists an' cunts with second homes said anything close t'tha'. Maybe Markie Phillips did, before someone set to un with a chainsaw.

'I'm off on me travels,' Tommy went, speakun' like some new Cousin Jack.

'Where ee off?'

'Well, I knaw you'm set fur Falmouth t'train as a teacher like... but I be goin' t'Mongolia...'

Sally 'ad t'think fur a bit t'work out where tha' wuz.

'South ov Russa, north of China,' went Tommy anticipatin' her thoughts.

'Whaas' on then?'

'Mining... Western United Mines've signed a deal with the government in Ulan Bator to develop part of the Oyn Tolgoi copper mine ebn' um...'

Ulan Bator in Oyn Tologi sounded like 'twas way down west somewhere – near Land's End - either tha' or somewhere close to Mount Doom from the *Lord of the Rings*.

'Matta, me an' a few others is goin' out fur a visit – they want my expertise as a Shift Cap'n out there Sal... How 'bout tha'?'

Sally nodded. Ut sounded impressive – just about the moast impressive thing t'ever 'appen in Tommy's life.

'With the agreement they've signed, they d'reckon there are tin, copper and gold resources out there worth about two billion pounds. Sal, y'd'knaw wha' tha' means – the plaace will be the new Cornwall. Give ut five years, an' 'twill be a world-class mining district, all developed on the expertise ov boys from Crofty...'

'What about Crofty then?'

'Well tidn' goin' t'go away is ut? This'll see my time out Sal... I wun't be out there all the time... Aw naw... A lot of the development work'll be done here with the Mongolians comin' over t'Cornwall. I'll be headin' tha' up...'

Sally Curnow looked at her husband. Ut seemd liked they'd turned a bit ov a corner. All the crap, all the pain, all the anger, all the extra-marital relationships seemed a long way away now.

'Whas' fur tea?' went Tommy, back in the real world ov the here an' now.

'Pasties,' said Sally.

'Lovely,' went Tommy, and held Sally by her waist, lifting her hair and kissing her neck gently.

So there 'twas. Tommy wuz back doin' wha' the Cornish dun best: deep in the earth diggin' fur stuff.

'You a'right?' asked Sally.

Tommy knew wha' tha' meant. Ut meant wuz 'is heart alright? Was a about t'keel over again and give um all a fright. 'Is time up Treliske had given Sally a new view ov her husband. Yes, pure twat ee wuz, but she cudn' help but love un.

'Sal... You knaw I've given up the fags... an' I'm cuttin' back on the booze... I'm makin' the right lifestyle choices... I'm doin' me five a day ov fruit... an' this week I'll be back on the exercise programme... honest...'

Sally opened the oven door and pulled out the fresh-basked pasties. The smell travelled around the Curnow kitchen and through the open window into the lanes and walkways of the surviving Trelawny estate. Sally scooped the larger of the two pasties onta' a plate and placed it down before her husband. Tommy took a knife and cut off a chunk, placing it on the end of a fork.

'There's more,' went Tommy, speaking as the chunk of pastry and beef hastily entered his mouth.

Sally joined him.

'They'm looking at Afghanistan too... Es, I knaw 'tes an impoverished and failed state...'

'Just like Cornwall then,' chipped in Sally.

'Well, maybe... but tell ee what maid, the untapped minerals in there is amazun'...'

'Will you be going there too?' asked Sally.

Tommy could see the worried look on her face.

'Boy Bluett says i's not tha' bad...'

'Not yet though Tommy... not while... 'tis still going on out there...'

Tommy understood.

He didn' say anymore. But Gerald Matta'd been through the statistics and the surveys. Ee'd had high-level meetings in London – with the Prime Minister and Hamid Karzai. Apparently one trillion dollars worth ov untapped mineral resources were out there. Afghanistan had even more potential than Mongolia. Tommy knew the Aynak Copper Mine in the Logar province wuz one of Western United Mines' next targets. So, there 'twas – from Crofty t' Kabul, an' back again.

'You heard from Charlie?' Tommy asked.

'Aw – they had some meetun' – about the band up the line somewhere... with tha' Pete Thomas. Y'knaw the one who offered um a deal backalong...'

Tommy nodded, laughing t'hisself.

'Nothun'll come ov thaa' – mark my words...'

'Bev's back in ut y'knaw...'

'Wha' – an' her up the duff... How's tha' goin' t'work?'

'Well, Charlie d'say tha' they've worked ut out – an' this time, tha' Pete Thomas is offerin' ov um a lot ov money... t'do ut proper-like – an' an really go fur ut.'

'I'll eat my bleddy safety helmet if they make ut...' went Tommy.

Tommy looked over at the wedding picture ov Jess and

Micky. Micky still looked a right fuckin' yob, even done up like a dog's dinner in a formal dress coat an' top hat. They didn' need t'worry 'bout they two though – now tha' Headönizm wuz reachin' new heights. 'Es, Jess had expanded, done very well indeed with her business an' products. She 'ad her Cornish-themed set of hairdressers' supplies all over the plaace. Organic, home-grown products with natural Cornish ingredients seemed t'be 'zactly what the world wuz after fur their hair these days. Fur Jess, ut seemed like everything 'ad been conditioned, detangled, moisturised, invigorated an' enhanced. Christ she even 'ad a pilchard product on sale. Tommy wudn' be usin' any of tha' muck though in the near future. Ee'd stick t'what he knawed best fur getting tin dust out ov his balding mullet – soap an' water – an' nothun' more.

An' Micky – well Micky'd dun pretty good too. A chain of tattoo shops in Cornwall an' the south-west ov England. Did Tommy knaw tha' a fifth of all British people have been inked at the start ov the twenty-first century an' tha' tha' figure wuz only likely t'grow? Naw, ee didn'. So yeah, 'is little maid 'ad shacked up with a tattooed millionaire who seemed t'knaw wha' ee wuz on upon.

'They'm mainstream now Tommy,' is what ee 'ad said.

The latest thing with they wuz building some eco-friendly plaace over Praze-an-Beeble. Ut wuz even goin' t'be powered by Wave Hub electricity.

'Fuckin' hell,' reckoned Tommy. 'Wha' wuz the world comin' to when cunts wuz buildin' grand designs over plaaces like Praze-an-Beeble? Fuckin' Traveller mansion that'll be...'

Ee didn' want t'say ut, but now wuz as good a time as any.

'Sally, well, now the kids is all sorted, perhaps 'tes time we had a look at somewhere else... I mean, we'm back on our feet again bain't us?'

Sally stopped eatin' and looked at Tommy inquisitively.

'I wudn' appy either about all tha' with the Trelawny Adit too... Well, there's no way we'm goin' t'spend the rest ov our lives living next t' a bleddy great black hole...'

'Are you saying we can move?'

'Es, I d'reckon so. Listen, there's one ov they Wain homes over Lanner fur sale in the West Briton. Shallus go look at ut? I mean the compensation an' my little find've sorted we out good an' proper...'

The shock ov all this made sure tha' Sally cudn' eat any more of her pasty. She gave a quick message ov thanks back t'her Virginia Woolf collection on the shelf, just like Tommy would t'the knockies underground.

'Do I get me own room?'

''Course,' went Tommy, 's'long as I'n have a bigger shed t'put all me memorablia in...'

By tha' ee meant 'is rare porn collection, rock posters an' Trura City Programmes. A few old flyers from Club Rhino too. Then ee remembered, just about all ov ut wuz now underground – somewhere deep in the Trelawny Adit. Never mind – ee cud collect ut all again ee reckoned – on eBay or Amazon.

In thanks, at such domestic harmony, the minerals ov Cornwall, Mongolia and Afghanistan seemingly eased themselves out of the rock – and made the process of hard-rock mining a little less tricky. Down Newlyn, fur the first time in years, shoals of pilchards in good numbers returned t'the Western Approches that summer. And over Godrevy, every ten seconds, the light assumed its age-old rhythm again.

Voodoo Pilchard Dry Wax – The Rule of cool is never look like you're trying too hard.
Texture and definition
• Waxed texture – Non-oily cosmetic wax provides an easy 'lived-in' look
• Pliable – Conditioners and softening ingredients help create a moveable finish
• Controls – Firm hold, formula of fish oil (no, really!) provides ultimate control

Charlie Curnow didn' knaw ut then, but three years later, on the weekend of June 14th, ee an' Yak, an' Neil an' Bev – as contemporary metal band Voodoo Pilchard - would be headlining the main stage at the Download Festival, Castle Donington, the culmination of a massive sold-out world-wide tour. A reformed, cocaine-less, Hendrix-less Spryer looked on from the side of the stage, proud as punch – now standing there as the band's official tour manager. Next to him wuz Pete Thomas. With them stood Micky an' Jess, there for the weekend, as special guests –

straight up from the latest launch of their Cornish hairdressing products range. Now, with deals all over the shop, an' supplying the largest salons world-wide, it wudn' a bad view from where they wuz standun'. There too, with Access-all-Areas passes were Druid Dave (clad in a Voodoo Pilchard limited edition roadie-only World Tour t-shirt, ee'd proudly be wearing next week over the scrapies over United Downs), Mel an' Kelvin, and not in a body bag, but back from Afghanistan, Boy Bluett. The whole event wuz bein' powered by Wave Hub electricity – all the way from the Atlantic t'the middle ov England.

As Charlie plugged in, an' the Donington crowd roared, ee gave his sister the largest smile she 'ad ever seen from her brother. The immense back-drop wuz in place – a new take on the Pilchard graffiti: the band's iconic logo found on all their albums an' merchandise. Their bad-ass intro-tape wuz rollin'. There were Papa Piran flags proudly raised in the audience from those in the west who'd made the pilgrimage to rock's Mecca. Just behind them stood Ally with Anthony and Megan. Anthony wudn' ever be 'zactly the calmest child goin', but never mind, with the money the band wuz makin' now, ee cud get the very best treatment. In her arms, she wuz holdin' Charlie and Bev Curnow's three year-old daughter, Molly, who wuz happily chitterin' on like there wuz naw tomorra'. Molly see, tha' wuz Mrs Williams' first name, an' who she wuz named after. An' Bev an' Charlie married now – a low-key event down Treslothan church in a break in the touring schedule, but with paparazzi interest from all over the world.

In the same week, knawin' the band had become tha' successful, Cornwall Council slapped a preservation order on some selected pieces ov graffiti around Camborne. An' Condurrow? Well, ut needed preservin' didn' ut – fur the Cornish nation? Now, 'twas rock 'n' roll history. 'Twas world heritage now, like the Cavern, the Marquee Club, or the studios at Abbey Road. *Senedh Kernow* – the small but potent, and now devolved Cornish assembly - had passed a motion on ut. Back Crofty, Tommy Curnow wuz shawin' 'round a delegation from Mongolia, an' cursin' hisself tha' ee didn't have more faith in his son.

All they from Outer Mongolia, had heard of Voodoo Pilchard, an' were suitably impressed.

'Ah yessh... We know Voodoo Pilchard. Good hard rock music, yessh? Number one album in our country right now... We like very much...'

Luckily, as they eased down inta' the levels, Tommy's safety helmet hadn' been eaten yet.

An' electric pastyland an' Obby Stanker Country would never be the same again. Every day, at 38 Trelawny Gardens, a bevy of tourists come t'look at where a rock legend began. They read new meaning inta' album covers, song lyrics an' the band's progress inta' rock 'n' roll mythology. The space at number 34 and 36 would be converted inta' a rock 'n' roll museum about their earliest days.

At last then, Charlie'd finished the job ee set out t'do. Ee cud thraw away his ladder, stencils and black-an'-blue aerosol cans. They got 'eaved in a skip over Crofty a while back. But if y'd'look close enough, the graffiti's still there.

Bewdie, me 'andsomes.

'Now, Donington,' went Charlie Curnow, turning to face his crowd, an' flicking the horns, 'let's rock...'

Alan M. Kent

ACKNOWLEDGEMENTS

'Photograph', words and music by Steve Clark, Pete Willis, Rick Savage, Robert John Lange and Joe Elliot. © 1983, Vertigo Records.

'Christian Heroism,' words by John Harris. © 1853, Hamilton, Adams and Company.

'Summer Nights.' words and music by Jim Jacobs and Warren Casey. © 1978, RSO Records.

'Block Buster', words and music by Nicky Chinn and Mike Chapman. © 1973, RCA Records.

'Changes', words and music by Ozzy Osbourne, Tony Iommi, Geezer Butler and Bill Ward. © 1972, Vertigo.

'The Unforgiven', words and music by James Hetfield, Lars Ulrich and Kirk Hammett, © 1991. Elektra.

'Here I go Again', words and music by David Coverdale and Bernie Marsden, © 1982 and 1987, Geffen.

'Man on the Silver Mountain', words and music by Ronnie James Dio and Ritchie Blackmore, © 1975, Polydor.

'Highway Star', words and music by Ritchie Blackmore, Ian Gillan, Roger Glover, Jon Lord and Ian Paice, © 1972, EMI.

'Round and Round', words and music by Robin Crosby, Warren DeMartini and Stephen Pearcy, © 1984, Atlantic.

'Eye of the Tiger', words and music by Frankie Sullivan III and Jim Peterik, © 1982 WB Music Corporation, Easy Action Muic, Holy Moley Music and Rude Music.

'Matty Groves', trad. arranged by Fairport Convention, © 1969, Island.

'The Lady of the Sea', words and music by Seth Lakeman, © 2006, iScream.